AUTUMN FALLS

The Autumn Series
Book One

A novel by E.S. Maria

Disclaimer
This book is a work of fiction. Names, characters, places, and incidents are products of the author's imagination or are used fictitiously. Any similarities or resemblance to actual persons (living or deceased), places, business establishments, events, or locales are purely coincidental.

ISBN-10: 0992477247
ISBN-13: 978-0-9924772-4-0

Cover art by Kellie Dennis at Book Cover by Design
www.bookcoverbydesign.co.uk

CONTENTS

DEDICATION

To those I love greater than the universe, this is for you.

I'm where I want to be ... I finally found my bliss.

CHAPTER 1

"Shit! I'm going to be late!" I mumble roughly to myself as I zip up my gray pencil skirt. Grabbing a simple red button-down blouse off the hanger, I make a dash out of my bedroom towards Ethan's room.

"Ethan, honey, we have to go soon so finish dressing up or you'll be late for school."

"Yes, Mommy." Ethan carefully ties his shoelaces. "Two bunny ears, cross 'em, one under the hole, and out again. I did it, Mom!"

"Well done, honey! Now let's go or we'll both be late!" Ethan puts on his backpack while I quickly grab my own black purse, and both of us head out the door. Hand in hand, we walk a few blocks, stopping right in front of Ethan's school.

"See you later, honey. Michelle will pick you up after school, okay?"

"How come you're not picking me up?" Ethan wonders with sadness in his eyes.

"I have a new job, Ethan. It's only a temporary thing, but Mommy needs this one so we can pay the rent. But I'm always on the lookout for a permanent day job so I won't have to work nights, and we can hang out more often," I explain as I brush a few strands of longish auburn hair covering his eye.

"I suppose ... good luck, Mommy! Can Michelle get me ice cream on our way home?"

I tap my forefinger on my chin as I pretend to think about it. "Well, that depends if you give me a big hug and a kiss!"

"Yay! I love you, Mom!" He jumps up to give me the biggest hug and the loudest kiss on the cheek, a gesture that always makes my eyes well up with joy. Holding it together, I manage to pay him back with a bear hug and a good-bye wave as he runs up the steps to school. He sees one of his friends, and with a short wave back to me, they both run off inside.

I check my watch while walking briskly to catch the train going to the city. Stepping off at Forty-second Street, I head straight towards the Grant Corp building which, thankfully, isn't hard to find at all. It's one of those tall edifices that look prewar from the outside and totally modern inside.

I nervously walk up towards the stunning lady behind the front desk. She has her brunette hair knotted tightly in a bun and is wearing a simple black suit with white shirt. She smiles warmly at me once she sees me approach.

"Hi, um, I'm here to see Lydia Parks. My name is Isabelle Morrison. She'll be expecting me?"

"Sure, have a seat, and I'll call her for you." She waves at the leather chairs in the lobby before picking up the phone, hopefully to call Ms. Parks.

"Thank you." Suddenly feeling self-conscious of my own auburn hair in a simple ponytail, I smooth it out hastily before taking a seat on one of the larger leather couches nearest to the elevators.

"Wow! Whoever designed this has really good taste," I whisper to myself while taking the interiors in. Gray and white marble tiles cover the floor, while an enormous chandelier with what looks like lit bubbles hanging off thin metal rods adorn the ceiling. The chandelier looks like a piece of art, but it also serves its purpose of lighting up the main foyer. A matte stainless steel sign etched with *Grant Corp* hangs behind the front desk and greets everyone coming in.

"Maybe I should've done my research about this company," I reprimand myself quietly. But since it's just a monthlong job, I quickly rationalize it's an exercise in futility.

My foot starts thumping on the floor. It's a nervous gesture I can't seem to get rid of. It has been a struggle trying to get a permanent job with the situation I'm in. So I'm anxious to do well in the hope that I can keep temping here for a little longer than my allocated time.

Sometimes I wish I never left home. Had I stayed, I would've graduated with a bachelors degree in business economics. Finding a job would have been so much easier, or I could've helped run Daddy's business. Instead I was only able to manage night classes in business administration. A good course, albeit limiting in terms of career choices. I couldn't afford to progress into a university degree, so I took what I could get.

"Stop it, Billie! No regrets. What you did was the best thing you could have ever done for you and Ethan." Shaking my head and closing my eyes, I quickly erase all thoughts of what could've been.

After waiting for about five minutes, a lovely, voluptuous lady approaches me with her right arm outstretched. "Hello, Isabelle! Welcome to Grant Corp. I'm Lydia Parks. I'm one of the senior accountants in the Finance Department and will be your supervisor for the four weeks you'll be working for us." She seems to be in her forties, with a chirpy voice and warm demeanor. I shake her hand firmly, knowing a good handshake shows good character.

"Oh, please call me Billie. Thank you for giving me the opportunity to work for Grant Corp."

"Of course. You have good references so it was an easy decision for me. Well, let's go up to the office, shall we?" I follow her as she walks towards the security turnstile. "This is your pass. You will need to swipe it here, like so." *Beep!* "Once you hear that beep, these dividers will open."

"Oh, like when I get into the subway." I follow her lead. I've never worked for a company with such high security. It makes me wonder what's so important within these walls that they have to be this stringent.

As if reading my thoughts, she continues, "They are very mindful of security here. Mr. Grant has always been very adamant at keeping his staff safe."

"Oh, okay. That's good to know," I nod at Ms. Parks with a small smile. Nice to know the big boss man cares. But I'll probably never meet the CEO anyway, so I don't think much of it.

She presses the elevator button going up. Once inside the mirrored cab, she uses her pass again before pressing Level 45. "The Finance Department is located on this floor. You might, however, need to go to the other floors for errands, like on the floor where the upper management will be. Just use your pass before pressing the *Call* button."

I notice the building has fifty floors. "Do I have access to all the floors? Or are they different companies?" I wonder aloud, my filter failing to work once again.

Ms. Parks gives out a tiny laugh while shaking her head. "Sorry, dear, the top two floors are not for all staff, only authorized personnel. Oh, and Grant Corp uses the whole building. Mr. Grant has multiple companies housed in here, but where you'll be working under is basically the 'head office' part." Ms. Parks does an open quotation with her fingers to emphasize her point.

"Oh, okay." I smile apologetically and make a mental note to filter my thoughts before opening my mouth. I really should have researched more about the company.

The elevator door opens to a large office space with tall windows, and almost all of them have great views of the downtown skyline. "Great office," I mention appraisingly.

"It's a great place to work for in general, actually," Ms. Parks explains as she leads me over to where my cubicle will be.

"This will be your area. If you need me, my office is two doors to your left. You will be assisting the team with general administrative duties, some filing, and some errands." She points to a small card on the table next to my office laptop. "This will have all your access codes for your laptop and the programs you need. You can't take this laptop home with you, but you can use it for personal e-mails and such, but please do try to keep that to a minimum."

I look around, trying to take it all in, before I look back at Ms. Parks to give her a smile and a nod. "No problems at all. Thank you Ms. Parks."

"Please call me Lydia. We're not that formal in here. I'll let you settle in first. If you need coffee or other refreshments, the kitchen is right over there." She waves at a room near the elevator. "You'll find the pantry is well stocked with a variety of beverages and snacks. I'll introduce you to the rest of the team during our morning meeting in fifteen minutes, okay? It would be a good chance to meet everyone."

"That would be nice. Thanks again, Lydia. I really appreciate it." She gives me a smile as she heads back to her office. I sink into my chair and switch on the laptop. Looking around in case anyone sees, I quickly sneak out a photograph of Ethan from my purse, and I give it a quick kiss before putting it back with a smile.

***

The team meeting goes smoothly, much to my relief. I get to meet the rest of the Accounting Department staff and personnel. One of the other senior accountants, Daniel Dean, is a big man, probably over six feet, with a strong chest, a kind face, and a dry humor which I like. Unfortunately we have to shake hands, but I retrieve mine as quickly as possible. Human contact, specifically *male* human contact, makes me feel uncomfortable and sometimes even physically sick. But in unavoidable situations like these, I do my best to tolerate it.

And then there's Marla, Jessica, and Boyd, all accountants who have different specializations. They all seem friendly and closer to my age.

I instantly warm up with the girls, but the men … well … as nice as they all seem, subconsciously I can't stand them. But if I want to keep this job, I need to just fucking try to get over my anxieties and act as normal as possible.

"I hope you enjoy temping with us, Billie. I like your nickname, it's pretty cool," Marla comments with a smile. She's cute and petite and wears her pinstripe shift dress well.

"Yeah, welcome to the team. We're not all stuffed shirts you know!" Boyd adds while jokingly pointing at Daniel. Daniel sees it and waves him off with a gruff.

As we're heading out of the meeting room, Boyd asks if I want any coffee so he can show me how the machine works. I nod with a smile, and I follow him to the kitchen. But then Boyd slows down so he can walk next to me. I instinctively move away a step but give him a small smile to cover it up. He seems oblivious to my reaction and gives me a big grin back.

"So, we're all going out for drinks tonight. We, meaning Marla, Jessica, myself, and a couple of the guys from Billing. Would you like to join us?" Boyd asks expectantly. He has warm brown eyes like caramel and is tall and fit with dark blonde hair, cut in a trendy, hipster style. He's wearing a slim-cut suit that works well with his slim build. He's actually good-looking, in a pretty boy kind of way.

"Thanks for the offer, but I have to head home after work." I intentionally leave out the part where I'm going home to spend some time with my son before changing my clothes so I can head out again for my second job.

"Well, okay … raincheck?" he insists, trying to mask his disappointment with a dimpled smile.

"Yes, please." I smile back as we make our coffee.

It will be nice to get to know them all outside of work. After all, I'm only twenty-five years young, and should be at my peak socially. But even though they seem to be a fun and friendly group of people, it's hard to make new friends at work when you're only able to stick around for a few days or a few weeks.

At exactly five in the afternoon, after checking with Lydia, I give her and everyone else a quick good-bye before heading home. *I hope I don't miss my train!* I rush out of the main foyer, and I'm on my way to the train station.

CHAPTER 2

"Mommy!" Ethan's eyes light up with excitement as soon as I open the door. I almost fall backwards from my son's weight as he jumps up and hugs me tightly. Moments like this make it all worth it … all of it.

"Well, hello there, honey! Did you have a good day in school?" I ask after giving my six-year-old little kisses all over his face.

"Yup! Ben and Jonathan played with me, and Ms. Olsen said I wrote my words really well," he tells me proudly.

"Of course you did, because you practice." I ruffle his hair playfully and kiss him on the head. "I'm so proud of you, honey."

"Dinner's ready in five. Eat something before you head out," a female voice calls out from the kitchen.

"Thanks, Michelle. I'll eat quickly. I don't want to be late."

Michelle shares the apartment with us. We've known each other since I first moved to New York seven years ago, when she lived at the apartment across from mine. A New Yorker through and through, she spent her childhood in Harlem, where her parents' interracial relationship were not welcomed with open arms by a few members of the community. They stood their ground and brought their child up to learn acceptance and compassion. And Michelle's lack of pretentiousness is one of the reasons why I found it easy to make a connection with her and to open up about my past. When my financial resources started running low, we've decided to move together into one apartment. It was an easy decision for us to make because she and Ethan get on like a house on fire. Being an only child like me, she doesn't have nieces or nephews, only cousins scattered all over New York and the tristate area. So she's become Ethan's cool aunt, a title she takes very seriously, much to my delight. She has been a very good friend and confidante. And even though we have other friends between us, she's the only one I can truly trust and has never judged me for my past. She is a blessing for Ethan and me.

It's also a blessing that she runs her own graphic design business from home so her hours are flexible, that it enables her to help out with Ethan. I don't know what I'll ever do without her. More than best friends, we're like sisters we've never had and always wished for.

"Tell me about work as well!" Michelle yells out again.

"Okay, will do when I come back!"

Time constraints can only afford me a five-minute shower, so I tie my hair in a bun so it doesn't get wet before I hop in. After I finish, I quickly dry off and rub on my moisturizer before putting on my uniform in record time. Not a big fan of makeup, I just apply some rouge on my cheeks and some lip gloss on my lips. After wearing my comfortable black flats, a quick glance at my mirror confirms that I'm ready.

I head towards the dining room where Ethan is finishing up his meal of mac 'n' cheese, his favorite. He looks up and upon seeing me dressed, he gives me a cute little pout.

"Are you going to the restaurant now, Mom?"

"Yes, honey. I'll just have some dinner first. But don't you worry. I won't have to go tomorrow. I get to stay home with you!"

"Yeah!" He gets me to fist pump him, more than satisfied with my answer.

Michelle comes out from the kitchen with our dinner—sirloin steak and buttered vegetables. She can cook quite well and knows how much I love steak.

"Thanks again, Michelle. I'll make it up to you by cooking dinner tomorrow, okay?"

"Girl, please. Just eat your dinner. You'll need it!" She smiles at me, but her eyes hint of sympathy.

We talk about our work while eating, and I smile back at my best friend. She *is* beautiful, inside and out. Her mom is Irish and her dad is African American, so the combination is amazing. Her eyes are blue, which is a gorgeous contrast to her dark curly hair and even brown skin. She also has a beautiful fit body, which is pure genetic lottery win since she never does a hint of exercise in her life. No wonder she hasn't any trouble with meeting men. In those rare occasions when I get to go out clubbing with her, it's unsurprising that she gets a lot of attention from men. For other women, this may be a cause for insecurity, but for me it's a good thing because it deflects the attention from me, and I won't have to deal with them.

Oh, and it helps that she's not fucked-up like me. I allow myself this sad truth as I kiss my son and say goodnight to both of them on my way out.

***

Back in the city, I still have a few minutes to spare before La Bocca opens. The french restaurant I work for is sleek and elegant—all glass, mirrors, and black and white interiors. I greet the manager and hostess, Annalese, who has shoulder-length, platinum-blonde hair and wearing a red knee-length shift dress with studded capped shoulders. It's an intentional and striking contrast that makes her stand out amongst the surroundings. She cocks her well-formed eyebrow at me.

"Cutting it close tonight, Billie?" she asks coolly.

I raise my hands in surrender. "So sorry, Annalese. No excuses, I'll come in earlier next time."

"You've worked here long enough, and I know your situation. But just be mindful of the time. Brooklyn's not that far away. We still have to prep before we open."

Actually you don't know my whole situation so don't even start. I sigh and close my eyes while I give her a nod. After depositing my purse in one of the lockers, I neatly put my black waist apron on to my hips and tie the strings at the back. We do our usual huddle before we open to confirm our stations, our responsibilities, and discuss any special requests from important clientele who made reservations with us tonight.

"Everyone," Annalese announces with her game face on, "one of our important customers, Mr. Magnus Grant of Grant Corp has a booking with us for a party of six. They will occupy your section tonight, Edward, so don't fuck it up, okay?"

My head jerks up to Annalese. *We've served Mr. Grant before? Maybe when I wasn't around.* I look at Edward's ashen face, which he promptly alters to a more determined one. He proceeds to nod. "You can count on me, Annalese."

"Good. We want Mr. Grant to keep coming back. It's good press and has done wonders to the reputation of our restaurant. If you need help with serving his group, let me know and one of the others can help you."

I roll my eyes, not noticing Annalese pick up my reaction. *Sheesh, is this Mr. Grant guy made of gold?*

"Actually, Billie, your section has the least bookings tonight, so if Edward needs help, you would have to do it. Mr. Grant is a good tipper, so I'm sure your share will be worth your trouble."

"No problem," I answer with a forced smile. I glance at Edward as if to say *Is that okay?* He nods slightly and gives me a relieved smile.

As I'm arranging the table settings at my area, I start to feel apprehensive. More people to serve means a bigger chance of someone, particularly men, touching me. This restaurant caters for the more upper class clientele, so the tips are amazing. But alcohol easily turns any rich men into rich grabby assholes.

I'll be fine ... plus it would give me a chance to see what this Mr. Grant looks like. I assure myself. Maybe I've seen him in the restaurant before but didn't know who he was.

"Okay, everyone, let's have a good night tonight, shall we?" Annalese announces. It's time to open the restaurant.

***

By 8 p.m., the restaurant is buzzing. I can see Edward making little adjustments to Mr. Grant's table settings. He tells me in passing that he normally comes to the restaurant on Tuesdays, when I have my night off. Although, he remembers him coming over on his own last Friday and sitting by the window in front. I was working then and my section doesn't have a clear view of the front part of the restaurant, so there was no way for me to notice him. And Friday gets quite busy, so it's no surprise my focus was with my own customers. This will probably be the only time I'll ever see him since I highly doubt we'll cross paths at work.

A small commotion at the front of the house pulls me back to reality. I look up after placing a basket of freshly baked rolls for a couple I'm serving, to see what the fuss is about. Suddenly I lock my eyes at the breathtaking man talking to Annalese. I notice the change in her body language towards this man in an almost sensual way. She keeps it professional, but it's hard to deny his sexual magnetism, so she automatically responds to it. I for one can't stop staring at him, not even knowing my mouth is agape.

He is tall, definitely over six feet. He wears his dark, almost black hair short on the sides and back, but wavy on the crown. It's inviting enough for me to want to run my hands through it, but he does it himself a couple of times. He has olive skin and a sculpted nose, and the way he wears his tailored suit could rival any GQ model. And what about those lips of his? Even from afar … wow, those lips. It twitches up ever so slightly in an oh-so-sexy way. He has a certain brooding quality in him, but wow … his presence commands attention, and boy does he know it.

I know it.

"Mr. Grant, welcome back to La Bocca. Your table is ready for you and your party. Right this way, sir," Annalese informs him in her sexiest tone as she leads Mr. Grant and the other suits towards the reserved table close to my area.

Holy shit!

"Double shit," I gulp as I'm overcome by his close proximity. For some unknown reason, I feel a pull coming from inside of me going outwards and towards the man in question. He must have felt my eyes on him because he raises his and fix them on me. Feeling crimson creep up my cheeks, I blink a little too rapidly before turning away and looking anywhere but at his direction. I go back to my section to check on my customers and distract myself from another embarrassing situation.

"Thank you, Annalese." From where I'm standing, I can hear his voice low and smooth, almost like warm liquid, surprising me as I feel the reverberation of it shoot straight to my core. *That can't be normal.* He nods at Annalese and gives her a slight smile, just enough to make her swoon a little.

"Excuse me, Miss!" A guy who is wearing a navy blue shirt and waving a menu on his hand calls my attention, forcing me to focus on my job at hand.

"Yes sir, are we ready to order?"

***

I continue to serve my customers while sneaking glances at the handsome gentleman sitting just a few tables from my section. How can anyone be that good-looking? And why do I feel so affected by him and not in a negative way? I try to push off the thoughts and remind myself that men are pigs and should be avoided at all costs.

He is in deep conversation with some suits. From their interaction, this is most likely a business dinner, and an expensive business dinner at that, noting the bottles of vintage wines on their table. I don't want to stare too long. I'm too afraid he might look up at me, and I'll be a goner. So I turn away and focus my attention on my customers instead.

I'm helping the busboy clean up one of my remaining empty tables when Edward walks up to me. "Billie, I need your help serving the main course. I don't want them to wait too long for their meals."

Admittedly I am a little hesitant, knowing I'll be serving the table of the CEO of Grant Corp, the same company I'm temping for. And the same man I've been discreetly ogling since he came in. But I sigh and say, "Sure thing."

We take the plates from the line and carefully carry them towards Mr. Grant's table. I'm mindful not to look at the man himself, in case I get distracted and drop my plates.

"Excuse me, ma'am, sirs. Your entree is served," announces Edward.

Most of them look up from their conversations and start to shift to accommodate us as we serve their food. Mr. Grant is the last to look up after checking his phone. When he does, he looks straight at me. I thought his eyes are nice from afar but up close … God, he has the most startling blue eyes—light blue, with silver specs, and long lashes to top it all off.

My normal reaction is to look away because if I can help it, I try to avoid any form of contact with men. But this time, I hold his gaze, surprisingly unafraid and completely drawn to him. His eyes widen, probably surprised at my boldness. Then the corners of his mouth lift into a smile. His smile crumbles my composure and practically renders me off balance, so I break away from his gaze and proceed to serve their meals, silently praying that I won't drop anything at all.

And just because luck isn't on my side tonight, the last plate I'm holding has to be his, of course! I carefully reach over and place the steak au poivre in front of him. Great, he likes steaks too.

"Enjoy your meal, sir," I say meekly, feeling myself blush once again.

"Thank you," he answers back, and his voice seems to resonate through me. I twist the plate around so the right side of it faces him, but as he reaches for the plate, his hand brushes accidentally with mine. That single touch makes me catch my breath, not because it is unwelcome but because I instantly feel the electricity surge through me. It's like nothing I've ever felt before … like my whole being has woken up from that one accidental touch.

It's impossible. Pulling myself up, I steal a glance at his handsome face. He seems unaffected, though his brooding stare is fixed solely on me. Did he feel something too? *Nah.* He must be thinking I'm just a little on the odd side.

"Enjoy your meals," Edward speaks to my left. Relieved at the interruption, I take his cue and leave the table but not before I see Mr. Grant nodding towards me with the corner of his lips curved up in a smile, tightening me up inside. I don't expect that hint of a smile to affect me like it does, and I don't want him to see, so I quickly turn back to my waiting customers.

As I'm walking away, I feel a weird tingling on my neck, like someone is staring at me from behind. But I won't dare turn around. I'm still in shock at what I felt after the slightest contact from him.

In the last seven years, I've perfected the art of avoiding a man's touch, unless I really have to. A man's touch brings back too many bad memories, awful memories I'm trying to replace with better ones. But it hasn't been easy, and it's one of the issues I've spoken with my previous therapist about. But I realize that as long as the contact is on my terms, it's somehow manageable.

"Mr. Grant looked weirded out after you served him. What was that about?" Edward asks me from behind. All I can do is shrug my shoulders. I have no words of explanation to give him anyway because I'm just as confused as he is.

I keep myself busy with my remaining customers. But once in a while I hear his deep voice, and something stirs inside of me. After finishing their desserts which, thankfully, Edward didn't need me for, Mr. Grant motions towards Edward, who rushes to him. I assume he wants his check, and I'm right. I try to remain invisible, still embarrassed by the way I reacted earlier and a little relieved that he's finally leaving. I'm still trying to figure out what the hell I felt back then.

When they finally start heading out, I feel somewhat relieved, yet sad at the same time. But before he leaves, Mr. Grant looks around for something … or someone, with a slight scowl on his face. I try to watch him without being caught, wondering if he's upset about the earlier incident and hoping he isn't. I really need this job.

So I discreetly hide out inside the kitchen, pretending to help wipe the cutlery while getting a better view of him through the serving window. Mr. Grant hands Annalese something which I assume is Edward's tip. She smiles at him seductively and nods. He looks around the restaurant again. I'm just thankful that my vantage point is hidden from the public. He leaves the restaurant with the rest of the suits, a look of disappointment written on his face.

As soon as he leaves, I breathe a sigh of relief. But relief turns to worry as I see Annalese walking towards the kitchen with Edward. "Billie!" she calls out as she opens the kitchen door.

"I'm here, Annalese. Look, I don't know what hap—"

She cuts me off, "Mr. Grant wanted me to personally give you this." Her voice is clipped as she hands me an envelope with a thousand dollars in cash inside.

I must look like a deer in headlights when Annalese hands me the wad of cash. "What? Why would he give me such a massive tip?"

She shrugs. "He said that this is on top of what he tipped Edward. Apparently he was quite pleased with your service and wanted to give you this tip himself, but, well, you're in here." She rolls her eyes at me. "If I were you, I'd give some of that to Edward. He was Mr. Grant's server, and he gave you a lot more!"

Edward, who is standing behind Annalese, surprises me with his response. "It's okay, he gave me more than enough, and I know Billie needs it. She didn't have nearly enough customers tonight." He gives me a friendly smile.

"Sure, whatever. Good job tonight, everyone." Annalese dismisses us with a wave of her well-manicured hand before heading back to the front of the house.

"Thanks, Edward. I owe you one." I offer him a smile, grateful for his understanding. But for the rest of the night, I'm left wondering why Mr. Grant would be this generous to someone like me and if I'll ever get a chance to thank him for it.

***

It is almost one in the morning when I get home and as tired as I am, I always make sure to check on Ethan before going to bed. He's sleeping peacefully while cuddling his beloved teddy bear. Walking oh so quietly towards him, I lay a light kiss on his temple. He stirs slightly towards me while still asleep, and it gives me a chance to admire him. His hair is slightly lighter in color than mine, and he has a pert nose and a small dimple on his chin. On the day he was born, I thanked the heavens that except for that dimple on his chin, he got his looks from me. I'd surely love Ethan unconditionally though, even if he'd look like his father, but not having a blatant reminder of *him* on my son's face helps with the healing process. I close my eyes and refrain from digging up the past, before quietly letting myself out of Ethan's room.

Back in my own bedroom, I strip and take a much-needed shower to remove the night's dirt and grime. As I rinse off, my thoughts drift to Mr. Grant. Mr. Magnus Grant. He's the first man in a long time who didn't make me feel disgusting with his touch. He's impossibly handsome and so damned sexy … and definitely way, way out of my league. I try to strike that one contact from my memory while changing into my pajamas, letting out a resigned sigh before lying in my bed and grabbing a novel I've been reading. As much as I love to escape through the books I read, I'm hoping sleep will claim me sooner. The sooner I sleep, the sooner Magnus Grant will be out of my thoughts.

CHAPTER 3

"Wake up, Mommy! Wake up, Mommy!" I open my eyes in slits towards the calm little voice I'm hearing, and I find Ethan lying on his stomach beside me, nudging my arm.

"Morning, Ethan." I give him a cuddle before checking the time. "Oh no!" I shout out, flying out of my bed. "I slept in! We're going to be late!"

Oh no! Oh no! Oh no! I'm screaming in my head, while running towards the kitchen.

"Mom, Michelle already gave me cereal. I'm full!" Ethan calls out. With a huge sigh of relief, I rush back to my room to get ready.

"Morning, Billie!" Michelle pops her head in on cue. "Now c'mon, Ethan. Let Mommy have her shower and get dressed, and I'll help you out with your clothes, okay?" She winks at me, mouthing *Go!*

"You're awesome, Michelle!" I shout out to her as I head to the bathroom.

"I know!" she laughingly shouts back.

I quickly shower and blow-dry my hair, deciding I'll let my natural waves fall, keeping my fingers crossed they stay manageable the whole day. I put on my black skirt, noticing how snug it is on my hips but in a flattering way. For my top, I choose my emerald-green sleeveless blouse with my matching black suit jacket to complete the togs. Happy with my outfit, I grab my purse, making sure my work pass and phone are inside before I head out to the kitchen to see Ethan all dressed up and ready to go. I give him a big smile as he pours me some cereal and milk.

"You're awesome too, little man!" I bend down to kiss the top of his head. "I'm going to eat quickly so I can take you to school. Michelle will pick you up and as soon as I get home, I will make you your favorite," I tell Ethan with a wink.

"Is it mac 'n' cheese?" he asks excitedly.

"Would you like mac 'n' cheese again or fried chicken?" I raise my eyebrows playfully.

"Fried chicken!"

"You got it, buddy!"

"Yes!"

***

By lunchtime at work, I feel my stomach rumbling. Cursing myself for forgetting to pack my lunch, I check my wallet hoping to pop down and get a sandwich. That's when I notice the thick bunch of bills inside. *Oh yeah, I have my ridiculously massive tip from last night. I can spare a few dollars for my lunch, then some to buy groceries tonight, and the rest to pay the rent.*

While mentally budgeting, a picture of the tipper himself, Mr. Grant, pops in my head. I frown at myself for my somewhat odd behavior last night. He probably thinks I'm a weirdo. Maybe that's why he felt sorry for me. Good. I hope it means he'll steer clear of me. Someone as handsome as him will have a string of women vying for his attention. I'm just a fucked-up runaway who's better off without any men complicating my life.

But why am I thinking he'll remember me in the first place? I dismiss it as part of my delirium, brought about by hunger and nothing more.

On my way to the elevator, Lydia calls out to me, "Billie! Hold up. Are you heading out to lunch?"

I nod at her. "Yes, would you like something from the deli?"

"No, I had lunch already, but thanks for asking. I was actually hoping you could take these files up to the CFO. He's not on this floor. You have to go up to the forty-eighth. If I didn't have the auditors with me right now, I would do it myself. He needs these files immediately for a meeting that's … already started!" she says, panicking after checking her watch.

"No problem, Lydia. And I'll introduce myself, as well."

"That's right. I forgot to introduce you to him! I'm sorry about that. I'm so absentminded sometimes! His name is Charles Dune, by the way. Just ask upstairs where his office is." She hands me the files. "Thanks again, Billie. Take an extra ten to fifteen minutes from your lunch break if you want." She smiles with relief before walking back to her office.

I push the *Call* button for the elevator to take me two floors up. As soon as the cab doors open, a familiar nervous knot forms in my stomach. *Must be the thought of meeting the CFO. I hope he's not a jerk … or better yet, I hope he doesn't want to shake hands.*

I ask one of the girls on the floor where Mr. Charles Dune's office is. She points at the direction of his office but also mentions that he's currently in a meeting, and the door is closed. So I tell her who sent me, and why I need to interrupt him, and she nods and motions me to go ahead.

When I reach Mr. Dune's office, I peek inside the semifrosted glass wall next to his door. Inside I can see him talking animatedly with someone sitting across the table from him. Because the office is closed, I can barely hear their voices, but I can confirm his guest is a male, judging by his expensive leather shoes, the only clue I have of the mystery person. Mr. Dune nods as if understanding what the other person is saying and suddenly starts to laugh out loud. *At least whoever he is, he seems funny.* But then, Mr. Dune looks up to where I'm standing, leaving me frozen by the door. *Uh-oh!* But he just smiles at me kindly and motions me to come inside.

"Um, excuse me, Mr. Dune?" I speak timidly while standing by the doorway. "Lydia asked me to send these files up to you for your meeting?"

"Oh yes, that's right. She did call to tell me her temp is coming up. She forgot to mention your name though. I don't think I've seen you around before. Did you just start recently?" he asks with calm interest. I notice his guest shifting in his seat.

I'm holding the folders of files across my chest as if they will somehow give me protection. "Um yes, Mr. Dune. My name is Billie, I mean Isabelle Morrison. I just started working here yesterday." My voice is shaky from the nerves. I'm still hoping he won't want to shake hands. He seems nice enough, but for me, it doesn't really matter. I know for sure I won't like it.

Mr. Dune motions for me to get closer. "Ah, you're in luck. You get to meet the big boss man as well."

I feel my blood rush up to my face. *Oh. Holy. Crap.* Not him. My feet feel like lead as I put one before the other. And my stomach is sinking at a very fast rate. My eyes leave Mr. Dune and lock on the tall, dark-haired man whose eyes are now fixed on me.

Oh. Holy. Crap of all craps. It *is* him.

Those blue eyes leave me static on the spot as they take me in from head to toe. He isn't even being discreet about it. If this were any other man, I might feel nauseous and worse, run away. But when he's looking at me like this, I feel that same pull that drew me to him last night. But what leaves me in shock is the tightness I feel *down there*. I can't believe how turned on he makes me feel! I continue to gawk at him, watching him stand up, with my eyes wide and unblinking. The corners of his lush lips rise up into a smile, reaching his eyes, like he's pleased to see me. Or maybe I'm just imagining it. He probably just remembers I'm that weirdo server from last night. Everything seems to be in slow motion as he takes a few steps towards me and raises his hand to shake mine. "Hello, Isabelle Morrison, it's good to meet you. I'm …"

Thud, thud!

"Oh shoot!" I yelp in a tiny voice when the folders holding the files slip out of my arms and straight to the floor, leaving a mess around my feet. I'm on my knees in no time, trying to salvage the files, thankful my bowed head won't allow them to see how embarrassed I feel.

The same pair of leather shoes I noticed a minute ago is now planted right in front of me. I must admit they are great-looking shoes … big shoes … he's got big feet which apparently means … *stop it, Billie!* One shoe disappears and replaced by his knee on the floor. And before I know it, he starts to help me pick up the files scattered everywhere. I notice Mr. Dune coming around his desk when I hear Mr. CEO's voice, deep and with a hint of mirth.

"I've got it, Charles." It halts Mr. Dune from proceeding and then Mr. Grant turns back to me.

"I'm Magnus Grant." He says in a strong yet soothing voice, and I can't help but sneak a glance at him as soon as I hear him speak. God, that voice is so warm it can melt the whole Arctic Circle. He offers his hand towards me, and I just stare at it with the memory of last night's touch still fresh in my head.

And then, as if my suffering isn't enough, his scent hits me. He smells of expensive aftershave, mixed with something I can't recognize, something distinctly his own. I suddenly feel my mouth water. This is going from bad to worse.

Then I notice his extended hand, still waiting to shake mine. So I raise my hand slowly to meet his, holding it steady and hoping to keep the contact quick. But as soon as we touch, I feel the same tremor between us. It feels even stronger now, like volts of electricity. I hold back my gasp as these tremors quickly make their way down to my stomach and finish down there … down … there.

I'm not used to this strange, yet pleasurable sensation. I try to let go, but he closes his hand firmly over mine. I look down at our hands held in what looks like an innocent handshake, and for the first time in a long time, I don't feel any panic or anxiety. I like how it feels ... and it scares me senseless. I muster enough courage to look up to his face ... that gorgeous face of his. His mouth is slightly open, like he's just exhaled deeply. His blue eyes, which are like light pools of water, are growing darker. But his brows are slightly furrowed like he's trying to figure this out. Did he feel it too? I doubt it. He probably just confirmed that I'm acting oddly. The moment is over as soon as I hear Mr. Dune's subtle cough. I try to let go of my hand again, and he finally lets me.

Oh. A sudden chill replaces the warmth I felt, making me hope he will hold me again. But as he gathers the rest of the files on his side, I can't help but feel relieved. As wonderful as his skin feels against mine, I don't trust myself around him.

He stands up with some of the files while I quickly gather the rest of them to put in their rightful folders. Then his hand is reaching out for mine again.

No way.

"It's okay, I got it ... thank you." I hold onto the files protectively with both arms as I begin to stand up. He replaces his hand in his trouser pocket, then chuckles discreetly at the awkward way I let myself up. *Douche.* Then I place the files on Mr. Dune's desk before smoothing down my skirt. I glance at Mr. Grant and his eyes are skimming over my body, like he's enjoying my actions. For some reason, I don't feel the least bit offended at his blatant admiration. Instead, I actually feel flattered.

What's going on with me?

I hand Mr. Dune his much-needed files and try to make a quick exit. "I'm so sorry again, sirs. But you'll find all of those files in order. I'll let myself out now." I try to focus my attention towards Mr. Dune alone and speak to him directly. But the goose bumps I'm getting from Mr. Grant's intent gaze are increasingly harder to ignore. I start walking backwards to the door. I need to leave now and distance myself from him and this crazy energy between us.

"Don't worry about it, Isabelle. And thank you," Mr. Dune answers in a kind voice. He turns to Mr. Grant and says, "So should we continue with our discussion, Magnus? We can go through the files I was talking about. Let me just find it ..."

"While you're doing that, I'll walk Isabelle to the elevators. I'll be back soon, Charles." Mr. Grant turns to my direction, and I panic.

"Oh, there's no need to, Mr. Grant. I ... I don't really want to inconvenience you at all." I raise my hand, hoping to stop him.

"But I insist, Ms. Morrison. It's not an inconvenience to walk my staff to the elevators." There is an almost wicked undertone to his voice. In no time at all, he's next to me, making my mouth water as soon as I breathe in his scent.

"I'm ... I'm only a temp here, sir. I'm not technically your staff." Great, now I sound like a smart ass. Luckily, he finds humor in what I said, and he lets out a chuckle. It sounds endearing and light, and a chuckle escapes my mouth as well. We pass by the girl I asked from earlier, who's now making googly eyes at Mr. Grant. I assume he must be getting a lot of this, all the time. We stop by the elevators, and I quickly push the button going down. I try to look everywhere else than his direction, but the only diversion I have is the frosted glass wall separating us from the rest of the office.

"Who knows, Isabelle, maybe something might open up and you'll be a permanent member of the staff for my company." He shrugs nonchalantly, looking directly at me with a coy smile, and both his hands in his trouser pockets.

When I am unable to respond, he leans forward ever so slightly so his mouth is close enough that I can feel his warm breath against my cheek. It takes a lot out of me not to turn my head so my mouth can meet his.

Wait, did I just really think that?

"And I don't really like being called sir by you. It makes me feel ancient when I'm not. Please call me Magnus." He speaks in hushed tones so only I can hear it.

Narcissist much? Good, this will just turn me right off.

I manage to straighten my back but still looking straight ahead. "I don't feel it's proper for me to just call you by your first name, sir. You *are* the CEO of the company, and you deserve all the respect from your employees."

"Hmm ... that's interesting." He pulls back, and he regards me thoughtfully. "I looked for you at the restaurant before I left."

He did? I feel myself blush once again.

"I had to help out in the kitchen. My section wasn't as busy as Edward's ... well, he was actually your server last night, sir. I was just requested to help out."

"Did you get my tip?" he asks with interest.

I turn to him slightly, nodding and offering a smile, "I did. And I wanted to thank you because that was very generous of you, sir. But I didn't deserve it. I only served your table that one time."

"That one time made a lot of difference. It made my night ... memorable."

I quickly turn my attention towards the elevator doors, trying not to appear like what he just said didn't affect me.

The elevator going down finally arrives. I hurriedly step inside and press the button for the lobby.

"Well, thank you again, sir, for the tip last night and for not firing me on the spot when I messed up the files at Mr. Dune's office." I shyly smile at him, trying to avoid his arresting blue eyes.

He holds the elevator doors as they start to close to keep them open. "My name is Magnus, not sir. You better start calling me by my first name because I'm sure we'll be seeing a lot more of each other." And with those words, he steps back to let the cab doors close but not before I catch him smirking at me, with his eyes confirming his intention. *Was that a threat or a promise?* The way he looks at me makes me feel utterly confused and extremely turned on ... again. Who knew smirking could look so sexy?

Well, shit. This cannot be right.

"Get yourself together, Billie," I whisper harshly to myself, slapping my thigh at the same time. "You can't be dealing with these things right now." I let out a deep sigh of relief as I head out of the building for some much-needed air and sustenance.

***

I am back at my desk after lunch, using the whole hour distracting myself from what just happened with Mr. Grant earlier. I'm about to sit down when I notice a small interoffice envelope at my desk with *Isabelle Morrison* handwritten on it. Because it's an internal mail, there's nothing to indicate who sent it. I pick it up and feel something hard and rectangular inside. Curious, I open the envelope carefully and find an access pass inside.

I already have one, why am I getting another one?

I'm about to walk to Lydia's office, when a business card drops from the envelope. As soon as I pick the card up off the floor, I notice something handwritten on it as well.

'Isabelle, use this card to access the top floor.'

My breathing accelerates as I flip over the card to confirm the details: Magnus Grant, CEO, Grant Corp.

I return everything back in the envelope as my heart pounds with excitement and apprehension. What does he want from me? Is this a joke? Am I in trouble from the incident earlier? Oh no, what if I'm fired? My excitement turns to panic. Shit, do I just ignore this or do I reply by e-mail or something?

I try to regain my composure as I log on to my laptop. That's when I notice a pop-up message confirming a meeting. I check the details and realize Mr. Grant booked a meeting in my calendar to block my time. It's for this afternoon at five o'clock. Location: his office.

Whoa, can he do that? And why will he want to meet me, in his office, no less! This is shady, and my alarm bells should be ringing by now. But instead, that tingling sensation I've been keeping at bay, is slowly creeping back. I breathe deeply, trying to expel them out. I stare at the appointment in my calendar, thinking this is highly unusual; therefore, it must be that someone is pulling a prank on me. Why would a CEO go through all this trouble to see me? He's a busy man after all and would probably not think twice about someone like me. Yup, this is definitely a prank.

I heave a deep breathe, place the envelope with the pass and the note inside my drawer, and click the *Decline* button.

The rest of the afternoon flies by quickly, with Lydia asking for my assistance in providing information required by the auditors. She also has plenty of back files that need organizing, which I get on top of. Before I know it, it's the end of my working day.

I'm in the middle of saving a file before logging off when my phone rings, making me jump with surprise.

"Good afternoon, this is—"

I am cut off by a low voice on the other end of the line. "You've declined my invitation."

"I'm sorry? Who, may I ask, is calling?" I close my eyes shut, dreading to hear the answer. How can his voice so easily give me a surge of electricity straight down to my core?

Long pause. I literally hear my blood pumping strongly while my ear is pressed against the headset. "Don't pretend you don't know who this is." I notice a slight irritation in his voice.

"Mr. ... Mr. Grant?" I can hear him exhaling loudly. Yes, he's definitely irritated. Then I remember what he told me earlier. "Magnus," I whisper.

"Good girl." Normally that remark will trigger something terrible inside of me, and I'll lash out. But for some reason, I'm feeling all sorts of warm and fuzzy, knowing I pleased him. But I try to maintain some composure in my voice, wishing my whole body will do the same. "What can I do for you?" I ask, managing to stop my voice level from rising.

"Didn't you get the envelope I sent for you?"

"Um yes, I did, but ... I thought someone was just pulling a prank on me."

"Ah, so that's why you declined my invitation. Fair enough," he concludes, pauses. And before I can say something, he follows through with what I'm hoping he won't follow through on.

"You're still expected in my office, Isabelle."

Damn.

"I ... okay. Will it be a short meeting, sir? Because I don't want to miss my train home." I leave out that I promised a home cooked meal for my son and best friend tonight. He doesn't need to know what I do beyond my work hours.

He lets out a small chuckle. And having that sound so close to my ear, like his mouth is actually pressed against me, sends delicious shivers all over. "So you're back to calling me sir, huh? Look, you could take my word that it won't be long. I just want to have a chat with you, but I would appreciate it if we could do this face-to-face. Don't worry, I'll make sure that you get home safe."

My mind starts to race on what he possibly wants to talk to me about. And all I can come up with is that right at this very moment, I don't care. I just want to see his face again.

"Okay. I'll be up shortly." I stumble as I try to get up from my desk, my heartbeat quickening with anticipation. I say my quick good-byes to everyone on my floor, making sure the elevator is empty before swiping the second card to go to the top floor.

I really don't have enough time to back out. Soon enough, I'm on the top floor. My eyes widen as I step out of the cab. It's like a smaller version of the main foyer. There's a small waiting area and a kitchenette with a high-end espresso machine, teas, and fresh fruits. In front of me is a small reception area, with an attractive lady behind the reception desk. Her bob is cut in an angular way that suits her high cheekbones and almond-shaped eyes.

"Hello. Isabelle Morrison, right?"

"Yes, that's me," I reply, surprised that I seem to be expected.

"Mr. Grant is ready to see you. If you would like to go through those double doors, it will lead you to his office. Denise Cann, Mr. Grant's executive assistant, will be able to assist you if you need anything at all."

Wow, it all seems so formal. I thought Magnus just wanted to ask me something.

"Thank you, um...?"

"Belinda, Belinda Lam," she answers with a personable smile.

The massive doors open automatically which I assume Belinda made happen. Inside is room with a hallway leading to another set of double doors, this time in dark timber. To my right, I notice an older lady typing steadily on her laptop. She has pleasant features, her light blonde hair cut pixie style, and a petite frame which is a contrast to her austere demeanor. The plaque on her desk says *Denise Cann – Executive Assistant to the CEO.*

But that demeanor changes when she raises her head to greet me. "Ah, Ms. Morrison," she says brightly, "I'm Denise. Mr. Grant has been expecting you. His office is just through those doors." She waves at the double doors at the end of the hallway. "Would you like me to get you any drink? coffee, juice, tea?"

"Oh no, thank you, Denise. I'm sure I won't be long." I smile at her nervously, giving her a wave before making my way towards Magnus's office.

To the right of the hallway, I notice a meeting room, and to my left, the wall is lined with photographs of what appear to be random things and places but presented so well that they look like works of art. But what stands out is an enlarged photograph of a younger-looking Magnus, somewhere in Africa, with a group of beautiful African children happily surrounding him. He looks so serene, laughing with the children as some of them give him a hug. At the bottom it says *Grant Foundation.*

Wow! So not only is he a business leader but also a big philanthropist. My heart swells at the black and white photograph, until I remind myself why I came up here in the first place. I hesitate before turning to knock softly at the door, still questioning what the hell this is all about.

"Come in, Isabelle," his voice is calm but commanding as he calls me in.

I make my way inside and close the door behind me. Somehow I know where to find him in his expansive office. It's almost like I'm drawn to his beacon of energy. He is standing by the window, but he turns to my direction. My feet, however, are glued on the floor, and I suddenly feel self-conscious as his eyes are now focused on me.

"I trust you had a good day today?"

Small talk. I can handle small talk. "Yes, I did. Busy, but I prefer it that way."

Magnus just keeps his silence.

"Big office you have here," I declare nervously, thinking I need to say something to break the ice. I let my eyes roam around his vast office. Half the office is made up of windows. There is a massive flat screen television on the other side of the wall, with two long black leather couches and a clear coffee table on top of a chocolate colored fluffy rug. He is standing by the minibar where there are two smaller black leather seats with table in between. A stunning piece of artwork hangs behind his impressive mahogany office desk. It's an office fit for a powerful magnate with extremely good taste.

"You don't have to stand there, you know. Please, the view is better from here." His voice is trying to hide a chuckle as he motions for me to walk over to where he's standing.

"Would you like something to drink? whisky? wine?"

"No, but thanks for offering." I walk slowly towards the windows and stand next to him but still keeping my distance.

He gives me a discrete once-over and a sexy smirk forms. "Thank you for coming to see me, Isabelle."

"Please call me Billie. And with all due respect, you kind of didn't leave me any other choice." I am hoping to sound defiant, but I'm only succeeding at sounding shaky with nerves.

"There's always a choice, and you chose to come and see me, and for that I thank you. And I also choose to call you Isabelle instead of Billie. I hope you don't mind." His hand reaches up to touch my bare, upper arm. It's an act that may be intended as a friendly gesture, but I can't help the gasp that escapes my mouth— not from my distaste at being touched, but from the surge of the same electricity that that one touch has created throughout my body.

Why did I forget my suit jacket downstairs? Damn it!

He pulls his hand back and bends his long fingers into a knuckle. I look up to him and see the same expression as last night's. Could he have felt it too? The electricity I felt, did he feel it too? Or did he just get offended with my reaction?

I begin to panic. It's probably the latter. Surely I can't stay. But I know that a part of me, that curious part of me, wants to, just to see where this is going. But the tension in the room is palpable, and I wonder if he's aware of it too.

"What did you want to talk about, Magnus?" I turn away from the beautiful skyline and face him with my arms firmly crossed in front of me.

His smouldering blue eyes meet my stare, and to my surprise, my nipples begin to harden. Not from the fact that I'm jacketless but because his gaze is doing things to my body. Thank goodness I crossed my arms to hide the evidence!

"Before I get into that, please, have a seat." He waves at the plush leather chair to my right. I sit myself down, but he remains standing. Instead, he just follows my movements with those stunning eyes of his.

"I have a confession to make. Last night wasn't the first time I saw you," he starts with a somber tone.

Okay. Right now, I don't know where this is going.

He continues, "I normally don't go out on Friday nights by my lonesome. I usually prefer the company of a ... friend."

Ha! Friend, my ass! Marla and Jessica have told me stories about Magnus and how he only dates the most beautiful women. Not just models, mind you, but celebrities and socialites. I suppose, only someone of that caliber is a perfect match for him. The thought makes my shoulders sag.

"But I decided to dine alone at La Bocca that night," he continues.

"Friday last week?" I ask. He gives me a small smile, but his eyes appear to read my expression.

"You were serving at the restaurant that night, but you were out
back so I was only able to see you when you were coming from the kitchen. Even from afar, you caught my attention. I found you … exquisite."

I feel my cheeks start to redden. "Right! That's me from afar, alright!" I joke nervously, cursing myself a little for sounding sarcastic. But I can't help it. How can he find me exquisite when I was run off your feet?

He continues, eyeing me intently, "I was drawn to you." The back of his forefinger, traces the line of my jaw. When I likely in this instance will flinch and move away, his touch leaves me hot and craving for more.

"Then last night, when I finally saw you up close for the first time, I knew I wanted to touch you, to feel you." I can't help the small gasp that escapes me. But I stay in place, unwilling to move. Without warning, he grazes his thumb over my lower lip, and my mouth opens slightly.

"And this morning, after you left Charles's office, all I could think about are your lips and how I'd like to taste them."

My hand instinctively covers my lips, a feeble attempt at protecting them. It only serves to make Magnus focus on them more. God, and here I contemplate I lack a filter between my brain and my mouth! This is wrong. So. Wrong. Then why am I not pulling away? Why am I still sitting here?

Then realization hits me. "Wait, did you know I was working there last night?"

"I asked Annalese about you before I left that Friday. I wanted to know what nights you worked. When I know what I want, I act fast, Isabelle. She didn't want to disclose anything, but a large tip helped matters."

I furrow my brow. "You what?" He asked for my schedule and Annalese gave it to him? Whatever happened to privacy? I guess money can buy that, as well.

"I knew I wanted to have you the first time I saw you. Last night confirmed it. This morning made it even clearer."

The butterflies that have decided to take residency in my stomach since I've met Magnus are now fluttering wildly. I mean, is this man for real? And why am I still not offended?

"What … exactly are you telling me?" I ask, not realizing that I'm holding my breath, waiting for his answer.

He sits on the small table right in front of me, his whole body facing me directly. And with him this close, all of my senses seem to be going on overdrive. He takes my hands in his and rubs his thumbs over my knuckles.

For a long moment, he just stares at our joined hands, and I can't help but do the same. Somehow, Magnus holding me like this is actually beginning to calm me down. But it's just so surreal that his touch can actually make me feel like this. Finally, Magnus finds his voice, "What I'm telling you is this—I want you. I want to kiss you. I want to taste your skin. And yes, I want to fuck you. And if I'm not mistaken, you want exactly the same thing."

My head jerks up, and my mouth hangs open, staring at him gobsmacked. I am dumbfounded by the words that have just come out of Magnus's mouth. It feels like a bucket of iced water has been thrown at me, and my knee jerk reaction is to pull away, which I do. For goodness sake, what do I say to that?

Does he really think he wants me when he doesn't even know me? And is he that arrogant that he thinks I'll just bow down and say, yes, please?

I want to set him straight, but all I can manage is, "No," while shaking my head repeatedly. "I don't. I don't want the same thing." It's a pitiful attempt at indignation. Even I am not altogether convinced myself.

"Why not? Aren't you the slightest bit curious about this … whatever this is between us?" he speaks in whispers, reaching out to touch me again.

"Stop it!" I stand up and away from him, knowing I may not be able to control myself if he touches me again. "I can't. This is too much … and way too inappropriate, for goodness sake." I try to step back once more, but my heel hits the chair's leg, and I fumble.

Suddenly I feel strong arms around me. I don't want to hold on to them. But my body betrays me as it succumbs to Magnus's warmth. I know I should pull away because this is so wrong in so many levels. So … many … levels!

I look up to his face with forced bravado so I can demand him to let me go. But how can I, when his eyes are so hypnotic? How can I, when his muscular body is pressed protectively against me and it feels so right ... and so safe? God, this is a heady mix pushing me to surrender.

Magnus licks his lower lip, a movement I've noticed him do a few times. And every time he does, I want to be the one to do it. I want him to kiss me. No, I *need* him to kiss me.

Holy shit, where is this coming from?

He sees the answer he wants in my eyes. "Isabelle, you want this," he groans, cupping my face as his lips dip to touch mine.

Now I understand part of the reason why I rejected those chances to interact with other men all these years. My body and soul have been waiting for this moment ... for this kiss.

His mouth is electric, like something dormant inside of me has been awakened with a jolt. I open my lips instinctively, and his tongue accepts the invitation like it's the most natural thing in the world. My stomach clenches as he gently strokes my tongue before licking my lower lip. I raise my hand and clutch his soft, wavy hair like I've always wanted to. A moan escapes me, pressing him for a deeper kiss. He gives in wholeheartedly and kisses me harder, his tongue massaging the inner depths of my eager mouth. He raises his hand and gently cups my nape, tipping my head up as he takes me, devouring me in a way that is overwhelming and mind-blowing at the same time. I do my best to reciprocate as my tongue sweeps the inside of his mouth, making him moan approvingly. I can't help but savor the delicious tingles that consume my whole body as they travel downwards towards my sex. It's a feeling I've never felt before, and it's fueling my greed for more.

"You taste so good, Isabelle. Just like I knew you would," he whispers in my mouth, at the same time biting my lower lip. I moan. Now *this* is exquisite.

My arms are around his shoulders so our chests are pressed together. I feel his heart racing, just like mine, and it must be our adrenalin kicking in. He starts to nibble the corners of my mouth, traveling towards my jaw. I sigh as he leaves small licks down my neck like small flames heating my skin.

"I want to take you right here, right now," he growls as both of his hands travel to the back of my thighs, slowly making their way up to the hem of my skirt, trying to push it up. He presses me closer to him, and oh my, he's hard!

The warning bells that were sitting dormant are now ringing in my ears. This is happening. Oh, my God, this is happening!

No, it isn't. My body may be waiting for *that* kiss, but I'm unprepared for what comes after.

My whole body stills. My God, this is going too fast … way too fast. How am I allowing it to go this far? My common sense finally takes over. He will just hurt me. I know he will. Just like *him*.

Just like him, Billie!

"No, … stop!" I mumble feebly as I hold on to both of his wrists, stopping his hands from going any further. But although he keeps them in place, he starts to draw small circles on my thighs with his thumbs. It gives me goose bumps, but I bite my lip hard, trying to hold my ground.

He stops kissing my neck, but moves to nibble my ear. God, it feels delicious, but I push my head back so he has no choice but to look at me.

"What's wrong, Isabelle? I know you want me as much as I want you." He is breathing as heavily as I am. And his eyes are fixed on my parted mouth like a predator hungry for his prey. He moves his head towards my lips again, and I start to panic. Why isn't he stopping when I said no?

I have to gain control. The last time I lost all control, I lost everything.

"I. Said. No!" I answer back through gritted teeth, finally finding my voice back.

With all my strength, I shove him off of me. He raises his hands in surrender, his face bewildered but his eyes still glazed with lust. He blinks and shakes his head slightly, trying to get his head on straight. I use this opportunity to back the fuck away from him, to grab my purse and run to the door.

"Wait, Isabelle, don't leave!" he says firmly, and I stop moving. A part of me wants to run back to him, but instead, I hold my place, closer to the door.

Before I know it, he bridges the gap. And his face is a mix of confusion and concern. "What just happened? Why are you running away? I thought you wanted this?"

I hold my hands up, preventing him from coming closer. "No, I don't. I *said* I don't want this. But ... but you took me by surprise."

A look of hurt passes through his eyes, but it's gone in a flash. "Your kiss betrays your words." I don't know how to reply to that. He's right. I wanted that kiss from him. But that kiss, no matter how good it was, will just ruin me. I can't let it happen again.

With all the control I can muster, I answer him back in an even tone. "Well, maybe you'll believe these words—I am *not* a sure thing, like your other women! You can't just *take* me just because you *want* me. And if this is how you'll be while I'm working for your company, then I should just quit right now." I blink away the tears that start to form, surprised at my own vehemence. I do need this job but not like this. Not if the price I have to pay is worth more than my dignity. It doesn't matter if I find Magnus extremely attractive. I can't have this kind of complication in my life.

"Wait, hold on," he urges back, raising a hand as if to hold me off. "First of all, I never wanted you to feel degraded, not for one second. And unless I read your signals wrong, which is highly unlikely, you *did* kiss me back. And third ... don't quit." Sighing, he runs his hand through his hair in resigned frustration. "Please ... don't quit because of this."

The way his voice breaks just then gets my attention. He seems lost, vulnerable even. Did I do that? Surely I didn't? But the way he's looking at me right now, it just makes me want to wrap my arms around his waist and lay my head on his chest. I mentally slap myself for even thinking of it.

"Good-bye, Magnus." I grab my things and inch towards his office doors. I need to get out of here so I can think clearly.

"Wait." I freeze at the firmness of his voice. I look back at him expectantly. "Maybe I did misread your signals. And for that, I sincerely apologize. But I also said I was going to take you home and that's what I'm going to do." His expression changes to someone who's now in control. Any trace of vulnerability is gone.

"Don't oblige yourself on my account. I can make my own way." Is he for real? I turned him down, and yet he still wants to honor his word? I feel my heart flutter for a moment.

"It's the least I can do, Isabelle. I went over the line, and it was uncalled for. And just so you know, I *will* accept full responsibility if you decide to take this further."

"No," I answer, shaking my head. "I'm not going to take it that far. But this can't happen ever again, Magnus." I can feel a small part of me protesting. That part of me wants nothing more than to feel his lips on me again. Well, it can just shut the hell up.

He takes a few tentative steps towards me, pushing his hair back once again. That's when I notice that same look of hurt pass through his face again, if only for a second. "I'll make sure it'll never happen again. Please … let me take you home."

Damn it, why is he looking at me like that right now? I will not win this argument, especially when this usually arrogant man is showing sincere remorse. Or is it hurt pride I see? He probably never thought someone like me would ever say no to someone like him. But it's not like I didn't want him in the first place. And if I'm being honest with myself, I still do. I'm drawn to him like a moth to a flame. But I can't allow myself to give in again … no matter how good his mouth, his hands, and his body feel on me. Even in this messed up head of mine, I know that this situation is all kinds of wrong. Why? Because like the moth to a flame, the moth will end up burned if it gets too close.

But then again, maybe I'm just a masochist.

"Fine," I answer with a sigh. "Take me home."

Checking my watch, I panic when I see it's past six. "Oh, shoot!" I slap my forehead at my slip up.

"What's wrong?" Magnus asks, seemingly concerned.

"Well, I'm … I'm supposed to cook dinner tonight. But it's getting late and I haven't bought anything." I choose my words carefully. Magnus doesn't need to know about Ethan, especially since there's not chance of them meeting anyway. I walk out the door briskly, not wanting to waste another minute.

I notice him take his tailored suit jacket off a hook next to the door, then proceeds to press some buttons, which effectively shuts down his office.

"We could get a takeout on the way." He rests his hand lightly on the small of my back. My body instinctively feels drawn to that hand, but I ignore it. We head towards the double doors and out to the elevators. I notice both Denise and Belinda are gone for the day. *Thank goodness!* I hope they didn't hear the racket we might have made from inside Magnus's office.

We step inside the elevator, standing side by side. His hand doesn't leave my back, and the warmth of his touch is soothing. I don't remember feeling this comfortable with another man. Ever.

"I know a great place that serves the best fried chicken," he says, thankfully breaking the tension. He looks down with a smile. "Everyone loves fried chicken, right? So for how many people are you cooking tonight?"

Okay, that's weird. Is he reading my mind or something? "Actually, I was planning on cooking friend chicken for … um, two of my roommates," I suck in air briefly. That was close. "Um, this place you're talking about, is their food expensive?" I ask, a little worried that his taste in food might not agree with my wallet.

"It doesn't matter if it's expensive or not. It's my treat, Isabelle. It's the least I can do."

"Least you can do for what? You're already taking me home. No need to bribe me with chicken." I sound brusque, and I instantly regret my tone. He's being contrite and I'm giving him shit for it.

Sighing, I continue in a more even tone. "Magnus, you don't have to make up for something that I … well, … a-allowed to happen," I stutter, hardly able to finish what I'm trying to say.

He opens his mouth to say something, but the cab doors open before he can utter a word. At the lobby, a security guard sitting at the main reception looks up in our direction.

"Good night, Mr. Grant … Miss …," the guard gives Magnus a respectful smile and shows me the same courtesy.

"Good night to you too, Johnson," Magnus greets back with a polite nod and a kind smile. There's an air of familiarity between them which I find endearing. Magnus works 'till late nights is all I can conclude.

As for me, all I can manage to do is smile shyly back at him, a little self-conscious at what he might think of at the sight of the CEO of Grant Corp leaving with a protective hand on my back. It makes me wonder if this is a common occurrence.

Outside, I can feel the chilly breeze on my bare arms. It's only September, the first month of autumn, and yet the air seems cooler than usual. *Maybe I should've gone back for my coat.* A light shiver runs through me.

"You feel cold. Here, wear this," he says while handing me his suit jacket. He gently puts it over my shoulders to warm me up.

"Thank you," I manage to blurt out while feeling the onset of a blush coming. I can't help but discreetly breathe in his custom-tailored jacket, knowing his scent must be imprinted on them. The coat still smells of his aftershave intermingling with his own musk. It is a mouth-watering aroma that is sexy and all him. I wonder if ...

"Did you just smell my coat?" he asks interrupting my thoughts with a look on his face that's a cross between curiosity and mirth. "It doesn't smell, does it?"

He's making fun of me. I can tell. And I just made it worse by turning redder. Stupid pale skin and overactive blood vessels!

"Um, no. It's not smelly. You smell great. I mean the coat smells great!" I hiss a curse word under my breath at my obvious lack of filter.

He chuckles softly, but when I look up to him in defiance, I realize he isn't making fun of me at all. He's actually looking at me in an adoring but not patronizing way. It's the kind that makes me feel warm and fuzzy all over. It's charming, but I shouldn't like it at all. When he looks at me like this, it's like he's holding a little hammer, and he's trying to chip away at the walls I've built so carefully around me.

I notice a big black car waiting in front of the building. It has black tinted windows, and it looks extremely expensive. It's like no other limo I've ever seen. And in Manhattan alone, limos are like a dime in a dozen.

I am just about to comment on the vehicle when a man in a black suit hops out of the driver's seat, and he comes around to open the car door. Magnus starts walking towards the car, but stops when he realizes that I'm frozen to the ground with my mouth open.

"*This* is your car?" I ask incredulously.

"One of my cars, yes," he answers with a modest smile, but I see the hint of pride in his eyes. "It's a custom-made Bentley Arnage." He takes my hand while the driver waits by the car door. "Ladies first," he says in a low voice. Damn him and his sexy voice.

"Good evening, Mr. Grant ... ma'am," the driver nods to me with a polite smile.

"Good evening, Alex. This is Isabelle Morrison. We'll be taking her home. But first we have to make a stopover at The Redhead. Could you call them ahead, please, and let them know we're picking up four orders of their fried chicken with all the sides included."

"No problem, Mr. Grant, Ms. Morrison."

"Please call me Billie," I answer back, smiling shyly and tucking my hair behind my ear.

My eyes, however, do not escape Magnus watching the exchanges with a slight frown. Alex must have seen Magnus's expression as well and puts on a more business-like front, closing the door as soon as I'm inside.

I let my eyes and hands wander at the luxurious interiors of the car—plush cream leather seats, more than ample leg room, and small tables for laptops that fold discreetly if not needed. The front part of the car is completely sealed off with a flat screen television hanging from it. The door on the other side opens, and Magnus takes his seat beside me.

"Magnus? I think you might have ordered too much food."

He laughs lightly, making my heart skip a few beats. "Well, if you need someone to help you finish it off, you could invite me up for dinner."

No way, uh-uh! I feel the blood leave my face. "Oh, um, I don't think ..."

He starts laughing again. He was teasing me, and he got the reaction he wanted. "Relax, Isabelle. I'm only kidding. I'll take the fourth chicken order home since now, I've got a craving for it."

I feel relieved, yet surprisingly unhappy at the same time. I internally kick my behind for hoping he was serious at his self-invitation. Instead, I just nod back and begin to scope my surroundings.

"I've never seen a car like this before. It's so, I don't know ... a little over the top?" I speak out aloud, stupidly forgetting whom I'm speaking to.

"Over the top, is it?" He cocks a brow at me, making me regret my lack of diplomacy. To my relief and utter bewilderment, he laughs out loud. The sound of his laughter echoes deep inside me, and I can't help but giggle back.

"Sorry, I have no filter. I shouldn't have ..."

"Don't be sorry. Your honesty is quite refreshing," he regards me with a smile, and I smile back at him. Somehow, it breaks the awkwardness between us from what just happened earlier.

And wow, I wish I can keep that smile of his with me always. The way his face lights up and the way his blue eyes sparkle. It's a sight to see, and I'm not even sure if I'll see it again. Not that I deserve it, anyway, after all …

"Isabelle?"

I blink a few times, not realizing I've been staring at Magnus the whole time.

"I think I lost you there for a second." He eyes me teasingly.

"Sorry, I um … got lost in a thought. You were saying?"

He smiles back at me, and the warm feeling is back. "Don't worry about it. I was telling you about the interiors of the car, but I realize it must be boring the hell out of you."

My eyes widen with embarrassment. "Oh, no! It wasn't that at all. You can tell me all about it … please."

He chuckles softly. "Next time, I will. To be honest, I heard myself as I was pointing out the many features of the car, and even I thought I sounded like a boring pompous ass."

Okay, I must admit that the only thing that stood out from what he just said is that there will be a *next time*. I don't know if I should do an internal jump for glee or make up an excuse to make sure there will be no next time with him.

I remain quiet instead, looking straight ahead to avoid myself from getting distracted by the way he's gazing at me. But the only thing in front of me is the divider with a small television. That's when I realize the implication of that divider. We are completely cut off from the driver and have complete privacy. A nervous current sears through my whole body. I turn towards Magnus and see that he's still watching me, but now with so much heat in his eyes that I feel hotness in between my legs.

"What? Why are you staring at me like that?" I ask, feeling self-conscious.

"I just think you look beautiful with my suit jacket on."

I know my cheeks are now definitely the same color as my hair. I try to avoid his gaze, not knowing how to take compliments well, especially from this man beside me.

"Yeah, right," I titter nervously before I start chewing on my lower lip absentmindedly.

I suck in air as Magnus reaches up, his hand gently pinning one side of my hair behind my ear. Then his fingers begin to trace the line of my jaw, making me sigh at how good his touch feels on my skin. Then he's tipping my head by the chin so we are face-to-face.

"I want to kiss you again, Isabelle. I know I said I'll stop all of this, but damn it, being so near you, I'm struggling." His darkening eyes settle on my lips. Then he shakes his head, sighing with resignation as he pulls away. "Damn it, I'm sorry," he mumbles so softly I barely hear him say it. He doesn't notice my shaky exhale at that moment he pulls away, thankfully. Why does he say these things that make me quiver inside? If only he knew how much I'm struggling too. All those years of caution are about to be thrown out of the window because of this arrogant yet irresistible man in front of me. But before I can do anything I might regret later, the car stops moving. I look outside and notice we're in front of The Redhead.

"Alex is getting the food. We can just wait here," Magnus says, his face now impassive, distant. My heart constricts at the change in him, but I reassure myself it's for the best.

"Okay. No problem," I answer back, but turning away from him so I can look out from my side of the window. It's busy outside with everyone rushing to get to their destinations, going about their business. It's one of the reasons why I chose New York City when I ran away those years ago. I welcome the anonymity that a big busy city brings.

After a few rather awkward minutes, I feel the car drive off once again. I sneak a look at Magnus, and he's reading something from his phone. I look away once again, not wanting him to think I'm being nosy. Then a thought occurs to me. "Wait, do you know where I live?" I don't remember giving him my address.

"Yes, I do," he answers distractedly, his eyes still on his phone. "You're working for my company so I've got access to your file. I hope you don't mind." He lifts his head to meet my now scowling face.

Why am I not surprised? He is quite adept at acquiring information for his own purposes. I wonder what other intel he has on me? Did he discover anything he shouldn't have?

"What else do you know about me, Magnus?" I ask, my voice a whisper, through gritted teeth. I don't know why I'm whispering since we're the only ones in this side of the car. But I can feel my anger rising and I'm trying to hold it back.

He answers with a voice flat and unaffected, "Whatever information you have on our file, that's all I know."

He must've seen the tension in my face, and he knows I don't completely believe him. "What's wrong now, Isabelle?" he asks me wearily, his hand combing through that lush hair of his.

"I just don't feel comfortable about you getting information about me without my knowledge."

"I was within my legal rights as an employer, Isabelle," he maintains his even tone. I'm almost impressed by how collected he sounds, but my anger over the intrusion of my privacy holds my emotion at bay.

"You could've just asked me," I mumble back, looking out the window. I do not want him scouring through whatever sources he's got at his disposal. If he finds out about my past, or it catches up to me because of his actions …

The tension inside the car is tangible for the rest of our journey to my apartment, since neither of us want to continue on with this line of conversation. But the whole time, I can feel his eyes on me, like he's trying to figure me out while staring at my back. I ignore the heat and the goose bumps I feel from my awareness of him. Instead, I force myself to turn my thoughts on Ethan. I have to protect him from my past. I've been working so hard for years so he'll never know about his mommy's history. Thankfully, we pull up in front of my building. Like in the city, I see passersby stop to gawk at Magnus's car. I can't blame them since the car is pretty impressive. But I have to get out here, now. If I don't, I might just slap him or kiss him, and either one will have dire consequences.

After a few more moments of silence, I place my hand on the door handle. But before I leave, I decide it's best if I end this on a civil note.

"Thank you … for buying the dinner and taking me home even though you didn't have to. I really think I should pay you back." I hate owing people anything. Personal experience has made me feel very uncomfortable about being indebted. Sometimes the price you pay back is much, much more than the actual debt itself.

"No, you don't. Like I said, you owe me nothing." He pauses, then he looks at me with sincerity in his strikingly blue eyes. "I'm sorry if I made you uncomfortable about me looking into your personal information. I wanted to know more about you, but my approach may have been a little gung ho."

"You could've just asked me," I remind him. Because then I may have the option to reveal what he may or may not know about me. But what's the point, anyway, when there's no hope of any kind of future between us?

So I continue on, "Could I be honest with you? Please don't waste your time on me because I'm not worth the trouble. But I ... but I hope we could remain in good terms at least while I'm working in your company. After that, we can leave whatever happened between us in the past. And if you're concerned that I'll talk, I won't. I know how rich, powerful people like you hate scandals. I need this job badly." I do need this job, and it won't be fair if I lose it because of tonight's events, especially since I was a willing participant. I hate sounding desperate for a job, but it is what it is.

"Please don't ever put yourself down like that, Isabelle. You're a good person. Don't ever think otherwise. And don't worry. Contrary to your belief, I know how to play nice. I am not a monster either." If he is hurt by what I just said, he isn't showing it. He'll probably just move on to the next woman he finds attractive, anyway. The thought of it gets me down, so I try to push the unwanted thoughts away.

"I appreciate that. Thank you." I move to open the car door and I notice him opening his side as well. "No, it's okay, Magnus. There's no need for you to leave your car." I hold my hand up to him as I open the door to step out. To my relief he stays inside.

"Good night, Isabelle. For what it's worth, I'm truly sorry for what happened earlier. I still don't know what came over me. I'll make sure it won't happen again." His voice is sincere, and it saddens me just the same. He gives me a smile that leaves me breathless. I really need to get out of here now.

"Good night, Magnus ... and thanks again for the dinner and the ride home. And if the circumstances were different, I'd be flattered that you even noticed me." And that is the honest truth. I close the door and start to back away, but I rush back to knock on the window, which he opens at a push of a button. "And for what it's worth, I never thought you were a monster. Never."

I didn't wait to see his reaction anymore. And as I move away from the car window, I see my son and Michelle with their mouths hanging open in shock, looking down to where the Bentley is parked. Thank God, Magnus didn't come out or he might have seen them. That will just lead to questions I'm not ready to answer … as in *ever*.

I walk towards the front passenger side to collect our dinner from Alex. I say my thank you, before stepping away from the car. I turn and look up to where my loved ones are waiting, raising my arm to show off the big bag of fried chicken with sides. Then with a heavy heart, I make my way inside as the car drives off, putting on the best smile I can muster for my son and my best friend.

CHAPTER 4

I wake up in a haze, barely able to open my eyes. My eyelids feel so heavy, and I'm not even sure they're open. I can't see a damn thing!

"Oh my God, what just happened?" I whisper, my voice husky. My throat feels like I swallowed nails. I blink a couple of times to try and focus on something, but still, all I see is darkness.

What the fuck? Am I blindfolded? I try to remove whatever it is that's covering my eyes, but I can't move my arms. They're above my head, and as heavy as my arms feel when I try to move them, they just won't budge. I think I'm tied up. And the pain ... shit, why am I so sore all over?

What the hell is going on? Is this some kind of a sick joke? I try to move my legs but even they are cuffed and tied ... and spread apart. I try to recall the events that can possibly lead me to this predicament, but my mind is too muddled to begin with.

My heartbeat quickens and panic sets in. I'm scared. Really scared. Suddenly I feel the air skim on my whole body, and it makes me shiver all over. Holy shit, am I naked? Where am I, and why am I tied up in the first place?

"Help! Help me!" I try to scream but only manage a croak. My throat hurts so damn much. I try to struggle, hoping to break free from whatever it is I'm tied to, but the damn thing won't budge!

"Is anyone there? Please, someone, please help me!" It hurts to scream, but I have no choice. I try to force my voice out. I can't help the onset of panic within me. Why am I here? Who's doing this to me? I try to shift my head, forcing myself to hear anything, any sound that will help me figure out where I am.

"Help! Help! Help me please, anyone. Please let me go!" I scream my lungs out hoping someone will hear.

All of a sudden, I can hear a door creak open and footsteps coming towards me. My head immediately turns towards the sound.

"Hello? Is anyone there? Help me, please. I don't know what's going on!" I cry out desperately.

"Ssshhh! Better hush now, sugar. The whole neighborhood might hear you." Then I hear a menacing laugh. *"For such a hot girl, you're pretty stupid. Scream all you want! There's no one around for miles!"*

I feel a chill run through me. I think I know that voice.

"Please let me go. My family will be worried about me," I plead with him.

"Don't worry, you'll see them eventually. Let's have a little fun first." I do know that voice, but my head is still fuzzy, and no one comes to mind. Then I feel him tracing his finger over my thigh so I try to jerk it away, feeling repulsed by it. But he grips my thigh hard to hold me down, and the sudden pain makes me shriek.

"Uh-uh-uh, lil' lady. It's so cute when you think you can fight me." He sneers next to my ear. It makes my skin crawl.

"You are such a fucking cock tease, Autumn. But it ends tonight. I finally got what you've been dangling in front of me all these years!" He prods his finger on my left cheek and then suddenly grips my face hard.

"Who knows, I'm not done yet, so you might enjoy it too." He laughs harshly before roughly letting go.

Oh my God, it can't be. Even with the blindfold on, I can picture his face in my head. It's Cooper Thornton! Surely it can't be the same person who professed his love for me ... the same person who wants us to continue as friends after we broke up!

I suddenly have the urge to vomit.

"Cooper? Is ... is that you?" I ask, trying to sound calm, but my voice is shaking. *"I'm sorry if you thought I was a tease. I didn't mean to. Please ... just let me go. I'll do what you want. I ... I thought you loved me!"*

"Who's Cooper, Autumn? Oh, is he that long-suffering ex-boyfriend of yours who you always keep at arm's length? It must be the same guy who has girls throwing themselves at him, but you can't even open your legs for. That's not love in my book." He laughs, enjoying his own sick joke. *"You can guess all you want, Autumn baby, but you can't prove anything."*

Oh my God, he could be right. It'll be impossible to prove it's him. I'm blindfolded, and my hands and legs are bound. But surely, he must still have feelings for me, right? And what about his family's reputation if they find out what he's done to me? Maybe I can talk him into letting me go.

"What ... what will your father think if he finds out about this? You are the son of the mayor." My heart is racing, and I am getting dizzy ... did he drug me?

"You're just assuming I'm Cooper when you have no fucking proof. You know what? Once you start talking shit, no one will believe you. You look like a whore all tied up and naked. You know what a sex tape is? Well, if anything happens to me, I'll release our sex tape on the Internet. You'll be a fucking star, and everyone will assume you're just a kinky whore! Is that what you want your church-going parents to see? Your family will be a laughing stock!"

I feel the urge to vomit once again. *"Sex tape? What are you talking about? I won't say anything, I promise, Cooper. Please, you know I'm a ... I'm a virgin,"* I remind him pleadingly, hoping he'll see this clearly.

He lets out a sickening laugh. It's loud, and obnoxious, and scares the shit out of me even more that I literally tremble.

"I know you're a fucking virgin! But guess what, princess? I took it over, and over, and over again. And the best part is, I have it all on tape!" His hands are all over my body, pinching, squeezing, and groping me like I'm some piece of meat. I try to shake him off, but I know it's no use. Eventually, I don't feel the soreness anymore, I just feel numb. And as the blackness begins to surround me, all I can hear is my muffled voice, crying out for his mercy.

***

I wake up gasping for breath, completely covered in sweat. My heart is racing, as I look around me, unable to focus. When I come to realize it was just another dream, I breathe out a sigh of relief.

I'm safe. Ethan's safe.

I hear a light knock on the door, and Michelle emerges from the other side. "Billie! Are you okay? Are you having your nightmares again?" she whispers softly, careful not to wake Ethan. She gets the box of tissues from my nightstand and hands me a few. I didn't even realize I was crying. She wipes my eyes and cheeks and puts the tissues in my hand so I can blow my nose.

"I ... I think so," I mutter, noticing my hands are still shaking. I can't believe that after all these years, my nightmares are as vivid as when it happened.

"I don't wanna remember anymore, Michelle," I sob, pulling my knees up so I can lay my tired head on them.

She opens her arms, and I allow myself to be embraced by her. I close my eyes as she gently rocks me soothingly.

"You need to see your therapist again," she tells me softly.

"I know, but I can't afford her," I answer back, still with my eyes closed, trying to stem the tears from falling again.

"I can dig into my savings …"

"No, Michelle. That's your money. I'll find a way. I can ask for more shifts at the restaurant."

"What about Ethan?" she reminds me gently.

"I know … God, I don't know …" My head feels like it's going to explode.

"Okay, shhh …," she whispers, her hand on my head. "We'll figure it out."

She grabs both of my shoulders and forces me to look at her.

"Right now, what you really need to do is to be strong. Do not let this take over your life, do you hear me, baby girl?" She is firm, looking straight into my eyes.

I nod. "I'm doing my best, Michelle."

"Good. Because you can get through this, I know you can. I've seen it before." She gives me a kind smile, and we hug it out for a few more moments. After I feel myself calming down, she lets me go and stands up.

"I'll prepare the breakfast. Get ready for work. It's almost seven." Sometimes, Michelle can be terribly bossy when she wants to. But her bossiness helps me when I need direction. She knows all about me and knows when I feel like giving up. Yet, she never does … on both Ethan and myself. She's an amazing, selfless human being, a product of two loving parents who taught her all the right things in life.

"I'll wake Ethan first so he can get ready as well," I manage to tell her as I'm getting off the bed.

***

I step off the train on my way to work, feeling a mix of worry and dread. The kisses Magnus and I shared from over a week ago have proven quite difficult to erase from my memory. Add this to my very vivid nightmare this morning, and I'm now left in a pretty weird headspace.

The good news is that Magnus is keeping his word, and I'm still working for Grant Corp as a temp. The bad news is, he is also true to his word when he said he won't try anything on me again. In fact, I haven't seen him at work or at the restaurant. Looking back at what happened that fateful afternoon last Tuesday, I still can't believe how easy it was for me to give in to my attraction to him. I'm still reeling from the feel of his lips on mine, his tongue caressing my own. It was breathtaking, and God, it felt so right ... and so wrong at the same time. But yes, definitely breathtaking. That's the word that best describes our kiss. But he's my boss. No, he's my boss's boss which makes it worse. And not only that, he's a *player* who's my boss's boss. That's way too many strikes against him.

The way I see it now is that I was just someone to pass his time with while he's in between women. So maybe it *was* a good thing I put a stop to whatever it was that happened that night. And as much as this whole situation depresses me, the only silver lining I can take from this is that because of Magnus, I know there's still hope for me. That maybe when that right man comes, I will be comfortable enough with him that I'll be willing to build a relationship with him.

I shake my head to remove any thoughts of Magnus as I step inside the crowded elevator. If he got over me, and it's obvious he has, then I should be able to get over him as well. I swipe my card so I can press the button for my floor. That's when I remember that I still have two access cards. I check the pocket of my purse, and sure enough, the card that Magnus gave me is still inside. *Damn!* I make a note to myself as I reach my floor, that I have to give back his card ASAP. I better make sure to call Denise later this morning and let her know I'm sending the access card off via internal mail. There's no reason for me to access the top floor on my last few weeks here.

"Good morning, Billie," Lydia is looking extra cheerful this morning as she pops her head out from her office to greet me.

"When you've settled in, would you come to my office, please?" Lydia sounds too serious for my liking. She's usually quite cheery in the mornings.

"Sure thing, Lydia. Oh, and good morning to you too." I smile back at her. But inside, I feel queasy, thinking the worst.

After a few minutes of psyching myself, I tap on Lydia's door. "Come on in, Billie," she replies.

I nervously step inside her office, which, although decent sized, is tiny compared to Magnus's colossal one. I push away any thoughts of Magnus as I close Lydia's door behind me.

"What did you want to see me about, Lydia?" I ask with uncertainty in my voice.

"Have a seat, please." She waves at the seat across from her desk, and I comply.

"Okay, I'm not even going to beat around the bush. I'm too excited so I'll just go ahead and say it. Mr. Charles Dune, our CFO, has advised me that he requires a full-time personal assistant and would like to offer you the role!"

What??? "I'm ... I'm sorry? Um, Mr. Dune wants me to work for him as his PA?" I am stunned. This is *not* what I'm expecting, not by a long shot!

"Yes! You must've made a good first impression." I look for any hint of sarcasm, but see none. After all, letting Mr. Dune's files fall all over his office floor does not a good impression make. I'm waiting for the punch line, but there isn't any. Lydia looks genuinely happy for me. But there's this niggling doubt at the back of my head that this sounds too good to be true. *Good impression my ass.* Magnus was in that office with Mr. Dune. Somehow I don't believe this is as random as it appears.

"Look," Lydia continues, sensing my doubt, "Mr. Dune and HR would like to have a chat with you about the role. You'd still have to go through an interview process, but I'd assume it's mostly formality. They want to give you until tomorrow to give them a decision, so I suggest you sleep on it. After that, they'll advertise the job," Lydia pauses and regards me thoughtfully. In the week since I've been working here, she's been nothing but nice to me. She's the only one in the company who knows I'm a single mother, though I didn't divulge anything else. Is she encouraging me because of this? It's not like I'm the only person in this company who can benefit from this promotion.

"Honey, if I were you, I would take the job. It's a permanent role, and a really good paying one at that," she reassures me.

"I'm just a little taken aback by the offer, I think. I would definitely have that meeting with Mr. Dune and HR about the role." I leave out the part where I have my doubts about how I got offered the job in the first place. I can smell Magnus's minty aftershave all over this. And if this is some Machiavellian act of his, and I'm quite certain that it is, then I don't think I should accept the job offer. It just means I'll be indebted to him, and it's a predicament I'd truly hate to be in.

Lydia claps her hands with delight. "Great, I'll let them know, and they'll set up a meeting with you."

"Thank you, Lydia. If I do take the job, I wouldn't want to leave you high and dry. If it all goes well, and there are any tasks you'd like me to do, I'll make sure to get them done before I go." I don't have to think twice about making sure I do the right thing with Lydia. I feel I owe it to her to finish up the right way.

She seems pleased with my offer. "That's definitely good to know. Speaking of tasks, I've put some documents on your desk that need to be sorted and filed. If you can start with those, that would be wonderful." She smiles kindly at me.

"Of course. See you later, Lydia. And thanks again." I get up from my seat and give her a smile back. Then I head back to my desk to start my work, silently anxious about what I've now decided to do on my lunch break.

***

After quickly eating my lunch, I call up Denise to check if Magnus is available. I might as well give him the access card back and talk to him about this dubious new job offer that just happened to land on my lap.

"Mr. Grant's office, Denise speaking, how may I help you?" a firm yet feminine voice answers from the other line.

"Hi, Denise, it's Isabelle, Billie for short? I met with Mag—, I mean Mr. Grant last week?" I don't know why I've become so nervous. Maybe it's the fact that I'm about to speak with the man I'm extremely attracted to but don't want to be.

"Oh yes, Billie," she replies warmly, instantly calming my nerves. "Would you like me to transfer you to Mr. Grant?"

Feeling the onset of panic, I start to backtrack. "Oh no, it's okay. He's probably very busy." What was I thinking? I'm really not prepared to hear his voice at all!

"Mr. Grant said to put you through if you call," she tells me matter-of-factly. "He's just in his office. Would you like me to patch you through?"

"Um, sure, if he's free. Thank you, Denise," I answer with a sigh. *Here goes nothing.*

I hear the call-waiting music as Denise puts me on hold to connect me through to Magnus. I recognize it as a cover of an old Coldplay song called "Sparks." *Fantastic.* I roll my eyes.

"Isabelle," Magnus's smooth, low voice cuts off the song, making my heart thud.

"Hey," is all I can answer back. I have to try and reign in the thrill of hearing my name spoken from his lush mouth.

"You have no idea how glad I am to hear your voice."

I ignore the way my heart jumped at what he just said. This is turning out to be harder than I thought already, and I haven't even explained what my call is about.

"I think you know why I'm calling you, Magnus." There's a long pause, and I hear shuffling of papers in the background. It's making me wonder if I caught him at a bad time. "Oh, if you're busy, I can just call y—"

"I know why you're calling me. Would you like to come up so we can discuss it?" he answers, cutting me off.

"Right now on the phone is fine, Magnus."

"I have time to spare. I can come down there, and we can talk by your desk." I can tell by the tone of his voice that he's only half-serious, but it doesn't matter now, he's going to get what he wants.

"Okay, fine. I'll be up shortly," I whisper harshly through gritted teeth, hoping I sound pissed off. I can't believe I'm attracted to a master manipulator. He knows full well people will get the wrong impression if they see us together. So now I have to go see him upstairs, in his office, alone.

"If you insist." He's teasing me with his answer. And I should be angry with him right now, but instead, a nervous energy stirs inside of me. Why am I so excited to see him?

I feel butterflies in my stomach as soon as I remember what transpired the last time I was up in his office. I don't know if I can handle being alone with him up there this time. But as much as I'd like to avoid being alone with him, I don't want prying eyes and ears seeing us together and listening in on our conversation either.

Shit. This won't end well.

"Fine, I'll be there in five." I hang up and grab both passes on my way to the elevator. I step inside where two women, a petite brunette and a tall blonde, are chatting animatedly about something I don't quite catch and don't really want to know. They both stop chatting when they see me swipe the card and press the fiftieth floor.

"Oh, you have access to the top floor?" the blonde one asks with an arched brow, giving me a once-over.

"Yes," I answer abruptly, not appreciating her tone of voice.

I sneak a glance at them through the reflection on the metal doors, and I suddenly become self-conscious of my appearance. I'm about five feet five, and though I'm not skinny, I look relatively proportioned and within a good weight range for my height. Motherhood did give me soft curves in places that used to be lean, like in the boobs, hips, and booty department, so I shouldn't be complaining at all. And right now, I think I look decent enough in my simple gray shift dress with a slim, red belt, stockings, and red heels. I absentmindedly smooth my ponytail, then curse myself for subconsciously primping for Magnus.

"Hoping to see Mr. Sex-on-Legs, are you?" the brunette's eyebrows raise curiously, while the blonde leers.

"Mr. Sex-on-Legs?" I ask, confused.

"Mr. Magnus Grant. He's got girls in and out of his office like a revolving door, honey. But they're usually model-types," the blonde one replies sardonically while eyeing me from head to toe. The brunette elbows her to make her stop.

"Don't listen to her, she's just bitter because she's tried to catch Mr. Grant's eye but failed," the brunette retorts, teasing her friend. The bitchy one purses her lips and pretends to ignore her.

Thankfully, the cab finally stops at their floor. I don't appreciate the territorial feelings I'm getting for Magnus. They both get out, but only the brunette waves at me before the doors close.

I finally reach Magnus's floor, and as the doors open, I exhale deeply. *Here we go.*

There's no one at the reception, but the sliding glass doors open as soon as I'm close to it. Inside, Denise waves me through with a warm smile. As I walk down the hallway to Magnus's office, I feel a nervous prickling all over my body. But before I reach his office doors, I halt mid-step when it opens and out comes Alex, the driver. He's wearing the same style dark suit he wore last time, with his coat hanging open. He's taller than I remember with light brown hair, in a buzz cut, with some grays showing. He has a crooked nose which I'm curious to know how he got. He's built like a heavyweight boxer or a wrestler ... scary and very intimidating. But when he sees me right there, he smiles warmly. He leaves the door ajar and puts his index and middle fingers up to his temple in a mini salute. As he does so, his coat opens a little, but enough for me to notice the gun in its holster. My smile freezes. I'm not a fan of guns, which is surprising since I'm from Texas. But if Alex is carrying, that only means he's not only a driver but also Magnus's bodyguard. I suppose I shouldn't really be surprised, since being the CEO of a multibillion company makes you a walking target. So a bodyguard is a necessary precaution. I watch as both Alex and Denise exit out of the glass doors, leaving Magnus and me all by ourselves yet again. This is suspicious as hell. And why am I still getting excited when I should be bothered about this whole set up?

After several encouraging words to myself, I open the door a little wider, and I find Magnus behind his desk with a frown on his face, a pair of black-rimmed glasses propped on his nose while reading something from his laptop. He looks up to see me, and his expression instantly softens into a smile ... a smile that instantly hits me like a punch to my stomach. How someone can look absolutely sexy and powerful in a pair of nerdy-looking glasses is beyond me, but Magnus manages to do so with ease. The tightness in my core definitely thinks so, anyway.

"Isabelle, come in ... please," Magnus greets me like he's truly happy to see me, standing up from his seat and motioning for me to come in. Then as if he's forgotten, he takes his glasses off. I have to stop myself from telling Magnus to keep them on.

Before I change my mind, I close the door behind me, and I walk across the room so I'm standing opposite his large office desk, ensuring a barrier between us.

"Thanks for seeing me. I'm not gonna stay long. Two things: first, I just want to talk to you about what Lydia told me this morning."

He raises his hand, gesturing at the seat next to me. "Please have a seat." And as I open my mouth to protest, he continues, his brow raised. "I'm not going to bite."

Underneath his polished demeanor, I notice that he regards me with slight nerviness. But if it was ever there, it's gone the moment I sink into one of the leather chairs.

His stare lingers at me seconds longer before he continues, "I know what you want to ask me. And yes, I may have a tiny role to play with regards to your job offer. But Charles has been looking for an assistant. I merely suggested that he considers you. You have previous experience and great references, Isabelle. I'm surprised no other company has taken you on board full time. I guess the economy and luck is on Grant Corp's side." His lush mouth breaks into a playful smirk.

I purse my lips in an effort not to smile at his offhand compliment. "But why me, Magnus? I don't get it. There are other people within the company that are probably better qualified," I sigh before continuing, "and now I feel I owe you for even mentioning my name. I'm just not comfortable with being indebted to anyone. Unless … I hope you're not doing this in exchange for sex, 'cos I'll quit right now if it is." I don't know what made me say that without thinking and why my voice rose, but as soon as those last words leave my mouth, my face reddens. Why does he bring out such extreme reactions from me?

If he's surprised by my outburst, he doesn't show it. Instead, he laughs, literally laughs. And I know I should be offended, but the way his face lights up is melting my resolve like butter. *Damn him.*

"If my motives were as bad as what you just said, I'd be pissed too. You know your accent amplifies when you're upset? Definitely southern. I almost think it's worth getting you worked up just to hear it."

Great. Seven years of trying to get rid of my accent and it keeps hanging on like a rash.

"My accent is irrelevant so please don't digress," I reply back with my best indignant stare.

"It could be so. But now I'm curious as to why you feel the need to get rid of your accent in the first place. I actually find it quite appealing."

"I'm sorry but with all due respect, why is it your business how I speak?" I ask, a little too defensively.

He's unmoved, obviously not threatened by my sudden rise in tone. "You're right. It's none of my business. But I'd like it to be."

If he meant to throw me off balance by what he just said, then he succeeded. "Wh—what do you mean you want it to be? Wait, you're trying to distract me."

"Now you know how I feel." He stands up, but his eyes don't leave me as he walks around his desk and sits himself on the chair next to me.

"Magnus …" I shake my head as I stand up, needing to keep a bigger distance between us. I just don't trust myself when he's too damn close. God, now I can smell him too. Why does he have to smell so ridiculously good? But before I can go anywhere, he grasps my hand with his. Now I know it's too late. He's got me literally in the palm of his hand.

"You don't need to distance yourself from me. I did say I won't bite," he says with a gleam in his blue eyes. Satisfied with his answer, I sit back down.

"I just need a straight answer, Magnus. Why me?"

"Okay, you're right, you deserve a straight answer. Take away the fact that yes, I do want you to take the job mostly for selfish reasons. I'm very attracted to you, and I think I've made that quite clear. And being Charles's assistant would mean that I would see you more often. Now, with that out of the way, I also know you will do brilliantly in the role because based on Lydia's feedback, you've been nothing but that. So, what I'm asking from you, Isabelle, is to take the job not because of me. I'm asking you to take the job for yourself, in spite of me."

Wow. I don't know what to say after that. And I don't know if I'm more thrilled to hear him say that I'm brilliant at my job or that he's truly attracted to me. But I know I can't have my cake and eat it too … no matter how delicious the cake … no matter how much I'm craving for that cake right now.

"First of all, thank you for your honesty." I pause to clear my throat, trying to convince myself that what I'm about to say is the right thing. "If I accept this job, I don't want you to expect something I'm unable to give you in return. I can't have that hanging over my head. *We,"* and I point to him and then to me, "can't happen."

He seems taken aback by what I just said. He closes his eyes and pinches the bridge of his nose as if trying to fix a headache. "Damn it, Isabelle, why does it have to be so hard with you?" He's looking at me directly, making my insides twist with the same longing reflected in his eyes. "You don't owe me anything, Isabelle. If and when you do accept the role, I *will* respect your boundaries."

"Oh." I should feel relieved by now, and yet I just feel that my heart drops. "Okay. Then thank you for thinking about me. For the job, I mean."

"Glad I could help." The corners of his mouth lift up in a smile, and I can't help but return it back.

I nod, but I break our stares, unable to look into his eyes anymore. He makes me weak, and when he's this close to me, God … I just want him no matter how much that bitch in my head tells me he's not a good idea.

From the corner of my eyes, I can still see him staring. And the look of longing on his face as he stares at my slightly opened mouth gives me a thrill.

"You have no idea how much I want to kiss you right now," he speaks in low tone that shoots straight into me, making me feel weaker. I catch my lower lip trembling. I know I want the same thing he does. But if I kiss him, all the shit I said about not wanting anything between us to happen will end up slapping me in the face.

"You … you can't say things like that," my voice is as shaky as my lips. Without thinking, I bite on my lower lip to stop the trembling. That's when I hear him hiss out a curse word. He leans forward, placing a tentative hand on my knee. The only thing preventing our skins from touching is the delicate nylon of my stockings. I feel the heat from his hand, and it slowly spreads from my knee to every part of my body.

How can he just flick that switch on me with just one touch?

I gather enough bravado to move his hand away, ignoring the delicious tingles that follow.

"I should go now." I stand up, but my legs feel like jelly. I falter back, and in one swift move, Magnus has me in his arms. Great, now I'm in the middle of a déjà vu! He straightens me up, and I find my hands gripping on his hard chest. Our faces are merely inches apart, close enough that I can feel his warm breath on my cheek. And if I turn my head slightly, our lips will easily touch.

I lick my now dry lips, not realizing that he's watching me.

"What I'd do to lick those lips with my tongue instead," he whispers, staring hungrily at his target.

My breathing becomes heavier as the heat between us becomes more intense. Maybe one last kiss isn't too bad. Consider it a good-bye kiss. Like an 'It's been nice knowing your lips' sort of kiss.

"You want to lick my lips?" I inch even closer, melding our bodies together.

He looks me straight in the eyes. And he's so close that I can see his pupils dilate at my suggestion. "I want to lick more than your lips, Isabelle. I want my tongue to explore your whole body. But we've set boundaries, remember?" The smooth edge of his voice is gone, now replaced with roughness that makes my insides clench.

"Just kiss me already," I answer back with a growl.

And with a hiss, Magnus's lips touch mine, fleeting at first. But it's enough to make my heart thud wildly. God, how can I keep a strong front around Magnus when I feel my defenses turn to mush at his single touch?

I open my mouth to meet his probing tongue, moaning as our tongues begin caressing each other. I raise my hand to cup his face, liking the feel of the slight scruff on his jaw. I also like the way his hands begin its path down the length of my back, leaving a hot trail in its wake.

He pulls away slightly, our foreheads touching, our breathing quick and shallow. "I know you told me to keep my hands off of you but having you here so close, it's just impossible, Isabelle. Tell me you don't feel the same, and I'll stop right now."

His eyes are fixed on mine, and I swoon. I should say no. I really should. I don't think I'm ready for this, no matter how much I want him. Maybe I should listen to that bitch in my head and not the slut living inside my body.

"I do ... I want ... you." Shit. There goes my damned resolve.

A look of relief washes over Magnus's face, and before I can smile back, his mouth is pressed against mine once again. It's a good thing Magnus is holding me securely against him since it's the type of kiss that's making me legless. His tongue pushes into my waiting mouth, as it begins to massage my own, pulling it towards him and sucking it softly. The sensation of his ownership makes my core feel like it's on fire.

"Have you had your lunch?" he pulls away, whispering against my lips and making me whimper in protest.

He breaks the kiss for such a random question? "Uh-huh. I had a sandwich," is all I can mutter as I stare down on his lush lips. *Just kiss me already!*

"I haven't had my lunch yet. Been busy," he continues as he leaves a trail of kisses on my neck.

Seriously? Does he want us to go out for lunch right now? Mmm, that feels good. Wait, why am I here again?

"So do you mind if I eat your pussy instead?"

A gasp escapes my mouth. Did I hear him right? I mean his voice *was* muffled from nibbling my neck. How am I going to answer that? But damned it if his words don't make my stomach tighten and my sex swell with excitement.

I'm still lost for words when he backs me against his desk, placing my hands on the edge to hold me steady. Then he leans over me and holds me close, kissing me hard and thoroughly, and pulling away just as quickly. He lowers himself in front of me, his blue eyes still fixed on mine. He moves his hands down to my ankles and widens my stance, his fingers exploring every inch of my stocking-covered legs. I feel his warm lips on my inner thigh while his hands continue their exploration, moving underneath my skirt which he now lifts up inch by inch so it gathers around my waist. The way he looks me over with those hungry eyes ... I feel like I'm going to crumble any minute. I wait with baited breath at what he'll do next, knowing full well how wrong and so right this is at the same time.

Magnus carefully removes my heels, kissing my instep in a way that makes me moan. Now his face is right smack in front of my crotch. He inhales me, making me bite my lip. Then his own lips make contact on that small patch of exposed skin between my apex and my nonstockinged inner thigh. The way he nibbles on that part of my body, so close to where I want his mouth to be, is driving me nuts! How I manage from telling him to back off, to letting him touch me like this is beyond me. All I know is that he's got me where he wants me to be, and I honestly don't want to be anywhere else.

"Hmmm. Who knew that my demure Texan is wearing a sexy garter belt underneath her dress?" He bites his lower lip in lust-filled appreciation of my choice of undergarments. God, the way he's looking at me right now is getting me so turned on!

I don't even know why I decided to wear the garter belt. I bought it on a whim one day, two years ago, as part of my healing process. I wanted something sexy to wear underneath my clothes when I eventually go out on dates. This is the first time I wore it, to work no less! I've stopped believing in fate a long time ago but now ... I don't know anymore.

I try to tone down the mood a little with humor. "Well, I do have a date tonight after work so ..."

His movement stills, and I notice his jaw clench, making me curse at my stupid choice of a joke. "Does that happen often … you going on dates? Of course, you're a beautiful woman so don't get me wrong. I just need to know if you're seeing someone else right now." His expression is unreadable, but there's a glint of menace in his eyes as he waits for my response.

I ponder his sudden mood change. Why is Magnus acting territorial all of a sudden? It's not like I'm dating *him*. Nor am I dating anyone else for that matter. But maybe he doesn't need to know that. Maybe this is the way out I need. If he thinks I'm committed to someone else, he'll leave me alone.

"I am. So I'm seeing someone. Now what?" I ask, hoping he doesn't see through my lie.

His fingers trace the waistband of my panties while our eyes are locked.

"Then I suggest you break it off with him." Now the same fingers curl around my waistband. He looks up to me with those pools of blue, and they are laced with an intoxicating mix of jealousy and hunger.

"I never share, Isabelle. After I finish giving you an orgasm you'll never forget, you will have no option but to break it off with him."

Is this man for real? Could he really be jealous?

But before I can answer that question, he unclips the garter belt and takes off my panties, surprising me with his deftness, and leaving my now drenched pussy in full view.

My breathing accelerates as he stares at my pussy, making me feel so exposed. Then he looks up at me, licking his lips as they form into a sexy smirk.

"You're beautiful," Magnus pulls me away from the desk and guides me so I can sit down on the chair again. Then he opens my legs so he can position himself in between. I am open wide and feeling way too defenseless as his eyes drink in every detail of me … of my sex. But before I know it, he dips his head towards my throbbing apex, leaving kisses on my mound first. Then I feel his tongue lap over the length of my slit.

"So wet and juicy. I'm definitely going to enjoy my lunch."

Oh yes, he's for real, all right. I'm a goner now!

I moan as he licks my clitoris with slow strokes at first, then he ups his speed, before his mouth closes in on the hardened nub. I can feel my belly spasms. I've never felt this sort of thing before. He moves his tongue down, catching every inch of my wetness. Then he targets my clitoris once again.

I tilt my head back in ecstasy. *Oh, that feels good!* Oral sex is the closest I've been to actual sex before *it* happened, and it was never, ever like this. Magnus is so skilful, and my whole body is appreciating it. Even my brain stops questioning my every move so I can focus on Magnus and what he's doing to me.

Magnus lifts my legs, so each one is sitting on an armrest, opening me wider. I know I should feel more embarrassed, but for some reason, he gives me confidence. He slips his tongue inside of me, making me gasp, while his thumb circles around my clitoris. I feel my lower torso shuddering involuntarily.

"Oh … Magnus!" I moan as I grip his head, forgetting all of my inhibitions. I can feel torrents of energy inside of me, my heart thumping hard against my chest. This is like nothing I've ever felt before, and it's so … damn … good!

Using his index and middle finger, he opens my inner lips wider, exposing my already swollen clit. "Damn, Isabelle, you have no idea how much you're turning me on. My cock is not happy he's missing out."

His cock! Did he say what I think he just said? Oh no! Does he want …?

"Magnus, are you? Are we?" he probably notices the panic in my voice.

"Don't worry about me. It's all about you right now," his voice is thick and muffled while his hands, holding my inner thighs, keep me steady. He continues to lick my clitoris, then he inserts one finger inside, quickly followed by the other.

"Ah, I can't believe I'm your lunch," I blurt out stupidly in a half-moan.

"M—hmm. I like hearing you moan," he looks up at me with a wicked smile, his lips glistening with my essence. "Good thing my office is soundproof. I get to keep all of your pleasure to myself."

I'm. A. Goner!

He circles his fingers around before he stops and starts to flick his fingers upwards, rubbing that unrealized spot inside … a spot I never knew existed but heard about. The sensation of it is so incredible that I know I'm done for. I let out a small squeal as I'm taken over the edge, climaxing like I never thought possible.

I grip on his luscious hair, needing to touch him while I'm trying to ride wave after wave of pleasure. His fingers are still inside of me and while staring at my glazed eyes, he slowly takes them out and puts them into his mouth to taste. As if not satiated enough, he licks me once again, but slowly this time, like a lion grooming his mate. It feels amazing, even nurturing. I lick my lips while gazing down at him, my breathing still heavy from my climax. Magnus seems so focused at his task, but if he carries on with what he's doing, I don't think I'll be able to leave his office in one piece. So I carefully pull my crotch away.

He gets the message, and looks up at me wickedly, sexily wiping the corner of his mouth with his thumb. "Hmmm. I couldn't seem to get enough." He stands up and carefully lifts my legs off the armrests. The stretch from my previous position has made my legs a little sore, but before I can do something about it, Magnus starts rubbing my thighs, most likely to recirculate the blood flow.

"Thanks," I tell him, feeling shy and awkward all of a sudden. He lifts my chin up to face him. Then he bends down to give me a soft kiss, and oh my, I can smell and taste myself on him. I don't know why, but it makes me giddy, like I've marked him with my scent.

"Judging from your expression, I did good, right?" he teases with a wink. He doesn't wait for my answer. Instead, he lets me go and walks over to a discreet door that conceals a bathroom.

I feel hotness all over my face, and I try to cover my cheeks with my hands. But in an instant, he's in front of me, placing a dish with a small, damp towel on his desk. Then Magnus places his hands on either side of the armrest, caging me in.

"So Isabelle?" his voice is thick and syrupy and hits me straight where it counts. "You now realize what you need to do, right?"

"What?" I stare back at him blankly, still dazed and now distracted by his still glistening mouth.

"You're breaking up with your boyfriend, right?" He nods at me slowly, as if urging me to do the same.

Oh … oh, that's right. I lied. Then, shaking my head, I answer, "No … I mean I don't have one." I breathe out loudly. "What I mean to say is, I don't have a boyfriend."

"I know," he calmly answers with a shrug, his face still inches from mine.

"You knew? So why ask if you knew?" I reply indignantly.

"Because I want you and I want to hear it straight from your gorgeous mouth that there won't be anyone in the way."

"And if I did have a boyfriend, what would you do?"

"I guess we'll never know, would we?" he shrugs again and gives me a mischievous smirk.

*Fuck me. This man is trouble with a capital T, in bold, and underlined even. **Trouble**.* I told him to stay away, and a mere one week passes and he's made me come with his mouth! I can't handle this. I can't handle *him*. I might not be able to tell the future, but I know for sure that this will end up with me getting **H**urt.

"I have to go," I blurt out abruptly.

He frowns at my sudden change in disposition. But he isn't moving an inch at all.

"Let me at least clean you up first. Open your legs." I blink a few times at the authority in his voice, but I comply anyway, curious at what comes next.

Magnus grabs the damp towelette and gently wipes my still damp crotch and inner thighs until I'm feeling fresher and tidy. It's a gesture I find extremely intimate, and surprisingly caring. I feel my heart skip a beat, and I can't help but smile at the warm fuzziness of this moment. He catches me smiling when he's done. And yet, I can't look away. He's not saying anything. Instead, he keeps his eyes on me as he picks up my panties off the floor, holds it up, teasingly waving it in front of me. I try to swipe it off him with mock indignation, but he gets the damned thing out of my reach with a chuckle. I practically swoon when he bends and helps place my legs through each hole, then pulls me up to stand, supporting me as he pulls my panties all the way up. Then he clips my garter belt to my stockings. He leaves me momentarily so I can straighten myself up to look more professional and less like 'lunched,' a feat proving to be a tad difficult considering my legs are still a little wobbly. But I'm not complaining. After all, with Magnus, I never feel anything but cared for this whole time.

But I'm not an idiot either. I know full well this is going way too fast. Tragedies happen when you go too fast because you crash. And sometimes no matter how hard you want to, you just can't survive it.

I observe Magnus while he smooths his unruly hair back in place. I smile from the inside knowing I was responsible for the sexy mess, but I bite my inner cheek to stop me from showing it.

Then I'm reminded of the fact that he just *had* me not long ago and needs some grooming himself. After all, he can't walk around with a part of me all over the lower half of his face. So I decide to give him the same courtesy he showed me. I grab some tissues, and I close our gap, tiptoeing as I wipe his mouth and chin. He's stunned at my gesture at first, but his expression softens, and he stares at me with tender regard. I feel my whole body reacting to the way he's looking at me right now. And it shocks me because it makes me feel good inside. Somehow, he takes my stillness as an invitation, and he dips down for a kiss. It's tender and sweet, and it leaves me giggling in that half-embarrassed way. He chuckles back, but in a more 'okay, I don't know what was that about' way. I pull away from him hesitantly, and he carefully adjusts his crotch, which isn't easy, judging by the tenting in his trousers. He's still hard. Very. Hard. He catches me staring, so I turn away, acting nonchalant and pretending to check my watch instead.

He laughs softly. "It's okay to look. I like it when you look."

"What? Oh, I wasn't. I mean I was but ... are you going to be okay? I mean ..." I wave at his crotch like an idiot. That's when he laughs out loud.

"I'm more than okay. Don't worry about me." He raises a brow and smirks that sexy smirk of his.

"Good ... well, thank you for ... um ... thank you for your time ... for what just happened," I start awkwardly, "but I should head back to my floor. I don't want to be late." I put on my black heels, picking up the access card I placed on the table earlier. I hand Magnus the card, and he looks at it like it's an alien life form.

"Would you like your access card back? I'm not sure if you still want me to keep it."

His brows furrow. "That's yours, Isabelle. And if you take the job, then you'll need it." He reaches for my waist and pulls me close.

I can feel his still hard cock on my belly. I stare at one of the buttons of his shirt, unable to look up at his face and down his crotch, no matter how much I want to.

He dips his head so close to my ear that I can feel his lips on my lobe. "Skip your work at the restaurant tonight. I want to take you out to dinner." Then he starts nibbling my ear, shooting jolts of electricity all over me. "Or better yet, I want to have *you* for dinner tonight. I seem to have developed an appetite for a certain Miss Isabelle Morrison." And he slowly and deliberately traces my back with his fingers, downwards to my ass, giving it a squeeze.

"No, Magnus, I can't. And I don't think it's a good idea." I should push away from him, but I can't even move. I don't understand why having him this close feels so good.

Magnus tips my head up and searches my face for clues, trying to figure me out. "I don't understand, Isabelle. We *both* allowed it to go this far because we *both* wanted this. Why do you pull me towards you one minute, then shove me away the next?"

I place my hands on his chest, doing what he just said, but it's an exercise in futility. It's like pushing away at a wall ... a wall of hard muscles.

I shake my head in frustration. "Yes, I admit that what happened earlier was mind-blowing to say the least. But trust me, you don't really want me. I'm not the type of woman for you at all. Thank your lucky stars I'm pushing you away." The truth hurts so much, especially when it's coming from my own mouth. But this only makes him hold me closer.

"How do you know that you're not exactly the type of woman I want? All I know right now is that I want to take this amazingly beautiful woman in front of me, out to dinner so I can get to know her better. Is that so bad?" I wish he doesn't look at me like this, like he's looking through me, and I have no place to hide.

"So what do you say?" he asks as he cocks his head to the side. Call me stupid but do I detect apprehension underneath that cool facade? I use this chance to pull away, and thankfully, he lets me go. I need to be without his touch if I want to think clearly.

"One date," I finally agree, knowing if I say no, I'll regret it for the rest of my life.

He looks relieved, and it's so adorable that I want to kiss him so badly. But I won't. I can't.

"I can work with that for now," he adds with a wry smile.

"Good. And let me be clear, you only get one date and one date only." I hold my forefinger up for good measure while backing away towards the door.

His eyes widen at my cockiness, then he shakes his head and laughs to himself.

"What?" I ask, pausing mid-step.

"It's just that I'm the owner of a Fortune 500 company. I've negotiated many deals, acquired companies, and at the expense of sounding like an arrogant asshole, I *am* extremely successful at what I do. But when it comes to you ..." He trails off, shaking his head.

I stand still, looking at him expectantly, and half-afraid of what he'll say. "When it comes to me, what, Magnus?" I ask softly.

He gives me a small smile and walks over to where I'm standing to give me a chaste kiss. "One date, Ms. Morrison. I'll confirm the details later. And you're still accepting the job offer, correct?"

"I'll talk to Mr. Dune and the Human Resources and decide from there." I open the door and turn to him. He has his hands on his pockets, his head bowed but his eyes focused on me with the sides of his lips upturned. That damned sexy smirk. I can't believe I have to walk out while he's looking at me like this.

"I guess I'll see you around."

"Oh, I'm confident you'll see me very soon. And thank you for the lunch. It's the best one I've had by far. Compliments to the chef!" he finishes with a wicked smile and a wiggle of his brows.

If he's trying to get a reaction, well, he's got it. I feel the blood reach up to my cheeks. How can he make a simple statement so dirty and thrilling at the same time?

I can play that game too. "The pleasure was all mine, obviously," I answer back with a wink. Magnus's reaction is priceless, and I quickly turn around and head out so he won't see me giggling.

I can't help the grin that's still on my face as I make it to the elevators. I'm relieved to see Denise and Belinda aren't back yet. It makes me wonder if they know what goes on in Magnus's office, or worse yet, if this sort of thing is a normal occurrence on this floor. The last thing I'd want is to be one of *those* women. But who am I kidding? I've just been intimate with the CEO of Grant Corp. I *am* one of those women!

I force myself not to overthink this. After all, if Magnus wants to take me out on a date, then surely, this can't be a one-off thing, right? Maybe he really is interested.

I get on with my work as soon as I reach my desk, checking my new e-mails first. That's when I notice I have two appointment reminders for this afternoon: one from Mr. Dune at three and the other from Ms. Lindon at the Human Resources an hour after. I continue on with my work, which is proving to be a challenge with Magnus constantly in my thoughts.

***

The scheduled meetings in the afternoon are a welcome respite. Mr. Dune discusses what the job as his personal assistant entails, tasks which I know I'm capable of doing without any problem. But what piques my interest is that there's an opportunity for professional growth. Unfortunately, the position calls for some days when I have to work long hours. Plus, there's the travel. As much as the travel opportunity sounds exciting, I'm not sure if I can bring myself to leave Ethan for long periods. Ms. Lindon, on the other hand, discusses the salary package. My jaw falls to the floor upon hearing the amount of money I shall earn if I accept the offer. That salary package will mean I can afford to leave my second job. It all seems so cut and dry. And even though I still have my reservations, knowing I can spend more time with Ethan makes me want to take the job right there and then. I ask Mr. Dune and Ms. Lindon, however, that if I do accept the job offer, if it's okay for me to start by Monday next week, so I won't have to leave Lydia in a lurch. Thankfully, they understand my situation. They expect me to give my decision whether or not to accept the job offer the following day.

There's only one thing that's truly keeping me from accepting the job right there and then. Knowing that Magnus has something to do with this isn't sitting well with me. It makes me feel like I'm stepping over someone who's more suitable for the job. And all because he's attracted to me. Not that the feeling isn't mutual, which makes it even worse! And what happens if he loses interest and moves on? After all, I don't think I'm his usual type of a woman. He's into models and actresses … glamorous women, while I'm just a single mother with a past. A freaking cliché! I haven't even told him I have a child. Will I get fired then? No, I'm sure I'll resign before it reaches that point. I don't think I'll be able to manage being around him when that time comes. I just hope I'll be strong enough to walk away when I should.

Okay, maybe I shouldn't quit working at my second job after all, just in case it all falls on the wayside. I'm actually glad that I'm working my shift tonight at the restaurant. It'll give me some welcome distraction and hopefully some perspective before I make my final decision about the job offer.

Before I leave for the day, I check with Lydia if there's any errand she wants me to do for her. We briefly discuss my meetings with Mr. Dune and Ms. Lindon, before excusing myself to leave so I won't miss my train home.

I manage to find a seat in an already crowded train back to Brooklyn. I grab the book I've been reading from my purse, but I can't concentrate because my thoughts keep reverting back to that lunchtime tryst with Magnus. I feel the warmth on my cheeks return, as I remember how achingly good his mouth felt. I have next to zero experience in oral sex, and until recently, I even balked at the idea of any kind of sex at all. So what I felt with Magnus is completely foreign, and scary, and, well, amazing.

God, I am in over my head here. How can he break down my defenses so quickly?

For years, I managed to keep men at arm's length. Love and relationships were out of the question. I couldn't handle being touched by any man since it brought back hideous memories, memories that I'd do anything and everything to forget. So I built my walls high to protect not only myself but Ethan as well. I made sure no one broke through because being vulnerable was never an option anymore. But then Magnus comes along and he's found a way to chip at the walls I've so carefully built. I can't deny how he makes me feel when he touches me ... when he kisses me.

Why is this one man affecting me so much? Why am I overthinking this? I have to get Magnus out of my crazy head. And maybe after granting Magnus this one date, I can finally get him out of my system. Ethan is the only person I should focus all my energy on, just like I've always done since he was born.

As I'm heading up to my apartment, I make sure to clear my head of all these manic thoughts. My little man is waiting for me inside, and he deserves my undivided attention.

CHAPTER 5

I am back in the city after a quick dinner and a catch-up with Ethan and Michelle. As I make my way towards La Bocca, a smile creeps up when I remember how proud they were about my job offer. Trust those two to always lift my spirits. I decide that I will throw caution in the wind and quit the restaurant next week. I have to let Annalese know after my shift tonight. Ethan was extra excited when I told him the news because we'll get to spend more time with each other. Seeing him so happy confirms I've made the right choice.

Annalese is by the bar, with a clipboard, doing a quick wine inventory. "Good evening, Billie. You're in time, great!" She gives me a quick once-over and a curt nod before going back to what she's doing. I ignore the usual rise of her condescending brow. I'm in a good mood, and I won't allow her to ruin it.

"Good evening, Annalese. You look lovely tonight." I give her a warm smile, and even though she reciprocates with an insincere one, I'm giving myself a mental pat on the back for choosing to ignore her negativity.

I head straight at the back of the restaurant where the staff lockers are and place my purse inside one of them, except for my phone. We normally don't have our phones with us, but I keep mine on silent mode and well hidden in my skirt pocket, in case of any emergency calls from home. After all, my son will always be my priority and if anything happens, I want to be the first to know.

We have our usual powwow before the restaurant opens. It's Wednesday, and it's usually not the busiest day of the week. But after an hour or so, the place is filling up. Unfortunately, I have a couple of cancellations at my station, which is disappointing inasmuch as I can always use the tips.

As I'm serving entrees to a group of customers, I see Annalese within my peripheral vision, seating a lone figure at one of my tables. For some reason, a prickling sensation overcomes me. It's weird, but I've felt this not so long ago, that sense of awareness, like my body has become conscious of something ... of someone. A ready smile is fixed on my face as I approach with a menu on my hand. But as soon as I see the person seated at my table, I freeze.

Well. Shit.

"Oh, come on, really?" I whisper incredulously to myself. Is he stalking me now?

"Good evening, sir. Welcome back to La Bocca. My name is Billie, and I'll be your server for tonight," I greet him with as much courteousness I can muster in between gritted teeth, knowing Annalese is still within hearing distance.

Those blue eyes are not the least bit discreet as they roam all over my body. And I can feel the heat of his stare, especially on that spot between my legs that came for him just a few hours ago. Goodness, my body has officially got a mind of it's own, and it's a very dirty mind at that!

"Good evening to you too, *Isabelle*. You look quite fetching tonight," he responds pointedly but soft enough as it's only meant for me.

"This is my work uniform. Hardly fetching," I respond in a monotone, handing him the menu and checking to make sure the coast is clear. "What are you doing here?"

"What am I doing here? Well, I'm hungry." His eyes on me are darker and hooded. I know exactly what hunger he's talking about. And I can't let him see that it's affecting me already.

"There are a million other restaurants in Manhattan. Why come here?" I ask, still in a whisper.

"Because what's on offer here is quite scrumptious." He meets my gaze with his wicked blue eyes, and it promptly makes me quiver down to my core.

"Well," I close my eyes briefly to break the spell he has on me before getting hold of the tablet we use to take orders in front of me. Then looking him straight in the eyes, I continue, "The *creeper* special is highly recommended. But take your time with the menu. I'll be back with your bread rolls, *sir*." And I give him a saccharine smile and walk off, not giving him a chance to reply. But then my heart starts to flutter at the thought that he came here for me. For me!

Damn you, heart, and your betrayal. Seriously, this is insane! Why do I keep getting affected like this? I shake my head as I take two dishes from the line towards a couple of customers waiting for their starters.

I breathe deeply before walking back to Magnus's table, grabbing a basket of freshly baked bread rolls and butter on the way. *Don't get affected, Billie. Just play his game.*

"Are we ready to order … sir?" I ask, placing the basket on the table. He takes his chance and holds on to my hand, making me stifle a gasp. I instinctively look around to make sure no one is looking.

He stares up at me as he lays a light kiss on my knuckle, eliciting a delicious shiver throughout my body. His blue eyes are luminous from the votive candles on the table. Strands of his hair have fallen on his forehead. I resist the temptation to push away those rebellious strands. I don't even realize that I'm biting my lower lip while staring at him, until I catch him staring back at my mouth with his eyes full of hunger I know is meant for me.

I quickly correct myself and pull my now shaky hand back, surprised in a bad way that he lets me go.

"Do you need more time? I can come back," I ask in a barely audible voice.

The way his eyes just stare at me like that is making my heart pound a little too quickly. I can't lose it now. He's not my only customer, for goodness sake!

"I know what I want to eat, but it's not on the menu. And I hardly think the creeper special would suit me." He's at it again with the double entendre, and I feel my cheeks redden even more.

I move a little closer so he can hear my hushed tone. "Magnus, if you're not going to order anything, then what are you doing here?"

"I wanted to see you," he answers in a matter-of-factly way, like it's the most obvious answer in the world.

I think my heart just did some cartwheels. Luckily, Magnus doesn't notice.

"Okay, now you've seen me. If you're not going to order anything, then please leave. I am missing out on paying customers." I try to sound firm, trying my best not to show how thrilled it makes me feel to know he's here for me. But he can't just show up like this, throwing me off with his sexy presence.

"I'll leave if you leave with me."

"For goodness sake, Magnus," I say, frustratingly. Seriously, is there anyone as pushy as he is? And why am I getting turned on when I should be angry with his ultimatum?

I can't handle him being here anymore though. If he stays any longer, we might create a scene, and that's the last thing I want.

I leave the table to ask Edward to mind my customers for a couple of minutes so I can go to the ladies room. I need space from him, to clear my thoughts. Maybe I'll just get someone else to serve him, maybe he'll leave then.

Inside the ladies room, I wash my hands and splash some water at the back of my neck, trying to cool myself off from the lingering heat inside of me. I stare back at myself in the mirror. My cheeks are pink from blushing, my green eyes are dilated, and my mouth is warm to the touch. Not once in years have I felt this attraction to someone. *Maybe I should just fuck him in the restaurant to get it over with.* I laugh a little at the ridiculous thought, but I know part of me would be all for it.

Screw it. I'm going back out to face him. I quickly wash my hands just as the door swings open.

There he is, Magnus, or at least his reflection, letting himself inside the ladies room like he owns the place. I keep still as I watch him close the door. He purposely walks towards me. I turn around to face him just in time, and he cups my face with both of his hands, guiding me backwards until my back hits a tiled wall. Then before I can say anything, he smashes his lips on me. His tongue urges my mouth to open, and I just let him in. His kiss switches something on inside of me, like it did before. The feeling is indescribable, like this moment is so right. We massage each other's tongues as my hands move from my side to his shoulders, then around his neck. I hear moaning, but in the confusion of our fused lips, I fail to recognize if it's coming from him or from me.

But then he stops kissing me just as quickly as he began, and I groan in protest. His hands are still cupping my face, with only our noses slightly touching. His eyes are closed and his breathing, heavy.

"Not here, Isabelle. Come with me. I need you. Now," he growls, his voice traveling straight down to my sex and making it quiver with want.

"I can't. I…"

"I took care of it. I spoke with Annalese earlier. You can leave right now."

"What? Wait, what did you do?" I suddenly panic. Did he just get me into trouble?

"In exchange for you having the rest of the night off, I paid for all the customer's bills, and left a pretty decent tip for all the servers working tonight."

"Are you kidding me, Magnus? I was planning to work here until next week. I can't come back after what you've done. They'll all ask questions I don't have answers to."

"Then I'll double your pay so you can quit right now. I'll also double the tips you'll earn up to next week."

With that, I push at his chest in frustration. "You can't buy me like that. I'm a person, not an object for you to take however you want to," I answer back, my voice rising. I'm not even sure if I should be offended or be flattered. But a bigger part of me is definitely offended.

He rakes his head in obvious frustration. Suddenly, the door opens and an embarrassed patron widens her eyes before huffing back out the door.

"I'm not trying to buy you, Isabelle. Call this your compensation package."

"I'm not comfortable taking your money."

"Then I'll just deposit it in your bank account. You'll get paid one way or the other." He is a shrewd negotiator; that, I can give him credit for.

"You're making me feel like a whore," I yell back with gritted teeth, tears threatening to fall. He's spending all this money for what? So he can have me? Damned if I'd let him see me cry from the hurt he's causing.

Stunned, he looks at me, shaking his head. "You seriously did *not* just call yourself that? Don't mistake my wanting to do whatever the fuck it takes to be with you as showing you disrespect. In fact it's exactly opposite to that."

He turns his back from me, roughly pushing his rebellious hair back with a muffled curse. And then he turns to face me again.

"God, Isabelle. I've never, *ever* pursued anyone because I never had to. If it got too tough, I'd walk away because it was never worth the hassle. But with you, with you, it's fucking worth it. How I feel by just being within your personal space ... Damn it, *you're* worth pursuing, Isabelle. Can't you see that?"

Oh. Damn it, he's good.

"I'm not going to win this, am I?" I ask resignedly.

"Never." He closes the gap and cups my face again, kissing me softly. I don't protest when his mouth travels on my jawline and up my left ear. He makes me feel so good that fighting with him hardly seems worth even a try.

"I wanted to see you, Isabelle. So I came here with the sole intention of having a quiet dinner without disturbing you. But as soon as I saw you ... God, I seem to lose my common sense when you're around." He leans further so his warm lips are grazing my ear. "And now I can't stop thinking about losing myself inside of you."

Holy shit, that's so wrong ... but so hot at the same time! I feel my insides clench at his words. "I ... I really don't know what to say to that."

"Say yes," he pleads, now with his mouth against mine.

"Why can't you play fair, Magnus?" I ask breathlessly.

"Say yes," he insists.

"Yes," I answer back, like a puppet to her puppeteer. And before I can say anything else, his tongue plunges in my mouth, showing me how much he appreciates my answer.

I pull away after a while, needing to catch my breath. "I need to get my things and say good-bye to everyone."

"Would you like me to stay and—"

"No," I answer back, cutting him off. "I just need to do this on my own, my way."

"I understand. I'll just be outside." He kisses my temple, then the back of my hand, smiling back at me before leaving the restroom.

I'm still shaky as I check myself in the mirror. *Oh my God, what did I just agree to? This is too crazy!* With my head still reeling, I head out to retrieve my purse from the locker and reluctantly say my good-byes to the chefs, kitchen hands, and fellow servers. I know I'm not coming back. Judging by the way they're looking at me, they have questions I don't plan on answering. This isn't how I want to leave, but Magnus seems to have a way of disrupting my plans.

With my things all in my hands, I walk up to Annalese warily. "Annalese, I'm really sorry, but I have to quit my job. I guess this is good-bye."

"Ah, so you've hooked yourself a rich boyfriend, huh. I've got to say, you've done very well. He's a major catch!" Her tone is sarcastic as she raises her perfectly formed brow.

Wow, bitch to the end. "Think whatever you want, Annalese. It doesn't matter anyway. Good luck with everything."

She shrugs before waving me off. "Bye, Isabelle. Oh and thank Mr. Grant for paying everyone's tab." I roll my eyes before turning to leave La Bocca for the last time.

Outside, Magnus is leaning by his Bentley, busy texting someone with his phone. When he sees me come out of the restaurant, he switches it off and offers me a big smile. He seems relieved. Is he unsure if I'm really going to go through with it? He closes our distance and takes my hand in his. God, the energy between us is so tangible, I'm sure he feels it too.

Alex is by the door in no time, and he opens it to let us in. Magnus guides me in so I scoot to the other side to give him more room. As soon as Alex closes the door behind us, my anxiety kicks in again. This feels surreal, and I'm not really sure I can do this. I know it's all going too fast, especially for someone like me. Magnus seems to sense my apprehension, for he raises my hand into his and kisses my knuckles. And just like that, I'm instantly comforted.

"Where are we going?" I ask Magnus, realizing just then that I quit my second job and allowed myself to get swept off without knowing what happens next.

"My place. It's not too far." He wraps his arm around me and holds me against him protectively.

I don't know how or why, but Magnus really does do weird things to my body. One of them is how my nipples seem to perk up just at the sight of him. It's embarrassing, to say the least, because my body's eagerness for him is practically out of my control. And the way he smells just sends my hormones into a frenzy. I think all of my five senses are jumping for joy over Magnus. Feeling a tad embarrassed at my hopeless situation, I avoid his gaze, hoping he won't notice his effect on me. But then with his other hand, he grazes my cheek and tilts my chin up, forcing me to meet his striking eyes. As if on cue, my mouth opens, and he reaches down to kiss me tenderly. The electricity between us is so powerful that I'm pretty sure we can light up Manhattan just from its sheer static.

I deepen the kiss, grasping the back of his head so I can push my tongue inside his mouth. He lets out a deep moan and meets my tongue once again. He feels so good against me. So soft yet firm at the same time. And his taste of mint and sweetness is dangerously addictive. Reigning in my inner bravado, I break the kiss, ignoring his groans of protest. My green eyes hold his blues as I shift positions so I can sit on his lap, straddling him.

"Well ... well," he murmurs, his smile so full of lust that I can't stop myself from tracing his lips with my tongue. He instantly captures my tongue with his lips, tugging it lightly. I gasp with pleasure, feeling the moisture of my sex increase. We kiss each other with so much hunger, like two deprived people needing only this kind of sustenance.

"You drive me fucking crazy, Isabelle," he groans in my mouth while his hands grip my thighs.

"Mmm, just kiss me." He does, and it's pure and utter bliss.

Time seems to stop while our lips are connected. So when the car pulls up outside a building, Magnus breaks the kiss with a whispered curse.

"We're here, baby," he announces while gently nipping me on the chin.

I look outside while I reluctantly disentangle myself from him. We're in the Tribeca district, I think. Magnus presses the intercom button to tell Alex not to get off anymore and to park the car after we get off. Magnus gets out first before holding my hand to help me out. Still holding hands, we walk up to the front of a magnificent art deco building.

"You live here?" I ask while looking up, impressed by the design of the building and the ornate glass windows.

"Yes, right at the top. It's a duplex penthouse," he says in a nonchalant way. Of course it is.

A burly-looking doorman with a gray moustache and equally graying hair quickly opens the door with a welcoming smile in his face. Magnus thanks him with a polite nod as he guides me in towards the elevator.

Inside the cab, he presses a code and Level P.

"So, penthouse, huh?" For some reason, I feel the need to make small talk to break the silence. He shrugs and gives me a small smile. But the heat from his eyes is unmistakable that I feel it running through me.

It's difficult to ignore the current that continues to run between our held hands. I look up to him, and he squeezes my hand and meets my stare, his face serious, contemplative. I wonder if he's nervous? Surely he's not. We stare at each other like so, just taking each other in. Without thinking, I press my body against his, grabbing his arms and wrapping them around my waist. He takes his cue, and he pushes me gently but firmly against the wall. His hands are now on my hips, positioning me so my lower torso is pressed against his crotch. There is no doubt in my mind that he wants me to feel his hardness, and boy, is he hard!

"I want to take you here, right now," he growls against my neck as he licks me up towards my ear, making me whimper with pleasure. "But maybe next time. Right now I want you in my bed." I hear a *ding,* and the cab doors open. Holding me close to him, we step out of the elevator and stop before the front door. He presses his hand on a panel beside it before quickly entering his code on the onscreen keyboard. It's not surprising that Magnus has one of these biometric thingies securing his home. Having learned more about Grant Corp, I found out that he owns a company that specializes in biometric security. The front door unlocks, and my thoughts on his home security is forgotten when he closes the door and presses me against it, kissing me like a man possessed. And just before I'm practically breathless, he pulls away, squinting his eyes like he's forgotten something.

"Where are my manners?" he says, breathing heavily. "Would you like something to drink?" He pulls me away from the door and laces our fingers together. I can barely see my hand inside his, and it makes me feel giddy. I haven't felt like this in years, and my brain has gotten fuzzy. All I want to do is be near Magnus. I inch my face closer to his muscled chest, breathing in his wonderful scent.

"I just want you," I reply back, the yearning in my voice surprising me.

"Good answer." Magnus swoops me up in his arms and kisses me. I wrap my legs around his waist and my arms around his shoulders, with one hand massaging the back of his head. I'm kissing the side of his neck and making him growl out my name as he hurriedly carries me along the hallway. He flies up the stairs, and I barely have time to appreciate the almost 360 degree view of Manhattan from the floor-to-ceiling glass windows. *Wow, Magnus sure loves his big windows.* Before I know it, Magnus opens a door from down the hall with one hand. I am now in his bedroom.

"Wow," I manage to whisper. He sets me down gently on the floor, and I stand in awe. The view of the city is even better up here.

I break away a little to look around me. "I've never seen the city skyline like this."

"It's not bad waking up to this." Magnus bends down a little and circles his arms around my waist so my back is pressed against his chest. Then he leaves small kisses on my neck, leaving delicious shivers in its wake.

"Let me give you a quick tour, and then I'm taking you to bed." I have to fight with every inch of my being to stop myself from jumping him. I'm taking this chance to reign myself in a little.

Slow down, Billie. Don't rush.

We lock hands once again while he walks me around his supersized bedroom. Floor-to-ceiling glass windows surround half of the whole room. A custom-made king-sized bed is at the center, and its transparent headboard ensures that the view of the Hudson River is not blocked. There are two seats and a small table next to it along the window. I follow Magnus down a hallway leading to a massive walk-in robe to my right. Straight ahead is the bathroom, honey-colored marble with timber and white interiors, and a modern bathtub with jets and fine finishings. The view from the window next to the bathtub is as breathtaking as the rest of Magnus's bedroom. The shower can fit two or more people, with no problems at all. The large showerhead is right in the middle. I imagine myself taking a shower there with him, but stop myself straightaway. I have to remind myself that this is just for one night. There was never any talk of a future beyond tonight.

Walking back to the bedroom, I take a peek inside his walk-in wardrobe. Rows of suits, shirts, and matching leather shoes on one side, denims, T-shirts, and casual shoes and trainers, with various accessories on the other. It's all very organized and luxurious, a reflection of the man who owns them.

"So this is what Grant money can buy, huh?" I comment, not realizing I said it out loud.

Magnus chuckles. "Well, Grant money can pay for a talented interior designer."

"Hmmm," is all I can reply back. I wonder if he thinks this sort of thing impresses me. After all, what girl won't be awestruck by all of these … especially a girl from Brooklyn?

I ran away from a house as luxurious as this. I know full well how money can buy one all the lavish trappings that can fit in a mansion or a penthouse. But none of these can give true happiness. Money makes people greedy. I know I still made the right decision of turning my back from it all.

"Is everything okay, Isabelle?" Magnus asks with concern. I must've been quiet for too long. I know I don't need to explain, no matter how easy I'm finding it to open up to him. Explaining will only lead to more questions, and those questions will be a lot harder to answer.

I turn towards Magnus with a crooked smile, then I slide my hands around his waist, placing my head on his warm chest. He wraps his arms around me, kissing the top of my head as we stand perfectly still. His steady heartbeat gives me comfort in ways I've never experienced before.

"Magnus?"

"Yes?"

"Are you happy? I mean, does having all of these ... luxury make you happy?"

He pauses, as if contemplating the answer to my question.

"I'm comfortable, and I do enjoy the fruits of my labor."

He didn't really answer my question. He tips my chin up gently, looking into my eyes with sincerity.

"But if you want me to be honest, I'm happy right now because you're here with me."

Oh. *Damn*.

In no time, with my hands fisted in his hair, I draw him towards my eager mouth, and we kiss deeply. I'm on my tiptoes, wanting more of him, his mouth, his tongue, all of it.

"I want you," I whisper against his mouth. This is it. I want him to make love to me. Goodness, I even want him to fuck me!

I look up to his eyes, and I see how much he hungers for me. He carries me towards his bed and sits me down at the edge. For a moment, I realize how completely open we are to the outside, thanks to the floor-to-ceiling windows in his bedroom.

He sees me looking worriedly at the windows, so he grabs a remote on his bedside table. "Don't worry. I'll get us some privacy." He presses a button, and automatically, all the blinds go down. It's one of those one-way view ones. "We can see them, but they can't see us," he adds.

He kneels in front of me, and he kisses me deeply, leaving me panting for more when he pulls away. But then his hands skim down the length of my leg, slipping both of my shoes off. He stands up, and his eyes never leave mine as he starts to remove his suit jacket.

Then he unbuttons his shirt and takes it off. At this point, my mouth is watering at the sight of all the rigid dips and planes of his naked torso. He takes his shoes and socks off and discards them next to his suit jacket and shirt. I can't help but notice his feet are large but narrow, with a good arch, and well-maintained. Damn it, even his feet are perfect! I push myself further onto the bed, enjoying the sight of his body from here—broad shoulders, lean muscles, a well-sculpted chest with light smattering of hair, a narrow waist and abdominals with a lean six pack, and that v-shape cut on his hip muscles … God, his body makes me want to cry. He leaves his trousers on, and I give him a little pout to show my disappointment. But he grabs both my legs and drags them near the edge again, making me shriek and forcing me to stand upright.

He kneels back in front of me so his face is right at my crotch. I start to breath heavily, anticipating his next move. His hands start caressing my legs, moving slowly upwards and over my buttocks. He gives them a soft squeeze, making me giggle.

Magnus looks up to me, a lazy smirk on his face. "I like your giggle. It's beautiful how your face lights up when you laugh."

"I'm already in bed with you. No need to butter me up," I respond back coyly.

"Oh, I intend to butter you up every chance I get." He proceeds to pull down my skirt zipper and takes it off. My black tights follow but not before he shakes his head at it. "These tights are an abomination. Burn them. They don't deserve to cover your legs."

"They're comfortable," I answer back in a half-assed attempt to sound indignant. I'm not exactly expecting something like this to happen tonight. I'm dressed for comfort, not for seducing Mr. Grant Corp himself. I am only wearing my nude panties now, so I cross my leg over the other self-consciously.

"Don't." He touches my left thigh, urging me to open my legs once again. "Nude panties. Who'd have thought they could look so fucking sexy?" He moves his head closer to my crotch and blows a kiss over the material. I inch closer, wanting more, but he stops me.

"Uh-uh." He hooks his fingers on both ends of my panties and leisurely pulls them down, leaving a trail of kisses on my lower belly, my pelvis, my inner thighs, but not my heated sex. His intentional snub is beginning to drive me insane.

"Magnus …," I plead with him.

"Shh, baby ... I want to undress you nice and slow. I want to see every sensual part of you."

He rises up and stands in front of me. My breathing is heavier, more impatient. He cups the back of my neck, forcing me to tilt my head up so we can kiss, satiating me with his tongue. He unbuttons my shirt before sliding them off my arms. He flings the clothing next to my skirt. His mouth starts to move down my jaw, nibbling me like I'm a delicacy he's been longing to taste. He squeezes my breasts gently over my bra, and I moan at the pleasure his firm hands bring. He takes my nude lacy bra straps down, and unhooks the back, letting it fall off my arms and down on the floor. He stands back to look at me from head to toe; his blue eyes hooded with apparent lust.

"So beautiful," he whispers. The sincerity in his blue eyes is daunting, and it forces me to appreciate that he means every single word. The realization gives me confidence. It's something I lost over the years and thought I'd never get back.

"Open you legs," he commands softly. I widen my stance.

"You know what else I adore about you?"

"What?" I ask back shakily, my eyes never leaving his as he thankfully sits me down on the bed. My already drenched sex is quivering with anticipation.

"You look as great as you taste." And in an instant, he's on his knees, and his tongue is on the slick apex between my legs.

I tilt my head back, moaning loudly. Magnus spreads my legs even wider, wanting to taste more of me. He licks my already sensitive bud gently, building up to a quicker pace. Then his tongue slips inside of me, making me tilt my head back because it feels too good. I hold onto his head with my hands, and I grip his hair while slowly grinding myself on his mouth, on his tongue.

"Magnus, oh ..." I look down on him, and the sight of him pleasuring me is enough to drive me over the edge.

"I couldn't stop thinking about doing this to you," he tells me, sucking my clitoris once again and inserting not one, but two fingers inside of me. My sensitive core feels every single thrust and every single flicker of his fingers inside of me. I have to lie down as shockwaves shoot through my body.

I know I won't last very long. I hold onto his sheets as I come in waves, screaming out his name. I climax so strongly that my lower half is shuddering. Magnus doesn't stop showering little licks and kisses on my satisfied pussy, as well as my inner thighs.

"Mmm, let's make that the first of many, tonight." He presses his body on top of my own, the hardness of his physique, a sharp contrast to my softness.

"You're overdressed," I breathe out, tangling my fingers in his lush hair. He dips his head so our mouths are touching, but only barely. Then I see a wicked gleam in his eyes.

"Let me fix it then." I watch eagerly as Magnus pulls himself up and unbuckles his belt. My hazy mind instantly clears up so I can focus on his every move. I'm practically panting with excitement. He's seen *me* twice now, and all I've seen of him is the hard outline from the tenting underneath his trousers. I can't wait to see how far that sexy happy trail of his goes underneath all the clothing. He's now standing with just his boxer briefs on, and my eyes widen at the shape of his hard cock underneath his underwear. It's like a wild animal trying to break free. His glazed eyes are fixated only at me, until he takes off the last scrap of material on his body.

"Wow," I croak out, locking into memory his incredible physique and his … glorious … cock. He is very hard … and big … very … big. I quickly get off the bed, finding myself on my knees before him. Only with him being this close, do I realize how perfectly fitting his name is.

He's Magnus, the Magnificent. There is no doubt about it.

I look up to see him staring at me, waiting for my next move. I close my hand around his cock, invoking a sweet groan from him. He feels so good in my hands as I stroke his long, thick length, and the urge to taste him overwhelms me.

My mouth lightly kisses the head first, surprised at how warm and firm it feels on my lips. I open my mouth and lick the pre-cum on the tip, tasting his arousal. I suck his head at first, then I try to put more of him inside my mouth. He growls, his eyes shutting momentarily, before returning his gaze back on me. I push more of him in, holding onto the base. I pull back once again, and I start to lick the head and the underside of his cock, flickering my tongue from the base to its swollen head. He groans out my name as he cups my face with his large hands, steadying me. I suck his cock once more, in and out. He starts rocking his hips now, moving inside my mouth slowly. His eyes are solely focused on me, savoring each stroke. I place both of my hands on his hips, holding his cock with my mouth as my movements quicken, trying to get more of him inside and tightening my hold as I pull away.

"Wait." He stops rocking his hips and hisses as he pulls out of my mouth carefully.

"Did I do something wrong?" I ask worriedly. I don't have much experience at all, but I hope it isn't that obvious.

"No. You were perfect. I just didn't want to come just yet." He lifts me up effortlessly, and I wrap my legs around his narrow waist, with his swollen cock cradling my ass. He carries me until we reach the middle of the bed, laying me down gently. Then he just kneels by my feet, his eyes drinking in every single detail of my body.

"Why are you looking at me like that?" I ask, breathlessly.

His gaze fixes on my mouth. "I'm just enjoying the view."

Magnus reaches over his nightstand, retrieves a condom, and tosses it beside him. I exhale deeply, knowing this is really happening, and I feel my heart palpitating with nervous anticipation. It's a feeling that surprises me because I truly want this to happen … but *only* with him.

He bends down and starts to kiss the inside of my knees. I never realized that part of my body's so sensitive! Then his mouth travels up, licking my navel, trailing kisses on my stomach, until they finally reach my heaving breasts. He squeezes them together, massaging them, while his tongue licks and sucks each of my hardened nipples. I arch my back, unable to get enough. He sucks my nipple harder, grazing it with his teeth. The combination of pain and pleasure makes me cry out his name repeatedly. His mouth and teeth give my other nipple the same treatment, leaving me whimpering with satisfaction.

"You like that?" his voice is muffled with my nipple still in between his lush lips.

"Yes," I sigh.

He growls, moving upwards until his mouth lands over mine. We kiss with so much passion that my toes curl from the intensity. His body is now wholly covering mine, and we are completely skin-on-skin. The feel of our naked bodies pressed together and his large cock digging on my belly are making me impatient for more. I want him to take me, to feel him inside of me.

When he nudges my legs further apart with his knee, it makes me wonder if he can truly read my mind. He positions himself in between my legs, and I arch my hips in anticipation. He reaches for the condom, rips the packaging open with his teeth, and expertly puts it on. My pussy quivers at the thought of Magnus's impressive cock filling me, and I wonder if he would actually fit. Call it inexperience, but I've never seen a cock as thick as his. I gasp when I feel his two fingers enter me, circling it around, like he's preparing me for what will happen next.

"You are so wet and ready for me, Isabelle," his voice is hoarse with lust.

"Fuck me, Magnus," I whimper impatiently, not even realizing my hips are moving with the thrust of his digits.

"You forgot to ask nicely," he teases, his eyes wickedly gleaming while his fingers continue to stroke me so close to the edge.

"Fuck me … please."

"That's my girl."

I feel the tip of his head gliding along my crevice, as Magnus bends down to give me a deep kiss, his tongue plundering my mouth with the promise of what his cock is about to do. At that moment, I know something isn't right. I start to tremble, starting from my lips, down to my hands. Is this excitement or anxiety?

He probably notices the shift in me. He lifts his head up, and he stares me deeply in the eyes. "Are you alright?"

"Yes," I answer, nodding. "It's been a long while, that's all."

Magnus kisses the tip of my nose before whispering into my ear, "Don't worry … I promise I'll be gentle."

My breath catches and my eyes widen as unwelcome memories begin to flood my thoughts. Just like that, I'm taken back to seven years ago, and I don't see Magnus anymore. All I see is complete darkness as I hear Cooper's voice in my ear saying the same thing.

"I'll be gentle, Autumn. I fucking promise I'll be gentle." But he wasn't. And he never was … every … single … time.

"You like it rough, don't you, you filthy whore?"

My hands form into fists against my tormentor's chest, shaking my head from side to side. *No.* My eyes are open, but all I can see is the darkness.

"Get off me," I sound oddly calm. But I'm not. I feel sick.

"Isabelle, wait, what's going on?" The darkness is gone, and I finally see his face ... Magnus's face. I should be relieved but I'm not. I can't do this. And why is he still on top of me? God, I'm really going to be sick!

"Get off me! I'm not a whore. Get the fuck off me!" I'm screaming, beating his chest with my fists. My eyes are beginning to fill with tears. He pulls away reluctantly, and that's when I shove him off with all my strength. It must have been the adrenaline kicking in, but I manage to push him off me. The feeling of nausea is gone and is now replaced by the need to get out of here. With my heart practically beating off of my chest, I use this chance to jump off the bed as fast as I can, picking up my clothes, wearing them in a panicked state. Bad idea. In the process of putting my panties on, my foot catches the edge of a leg hole, and I trip over.

With a curse under his breath, Magnus quickly holds me in his arms and helps me up to my feet.

"No, just ... don't touch me, please ... just ... leave me alone!" I try to push him away until he gets the message, and he steps back, his hands falling to his sides.

In the corner of my eyes, I see him raking his hands through his hair, a mixture of panic and concern written all over his face.

"What's going on, Isabelle? Why the hell was that rant about? Did I do something wrong?" He sounds so desperately concerned that my heart tightens for him. But I can't tell him why I can't do this. I can't tell Magnus how fucked-up I truly am. The last thing I want to see is the look of disgust that will certainly appear once he realizes how *dirty* I truly am.

I swipe the tears off my face, unwilling to answer his questions, continuing to dress up as quickly as I can instead. Magnus thankfully respects my wishes and lets me be, reluctantly putting on his boxer briefs but nothing else.

"Tell me what I need to do to stop you from leaving." He comes to gently wipe the stray tears with his thumb, and I can't ignore the pleading in his voice. I pull my head away. Magnus Grant doesn't plead to anyone, right? He doesn't need to.

"Nothing. There's nothing you can do. I ... I have to go. I'm sorry. I just ... this isn't right," I'm stuttering, and a part of me wants to tell him why. But I need to leave him with at least some of my dignity intact.

This is the right thing to do.

"Well, there's clearly something you're not telling me," Magnus exhales loudly as he pushes his unruly hair back, waiting for me to answer. Instead, I remain steadfast in my silence. "Look, I'm not going to push you if you're not willing to tell me," he sighs again, "but I won't let you go alone especially in this late an hour. I'm taking you home." And just like that, he sounds detached. Contrite, but detached.

"I can manage," I insist.

Buzz! Buzz! Magnus's phone starts to vibrate. He presses a button and lets it go to voicemail. But then it beeps again, and I notice a message appear on his screen.

"Shit. It's from my Japanese subsidiary. I'm sorry I have to call these people back. But please, stay here or wait for me downstairs. I'll be at the study for a couple of minutes, then I'll come back for you."

I'm still standing, all dressed up on the same spot, watching him walk briskly towards his walk-in closet while greeting the person on the other line in Japanese. If I weren't so distressed, I will compliment him with his multilingual skills. In no time, he's back with a pair of blue jeans and a gray knitted sweater. He doesn't wear them straight away. Instead, he just clutches them with his free arm before standing in front of me. He excuses himself again in Japanese and presses the *Hold* button, before locking his eyes on me, his expression solemn.

"Will you wait for me?"

I just shrug my shoulders, but I can't look him in the eye. He opens his mouth as if he's about to say something to me, but then he breathes out a curse instead before stepping out of the bedroom half-naked. The door has barely closed when I hear him speak in Japanese again.

"Fuck!" I exclaim to myself, stomping my foot in sheer frustration. This isn't right. He shouldn't be this nice to me after what just happened. Why does he insist on taking me home? He should be kicking me out right now. Maybe that will be easier to accept.

Maybe he thinks I panicked from inexperience. Now he feels obligated to take me home out of pity. Well, I don't need pity.

Good-bye, Magnus. I walk out of his bedroom without closing the door. I don't know where his study is, but I don't need the risk of him hearing me leave and coming after me.

I pad down the hallway, but before going down the steps, I pause, my eyes and mouth open in awe. Magnus's penthouse is literally almost encased in glass. The views of Manhattan and the Hudson River are spectacular. I drink them all in—the view, the apartment, and the art collections all around me, and I store them all into my memory. This will be the last time I'll be here, after all.

I quietly make my way down the metal and glass spiral staircase, a fixture of the penthouse that may have cost a pretty penny. Still carrying my shoes, I continue down the hall towards the elevator, stopping at one of the couches to grab my purse which I had thrown earlier on our way up. Just as I'm by the elevator, I hear someone cough softly behind me.

"Ms. Morrison?" An unexpected voice calls out.

I jump in shock before turning around, probably looking like a deer in headlights. It's Alex, Magnus's driver and bodyguard. And he's standing there with a curious look on his face. He must've heard me on my way down. Shit!

"Ma'am, is everything alright? Are you leaving?"

"Yes, I am. I really don't want to overstay my welcome." I press the *Down* button of the elevator twice.

"Does Mr. Grant know you're leaving? It's just that I didn't get any instructions to take you home." For a tough-looking man, he seems concerned. But he works for Magnus, so of course, he'll be concerned.

"I really didn't want to disturb him so I thought I'd head out. It's okay, Alex. I can go home on my own. I'm used to it, what with working late shifts in a restaurant and all," I reassure him softly, not wanting to make too much fuss.

"Well, with all due respect, ma'am, he will have my head on a plate if I at least didn't confirm with him first, and I like my head where it is right now." He smiles but eyeing me cautiously. I'd really want to leave with some ounce of dignity, but I can't let Alex get into trouble with Magnus because of me.

"Isabelle?" *Shoot! Well, at least Alex doesn't get into trouble.*

Magnus comes out from his study and is walking towards us. It appears he's now fully dressed. And he is a vision, even in something so simple. He looks so sexy I have to restrain myself from jumping him. I can't believe this is the last time I'll be able to feel his body. And I have no one to blame but my fucked-up self.

"Were you leaving just now when we agreed I'd take you home?" His brows are furrowed, and a scowl is forming on his face .

Why does he feel obligated to be nice to me when I'm trying to make it easy for him by leaving on my own accord?

"Yes, I just didn't want to be a bother. I can make my way home; I'm used to it, for goodness sake!" I know I sound defensive, but that's what happens when I feel cornered. Fight or flight.

We barely notice Alex discreetly slipping out back, leaving Magnus and me alone. Our eyes are fixed on each other, and neither of us seems to want to look away.

"I'll take you home myself. I'll just get the keys." He walks back to what I assume is his study.

"Magnus ... no." He stops. This is it. I'd rather feel this pain now than risk a far greater hurt if I allow myself to go deeper with him. "Let's just end this here. Right here, right now. Okay?"

He turns back to me, and I can see hurt and confusion in his face. When he stops only inches from me, my body reacts to him like the traitor that it is. But I hold back. I have to hold back.

"Make me understand." He searches my face for answers, and a part of me just wants to open up and tell him everything.

But instead, I try to choose my words carefully. "I know we both had the same intention tonight. And for the most part, it was ... amazing ... you were amazing. But I freaked out. And I know for sure it will happen again."

He doesn't say anything, but he stares at me like he's waiting for me to continue. And so I do.

"Magnus, I've ... I've got issues I'm still working on. And I'm sure a woman with baggage as big as mine would be the last thing someone like you would want. So let's leave it at that and move on. I mean, you're *Magnus Grant*. Women flock to you. One day you'll look back, and you'll be grateful you dodged a bullet." I try to make it sound lighthearted, and I hope I've succeeded because on the inside, I'm deeply hurting at the very thought of Magnus moving on with other women and laughing me off as a mistake.

"That's all you have to say?" The coldness in his voice throws me back. But I ignore it because I want to end this in good terms.

"Actually, I wanted to thank you for recommending me to Mr. Dune. I'd be honored to take the job if it's still on offer, despite of what happened tonight. Please believe me when I say I'm very grateful for your help."

He rakes his hand in his hair again. Then he chuckles softly, but the laughter doesn't reach his eyes. He grazes his finger on my cheek, ever so lightly that it makes my breath hitch. "Funny that," he says with no humor in his voice at all. "You see, the only woman I actually want to *flock* to me is about to run out on me. I'm not the one dodging anything here."

"Magnus…"

Magnus drops his hand to his side. "At least for my peace of mind, let Alex drive you home." He turns and walks away. But then he pauses and looks straight at me.

"Have a good night, Isabelle. I truly am sorry it didn't work out no matter how much I wanted it to. Good luck with your new job with Charles next week," he says softly, but sounds so detached that I might as well be talking to a wall. It hurts me to see … to hear it. And then he walks off.

My heart lurches as I watch his figure disappears. But this has to happen, no matter how gut wrenching this feels. It's for the best.

At least that's what I try to tell myself as Alex is driving me back home for the last time.

Back in my lonely old bed, I think about how Magnus wished me luck for next week. At least he's not bitter enough to involve work in this shit-storm I've created. But obviously, it's quite clear that he won't see me again. The thought saddens me immensely though. I realize that as much as I hate to admit it, my feelings for him are not going down without a fight. The thought depresses me even more because I'm the one who pushed him away. And after tonight, he most likely *will* stay away. The worst part is, I know he'll move on easily, and I'll stay stuck alone in my rut. My only silver lining is at least I have my son to visit his old maid of a mother in the nursing home.

Out of sight, out of mind. I repeat the words in my head. If only my stubborn heart does the same.

CHAPTER 6

"Wake up, Mommy! Wake up, Mommy!" *Bounce! Bounce!* I open my eyes a crack to see Ethan jumping up and down on my bed. It amazes me how much energy he has this early in the morning. I check the time … 6:45. *Damn.*

I feel exhausted, still reeling from another awful episode in my sleep. I try my best not to show my distress in front of my son. Hopefully a good scrub in the shower will remove the dirty feeling I'm left with every time *he* comes back to haunt my dreams.

"I need a hug so I can get my powers, honey!" I flail my arms about, still lying in bed.

"No problem! I'll save you, Mommy!" Then he gives me the best hug and a wet kiss on the cheek. *This really is the best cure for my troubles.* My son, in all his sweetness and love, beats therapy at any given day.

I sit up, giving Ethan a tight squeeze and trying to ignore the small knots that have formed in my stomach from last night.

"C'mon, it's breakfast time." Ethan runs out of my room, yelling to Michelle that I'm up.

I get off the bed, slowly making my way out to the kitchen where Michelle just finished cooking what looks like a cheese and spinach omelette with toast.

"Geez, baby girl, what happened to you last night?" She wrinkles her nose at my run-down state.

"Mornin' to you too, babe. Can we please talk about it later?" I drawl back, rolling my eyes at the same time. I'm not in the mood to talk about anything depressing so early in the morning, especially since Ethan is right beside me. I lay a kiss on the top of his head, and he beams right back at me, his mouth full of excess bits of cereal.

"Sure, we can talk about it, but I can't tonight," Michelle tells me hesitantly.

"Oh?" I raise my eyebrows questioningly, relieved that the attention is off me.

"Mom, Michelle really, really likes my friend Tasha's dad and they're going on a date tonight!" Ethan chimes in excitedly.

"Ethan!" The way Michelle's eyes bug out makes me laugh.

"So Michelle, does Tasha's dad have a name?" I ask, fluttering my eyelashes comically.

Michelle sighs with a smile. Obviously, this is not how she wanted to break the news, but she seems happy to finally let it out.

"Well, his name is Nathan. And like what your brazen little son here said, he's Ethan's friend's dad," she explains as she playfully pinches my son's nose.

"He's divorced," she continues, "and a vet. You know how much I love animals, girl! He owns the local practice down the road." She looks at me with a twinkle in her eyes. "We met while picking up the kids. I've seen him around before, thought he's pretty cute, but then we started talking over at the school, which progressed to talking over coffee."

"You like him?" I ask, eyeing my best friend happily.

"Mm-hmm. He's intelligent, funny and ...," she blocks her mouth from Ethan, making sure he doesn't catch what she's about to say. "His kisses? Lawd, have mercy!" she whispers theatrically.

"Oooh, a hot vet! Girl, it's so on!" I squeal back, making Ethan curious.

"What did she say, Mom, what did she say?" he asks while tugging at my arm.

"Michelle said Nathan is super duper cute!" I pretend to whisper to him, and he just shrugs and continues to eat.

"So yeah, he's picking me up at eight tonight," Michelle says like its no big deal, but the smirk on her face tells me otherwise.

"Well, I look forward to meeting this Nathan." I stand up and give my very best friend a hug. "You deserve to be happy, babe. You know I love you, right?"

"Thanks, baby girl," Michelle says, hugging me back. "And I love you back. But you deserve happiness too, don't forget that."

I give my son a tight hug, making him squeal out aloud, "I *am* happy! See?"

"Mm-hmm!" Michelle raises her brow like she's challenging me. That's the problem about having an intuitive best friend; she knows me too well. But one of the best things about her intuitiveness is that she knows that I'll open up when the time is right.

***

I'm in the middle of organizing some contracts when Jessica approaches my desk with a big grin on her sweet face.

"Hey, Billie, guess what we just heard? Is it true that you're going to be Mr. Dune's personal assistant?"

"Um, yeah I am," surprised at how quick news travel. I just officially confirmed my acceptance of the job this morning, and that was just a few hours earlier.

"You sly, little thing! Well, I think this calls for a celebration. Marla, Boyd, and I would like to take you out to dinner and drinks tomorrow night. And don't try to excuse yourself out of it!"

"Tomorrow? Um, I don't know," I answer tentatively.

"C'mon, it's going to be fun! I'm thinking Japanese for dinner and clubbing at this new joint that's so hip, it hurts!" Her enthusiasm is contagious, and I must admit I'm getting tempted.

I guess it won't hurt, and it would be nice to have new friends within the company I work for. I need the distraction, especially after that little thing with Magnus is over. Not that he has a little thing … far, far from it in fact.

I really need to stop thinking about him and his thing!

Jess continues on, "And you know who's really going to be excited if you join us tomorrow night? Boyd!" I notice her smile doesn't reach her eyes. "I think he's got a thing for you. He can't seem to stop talking about you."

Boyd? Really? I mean he's pretty cute but he's not my type. I look at Jessica and as much as she tries to sound excited about Boyd and me, her forlorn eyes betray her real feelings. Is she baiting me?

"Jess, I'm not interested in Boyd," I reassure her and her eyes perk up. "But I guess a good night out won't hurt. Let me just check at home, then I'll let you know, okay?"

"Oh, boyfriend? husband?" Jess asks.

"Son," I answer back, but not elaborating further.

Her eyes widen slightly, probably not expecting that answer. But she smiles back kindly, "Oh cool. So I'm putting you down as going, okay? Well, I mean, once you get a babysitter or something," she adds hesitantly.

I confirm with a smile, "Uh-huh, put me down as in, girl!"

She claps her hands excitedly and rushes back to her desk. I'm starting to get excited about tomorrow night, as well. I need to start opening myself up to new possibilities. Maybe, eventually, I'll find that person who will love me regardless of my past. Magnus's face suddenly appears in my thoughts but I quickly shake his image off. Not him … definitely not him.

By lunchtime, I decide to pick up the phone to call Michelle about tomorrow night. I also want to know more about Nathan. She's at home, working on a new project all morning, so she's happy to have a chat and to take a little break. We end up making plans to head up to her parents' house in Long Island for Thanksgiving, even though it's still a month away. Michelle's parents have always treated Ethan and me like their own family, so any excuse to come and visit them is always something I look forward to.

With my lunch break almost over, we say our good-byes and hang up. Michelle said I should definitely go out tomorrow night and allow myself to relax and have fun. She even joked that if I meet a guy I'm not completely repulsed with, then maybe I should hook up with him.

If only she knew …

In all the times that I've been honest with her, I decided against talking about Magnus. She'll make a big deal about it, and it'll be something she'd want to talk about at length. But I just don't want to dwell on something that's finished before it even started.

So maybe it's a good idea to go out more. After all, Ethan is getting older and becoming more independent. I'm confident about leaving him with Michelle or Riley, our neighbor's daughter, who babysits Ethan once in a while.

Also, Ethan is starting to get curious about his father and why he doesn't have one, and it breaks my heart. Maybe I'll meet someone who can be a good father figure for him if I put myself out there more often. As much as I try to be both mother and father to him, sometimes, it's just not enough. But that will be a long way away. I still have to get over my fucked-up reaction to getting touched by men.

***

"Wow, where'd the time go?" I blurt out aloud as I check my watch. It's almost the end of the day. I finalize the e-mail Lydia wants me to send out to the accounting staff about some changes in our accounting software, which will affect the way we pay our suppliers. As soon as I click *Send,* I pack up to make my way home. On my way out, I confirm tomorrow night with Marla and Jessica. I'm actually looking forward to it now.

In the subway, I'm holding my book open, trying to read one paragraph, but nothing seems to register. At work, it's easier to focus my attention elsewhere but on my own, my thoughts keep returning to Magnus and the sad fact that he never attempted to contact me today. And why will he when I drove him away? But as much as I want to deny it, I miss him. I miss him a lot. I recall the times we were together, and although you can count those times with one hand, our encounters left me with emotions I never know existed. But I'm also aware that in almost all of those times, I was pushing Magnus away. Maybe he finally got the message. It definitely sounded like he did last night. And why will he want to hang around with me anyway? I offer him no incentive to stay. I'm a single mother with a shitload of baggage that even a shipping container may not be able to hold.

I let out a deep sigh. Life was a hell of a lot simpler when it was just myself, Ethan, and Michelle. Yes, I have an ongoing problem with men touching me. But not with this beautiful man whom my body eagerly responds to, and yet I know I can't keep him because my past won't be appealing to someone like him. I'm damaged goods and he's ... well, he's top shelf. Looking up and shoving the book in my purse, a bitter laugh escapes me at the fact that I've been thrown yet another curveball in my life. Suddenly, something catches my eye, and I look across myself to a passenger reading *The New York Times*. Surprise, surprise, Grant Corp is on the cover of the Finance section. From the title, it looks like it's about a new acquisition. I notice there's a small photograph of Magnus, and my heart immediately skips a beat. Even a small photograph can affect me this much.

I close my eyes and look away, trying my best to avoid looking back at the paper. Finally, I get to my stop, and I walk my way home. God, who am I kidding? How can I get him out of my mind when he not only owns the company I work for, but he's also relevant enough to be in the news all the damn time!

I open the door to our apartment, and the first thing I see is my son running towards me with his arms outstretched.

"Mommy, you're home! Yay!" Then he jumps up to my own outstretched arms, and I stumble backwards, losing some of my balance. I keep forgetting that my little boy is growing and getting bigger and heavier every day. But I don't care if my back aches, and as long as he still welcomes me this way, I'm a very happy mommy.

"Hello, Ethan!" I give him a big kiss on the cheek, and he lays a wet one on my lips.

"Eww, it's a wet kiss!" I laugh, teasing him. He laughs out aloud, enjoying the trick he's played on me before running back to the living room to play.

"Hey, Michelle! You didn't cook, did you? You should be getting ready for tonight!" I give my best friend a big grin as I make my way to my room to change into my favorite sweatpants and a T-shirt.

"Don't start." She laughs. "I had to do something, I'm a pile of nerves right now! Anyway, I just cooked some taco filling. You have to prep the lettuce, tomatoes, and the guacamole, okay? Oh, and I've done two loads of washing and folded all of them. Your pile is still inside the basket, but I've packed Ethan's away already."

"Sure thing, babe." I beam at her as I come back to the kitchen to get plates so I can set the table. "I got this, Michelle. Go and get all pretty for Nathan." I shoo her off, and give her a wink.

You see, this is how my best friend deals with stress—she does the house chores. And as much as I don't like seeing her stress out, I can't fault her method of dealing with it.

"Michelle, are you going to kiss Nathan?" Ethan asks innocently. I give him a mock surprise expression. It's refreshing how he just gets to the point.

Michelle freezes on the way out of the kitchen, and her eyes widen at me for help, but I just shrug my shoulders.

She rolls her eyes at me. "Well, honey, it depends if I really, really like him."

"How about we just let Michelle get ready?" I step in, waving her off, mouthing '*Go!*'

The buzzer goes off as Ethan and I are eating Michelle's homemade tacos. I look down from our front window to check.

"Michelle, is Nathan tall, dark, and *muy caliente*?" I yell out to Michelle, knowing the attractive man smiling up at us can hear.

Michelle comes scrambling out of her bedroom, still barefoot, but wearing red skinny jeans, a snug black wife beater, and a black crop blazer with the sleeves folded showing off her arms. Her hair is a sexy mess of tight curls that help show off her figure. The only accessory she's wearing is an animal print scarf wrapped around her neck. She looks out the window, down to where Nathan is.

"Hi, Nathan, you'd have to excuse my friend here, she's a little cray-cray! Come on up."

I giggle as she hits my arm playfully, before pressing the button to let Nathan in.

"Behave, please. Tell him I'll be out shortly," she begs, as she runs back to her bedroom to finish up.

I open the door, just as Nathan is approaching our apartment door. Ethan runs next to me and holds on to my arm … his standard stance when he's feeling shy.

"Hello, Nathan. I'm Billie, Ethan's mom, and Michelle's crazy friend." I tap on my head flippantly, before stretching my hand out to shake his. Funny thing is, I'm only half-joking. "Come on in."

"Hi, Billie. Michelle's actually talked about you a lot. Don't worry, I didn't get the crazy vibe either," he replies in a warm tone, shaking my hand firmly. I note that I have no violent feelings of repulsion after our contact, just a slight nervousness … this is a very good thing. I'm beginning to like Nathan for Michelle already.

"Hello, Mr. Vasquez," Ethan waves up to Nathan. "Where's Tasha?" he asks, and I notice the hint of disappointment in his voice.

"Sorry, little man, Tasha's actually at her grandma's tonight."

"Hi, Nathan," Michelle walks out of her room, now wearing her animal print high heels that match her scarf and her favorite black Alexander McQueen clutch. She looks phenomenal. And Nathan definitely thinks so too as he gives her an awestruck once-over.

I can't help but smile as they stand side by side. They look hot as a couple. Nathan is tall, with an athletic build, a clean-shaven head, beautiful dark skin, light, brown eyes, and a warm smile with a dimple on one side. They can't seem to take their eyes off each other.

"Well, you guys better go, or you might be late for whatever it is kids do on dates nowadays," I finally break their little stare-off, wanting them to get on their merry way.

Michelle walks over to gives Ethan a big hug and me, a kiss on the cheek.

I put my arms around her. "I like him already, babe. Have fun tonight," I whisper to Michelle softly.

"Don't forget to give your server a nice tip," I yell out teasingly before closing the door behind them.

Ethan is waiting for me at the dining table, and we finish our meal together, talking about school, his friends, and my job.

After brushing his teeth and changing into his pj's, I tuck Ethan in bed so I can read him his favorite book, *The Cat in the Hat* by Dr. Seuss. Not long after, he's fast asleep. So after a kiss on his forehead, I head back to the kitchen to clean up.

Once the kitchen is looking spic-and-span, I decide to watch the late news on TV before calling it a night. I get myself a glass of white wine and settle on the couch before switching on the TV. I scour through different channels and stop when I catch a glimpse of Magnus on the screen. The newsreader is talking about the acquisition that Grant Corp had made with SonneSys, a company that's leading the way in research and development with harnessing the energy from the sun into a greater scale. It's the same news I saw on the paper on my way home. Apparently, the acquisition enables the start for the production of window panels that can be used for home and industrial use. The panels soak up the energy from the sun and converts it to power. The windows are strong and safe enough to be used for skyscrapers and houses. I can just imagine the impact this will make towards green energy, and I can't help the pride I feel for being an employee in a company that has an environmental conscience … or the pride I feel for the man behind it.

I watch intently, as they show stock footage of Magnus Grant, doing a speech in front of a conference, looking so dapper in his black suit. At the young age of thirty-two, he's going from strength to strength with his achievements.

Then my heart clenches at the last clip they show of him. He is at a charity event, and his arm is around a beautiful statuesque blonde. I recognize her instantly. Her name is Sofia Meier, a famous model who has graced the covers of *Vogue* and *Harper's Bazaar* to name a few. They look beautiful together, with her blonde hair and fair skin that complement Magnus's dark hair and olive skin. The newsreader says the couple are involved in an on-off relationship and also comments that the footage being shown was taken only less than a month ago.

I feel a stir of something unwelcome inside of me, like a desire to inflict harm on that woman when she hasn't even done anything wrong with me except that of being Magnus's sometimes-girlfriend. Then a thought occurs to me—does this mean that Magnus only wanted me because he and Sofia were possibly 'off' at the time?

The thought makes my eyes well up with tears but not because I feel sad. No, I'm angry. I'm angry with myself. I am such an idiot for giving in to him and his smooth lines so quickly. Of course, he's a player! And I let myself get played by his looks and his sweet talk. I should've known better.

I roughly wipe off the tears that start to fall. I vow never to make the same mistake again … ever. I'll find someone who I will be comfortable with, on my own terms, and I will have a fun time doing so. And I'll start when I go out with my new friends tomorrow night.

Screw Magnus and his skinny ass girlfriend!

I drink the last of my wine before dragging my feet back to my bedroom so I can get ready to bury myself under the covers.

Tomorrow is a new day. Tomorrow will see a braver, less naive me. I'm over playing the victim. With that, I close my eyes, hoping to fall into a dreamless sleep.

***

Friday comes and goes like a blur. After finalizing my tasks with Lydia, the accounts team gives me a small surprise party with cake and drinks to congratulate me and to wish me luck on my new job with Mr. Dune. Magnus isn't there, but then again, why will he even bother?

By five in the afternoon, I can feel my nerves going haywire, anxious at what tonight will bring. After logging off, I head over to the ladies restroom to freshen up before meeting Jess, Marla, and Boyd. I check myself in front of the full-length mirror and decide I look decent enough.

I am wearing my red dress which is fitted in the right places and sits a few inches above my knees. It has a low neckline that accentuates my cleavage, but the back is even lower. So during the day, I covered my back with a slim-fitting, black tuxedo-style jacket. A simple three-strand, long necklace and a pair of black heels finish off my outfit.

Not too skanky, but not too demure either. I give myself a mental thumbs-up as I leave the restroom and head towards the elevators. I'm supposed to meet my new friends at the lobby by five and I'm now ten minutes late. I keep my fingers crossed, hoping that I won't see … you-know-who … at the lobby.

I don't know what will happen when I start working for Mr. Dune, but for now, I'm relieved that I have a buffer to give myself some time to heal and move on.

"Hey, Billie, over here!"

I see Jess waving at me, in the middle of a sea of employees heading out the door. I walk up to them with a contrite smile, feeling a little self-conscious at the manner Boyd is staring at me.

"Sorry I'm late, guys. I just had to tie a few loose ends at work," I announce apologetically.

Boyd gives me a thorough once-over. "Wow, you look—," Boyd says, interrupted.

"Thanks," I cut him off before he can continue, hoping to make up for the abrupt response with an embarrassed grin. "So what's on the agenda tonight?"

Marla's face lights up. "Okay, well first, we have a dinner reservation at this yummy Japanese restaurant in the East Village. Then we're going to *the* trendiest nightclub at the moment ... Cirque!

"Cirque?" I ask, looking puzzled.

"Cirque!" Jessica confirms.

"Pretentious enough for you?" Boyd asks sarcastically, and I have to laugh.

"Well, I *have* been living in a cave for a while," I add lightly, putting on my bravest smile.

All four of us leave the building in good spirits, but I freeze at the sight of Magnus's Bentley parked in front of the building. I don't know if Magnus is inside, but I feel a small volt of electricity goes through me just at the mere idea of him being so close.

I'm not going to hang around because if I do, I might just turn my heels around and peek inside the car to check. Or worse, I might see Magnus inside with someone else. So I bypass the group and hail a cab for us instead. Luckily, a cab pulls immediately, thankfully avoiding a potentially awkward moment. After Marla gives the address of the Japanese restaurant, our cab finally drives out and away from Grant Corp and Magnus's Bentley.

"Damn, how awesome is Mr. Grant's car? That's a fucking Bentley Arnage! You know those cars cost a fortune because they're custom-made? To ride in one of those cars would be sweet!" Boyd exclaims excitedly.

"Yeah, it's a pretty sweet ride," Jessica agrees with Boyd, batting her lashes at him. I keep my mouth shut, only nodding and trying to keep a straight face.

Marla leans over. "Hey, Billie, have you met Mr. Grant? Well, I have and let me tell you, if he so much as gives me a fuckin' wink, I am so dropping my panties right there and then. He is so hot!"

I notice the driver curiously checking out Marla from the rearview mirror. A part of me wants to shake her and tell her to keep his hands off, but I try my best not to get affected instead. I know I'm being ridiculous. I don't even know why I'm pissed off. It's the same thing I felt last night when I saw Magnus with Sofia, and I feel like an idiot for it.

Then I realize all three of them are looking at me expectantly, waiting for my answer. "So ... have you met him, Billie?" Marla asks me once again.

I choose my words carefully. "Yeah, actually I've met him but only briefly. He was having a meeting with Mr. Dune at the time and I had to drop off some files he requested." At least that's mostly true, especially the dropping part.

"Oh, my God, isn't he just beautiful? And those eyes ... swoon!" Jessica sighs, looking like she's daydreaming and seemingly forgetting about Boyd. Or maybe she didn't forget but she's trying to see if Boyd is affected. Out of curiosity, I turn around to check. Boyd is looking at Jess with a cocked eyebrow ... interesting.

"Yeah, he's alright," I answer with my best indifferent tone.

Boyd thankfully decides to change the topic as we make our way to the restaurant. He talks about his plans for the weekend and about a funny incident at work. As for the girls, well, the girls are mostly bitching about work. I'm at the front seat, so I'm happy to just listen and laugh with them.

We finally make it to the Japanese restaurant they were raving about, after half an hour's worth of shitty traffic. You wouldn't actually think there's a restaurant there because of the nondescript façade. A small *Open* sign on a small gate tells me the restaurant is underneath the building. We head down the steps where a pleasant-looking lady confirms our reservation and guides us to our table.

Marla sits next to me while Boyd and Jess sit across from us. I catch Boyd openly staring at me, but I choose to ignore it, even if it makes me feel uncomfortable. Thankfully, our server arrives and hands us our menus.

Before we know it, two hours just passed. We finish our food, and our sake bottle is now empty. The server hands our bill, and I'm on the verge of tears upon seeing the total, realizing how much I need to contribute. But thank heavens they insist on paying for my share, explaining that it's a treat for my promotion.

I'm already feeling the after-effects of the sake, so I can't wait to get upstairs and breathe in the cool, crisp autumn air. By the time Boyd hails another cab en route to Cirque, I'm feeling less uptight and raring to go.

We get dropped off in a warehouse-style building, but there's no actual signage. What is up with these establishments with no signage? Boyd is right. It's already looking pretentious as hell. Close to the door, all I can see is a long line of people waiting to get inside. At the door are two burly bouncers who decide the fate of the people in line. So far, no one's getting in.

Marla leads our group right at the door, bypassing the long line of eager clubbers. One of the bouncers sees her, and his face instantly lights up.

"Hey, baby." She winks at the muscly guy in black with a shaved head, who gives her a lingering kiss on the cheek as he unhooks the velvet rope to let us in. I turn to Jessica with wide eyes, but she waits until we pass the door before whispering to me, "Marla hooks up with that bouncer once in a while. She has a thing for bouncers, especially the ones that work at really cool bars and clubs." She rolls her eyes while giggling.

Marla overhears Jess, and she shrugs her shoulders. "You're welcome, bitches!" She winks before laughing with us.

We walk through a mirrored hallway lit with fake flames encased in glass, that runs through the bottom part of the wall. It's pretty dramatic, and it gives one a taste of what the club has to offer. I can hear the music pumping at the end of the hallway, and it gets my heart racing. It's been a while since I've danced in a club. I'm actually looking forward to this.

"Holy shit!" I exclaim in awe. Inside the club, there are performers in platforms of various sizes, either swaying in the elaborate-looking swings, or pyro's who spit out fire. There's a gigantic screen behind the DJ, showing videos of vintage circus acts. It's seriously like being inside a very decadent circus. I've never seen anything like this before. The club screams expensive. Everywhere I look, from the people inside, to the vibe, it's just pure hotness.

"We have a table reserved for us ... there it is!" Marla leads us to a circular booth on an elevated platform which has full view of the dance floor. Boyd let's me in first, before moving inside to sit next to me. I notice how close he is, with his leg brushing against mine. It makes me uncomfortable, and I shift away, keeping some distance between us.

We're sitting around just enjoying the vibe, when a long-legged server wearing a sexy showgirl costume, shows up with a bottle of Veuve Clicquot and four champagne flutes. She opens the bottle in front of us and pours the pricey liquid in each glass.

"Compliments of the owner," she says with a smile.

"Who's the club owner? Where is he?" Marla looks around, obviously intrigued. The server doesn't answer but only gives us a smile before leaving.

Boyd takes his phone out. "Maybe I can look it up," he says before using Google in his phone. "Hmm, it says here the owner is a Jacque du Plac. And he's usually based in Paris but only comes over to New York once in a while, since he's got a local silent partner or some shit," Boyd informs us while reading from his phone before showing us Jacque's picture. He looks like a sugar daddy, or whatever the hell a sugar daddy looks like.

"Oooh, so is he in the club right now?" Jessica chimes in, looking around, as well.

"Well, what are we waiting for? Who cares who gave it to us? It's fucking expensive champagne, and it's free!" Marla takes a flute and raises it up, and we all follow suit.

"Cheers, bitches, and gentleman! And congratulations on your new job, Billie!" Marla proclaims aloud, and we all clink our glasses and drink. It's crisp and has a good finish. I've had these before, back in the days when my friends and I used to throw epic parties where underage drinking and expensive alcohol were prevalent. Look where that shit got me.

I better make sure I keep my drinking to a minimum. So I focus my attention at the club and its ambience instead, welcoming the distraction.

"Wow. This is pretty cool," I tell Marla, trying to speak over the music. I'm still curious if the generous owner is around. Maybe we'll get to meet him later.

"I know, right? And this is the first time we've ever had a free bottle of anything served to us. Must be our lucky night!" She smiles at me enthusiastically. "And Blaze, that's the bouncer up front, made sure we got this table. We're near the VIP section but close to the dance floor as well. We can see everything and everyone in here."

I nod back at her. "So who gets in the VIP area?" I ask, looking at the direction she's pointing at.

"Mostly people that can afford the membership. Then, there are the celebrities, models, the usual people." She shrugs at me.

I squint my eyes a little, trying to see through the dimmed lights, hoping to recognize any celebrities in the VIP area. But then I feel cold all of a sudden, and my mouth gapes, when I realize who's actually in there. I'm not even noticing the rock star or the actors playing vampires on television. My eyes are fixed on the man they're having a conversation with.

And he's with her.

"Whoa, look who's decided to grace us with his presence!" Jessica exclaims, looking at the same direction as I am.

Boyd confirms my fears. "Shit, that's Mr. Grant and Sofia Meier! Wow, she is so hot! They look good together, don't you think?" he turns to ask me while casually placing his arm behind my back, his hand brushing on my right shoulder.

But Boyd is the least of my worries. Right now, I'm unable to keep my eyes away from Magnus. He is seated across where we are and seems distracted with his cell phone. And as usual, he looks incredibly handsome in his black button-down shirt, with his hair slicked back but still a little messy, like his fingers have been through it so many times. *Or was it Sofia's hands?* The thought makes me want to throw up.

Sofia's arm is draped around his shoulders, and she keeps whispering in his ear. He smiles at her and whispers something back. The sight of them so intimate together, and right in front of me, is something I'm not prepared for and I don't think I ever will be.

I guess they're 'on' again.

I have to stop staring at them like an idiot or risk being in tears. I pull my eyes away to check out the dance floor instead. The song playing is something I'd like to dance to. And right now I really need the distraction.

"You guys wanna dance?" I ask the group.

Boyd's face lights up, and he gives me a big grin. "Sure!" He takes my hand, and I initially hesitate but I breathe deeply and hold on to his hand as he leads me to the dance floor. I look back at our table, and I wave at Jessica and Marla to join us, but both of them shake their heads 'no.'

Luckily, they're playing "Earthquakey People" by Steve Aoki which is fast enough so I'll be able to keep Boyd at arm's length while we dance. He's actually quite a decent dancer which is great because it keeps me motivated enough since I don't have to 'dumb it down' for him. I turn around so I'm dancing with my back against Boyd, closing my eyes for a moment so I can feel the rhythm, moving my hips to match the beat.

"Looks like the boss is leaving," Boyd holds me by the waist as he whispers in my ear. I flinch at the contact, but I use my dancing to subtly move away so I can turn and face the VIP section. I see Magnus and Sofia exit the closed off area on their way out of the club. I don't know if he's even aware that I'm here and part of me wishes he does. But then again, I pushed him away. Now he's back with Sofia, so even if he saw me, it won't make a difference at all.

"Good. Now we can really have a good time!" I try to sound carefree, when in fact I'm hurting inside.

The song changes to "Lights" by Ellie Goulding. It's great to dance in but it's on the sexy side, so I'm not looking forward to what might happen next. As predicted, Boyd presses himself against my back, his hands firmly on my hips. I stiffen a little, but when he bends his head down too close to my neck, I break into a cold sweat. With a forced laugh, I turn around and pull away at the same time.

"I'm thirsty. Let's go back so I can ask the girls what they want to drink. I think I prefer a cocktail than champagne right now. And I owe you guys a round!"

We walk over to Marla and Jess. Jess looks a little hurt, but her face lights up when Boyd sits next to her. I remain standing up. "Okay, second round of drinks are on me. What would you like?"

They give me their drink orders—two apple martinis and a Bud Light. Feeling warm after all the dancing, I take off my blazer before making my way to the bar.

"Hey there, sexy back!" Marla wolf whistles. Feeling playful, most likely from the sake and champagne, I do a sexy little twirl before putting my index finger up my lips in a hush. As I turn to walk away, I hear Boyd call my name.

"Would you like some help with the drinks?" Boyd offers expectantly, his stare lingering a little too long at my exposed back.

"Um actually, I'm hoping Marla could help me. You look like you need to take a breather from me outdancing you and all." I look over at Jess, and I give her a knowing smile and a wink. Hopefully, Jess will see my gesture as a way of proving to her that I'm not her competition with Boyd.

Marla and I head towards the crowded bar, checking out the clientele on the way. Most of them look a little uppity for my taste, but I must admit that majority of them are definitely good-looking. Will I meet someone nice in this bar? Highly unlikely but I need the distraction if it means pushing Magnus away from my thoughts.

We find an empty spot close to the middle, and I squeeze myself in. Marla finds a couple of her old friends standing next to the bar. She introduces them to me, but before I know it, she ditches me to play catch-up with them. *Great.* Maybe Boyd was a better idea. I sigh frustratingly before waving my hand to get the bartender's attention, which is proving to be more difficult since everyone else is doing the same. I lose some of my balance from all the pushing around, and I accidentally elbow the guy beside me. *Uh-oh.* He turns around with his brows furrowed, which turns to a sleazy smirk after giving me a slow and very creepy once-over.

"Hey, cutie. Need help getting your drinks?" The guy is built like a brick wall and looks intimidating. He also reeks of strong aftershave mixed with spilt beer. And the way he's leering at me is starting to make me feel sick. Ugh, tonight just keeps getting better.

"Sorry, I got pushed. And I don't need someone helping me with the drinks so thanks, but no thanks," I try to dismiss him curtly.

"C'mon, let me buy you one drink. You can thank me later if you want to." I realize he's probably had too much alcohol in his system, judging from the way he's slurring his words. He raises his hand towards my right arm and brushes it with his knuckles. His clammy touch makes me feel queasy.

"Don't *touch* me!" I push his hand off, needing to move as far away from him as possible. But he suddenly clutches my arm, making it impossible for me to escape.

"Stop being such a hard-to-get bitch! Now let me buy you a drink so you can properly thank me later!" He roughly pulls me against him.

I can't breath! Oh God, I can't breath!

"Let go of me ... please!" I plead with him, my eyes welling up with tears as extreme panic sets in.

"Unless you want to leave this club with a broken arm, you will do what this lady tells you." The voice behind me is enraged, menacing even. But it's the awareness I feel upon hearing *his* voice that triggers something inside of me. I don't even need to turn around to know who it is.

CHAPTER 7

"Who the fuck are you? Why don't you mind your own damn business!" the sleazebag responds, his hand gripping me tighter and making me wince.

"*I'm* the owner of this club, so this *is* my business. I'm giving you one more second, then I'm done asking nicely." The gravel in Magnus's tone is threatening, but it's doing the opposite with me. I can't even bring myself to look up to him because I know I'll give myself away. Just the sound of his voice, albeit hostile, is actually helping me calm down. And I don't want Magnus to calm me down because I'm angry with him.

But something he said, sticks. Did Magnus say he's the owner? So this means, he must be the silent partner, which means he sent for the champagne, which means, he knows I am here all along! But he left with Sofia. Why did he come back?

"Fuck. Off!" This guy still won't let me go, and now he's pushing Magnus back with his free hand. I try to pull away, but his grip is too strong!

And then it all happens too fast. One minute the other guy is holding me, and the next, he is knocked out and slumped on the floor. I feel Magnus's hand on my waist, stopping me from falling with that guy he just knocked unconscious. I clamp my mouth with my hand, trying to hold the scream that escapes my mouth, unsure if I'm more affected by the unmoving figure on the floor, or the fact that Magnus is holding me so close to him that I can feel his heart beating strong and fast against me. A crowd has gathered around us, and not long after, two bouncers pick the half-conscious man off the floor so they can kick him out. I'm still in shock, but I'm also aware that he's still holding me close. I need to put some distance between us because the way Magnus is holding me may be misinterpreted by my new work-friends. And I've seen how fast gossip travels at work.

So I push myself off of Magnus's embrace. As much as I want to stay in those arms, the fact is, I can't allow it to happen. I notice he's breathing heavily, his hand still formed into a clenched fist. But it's the way he's looking at me ... a mixture of bewilderment and ... is it annoyance?

It's written all over his face. I can understand the surprise because I pulled away from him so hastily. But is he annoyed that I'm here or that he is obliged to help me out to save his club's reputation?

Of course, it won't be the former. Magnus only helped because it's his club. He's back with Sofia, obviously. I suddenly feel choked up, and I can't breathe. He calls out my name, but I'm already stepping backwards and away from the scene, mumbling a thank you that's too soft for him to hear. I turn around and head straight towards my friends. I need to tell them I'm leaving. I can't stay here any longer. Thankfully, Magnus doesn't attempt to follow, but I know his eyes are still on me because I can feel the heat of his stare on my whole body. I hear Marla's voice closing in. She asks if I'm okay, but I can't speak a single word until I reach our booth. They're all staring at me, standing, stunned at the scene they just witnessed.

"Holy shit, Billie! What just happened in there? I left you alone for one second, and you get harassed by a dick, and rescued by our boss. Our fucking hot boss!" Marla sounds like she's going to hyperventilate.

Boyd joins in, "I was going to help out but next thing I know, Mr. Grant has knocked that loser down on the floor."

I answer while shaking my head, "I don't know what happened either. I guess Mag— Mr. Grant didn't want any of his employees getting harassed in his club?" For some reason, I feel like I'm outside of my body, numb, still in a state of shock.

"What? So *he's* the silent partner? That means the champagne came from him!" Boyd concludes.

"No shit, Sherlock," Marla chides back.

"I think I've had enough excitement for tonight. I'm going home. Sorry, guys." I grab my coat, and I put it back on, amidst their groans of protests. I really don't want to stay here and talk about Magnus in case I say something I might regret.

"Oh, come on, Billie! We should thank Mr. Grant for the champagne and punching out that loser. I saw the way he was looking at you and daaamn, girl!" Marla excitedly shakes my shoulders a little too roughly.

"That was a look of disapproval you saw, and possibly anger, nothing else. You can thank him for me if you like. I'm going. But you guys should stay and have fun. We'll do this again, yes? I still owe you all a drink." I know I'm blabbering, but I have to leave, I can hardly breathe as it is.

"Of course! But we'll probably move on to another club soon. Too much drama in this joint if you ask me. You sure you don't want to come with us?" Jess asks hopefully.

I shake my head and give them an apologetic smile. "Next time." Then I hurriedly grab my purse and with a wave good-bye, I make my way out.

I'm walking down the mirrored hallway leading out of the club when out of nowhere, an arm grips me by the waist, making me screech out in panic.

"It's me. We need to talk," the familiar voice whispers gruffly in my ear. My panic is gone, but my heart begins to thump the way it does for only one person—fast and all-consuming. I let him take me through a concealed door and into what appears to be the backroom of the club where the office and staff room must be.

But as soon as we're alone, my anger flares back up. "What the hell do you think you're doing, Magnus?"

"A simple 'thank you' would have sufficed," he answers, with calmness that just infuriates me even more. "But are you alright? You walked away, and I didn't get a chance to ask you."

"Are you sure you want me to say 'thank you,' or 'I'm sorry for causing trouble in your club?' It's unfortunate you thought I needed to be rescued, but I can take care of myself. Now run off and go back to your girlfriend!" And I wave him off before reaching for the door. But Magnus blocks my way and even if I want to push him off, what's the point? He's practically twice my size! So I do what any self-respecting woman will do, I stomp my feet and snarl at him with gritted teeth.

He raises his brows in response, but the way he's looking at me is practically predatory. "Why the hell are you so angry at me? But snarl like that again because it's fucking sexy."

"What do you want, Magnus?" I ask, stepping back with my arms crossed, hoping to appear defiant. But what I'm actually doing is covering my nipples because they're standing in full attention.

He takes a step closer. "Like I said earlier, I want us to talk."

"I'm not having sex with you." What the hell made me say that? Magnus didn't even mention anything of the sort. But I stand my ground, raising my chin, and meeting his stare head-on.

Magnus closes his eyes briefly and lets out a big sigh, "Thank you for clarifying that. Now let's go to my office. The staff walks through here all the time, and I prefer to talk to you without anyone listening in on our conversation."

"Whatever, let's get this over with. I want to go home soon." I roll my eyes as he leads me by the elbow to his office a few paces away. I try not to focus on the feel of his fingertips on my skin, but it's proving impossible.

Once inside, he ushers me in and closes the door behind us. He leans onto it for a short while, just drinking me in with those stunning blue eyes of his.

"Did you get my message?"

"What message?" I ask with exasperation.

"Check your phone."

"How'd you get my number? I never gave it ...," my voice trails off, and I let out a big sigh. *Of course, he knows my number.* I grab my phone from my purse and true enough, there's a message from an unknown number.

"I assume this is you?" I show him the notification. He nods, his eyes fixed on me.

I shake my head and take a deep breath before unlocking my screen. *'You look breathtaking tonight. I miss you...M.'*

My hands start to tremble, and I switch off my phone. What the hell is this? Is he playing me for a fool? He's on a date with another woman, and he's sending me this sort of text message? He must think I'm so gullible!

"How dare you," I say with gritted teeth, trying to hold back my tears. "You miss me? Do you think I'm a moron? I saw you at the VIP section with your girlfriend, Sofia Meier! Had you even broken up with her when you and I were ... you know what? Don't tell me!"

"Sofia's not—"

"Save your explanation to someone who gives a shit. Now if that's all you wanted to talk about, then I'm going." I move towards the door, but I barely make two steps when he closes the gap and we're standing just a few inches apart from each other.

I close my eyes for a second, trying to stay focused and not letting his scent, his energy, his *everything*, distract me.

"Open your eyes and look at me, Isabelle." He lifts my chin, and I force myself to open my eyes, steeling myself. "I stayed because I wanted to keep an eye on you, even if I had to distance myself. But I saw black when that motherfucker kept harassing you. I couldn't just sit back, Isabelle. I'm actually glad I knocked him out. I could've done worse, but I was holding you and I wasn't willing to let go. And as for Sofia ... Sofia is *not* my girlfriend. We're just friends going out once in a while ... only as friends. And I told Alex to take her home. You seriously can't expect me to leave when I know you're right here."

"That sounds fucked-up and so wrong," I tell him bluntly. I'm not sure how I feel with knowing he was watching me while Sofia was next to him.

He sighs. "Sofia and I have a platonic relationship. We are just good friends, and we've known each other for quite a while. I have no romantic intentions with her."

Bullshit. "Oh, so you've *honestly* never had sex with her?" I ask, eyeing him full-on.

And as expected, he doesn't answer me and looks away. I snort out cynically. "Okay, I guess that answers the question. Now if you'd excuse me."

"Once," he answers somberly, but looking me straight in the eyes. I can't answer back. But I hold his gaze because he's got me locked in no matter how much I want to resist. I offer no resistance either when he reaches up to brush his thumb on my cheek.

"You wanted honesty, and I'm telling you I had sex with her once, years ago. I don't even remember when. And it was only after a very long night of drinking."

My heart twists with jealousy, and it fires me up even more. "I don't want to hear about it. You don't need to feel obliged to give me an explanation."

"But I want you to know if it helps ease your mind." Now both of his thumbs are caressing my cheeks while the rest of his fingers begin massaging my nape. It feels too good.

He feels too ... damn ... good.

"Isabelle, Sofia's a lesbian. It was her one and only sexual experience with the opposite sex." *Oh.* Suddenly, I'm finding it hard to breathe, and I know it's not due to panic. This is a different kind of breathlessness. I open my mouth slightly, instinctively inhaling Magnus, tasting him in the air we're sharing. That's when I see Magnus's eyes drawn to my mouth, and without warning, his lips press against mine. But he doesn't smash my mouth like in previous times. Instead, he's gentler, even hesitant, as he brushes our lips together. I have to close my eyes when I feel myself shudder against him, like every single cell of my body that remained stagnant without him are now awake and jumping for joy.

But I know that if this progresses, I'll be unable to resist him. And that will just lead to heartbreak for me because eventually he'll know my past and he'll leave. That's why I have to protect myself now. I have to protect my heart from him. *Oh God, since when did my heart come to the fold?*

I turn my head to the side, breaking the contact from our lips. "We should stop." Damn it, even I think I sound unconvincing.

He leans his forehead against my temple, and I feel his ragged breath warming my cheek. Is he affected by our kiss as much as I am? "I'm trying to forget you, Isabelle, and I know it's only been a day, but I can't take you off my fucking mind. Were you jealous when you saw me with Sofia?"

He gently turns my head to meet his intense gaze, and there's no place for me to hide. Why does he have to make this even harder?

"Maybe I was jealous. And I know I shouldn't be because I ended whatever the hell this is, right?"

"Is that why you were dancing with that Boyd fellow? You're moving on? Are you seeing him now?" He pulls away, and I can't help my heart from twisting once again at the sight of his scowl. I want to kiss that scowl away so badly.

"And if I am? Maybe I'll have sex with him too and call it a platonic relationship," I instantly regret the unfiltered words that had just spilled out of my mouth, even if I merely wanted it to sound like a joke. The look on his face makes my heart plunge. He slowly removes his hold on me, and I want to grab his wrists so badly so I can put them back to where they were. But I've hurt him with my words. Something I've known to do a lot as a coping mechanism. Something I use to push people away.

"That's low, Isabelle. Especially coming from you."

"I'm ... I'm sorry. I meant for it as a joke. You were honest with me, and I threw it back in your face. But if you still want to know the truth, then I'm not seeing him, or anyone." I know I'm blushing at my admission. So I turn around, and I walk towards the plush-looking couch so I can sit down. All the tension in such a small period of time is making my legs wobbly.

"Good, because I was this close to calling his boss so he could get transferred. I've seen how he looks at you, and it makes me want to smash something."

I look up to him in shock, but noting that my heart skips a beat at his show of proprietorship.

"Haven't you had enough smashing for one night? You just smashed that douche barely an hour ago, remember?" I add with a shaky laugh.

Magnus's lips turn up on one side, giving me a lopsided smile. And before I can recover from the effect of that smile, he is already sitting on the couch next to me.

"If it means getting rid of my competition, then I'd smash the hell out of anyone and anything."

I gulp, hard. "Why would you do that?" I croak out. The last thing I want is for him to be in another fight because of me. I'm hardly worth fighting for.

He puts his arm on the back of the couch right behind me before leaning forward, his nose against my neck. He breathes me in, and my body responds rousingly.

"Because, Isabelle, I'm not ready to end this. I don't mind complications. As a matter of fact, I thrive on them."

Before I can reply back, Magnus places his hand on the back of my neck and pulls me to him. His mouth is now on me, and he kisses me like a man taking what he wants without apologies. His tongue glides in between my wanton lips and caresses my own. He moans at our union of wet tongues and soft against firm lips.

I shouldn't be doing this, right? I should be stopping him, right? right?

"Magnus ...," I whisper against his lips. I place my hand on his chest so I can push him away, but my fingers have a mind of their own as they glide over his hard chest and into his hair.

"I want you, Isabelle. Tell me you don't mean it when you said you want this to end," he's talking in deep breaths, his voice thick with desire.

"I should stop you, Magnus. I really should."

"But I know you won't because you want me just as much as I want you."

"Magnus, I'm not—"

He nips my bottom lip, the pleasure and pain instantly halting any further protests. Then he glides his tongue over it, making me close my legs shut as my core clenches with desire. But Magnus places a hand in between my thighs and pries them open, circling the inner part with his thumb. I close my eyes, sighing softly at his sensual attack on my mouth and my skin. But just as quickly, he pulls away, leaving me needy for more.

"Open you eyes," he commands, and I do. But the way he's looking at me with those darkened blue eyes is hypnotic. That's when I know I'm done for. "I want you to see … to feel how much I want you. Will you let me?"

I breathe out a 'Yes,' nodding slowly.

He kisses me once again before kneeling in front of me. He opens my legs and positions himself in between so we are face-to-face. His hands are on both sides of my hips, holding me securely. I should be freaking out right now and putting a stop to this. But I can't help that I actually feel safe, right here with him. It's like nothing I've ever felt in years, and it scares and excites me at the same time. And his lips, his hungry lips are kissing me once again … with his tongue exploring the inner recesses of my mouth.

"I love how delicious you taste, Isabelle. I want to taste you every fucking day," he murmurs a hair's breadth away from my mouth. Then without breaking contact, he takes my other hand and places it over his sculpted abs, on the way to his chest. I can't help but follow its movements.

"Isabelle, look at me," he urges, his voice low. I look up at his blue eyes, drowning in those blue pools.

"This is what you do to me when you're close, when we kiss, and when you touch me." He takes my hand and presses down so I can feel his strong heart beating hard and fast. I can't help but stare at our joined hands placed against his heart, and I'm staggered by my effect on him because that's exactly how Magnus affects me too.

"And this is what happens because of what you do to me." He guides the same hand downwards, and I follow with my eyes. He guides it lower, down past his sculpted abs once again, and onto his swollen crotch.

I suck in my breath as he wraps my hand over his hardened cock. Even over his denims, I cannot only feel but can see exactly how I affect him.

"Can you feel how much I want you?" His mouth is over my ears, half-groaning his words and making me feel all sorts of wet in between my legs.

I struggle to stay unaffected by him, and it's not easy when he affects me the way only he can. I pull my hand back from his grip.

"But what if I can't give you what you want? Maybe we shouldn't do this."

With both hands, he cups my face, locking my eyes into his.

"Why do you keep pushing me away?" The confidence I saw earlier in him is gone, now replaced with uncertainty. It's heart melting that a man like Magnus seems nervous to hear my answer. It makes me want to kiss that look away.

And so I do. I kiss him with all my pent-up longing for this man. I kiss him to erase any doubts he has that I don't want him. Because I do ... damn it, I really do. But my kiss has a hidden agenda. I can't answer his question. I'm not ready to say it, and Magnus will never be ready to hear it.

With a groan, he lets my tongue in, and our tongues begin their slow dance. My arms are now wrapped around his shoulders, pushing him closer, wanting more contact. He moves his hands to my back, feeling the naked skin with his fingertips. His touch leaves tingling sensations. It's addictive, and I can't get enough.

Then I find myself getting lifted off the couch as Magnus carries me. We swap positions, with him sitting down and me on his lap, straddling his legs. I begin gyrating against his crotch to the beat from the dance music in the club. I don't realize that my skirt is hitched up to my hips, exposing my panties. I've come to that point where I don't care anymore. Right now, I'm grateful for the friction Magnus's denimed crotch is giving my wet pussy. I feel my whole body pulsating, and I know it won't be long before I come.

Magnus doesn't miss a beat. He places a hand between us, pushing my panties aside so he can feel my throbbing warmth. When I feel his forefinger glide over my soaking pussy, circling over my clit, I let out a whimper. Then in one quick motion, his two fingers are inside me. I push my head back, closing my eyes, moaning his name. I let my insides tighten around him, thrusting myself down on his fingers until it becomes too much, and I shatter around him.

I cry out his name as his fingers feel every single spasm. After a few more moments, I slow down, my panting easing out. That's when Magnus removes his fingers from inside of me and inserts a forefinger in his mouth to taste me. God, its ridiculous how that gesture can prolong my orgasm further, but it does.

"Mmm, so wet and so sweet. Was that all for me?" he growls as he buries his head in my neck, inhaling me deeply. All I can do is nod my head, a goofy grin most likely plastered on my face.

"Would you like to know how good you taste?" he asks, with his eyes still hooded in lust. I nod and lick my lips. He gives me a sexy smirk, as his middle finger glides over my lips, mimicking a lipstick with his action. It's sensual and intimate, but it's not enough. So I grab hold of his wrist and I suck his long middle finger inside my mouth, letting my tongue twirl around it as a promise of what I want to do to him next. He bites on his lower lip, and I know he wants it too.

"You are so sexy, Isabelle. You're driving me insane." And with that, he holds me by the back of my neck and kisses me deeply. I can still taste myself on him, and it's such a turn on, I think I might have oversaturated my crotch. I won't be surprised if Magnus's jeans are soaking with my own juices as well.

Thinking about Magnus's wet crotch and the thick hardness digging at me makes me want to free him from his restraints. He has made me come so many times, and yet he never forces me to reciprocate. I've never felt safer with anyone than I do with him. Whether or not, we progress into something deeper won't matter anymore. All I know is deep inside, I'm ready for him. No, I've *been* ready for him since our last encounter. But I let fear overcome me.

Now, I want to regain my courage back.

"Magnus, make love to me." His lips are traveling to my neck, tasting me with flickers of his tongue. But when he hears me, he stops and looks me straight in the eyes, moving his hand from my nape so he can cup my face.

After a moment of him studying my face, Magnus shakes his head before answering, "No."

I'm confused and hurt, and I'm sure it's all over my face. "What? But I ..."

"No. Not here, not tonight."

"I thought ... I thought you wanted me. You said ...," I feel like a blubbering idiot and so embarrassed. I try to pull myself off of him because I can feel my face redden, and I don't want him to see. But Magnus refuses to budge.

"Let me go, Magnus," I plead softly, my head down, still unable to look at him.

"I will, but not until you look straight at me so I can explain," he speaks in such a gentle tone that I heed his request.

"I am not going to take you until you're really sure that this is what you want."

Is he serious? I'm practically begging to be taken! "Magnus, I've never been so sure in my life. I want you. But if you've changed your mind, then I understand. I mean I did run off last time and that must've freaked you out too, and—" Magnus presses his mouth on mine, but he pulls away just as quickly. It's his subtle way of shushing me, and it works. *Touché*.

"Clearly, there are some issues we need to resolve first, questions that need to be answered before we move on to the next step because, Isabelle, if I wasn't clear before, then let me be clear now. Once I take you to my bed, you're mine. I won't share you with anyone."

Oh. It's beyond flattering that Magnus wants me exclusively for him. I know I don't want to be with anyone else because the way I feel about him goes beyond what I've felt with any man. But I'm not stupid. I know my feelings for Magnus may develop into something deeper, and it scares me because his condition feels completely one-sided.

I must be so transparent to him because he tips my chin to face him, and the sincerity in his eyes is clear.

"Isabelle, you do know that this also means I'll be all yours and yours alone, right?"

"No sharing?"

Magnus gives me a lopsided smile again, and I can't help but smile back. "No sharing."

"But what about Sofia? I know you said she's a lesbian but there are other women equally if not better looking than her. I've seen the photos, Magnus."

"I'm pretty sure I said 'no sharing.' That applies to all the Boyds as well." He raises a brow, but he's still smiling. It makes my heart flip again.

"Okay." The thought of having Magnus all to myself makes me want to bounce off the walls with happiness. But then a thought comes up that makes me crash down with a thud.

My past. If I want us to move forward, I need to come clean with Magnus about my past. I feel a cold chill down my spine at the thought. How will I even begin to start that conversation?

"Maybe we should start things off by going out on a proper date so we could get to know each other?" he suggests with a lopsided grin.

"A date? Like, as in going out and being seen together?" I add another shaky laugh to my questions, hoping to sound lighthearted about it.

"Well, I have varying options for our dates. But yes, it would also include going out and being seen together."

"Oh." I look away, trying to weigh the pros and cons. It's not that I don't want to go out with him, but I do have some obvious concerns.

He must have misinterpreted my hesitation because he's watching me with his brows creased in a slight frown.

"Are you having doubts, Isabelle? Do you not want to be seen with me?"

"It's not that at all, Magnus. It's just … well … you're kind of the big boss of the company I work for. I just don't want people to get the wrong idea." Yes, I'm concerned about being called the office tart, but my bigger concern is if word gets out to Dallas … to my hometown. I don't want anyone to find me here. I don't want *him* to look for me in here.

Magnus brushes my cheek with his hand, and the comfort I feel is instantaneous. It's almost like his touch is magic on my skin. "I for one don't care about what other people think of me. But I don't want you getting hurt in all of these. We'll keep it discreet and indoors for now. But you can't blame a man for trying to show off. I mean, look at you." Magnus's eyes sweep me from head-to-toe, and I'm pretty sure I'm swooning right now.

"I guess we'll cross that bridge when we get there." I offer him a smile, hoping my cheeks aren't too pink from blushing.

"Thank you. So, Isabelle Morrison, would you do me the honor of going on an indoor date with me tomorrow night?"

"Oh, why so soon?" I hesitate. The first thing that comes to my mind is Ethan. Saturday is my mother-son bonding day.

"I don't think I can wait." He doesn't have to explain what he means by that. I can feel his impatience against my crotch. And boy, this man is very, very impatient indeed.

It nearly makes me forget to explain why Saturday is a bad idea. Thankfully, Magnus lets me ease off him, but still pulling me close. Maybe this is the best time to come clean with Magnus about my situation, at least about my son anyway.

"I can't on Saturdays." I feel nervous, knowing that what I'm about to tell him can make him run for the hills. And I'm not even telling him everything!

Band-Aid effect, Isabelle—rip it out fast. It'll be painful, but the wound will heal a lot quickly.

Here goes nothing. "I have a son. To support us both, there were times when I worked two to three jobs. But I always made sure that I have Saturdays off because that's our special day."

I notice Magnus's eyes widen ever so slightly, as soon as I tell him about my son. But there's not even an ounce of judgment on his face, nor is he running out the door. He nods in understanding, then reaches for my hand. "Okay, I honestly didn't expect that at all, but I completely respect the bond you want to keep with your son. Maybe we could go out on Sunday then?"

I regard him suspiciously. "You're not freaked out?"

"Why would I be? When the time is right, I hope we'll get a chance to meet."

Magnus sounds so sincere, and as much as I'd like to take him up on his offer, I've chosen to be more cautious.

"Sure, one of these days," I answer back with a small smile.

"So what's your son's name?" he asks gently.

"Ethan. His name is Ethan Morrison. He's a precocious little six-year-old, and he's in kindergarten now." I'm sure the pride is evident in my voice. He's the best thing that came out of the hell I've gone through and in that way, I feel blessed.

"And is Ethan's father ... involved?" Magnus must have noticed my smile disappear at the mention of Ethan's father.

Use the Band-Aid effect, Billie. The sooner I get this over and done with, the better.

But as I look into Magnus's eyes, something stops me. The way he's regarding me right now, like he's seeing me in a new light, is forcing me to rethink this through. The last thing I want is to see disgust in those eyes. And it will be disgust if I tell him everything.

I was about to open my mouth to speak, when his phone rings. He scowls at the sound, but takes the phone from his pocket. I stand up, inwardly thanking the universe for his distraction. He doesn't answer the call but stands up as well and puts the phone back in his pocket.

"Sorry about that."

"It's okay. Maybe we should go. Well, I should go anyway." I start walking to the door but pause when I feel his hand on my exposed back. My body reacts, as it seems to always do when he touches me.

"I'll take you home." He seems tense, and the clenching of his jaw is a giveaway.

"Thanks, I'd like that," I answer back, smiling at him. I notice his features soften, and he turns to me with a smirk and a raised brows as he opens the office door for us.

"What? No arguments this time?" he teases.

"That could be arranged," I answer back dryly. He laughs out aloud at my quip, throwing his head back with abandon. It's so infectious that I can't help but laugh back with him.

Wow, he just brought his hotness to another level when he laughs. I have to make him laugh more often.

Halfway down the hall, he pauses to readjust himself. By readjust, I mean moving his crotch around, possibly to ease his comfort level.

"Need help with that?" I ask coyly.

"As much as I'd love for you to help, your hands going anywhere near this area will just make it worse." He winces.

Just as we reach the club's mirrored hallway, I hear the intro to "Feels So Close" by Calvin Harris from the outside. It's one of my favourite songs at the moment, but the last time I danced to it was while I was cleaning the whole apartment.

"I love this song! Dance with me?" I give Magnus no chance to answer. I hold on to his hand, and I lead him back to the dance floor. He tells me to go ahead when he sees the floor manager. Now, I find myself dancing on the dance floor, the same place where Magnus saw me dancing with Boyd a while ago. I cautiously look towards the booth where we were seated before and luckily Marla, Jess, and Boyd are already gone. The last thing I want is….*Oh!*

I feel two warm hands coming from behind, gliding over my stomach. A whiff of that unique scent of his only confirms who my back is pressed against. I raise my arms up, waving them in the air while swaying my hips. Magnus surprisingly mirrors me from the waist down, and we're dancing in unison. Wow, he can definitely move. I sway my hips more provocatively, just at the point where the song peaks. Then I wrap my arms backwards around Magnus's neck, sashaying down and back up again with my hands sliding over his hard torso. With my hands now clasped around his neck, he bends down and inhales me. I feel his tongue slide over my earlobe, making my nipples stand in attention. And boy, it's not just my nipples standing so rigidly. Through his jeans, I can feel him thicken once again against my lower back.

"You drive me insane, woman. I am this close to taking you right in the middle of this dance floor if you don't stop swaying those sexy hips of yours," he's growling against my neck. It's guttural and emanates a chain reaction straight down to my core.

"Then take me right here, Magnus. There's nothing stopping you," I answer back, rephrasing the song's lyrics.

Just before the song ends, he whispers in my ear, "Let's go." I feel my insides tighten at the sound of his voice, strained with need. So he leads me out of the dance floor and out of Cirque.

He gives the bouncers a quick nod, walking faster than normal, with my hand still laced with his. We don't say a word, but there's an unspoken urgency between us to be away from here so we can be alone. A sleek-looking sports car is disarmed, and as we move closer, I realize it's another one of his.

"Seriously, how many cars do you need in a city like this?" I ask incredulously as he opens the passenger door.

He chuckles, shaking his head. "This is a Tesla S. The carbon footprint on this one is basically zero. So I think I can safely add this in the garage guilt-free."

I roll my eyes as soon as he closes the door, but a smile sneaks up on my face. He's arrogant but charming—a combination I'm finding extremely fascinating.

"Do you drive yourself most of the time?" I ask as he gets in the driver side.

He shrugs, "Weekends, I do most of the driving. Weekdays, it's easier if Alex does it, so in case I get stuck in traffic, I could still continue on with work."

"I didn't know you were part owner of Cirque. You must have so much on your plate, working practically twenty-four seven." I sneak a look at him while he's driving, and it gives me a chance to just stare at his handsome profile without being too obvious.

He turns to me for a few seconds, catching me staring anyway. "I was just trying to help out my friend Jacque. He wanted to set up the club in New York, and I helped finance the whole thing. It's not a bad investment, and I'm happy to let him get all the press. He owns several clubs all over the world, so this is his forte, not mine."

"That's pretty cool of you to do that. Don't you like getting press?" I raise my eyebrow, remembering how he's constantly on the news or magazines.

"Only if it's something important for me. Otherwise, it's all trivial." He looks at me again with a smile.

"Oh, like that solar panel company you bought. What's its name again? Sonne … SonneSys?"

"You heard about that?" he asks, with surprise in his voice.

"Why so surprised? It was in the news last night."

"Of course." He nods with a smile, looking straight ahead.

We stop at the lights, and then Magnus turns to me with a big grin on his face. "Texas! You're from Texas, aren't you?" He exclaims like he just found a cure for cancer.

"Yes, why?" I ask hesitantly.

"Ever since I heard the twang, I've been trying to place it, which isn't easy since it's barely there," he teases, reaching out to squeeze my knee. The contact sends jolts of electricity all over.

"I moved here years ago and didn't feel the need to keep the accent." I brace myself for the onslaught of questions with well-rehearsed answers.

"Did you move with your family?" He looks at me momentarily, his eyebrows raised.

"Wait, is this the getting-to-know part? I thought we'd wait until we actually go on our date?" I try to distract him by squeezing his knee, just like he did with me a minute ago. He steals a look down at my hand, now over his thigh, and I hear a rough sound come up from his throat.

"Hmm, you better watch it, or I'll pull over so I could do dirty things with you."

I gasp, giggling a little. Okay, so the distraction works.

After a few moments of comfortable silence, I notice Magnus glancing at me with a slight wrinkle between his brows.

"What about Ethan's father? Is he still around?" he asks, with a trace of grimness in his voice.

I sigh, shaking my head. I guess distraction tactics can only work temporarily.

"No. He doesn't even know about Ethan, and I prefer to keep it that way," I respond, trying to cover up the loathing in my voice.

"You had your son at a young age. Was he not ready to have a child himsel—?"

"What happened between Ethan's father and me was in my past, and I prefer to leave it there ... in the past!" I know I sound blunt, but I just do not want to talk about *him* ... ever. The last thing I want is for people to look at my son differently just because his father was ... and most likely still is, a sick human being.

He looks at me momentarily, trying to read my expression. I know he has more questions, but I am not about to give away any more answers. So I turn my head out to the window to watch other people go about their business instead.

After a minute or two, I manage to find my voice. "Look, Magnus ... I'm sorry for snapping at you. It's just that—"

"Shhh, it's okay, baby." Magnus reaches out for my hand and laces it with his while he drives with the other. He holds our linked hands up to his mouth and lightly kisses my knuckles, making my breath hitch and my heart jump up to my throat. "You don't need to explain. I'm sorry for pushing you."

I squeeze his hand in silent acknowledgment.

We make the rest of the journey to Brooklyn in silence. But occasionally, he kisses the back of my hand, as if reassuring me that it's going to be okay.

In what feels like the shortest trip back to my borough, we find ourselves in front of my building. Still holding my hand, he takes it up to his lips and leaves one last lingering kiss on my knuckle. I feel the effect of it all the way down to my toes.

"So dinner Sunday night?" Magnus asks, still not letting go of my hand. The feel of his hand on mine is so ... right. I just don't want to let him go.

"I have to check with Michelle if she has plans on Sunday. If she doesn't, then dinner it is. But I'll call you tomorrow to confirm." I unbuckle my seat belt before opening the door.

"Hold on." He grabs my hand again as I'm trying to step out, tugging me back in.

"Oh, why are you—?" Before I can finish my question, he holds me by the back of my neck and presses his mouth on mine. He tilts my head, and my mouth opens involuntarily, letting his tongue in. All thoughts of passersby and the possibility of Michelle or Ethan seeing us kissing inside the car are forgotten. *God, this man can kiss.*

We're both panting when he breaks away, our foreheads touching while we try to get our bearings back.

"Go. Now. Before we take this any further and give your neighbors a show," Magnus sounds close to breaking point with his voice rough and ragged. I can't help but giggle, still in awe that I can affect him this much.

I step out of his car and just as I close the door, I notice him adjusting himself again. *Poor Magnus, looks like I affected him more than I thought!*

Magnus gives me a sheepish wave as I head up the steps to my building. As soon as I'm inside, I hear his car drive off. I can't erase the smile on my face on the way to my apartment. I feel like a giddy schoolgirl after finding out that the guy he's crushing on likes her back. But the difference is, this hot guy has already given me mind-blowing orgasms, yet our first date won't be until this Sunday.

If you asked me seven years ago if I'd ever be in this position, I'd most likely say no. But Magnus is different. He's helping me realize that not all men are assholes … that not all men are like my sick ex. I can see myself opening up to him. It may be a slow process, but he makes me feel safe. My whole body warms at the thought of his arms around mine. I look forward to having those arms around me again.

After a quick peek at Ethan sleeping, I shower, brush my teeth, and change into my nightclothes. I feel very tired and sore, but in a good way. I smile languidly as I lie down to sleep. I'm still unsure where Magnus and I are going with this. All I know is that we both want to get to know each other better.

But what happens when I tell him everything? And what about Ethan? These troubling thoughts run through my head as I drift off, hoping for a deep slumber.

CHAPTER 8

I can only manage to open my eyes in slits, and my heart sinks when everything is still in complete darkness. My head is throbbing, my body feels like lead, and every part of me is sore. I try to focus my eyes, and my heart starts to race.

I'm still bound, and my eyes are still covered. Feeling a chill, I realize I'm also still naked.

Oh God, I'm still here! I wince when I try to move my legs and my inner thighs. I hurt so much down there! What happened to me when I blacked out ... was I raped? My God, did Cooper say he raped me? I try to listen around me for any sound, just in case someone's in the room with me. Nothing. I try to struggle out of the cuffs on my wrists since they feel soft enough. Maybe I can get out of them. I try to slide my hands off, but the more I struggle out of it, the tighter the cuffs get and now my wrists hurt.

I am exhausted, my wrists are probably bruised, and I am in a whole lot of pain. Then I hear footsteps, and I freeze up, my heart beating twice as fast.

"Is anyone there? Cooper?" I ask tentatively.

"Rise and shine, Autumn, baby. How does it feel to officially be a woman now?" He is laughing at me. Suddenly, he pulls my hair back, and I gasp, tears about to spill out.

"Say thank you, bitch!" And he pulls my hair harder.

"Oww! Thank ... you," I whimper.

"Awww, you're welcome, Autumn," he gnarls at me, his voice beastly. Then he roughly lets go of my hair, making my head flop back on the bed.

I am sobbing uncontrollably, my face and hair all wet since I have no way to wipe them.

Why did he do this to me? Why can't he let me go? He's already taken something so precious that was supposed to be mine to give to someone I love. He took it away, and I'll never get it back!

The bed creaks, and suddenly he is on top of me again!

"I'm not finished with you yet, baby." His voice gives me cold chills, and I shudder.

I try to shake him off me, but he roughly holds me tight and hisses at my ear, "Stop struggling, you'll make it worse."

He presses his mouth on me, trying to stick his tongue inside my mouth. With brevity, I open my mouth and bite hard on his tongue, cutting the surface. I taste some blood, and I spit it out.

"Fuck, you bit my tongue, you fucking bitch!" he screams, his words muddled from his hopefully injured tongue.

"Let me go, Cooper, you motherfucker!" I scream as hard as I can. Suddenly I feel a sharp slap on my face. It throws my head back to one side. Then I get a blow on my stomach knocking my air out. It leaves me in a daze but then I feel warm liquid trickling out of my mouth, and I know I'm cut.

Please God, just take me away from here. Just let me die, please ...

He is on top of me again, straddling me with his legs against my hips. "You'll pay for that, bitch," he screams at my face.

I can't fight him anymore. He'll just hurt me again.

I start to feel numb, and I can't feel the pain anymore. Maybe I should be thankful for at least that. Just as he invades my core, coldness start to engulf me, and I black out once more.

I open my eyes wide with a gasp, my body frozen, refusing to move. My body is covered with sweat, and my face is wet from the tears that shed from my eyes. Shame, fear, anger, awash me and I can't stop sobbing. My body is buckling from the memories that keep tormenting me.

I know I'm not in that place anymore. I'm back in my own bedroom. It was just a dream. But I feel like I'm still in that small room ... where he kept me for days even after he was done with me. He kept me there until my bruises and any traces of his violence towards me have disappeared. I can still remember when he visited that room, wearing a stupid mask because he took off my blindfold. But I knew it was him. We were childhood friends for goodness sake! He would leave food for me, and he kept saying sorry, saying it was because of the 'bad shit' he took. God, I didn't even know he took drugs! But he also said no one would believe me if I told the police. And if I'd tell my parents, he would make sure Daddy's business would be ruined, and he'd release the sex tape.

But I told my parents. And guess what? My own father and mother didn't believe me. They were more concerned about the contracts that Cooper's father threw at my father's construction firm.

They believed Cooper's story instead—that after the Thornton's New Year's Eve party, he took me on a surprise vacation to Cancun in Mexico. That was why I was gone for over a week. I was gone for over a fucking week, and my parents didn't care because apparently, I've been sending them e-mails and texts through my fucking phone. And by the time I realized I could actually get someone to trace the location of those alleged texts and e-mails, I was already in New York. I left everything in Texas, including my phone because I didn't want to be found. I only brought my ID, some clothes, and all the money I've saved. As soon as I arrived in New York, I created a whole new identity so no one could track me down.

I try to muffle the sounds of my sobbing with a pillow. I don't want Michelle or Ethan to hear me. This is my pain, this is my grief ... this is my fault ... because Cooper said it was.

I just want it all to go away. I just want it all to go away. I just want it all to go away ... please. I chant to myself, wishing this heaviness inside of me will disappear, but I know it never will. And in times like this, I've never felt more alone in my life.

I know I have to go back to my therapist. Dr. Mitchell has helped me deal before. But she's expensive so I can't see her regularly. But I know that if I don't talk to someone soon, I might not be able to get out of this dark space again. For Ethan's sake, for my sake, I need to continue with my therapy.

I begin to concentrate on my breathing while counting backwards at the same time, an exercise I've learned from Dr. Mitchell whenever I feel an anxiety attack coming on. It helps as I start to calm down, my sobs now only involuntary trembles.

My new job pays really well. I'll be able to see Dr. Mitchell again. But right now, I just need to concentrate on my breathing.

After what seems like a lifetime, I slowly sit up. I check the time: four o'clock. I might as well get up, knowing I can't get myself to go to sleep again. I close my eyes for a second. *You can do this, Billie.* I get off my bed and make my way to the bathroom.

I wash my face, needing to feel refreshed. I look in the mirror and wince at the image in front of me. *Thank goodness, it's Saturday. I won't have to go to work looking like shit.* My eyes are puffy, practically bee-stung in appearance, my cheeks look blotchy, and my lips feel too swollen. I wipe my face with a towel and quietly head towards the kitchen. I check the fridge, and thankfully find a small piece of cucumber inside the vegetable crisper. I slice two round pieces and sit on the couch. I turn on the TV, making sure the volume is low enough that only I can hear. I put each slice on my eyes and give myself half an hour to reduce the swelling. Hopefully, by the time Ethan wakes up, my eyes will be back to normal.

After an hour, my mind is clearer and my eyes are slightly looking better. I decide to cook breakfast since I'm already up. I prepare myself a mug of hot chocolate, before I put on the kitchen bench the ingredients of Ethan's favorite Saturday breakfast of chocolate chip waffles.

I still have at least a couple of hours to burn before I have to prepare breakfast, so taking my hot chocolate, I head back to the couch to watch a rerun of a cheesy TV sitcom from the '90s. I switch the channel, but nothing interesting is on at the moment. I look around my living room, wondering what else I can do. I notice my purse on the table next to the couch.

I suddenly have the urge to reread Magnus's message to me from last night at the club. I grab my phone from my purse, and I search for his message. I feel butterflies fluttering in my stomach while reading his text, and I feel like a giggly schoolgirl once again. I fight the urge to text him back, knowing how ridiculous the time is. And although it may sound incredibly selfish, I just want to have that connection with him, even if it's restricted to text message.

'Hello Magnus, I hope I didn't wake you. I just wanted to say I miss you, and that I would love for you to come over and kiss me right now. Too forward? Oh well … I'll call you later. ☺Isabelle.'

I reread my message before pressing the *Send* button. I decide to sign off as Isabelle, realizing now how it thrills me when he pronounces my whole name. I check the time again: five-thirty. I have plenty of time to spare, so I decide to revisit the novel that I'm halfway into finishing.

After a while, I'm now fully engrossed in my book, when I jump at the sound of my phone vibrating next to me. I pick it up, my heart beating a little faster, knowing exactly who has messaged me. *Did I wake him up? I hope not. What if he's pissed off? Shit!*

I press the button to open up the screen and sure enough, it's from Magnus. I swallow hard as I open his message.

'Look outside.'

That's all it said. *What? Outside? Like, as in outside my building?* I place my book on the coffee table, and I slowly walk towards the front window to look down. That's when my eyes widen, and my mouth gapes in shock.

There he is, Magnus, outside my building, staring up at me with a sexy smirk on his face. He drove here on his own, as I notice the Tesla parked across the road. It's still dark outside, but the streetlights illuminate his handsome face.

Holy shit! He's here! My heart is pounding a mile a minute. This seems surreal. But I can't let him in. Michelle and Ethan might wake up, and they have no idea about Magnus.

I give him a little wave, still stunned that he's here. I move away from the window, my heart still pounding but with a big smile on my face. And then realization strikes.

Oh no, I look like crap! I quickly check the mirror hanging next to the front door to check myself. Okay, my eyes are not as swollen, but I still have bags under them. *Great.* I tie my messy hair into a ponytail, breathing a few steady breaths before opening the door to meet him outside.

As soon as I open the main door of the building, he's right in front of me, with a big smile on his face. I take a second to appreciate how good he looks in a slim-fitting, charcoal T-shirt and black track pants. Even in what looks like gym gear, he looks hot. *No one* should look this good in gym clothes, and at this ungodly hour!

"Magnus, what are you doing here?" I sound breathless, my heart beating too quickly. "Come in, it's cold out."

As soon as he steps inside, he cups my face with both of his hands and kisses me. His mouth is warm on mine, his tongue wet and inviting. Still locked in his embrace, I step backwards, onto the main foyer, the door closing behind Magnus. I moan softly. I can kiss him all day, every day if I could.

But before the kiss gets any deeper, I place both palms of my hands on his chest and move back, wanting an answer to my question.

"Seriously, why are you here?" I ask again, not wanting to make too much noise in case our nosy neighbors hear us.

"I'm here because I got your text message, and I couldn't wait until you called me so ..." He nuzzles on my neck. "Lovely choice of sleepwear by the way," he whispers in my ear, holding my waist with both of his hands.

"Oh shit, I'm still in my pajamas!" I say a little too loudly, instantly regretting it.

"I prefer you wearing something I can take off easily." He's kissing my lips while his hands travel on my ass and gives them a squeeze. I giggle because of it, and that's when I realize .

"Magnus, stop! I haven't brushed my teeth yet, sorry," I tell him embarrassed, covering my mouth.

"So what? I don't care. You actually taste like chocolate ... yummy!" he states with a low growl.

"What? Okay, ew?" And I slap him playfully on the chest, making him chuckle. Maybe it's a good thing I indulged on a mug of hot chocolate earlier.

"Aren't you going to invite me in?" His hands move on my hips, pulling me close so our lower bodies are against each other.

I shake my head apologetically. "You know I can't, Magnus." What would Michelle say? And I can't even fathom how Ethan would react if he wakes up and sees another man he doesn't even know yet in the apartment.

He sighs out loud, obviously disappointed.

"I'm sorry, Magnus. I feel bad that I woke you up, and you had to come all this way. That wasn't my intention. I mean, I wasn't expecting you to come all this way ..."

He tilts my head and gives me a little smirk—the type that gets me weak in the knees.

"Don't worry, Isabelle. I was already awake and about to hit the gym when I got your message. Besides, it's worth it." Then he kisses my lips, and I close my eyes, savoring the tenderness of his lips.

Who does this? Who drives all the way from his comfortable abode in Tribeca to Brooklyn, on account of a text message, at an odd hour no less? Not that I'm complaining. This is incredibly sweet of Magnus to do. A little bizarre, maybe, but still incredibly sweet. I wonder if this is his way of showing that he cares for me? With these thoughts in my head, I break free from his embrace to sit down at the foot of the stairs. He follows and sits beside me.

"Thank you for coming over, even if you didn't have to. It's awfully sweet. And as much as I want you to come inside my apartment so I can repay your sweet gesture properly," I say while raising my eyebrow suggestively, "maybe now's not the right time. I mean, I haven't even told them about you yet."

He frowns. "Why not? Were you planning to tell them about me at all?"

"Yes, but these things can't be rushed. I mean, it's just ... it's just that I'm not good at this, and it's been a while ...," I explain nervously, shaking my head.

His expression softens as he cups my face with his hand, his thumb caressing my cheek. He doesn't say anything, but the way he's looking at me, like he's remembering every part of my face, sends delicious shivers all over. Right then I know I can't wait until tomorrow night. I need this man in bed, with me, as soon as possible! Maybe now's the time to throw caution in the wind.

"Okay, so how about this. How about if *I* ask *you* to dinner tonight?" I can't believe I just asked a man out! I just asked Magnus Grant out on a date!

His eyes light up and a smile begins to form. "You know my answer will be yes. But I'm still picking you up, and the plans I had for tomorrow will just be moved for tonight."

I can't help but smile back. I just hope Ethan will understand. I'll make it up to him tomorrow.

"So you'll tell your son about me?" he asks, as if reading my thoughts.

I give him a wicked smile. "Well, I can't just let you wait outside. After all, a gentleman always meets the lady's family on the first date."

"Is that a Texan thing?" he asks softly, tilting my chin up with his fingers.

I giggle before shaking my head. "No, it's just an Isabelle Morrison thing."

"Come here." He lifts me up and sits me on his lap so I'm straddling him. We kiss softly, and before long, our kiss become passionate.

"Ahem!"

I jump, and my face turns to crimson. Behind us is one of my elderly neighbors from the same floor, Mr. Fatone, frowning at us. He is wearing his running gear, obviously about to go for his morning walk.

"Oh, I'm so sorry, Mr. Fatone," I whisper, my voice barely audible as I scoot up from Magnus's lap and move to the side, so I can give him room.

Magnus, on the other hand, keeps his calm. He looks directly at my neighbor, before standing up and moving aside. He gives Mr. Fatone a small nod as he huffs down the last step. He shakes his head in disapproval before finally leaving the building.

I look up at Magnus, and he looks back at me, and as if on cue, we both laugh out loud.

"Shushh!" Giggling, as I put my forefinger on my lips, trying in vain to stop us from making too much noise and waking up the rest of my neighbors. He takes my hand and kisses its palm, sending tingles down my spine.

"Well, on that note, I'll take my leave, Ms. Morrison." His handsome face is lit up as he kisses the back of my hand in that old fashioned 'gentlemanly' way.

Still giggling, I wrap my arms around his waist instead. "I think you just got me in trouble."

"He's just jealous because I got to make out with you," he says with a wicked smile.

I playfully smack his chest. "Yeah, whatever, Magnus. I'll see you tonight. Go … now." I point at the door, playfully stressing my order.

He grabs the same hand and makes a move towards the front door. "I'll pick you up at eight?"

"Eight it is," I confirm with a smile, excited at the promise of seeing him again in a few hours.

He lands a chaste kiss on my lips. Then he opens the front door, and with a small wave, he closes it behind him.

I head back upstairs to my apartment, hoping to catch a glimpse of him before he gets in his car. He is talking on the phone but looks up to my window as he opens his car door. I give him a smile and a wave, and he returns the gesture. As I see him drive off, I can't stop the sadness I feel because I'm missing him already.

The sun is rising, and daylight starts to flood our apartment. I check the time and decide that it's time to prep up the waffle batter, so off to the kitchen I go. As I am mixing up the batter, I hear footsteps coming down the hallway.

"Oh, good morning, Billie. I didn't hear you get home. You cookin' breakfast?" Michelle greets me, her bed hair wilder than usual.

"Good morning to you too. Yeah, I'm cooking choc-chip waffles, Ethan's favorite. You want something else?" I ask her with a smile, trying to get her on my good side before I drop my bombshell.

"Nah, I'm in the mood for something chocolatey, anyway." She gives me a sleepy smile back, before she starts grinding the coffee beans for the coffee machine.

"What time did you get home last night? You had fun? Met anyone?"

Great, she just woke up, and she's already asking questions.

"Um, I came in at about past one, I think. And yes, to answer your question, I had a great time with some new work-friends," I answer while pouring some mini chocolate chips in the batter and folding them in.

"That's great, Billie. So, anyone interesting? Oh, how about Boyd? I remember you telling me he was crushing on you, right? Well?"

"Whoa! That's a whole lot of questions, way too early in the morning," I reply, shaking my head. "I'm not really interested in Boyd."

I put down the small knife and let out a big sigh. "I did meet someone. But it wasn't from last night. Actually, I met him two weeks ago."

"Oh? And you're only telling me now?" She sits on one of the bar stools by the kitchen bench and stares at me with a raised brow. I just shrug my shoulders in reply. "How did you meet? And most importantly, how *were* you around him?"

I try to be as nonchalant as possible. "The first time I met him was at La Bocca. He was a customer. Apparently, he saw me working there last Friday and decided to go back on Monday on the off chance that he'd see me." I intentionally leave out the part where Magnus asked about my work schedule. Details like that may get misinterpreted.

"Yeesh, a little on the creeper side, don't you think?" I'm definitely feeling better about leaving that info out.

"I thought that was odd too, but now I think it's flattering. Anyway, he was there for a business dinner with other suits, and they weren't seated at my station. But Annalese asked if I could help out since I wasn't really busy."

I take a deep breath. "Anyway, I served his entrée, and our hands sort of touched ..."

Michelle's chin is resting on her interlinked hands, and she's studying me with her carefully.

"How did that make you feel?" she asks, concern now showing on her face. She knows about my past, and she knows the effect a man's touch can do to me.

"That's the thing—for the first time in many years, what I felt was completely different from the usual. When our hands touched, I didn't pull back, I actually liked it."

My best friend's smile is from ear to ear, relieved at my revelation.

"So did he come back to the restaurant again? Did he ask for your number?"

I swallow slowly. "Well, here's the thing, you obviously know I started temping at Grant Corp on Monday, right?"

She nods before her face lights up with excitement.

"Oh shit, don't tell me he's working at Grant Corp too? What a freaky coincidence!" Michelle concludes with a big smile on her pretty face.

Oh boy, it's going to get even freakier than that, Michelle.

"Actually, this guy that I'm talking about, his name is Magnus Grant."

It takes a couple of seconds for her expression to change from a smile to utter shock, her mouth in a big 'O.'

"Ho ... ly shit! THE Magnus Grant is the creeper???" Her eyes are wide open, and they're almost as big as her gaping mouth.

"He's not a creeper, Michelle! We were introduced by my new boss, Mr. Dune. You see, Lydia asked me to send some files up to his office since he needed them for his meeting with Mr. Grant ... Magnus."

"Wait, wait. So did he know you were working as a temp there before you met him?"

"I doubt it, he looked just as surprised to see me. But he seemed happily surprised, you know, like I was. I just wish I didn't make such an ass out of myself. I dropped the files on the floor as soon as I saw his face!" My cheeks are crimson, a little embarrassed at my admission.

"Oh, baby girl, that's freaky and wonderful at the same time!" She pauses. "So did he ask you out already? I hope he didn't wait too long to ask you."

"That's another thing, Michelle." I take in a deep breath. "In the short time we've known each other, I've been … intimate with him." I wince, bracing myself for her reaction.

She dips her head, peering at me with a hint of disapproval in her eyes. "What? I remember telling you previously that it's time for you to move forward, with baby steps, not giant leaps. Billie, I don't want you to get hurt."

"I know, and I think about that every day since I've met him. I wanted to slow down but when I'm with him …" I close my eyes, and let out a deep sigh. "Michelle, he makes me feel safe. And I've never felt safe with any other man since …," my lips start to tremble, and I'm unable to continue.

Michelle jumps off the bar stool and rushes over to give me a hug. "I'm sorry, Billie. I didn't mean for you to bring those awful memories back." She strokes my hair gently, her voice soothing.

"I just want you to be careful. You've just met him. And if he fucking hurts you, it doesn't matter who he is or what he does, I'm gonna fucking make him bleed! And that's real talk, baby girl."

I giggle. "I know, I'm counting on it. And if it makes you feel any better, when I said intimate, it's not like we had sex yet, but um, it always ends up with me very, very satisfied." Michelle covers her mouth to muffle her excited scream. She asks for details, but I don't elaborate, telling her, a lady never tells.

When our giggles have settled down, I continue, "Beyond his name and whatever he's got, he's pretty amazing. And I really like him, Michelle. He's asked me out on a real date tomorrow night because I told him Saturday is my day with Ethan. But then he actually came over from his place in Tribeca this morning when you guys were asleep, just because I sent him a text message telling him I miss him. I got all excited and moved the date to tonight instead."

"Holy shit, no way! I thought I heard something this morning, but I thought it was just our neighbors. Girl, you're right. He is so into you. I'm still putting him on the creeper category though. I mean, who does *all* of that, seriously?" she teases. "So why didn't he stay?"

"Because I wasn't expecting him at all. I was in shock. I still am, actually," I explain, shrugging. "Plus I didn't want Ethan to see a stranger first thing in the morning."

Suddenly, Michelle's expression changes, and she becomes more serious. "Are you going to tell Ethan soon though? You know Saturday's your day with him, right?"

I get the waffle maker ready and wait for it to heat up. "I know. But anyway, Ethan and I still have the whole day today to bond. But I'll tell him and make it up to him tomorrow. I want Magnus to meet my son, so he knows what he's getting himself into."

Michelle nods. "Okay, so he's coming to pick you up tonight?"

"Yes. Girl, I'm sorry to hijack this onto you so last minute. I didn't even ask you if you had plans tonight."

"Well, I was supposed to go over Nathan's place for dinner and some desert." She winks at me twice, stating the obvious. "But he can just come over with his daughter, I'll cook some dinner, and he can bring an actual desert!" she says, rolling her eyes at me.

"Oh, Michelle, you don't have to." I don't want her to stop having a good night on my account.

"It's okay, I'm sure the kids would love hanging out anyway. And this is important to you. You need to make this step. I'm just happy you met someone who makes you feel safe. It's just a bonus that he's a sex-on-legs gazillionaire. Yeah, I know what Magnus Grant looks like." She purses her lips and nods slowly.

"Michelle, you know money has never been important to me. As long as there's enough for what's necessary, then I have nothing to complain about."

"I know, girl. I know!"

I put both of my hands on Michelle's shoulders. "Have I ever told you how I'm the luckiest person in the world, having you as my best friend?"

"No, but maybe you should start telling me every day!" She snaps her fingers and goes back to her seat.

We laugh together, and I start pouring the batter for the first chocolate chip waffle.

After a while, my little man starts padding down the hallway.

"Good morning, Ethan!" I walk over and give him a bear hug and a loud kiss on the cheek.

"Morning, Mommy. Morning, Michelle." He puts his nose in the air, and I wait for his reaction.

"Are you making choc chip waffles, Mom?" he asks excitedly.

"You got it, little mister," I reply as I give him another squeeze. "Want to help Michelle set the table?"

Ethan nods and walks over to Michelle who gives him a big hug as well. Then Michelle and my son begin to set the table together.

I finish off the batter and start to plate the breakfast: two waffles each with a healthy serving of chopped fruits on top. I leave the maple syrup and whipped cream on the dining table for them to use at their discretion. I decide to wait until all of us are at the table before talking to Ethan about Magnus.

"Mom, this is so yummy!" he says in between mouthfuls. I want to tell him not to talk with his mouth full, but it never gets old when he enjoys what I prepare for him.

"Ethan, Mommy has something to tell you," I start gently, brushing a wisp of his hair off his eye.

"What is it, Mom?" His voice garbled from the unchewed waffles in his mouth.

I look over to Michelle, who holds my gaze and nods.

"Honey, I met a new friend. And this new friend of mine is a really nice man."

He looks at me, confused. "But Michelle's your best friend."

I smile at him gently. "That's true, and that will never change. But this new friend of mine is a man, and he invited me to go out with him. And I want you to meet him, if that's okay with you?"

"Who is he, Mom?"

"His name is Magnus Grant, and he's kind, and sweet, and I really think you'll like him."

His face is thoughtful, and then he looks up to me. "You've never been on a date before. Do you like him? Like, really, really like him?" he asks.

It's a simple question, asked by a six-year-old who probably wants assurance. It brings tears to my eyes because I know without a doubt, what the answer is.

"Yes, I do because he makes me very happy, baby." I blink my eyes quickly, stopping the tears from falling.

"Ok," he says with a wide grin on his face. Little does he know how his blessing has lifted a heavy load off my chest.

"So little buddy, I'll invite Nathan and Tasha over for dinner so Mommy and Magnus can go out and have their date. You cool with that?" Michelle informs Ethan, winking at me mid-sentence.

"But Mommy's not staying tonight? I thought Saturday is Mommy-Ethan day." He crosses his arms and frowns, making my heart drop.

"Well, we're still going on our 'Saturdate' today. And I'll make it up tomorrow. How about we go to the Brooklyn Children's Museum today, then to the Central Park Zoo tomorrow? It's been awhile since our last visit."

"Yeah, the zoo! I love seeing the animals." He throws his hands up with excitement.

"So is it okay if you meet Magnus tonight before we go on our date?'

"Yup." He nods, going back to his waffles.

I look at Michelle and mouth a 'Thank you.' She gives me a smile and a discreet thumbs up. With that, we continue on with our breakfast.

After breakfast, Ethan and I prepare for the day ahead. I dress comfortably in jeans, a white tank top, and a bomber jacket. This fall has been particularly chilly at times, and today is one of those days. As I'm putting on my sneakers, Ethan comes charging inside my room. He shows off his interesting choice of outfit: blue jeans, a muscly Spiderman top, which is supposed to be part of a costume, and his black rain boots. I convince him to wear his Spiderman hoodie instead with a pair of sneakers, since the rain boots won't be particularly comfortable for walking.

Before we leave, Michelle confirms that Nathan and Tasha are coming over. She says good-bye to us before planting herself in her little nook of a home office, to continue her work on a print ad she was commissioned to design.

We make our way to the Brooklyn Children's Museum to explore different exhibits. He especially loves all the hands-on activities on offer. I let him have free reign to play at his own pace, knowing how much he enjoys the interactive displays.

By lunchtime, he's hungry and ready to leave. We make our way to East Williamsburg to one of Ethan's favorite places to eat, the Brooklyn Mac. The trip to the museum has whetted our appetites, and as soon as our food is ready, we start digging in.

I am scoffing down my carb and cheese laden lunch when I start to wonder if I should begin to be more mindful of my body … like, maybe I should lose weight so I can somehow be more like Magnus's exes. I am definitely not toned enough, and having a child without any time or money for exercise has made me slightly on the fleshy side. I mean, I may not be overweight, but I'm not model material either. My rounded bottom would attest to that.

Times like these get me wondering what Magnus truly sees in me. Magnus keeps calling me beautiful … even when I'm naked. I bite on my lip without thinking, as the images of me with Magnus start swimming in my head.

The sharp sound of a car horn brings me back to reality, and I feel my cheeks blush and my heartbeat quickens. I quickly glance at Ethan who is enjoying his lunch.

Well, maybe I should make a little more effort and start getting fitter. Looking at my finished lunch, I resolve to start next week.

We still have time to spare after lunch, so Ethan and I decide to watch a movie. He's been asking to watch that new superhero film, so now is a good time to do so. We take a bus ride to the cinema closest to our place, playing *I-spy* on the way.

I'm at my happiest when I'm spending time with Ethan. Since he was born, I've worked two, sometimes three jobs, just to be able to provide for him. Michelle, thankfully, has been helping me and has even been like a second Mom to Ethan. But now that I have a permanent job that'll pay well, it gives me a chance to make up for lost time.

I am also looking forward to tonight, although I'm a little apprehensive about the whole date thing. It's been quite a while since I've been on one. Our friends had set me up on a number of dates that never go past the first. I wasn't comfortable with the idea in the first place, but I agreed to indulge my friends. I didn't want to be touched by men, and in the back of my head, I kept thinking, *What if it happens to me again?* I had major trust issues. Major. I knew it, and my whole body knew it. And I'm still trying to fix it. And now the blind dates dwindle, but I'm not complaining at all. Then Magnus comes out of nowhere, and like a Mack truck, he knocks the breath out of me. I've never felt attracted to anyone like I have with him, and it scares and excites me at the same time.

We make our way to the movie theater, and Ethan helps find us good seats. Before the movie begins, I turn to my excited son, with a warm smile on my face.

"So how's your day so far, honey?"

"I'm having a great day. Our 'Saturdates' are the best! I love you, Mom!"

My smile gets wider as I put my arm around him and kiss his hair. "I love you too, Ethan…very much!"

It's close to six in the evening by the time the movie ends. I feel a nervous anticipation, knowing I'll see Magnus in two hours. In the meantime, Ethan is in superhero mode, recreating the action sequences as we walk to our apartment.

"Mom, you know Iron Man's my favorite superhero. Can you get me an Iron Man action figure … pleeeeaaase? One of my friends has it, and it lights up and everything, just like in the movie!"

"Well, your birthday is coming up in a few weeks, buddy. If you continue to do well in school and help with the chores at home, then I might, just might, get you all of the Avengers action figures! I can't promise you the one that lights up, but I'm sure you'll love them still." I give Ethan a playful squeeze, making him giggle.

"Yaaayyyy! I promise I'll be good and do my chores all the time." He happily skips beside me while still holding my hand.

I know every parent thinks this, but I have to say my son is the best. Ethan's not the type to ask for whatever he likes. In fact, if he wants a toy that's out of my price range and I have to say no, he accepts it, and he doesn't complain. I'm blessed with a child who is kind, sweet, and at times, mature for his age. So if I can afford it, I spoil him a little. After all, he deserves it.

We reach our block, and I notice all the lights are open in our apartment.

"I wonder if Nathan and Tasha are at our place already," I ask aloud.

Ethan shrugs, not saying anything as he concentrates on jumping over the lines and cracks on the sidewalk.

I open our apartment door, and I see Nathan with his daughter Tasha sitting on the couch in our living room, watching TV. They both look up, with Nathan standing up to give me a small wave and a smile.

"Hey, Billie. What's up, girl?"

"All good, Nathan. Had a wonderful day with my little man, right here." And I ruffle Ethan's hair as he hugs my leg. He lets go as soon as he sees Tasha, running straight to her so they can play.

"Billie, is that you? Can you come over here for a second, please?"

"Excuse me, your girl beckons." I nod at Nathan before walking to the kitchen where Michelle is in the middle of doing the layers of her signature lasagne dish.

"Oh, yum! Save me some of your lasagne, okay?" I ask as I swipe my forefinger on the side of the pot of her special pasta sauce.

"I already put your batch in the fridge, ready to be baked when you want it."

I kiss her on the cheek. "You're the best."

"I know," she says with a wink. "You ready for tonight? Make sure you're scrubbed, shaved, polished, okay?"

I pause, and my heart skips a beat. I know where this is going.

"The kids are just in the other room," I whisper while rolling my eyes at her.

Michelle lowers her voice as well. "And what about ... well, you know. Are you going to tell him tonight?"

"I don't know, this is technically only our first date. I don't want to scare him off," I speak in hushed tones, becoming uncomfortable at Michelle's line of questioning.

"But you like Magnus, right?"

I nod, knowing how true that is. "We'll see how this goes. I'll play it by ear."

"Just do what you feel is right, okay? If you feel what you have with this guy is real, then I suggest you better open up before you get too deep with him."

"I know. I have to go, get ready." As much as I love Michelle to death, sometimes her pushiness annoys the shit out of me. It doesn't help that she's right most of the time either.

"Alright. See you later."

I shut the door of my bedroom and quickly hop in the shower, mentally running an inventory in my head of suitable outfits to wear. Eventually, I decide on my dark burgundy camisole with a cropped blazer and my favorite pair of skinny jeans. I'm going for the more conservative route. After all, this is my first date with Magnus, and I want to make a good impression. Granted that we've seen each other naked, I still want to make a good impression. I want to look good for him, and it's odd because I usually didn't give a shit on my other dates before.

After dressing up, I check the mirror to make sure the look works. I normally don't like wearing makeup, and I'm not much of an expert either. So I just put on some blush, mascara, and some lip gloss. I grunt with frustration as I try to wrestle my hair into something decent, settling on just a few big curls at the ends. Lastly, I put on a long necklace, a spray of my favorite perfume, and my black heels. I am officially ready to go.

It's almost eight by the time I'm done. The butterflies in my stomach are now officially awake and flying wildly. I jump as I hear a knock on the door. I'm definitely a nervous wreck by now!

"Mom? Are you finished? Can I come in?"

I open the door, and my son is standing by the doorway.

"Well, honey, how do I look?" I ask while doing a twirl.

"You look pretty, Mommy," he answers with his sweet smile, and it never fails to make me feel warm inside.

"Thank you, honey." I bend down so I can put my arms around him for a hug. "And thank you for being so understanding about tonight when it's supposed to be mommy-and-son-day today."

"That's okay, Mom. We still had our 'Saturdate.' Guess what? Tasha said they're sleeping over tonight!" His eyes light up with excitement.

My eyes widen in surprise. "Who? Both Nathan and Tasha?"

"Uh-huh." Ethan nods. "Tasha and I will sleep in my room, and we'll build a fort. It'll be so cool!"

Just then the buzzer rings. *He's here!* My heart practically leaps out of my chest. I grab my purse and hold onto Ethan's hand, just as Michelle comes rushing towards my bedroom, pointing at the door with her thumb, her face showing a hint of anxiety.

"Your date's here."

"Thanks … Sleepover tonight, huh?" I cock my eyebrow at her, as we walk down the small hallway towards our front door.

She shrugs sheepishly. "It was an impromptu decision. So sue me."

"I just want you guys to have a great night." I lean over so only she can hear me. "Just no loud sex noises, okay?" I wink at her and she punches me lightly on the arm. I wince a little. She's always been heavy-handed.

This momentary distraction is what I need as I press the intercom button to open the front entrance. But as soon as I open our door and see him walk up the stairs, my heart starts beating a million miles a second. I can't believe how much I missed him since this morning. He looks so handsome with his tight, dark blue jeans and a slim-fitting, gray, checked button-down shirt which he wears untucked. He tops it with a charcoal wool blazer and a scarf. It's effortlessly sexy and making me want to purr like a cat in heat.

"Hey." I meet him at the landing, giving him an awkward wave. Why am I feeling shy all of a sudden?

"Hey yourself. You look stunning." He drinks me in from head to toe and back, and his appreciative smile makes me blush. Then he bends down to give me a chaste kiss on the mouth.

"Come in, I'll introduce you to everyone."

He nods and fixes a smile. "Okay, I'm ready." He seems a little anxious. Is he nervous about meeting my son?

"Are you sure you're okay to do this?" I ask in hushed tone. I look at him questioningly, trying to read his expression.

"Of course, yes," he answers reassuringly.

Before I can speak, he brushes my cheek with his hand. The warmth of his touch sends delicious shivers all over my skin.

"This is a big deal for me too, Isabelle, just as it is with you. I just want to make a good impression."

I reach for his hand, and I lock our fingers together, giving him a reassuring smile.

"You will, just like you have with me."

That's when his nerves seem to dissipate. I can't believe that this man in front of me, a power player in the business world, is nervous about meeting my six-year-old son. I almost want to giggle at the thought.

Still holding his hand, I walk him inside the apartment. Ethan and Michelle are standing together, with Michelle's arm protectively around him, while Nathan and Tasha are standing nearby. It must be an intimidating sight, but the welcome smiles on their faces should ease any nerves Magnus may have.

Ethan walks towards me with some hesitation, but he relaxes as soon as I take his hand.

"Honey, I want to introduce you to my friend, Magnus. Magnus, this little man right here is my son, Ethan."

Magnus lowers down to his level and gives Ethan a friendly smile. "Hello, Ethan. My name is Magnus. May I shake your hand?" He offers his hand out, and Ethan slowly takes it.

"Hi, Magnus." He smiles shyly as he shakes Magnus's hand.

"Whoa, you have quite a grip on you! You sure you're not Superman?" I chuckle as Magnus feigns a wince, shaking his hand as if in pain.

"I'm not Superman, I'm Iron Man!" My boy has come to life, pretending to be his favorite hero.

"Ah, that explains it." Magnus stands up. "Good to know your mom will always be safe knowing Iron Man will protect her."

Ethan beams at him, and so do I, touched at what he said. Michelle catches my eye and smiles, impressed at what she's observing.

Then she raises her hand out to Magnus. "Hi, I'm Michelle, Billie's best friend. I'm a big fan of your work but an even bigger fan of Billie's." She smiles at him as they shake hands, but I notice Michelle's pointed stare. She's basically warning Magnus with her eyes. I gotta give her props for her loyalty.

"Thank you, Michelle. I appreciate that. And it's a pleasure to meet you too," he answers, giving her a friendly smile. Whether he picks up on Michelle's vibe or not, his face isn't revealing anything.

"And this is Nathan and Tasha. Nathan is Michelle's ..." I smile at Nathan expectantly, and I notice color reaching his cheeks.

"Boyfriend. It's an honor meeting you, Mr. Grant. Your business ventures towards more greener and more animal friendly companies are quite admirable," Nathan gushes.

"I appreciate that Nathan, but please call me Magnus." He gives Nathan a firm handshake and waves at Tasha.

Michelle thankfully interrupts, "Well, now that we're done with the formalities, it's time for you guys to get on with your date!"

"You're right, we have to go. It was a pleasure meeting all of you." He bends down and extends his hand towards Ethan again. "Iron Man, it's been an honor. Thank you for meeting me."

"Next time, I'll show you my toys too," Ethan says proudly before coming over to give me a hug.

"See you, Mom. I love you."

"Love you too, baby." I kiss him on the cheek before waving to everyone else.

Once the door is shut, Magnus and I breathe out a sigh of relief. I turn to him, and I give him a kiss on the cheek. "Thank you."

He furrows his brows slightly. "For what?"

"You know, that went so well up there. I think Ethan likes you."

"Really? I hope so. Ethan's a cool kid. And thank you for introducing me to your son. I know how big of a deal that is," he gently adds as he cups his hand at the back of my neck, and he kisses me tenderly.

The kiss is broken so quickly when we hear the main door open. Our neighbor, a woman in her thirties whose name I've forgotten, comes in with her groceries. We move to one side as she tries to get up the stairs, and she glances at us to say her thanks. She double takes at Magnus and flashes him a big smile but just completely ignores me on her way up. I roll my eyes, but I choose to ignore it, not allowing anything to ruin this night. After all, he did ignore that woman's obvious flirtation. Outside, he leads me towards yet another car. This one is a Porsche Panamera. I look at him disbelievingly, shaking my head.

"What? I'm trying to impress you on our first date. C'mon, I'm sure, deep inside, it's working." Magnus opens the passenger side and lets me in, giving me one of his trademark sexy smirks before closing the door. I can't help but chuckle at his playful side. Boys and their big toys, indeed!

"You drove to pick me up, and you didn't go the chauffer route. So yes, I'm impressed."

"That's only because I want you all to myself, Isabelle. Now where were we?" Then he leans forward, as do I, and we kiss more deeply this time.

Oh, how I love kissing him, feeling his tongue inside me, slightly grazing my teeth. My lower core starts to quiver. And just as I meet his probing tongue with mine, he breaks our contact.

I moan in protest. Still leaning forward, wanting more.

"This is our first date, Isabelle. I really want to do this right." His voice is labored, most likely affected as I am. Then he shifts back to his seat and I follow suit, putting on my seat belt.

"So, where are you taking me tonight?" I ask, trying to make conversation before I let myself go and jump him.

"You'll know soon enough." His eyes are on the road, and he's got his poker-face on.

I reach up to smooth his hair, unable to help myself. "Did you have a haircut? It looks really good … You look really good," I try to not sound like I'm gushing.

"Thank you. Well, my hair is a nightmare sometimes." He self-consciously rakes his hair, and some strands escape and fall on his forehead.

His hand finds mine, and he kisses the back of it softly. It gives me such a warm feeling, and I can't help but smile. He quickly glances back at me with mild curiosity in his eyes.

"Why are you smiling?"

"Oh, nothing. I'm just happy," I answer honestly.

He squeezes my hand gently. "So am I. I hope you'll like what I have in store for us tonight."

"What is it?" I ask as we cross through the Brooklyn Battery Tunnel.

"Like I said, you'll find out soon enough," he teases.

I decide to leave it at that, not wanting to push him. I don't mind surprises as long as the intention is good.

After a while, I realize we are on our way to Tribeca. My butterflies are back, and I look up at Magnus.

"Your place?"

CHAPTER 9

We pull up by the side of Magnus's building as the big roll-a-door opens, leading to a garage underneath the building.

He parks the car at his reserved space, next to his Bentley. My heart is racing, remembering what happened the last time I was in his apartment. He unbuckles his seat belt and quickly gets off the car, coming around to open my door. As I get out of the car, Magnus holds my hand and helps me out.

He leads me towards the elevator that leads up to his penthouse. Once we're in Magnus's penthouse, a fifty-something lady is waiting for us at the foyer. She's smartly dressed and wearing a kind smile.

"Good evening," she greets us with a soft but almost melodic voice.

"Isabelle, I'd like you to meet Rosa. She's not only the best housekeeper in Manhattan, but she's an amazing cook. She'll assist you with any requests you may have."

Rosa laughingly waves him off. "Magnus likes to exaggerate. It's a pleasure to meet you, Isabelle." She shakes my hand, instantly making me feel comfortable with her.

"Thank you, Rosa. Pleasure's all mine," I answer mirroring her smile.

"C'mon, I want to give you an overdue tour." Still holding my hand, Magnus leads me down the hallway, pointing out the empty dining room before moving on. *Okay so we're not having dinner there.* He shows me his gorgeous living room, actually make that two living rooms. Then he leads me out through the glass doors, where an enormous wrap-around balcony awaits. I pause at the sight that beholds me, blown away by the views. I never really got to appreciate this the last time I was here.

Who'd have thought I'd be back?

"It truly is beautiful here, Magnus," I say, still in awe.

"Thank you, but I actually have something else to show you." He leads me around the corner, and I gasp as soon as I see what is waiting for me.

On a hardwood deck outside the main kitchen is an outdoor dining area with wooden poles holding sheer white tapestries that serve as its marquee. The table has been decorated and set up with white tablecloth, polished silverware, delicate china, and crystal glasses. There are a couple of outdoor heaters on the deck to help with the autumn chill. It's like I've stepped into one of those romantic movies. It feels so surreal.

"Did you …?"

"As much as I'd like to take credit for the whole thing," he explains as he pulls the chair out so I can sit down, "let's just say this is the reason why Rosa is the best. I relay, she executes."

"Oh, I must tell her she did a wonderful job. It's all beautiful, Magnus." I beam at him.

"I'll let her know." He bows down to kiss me. "Now, I would like you to just sit right here, and look amazing."

Before I can respond to what he said, he goes inside the kitchen. I notice Rosa is cleaning up. Magnus removes his jacket and drapes it on one of the bar stools at the breakfast bar. Then he starts rolling up his sleeves.

What the? Is he cooking? This just gets more interesting!

He walks over to the stove and grabs a ladle, before lifting the lid on one of the pots to add other ingredients in. He mixes its contents before tasting the mixture. Satisfied, he asks Rosa to get two soup bowls then proceeds to fill them up with the soup. He adds some finishing touches, and once done, he carries the bowls to our table with a proud grin on his face.

"First course is served, Miss Morrison. It is split pea soup topped with crunchy prosciutto," Magnus announces proudly, as he carefully places my soup bowl in front of me first, before setting his bowl down next. He grabs my table napkin and lays it on my lap, deliberately grazing my thigh with his fingers. I pretend not to notice, but the tingles I feel all over is not as easy to ignore.

I bend down to inhale the inviting scent of the soup. It smells delicious and mouthwatering.

"Did you cook this?"

"Rosa helped with the preps, but yes, I did. Surprised?" He raises his eyebrows teasingly as he sits down across from me.

"As a matter of fact, yes, I am. Who knew?" I tease him back. "So shall I?" I ask, my spoon ready.

"Please." He smiles as he opens a bottle of Australian Sauvignon Blanc and pours me a glass.

The soup is delicious and well balanced—creamy with the prosciutto adding some salt and texture. Yes, I love food, and this is very good.

"Mmmm." I smack my lips loudly as I finish off the soup.

He chuckles, and the light from the candles on the table gives his face a wonderful glow. Seeing him smile is definitely one of my favorite things.

He raises his glass, and I follow suit.

"To our first date." And we clink glasses. The wine tastes crisp and light, making it a good starter.

Rosa comes out from the kitchen after a while, and takes the now empty bowls from our table. I turn to her before she leaves. "You did a wonderful job with this setup, Rosa. Thank you."

"You're welcome, dear," she kindly replies, her accent giving her voice that melodic quality. She nods graciously before walking back to the kitchen, leaving Magnus and me alone again.

"I'm just giving the lamb a few more minutes of roasting time." He reaches across from the table and holds my hand. I can never get over the feeling when he touches me. The electricity between us is undeniable.

"You feel that, don't you?" he asks, his blue eyes staring intently at me.

"Yes ... yes, I do," I answer breathlessly.

"So do I."

My cheeks redden, and a smile arises on his face.

"You're used to this," he says all of a sudden.

I look at him, puzzled. "What do you mean?"

"You know your way around a formal setting—from your manners, to the way you use the utensils. You know what you're doing," he says matter-of-factly.

I tense up. "It's not exactly rocket science, Magnus."

"True." He nods. "So, tell me about your family, Isabelle. Are they still living in Texas?" He leans back but not letting go of my right hand, caressing it with his thumb.

I am not prepared to talk about myself just yet. Plus his touch is distracting me.

"Wait a minute, whatever happened to ladies first? I should get to ask you first." I coyly smile at him.

"Okay, okay. Fair enough, m'lady." He chuckles.

"Good. So tell me about your family, Magnus," I ask, copying his inquisitive tone.

He looks away for a moment. "Well, how about we start from the beginning. Let's see … my great-grandfather was a migrant, a hard worker, doing whatever jobs he could get hold of. He was also very prudent with his money. Each time he'd earned enough, he would buy run-down properties, then he'd fix them himself and resold with profit. Grant Properties was built from the ground up. He got married here in New York. Then the business was handed over to my grandfather, then my father after that. My mother, on the other hand, was a highly respected prima ballerina at the New York City Ballet. Now, she lives her life hosting charities and fundraisers. I have a sister, the youngest of the three. Her name is Regan, and she's currently studying medicine. And then there's my younger brother, Gerald. He works with our father." His voice seems hard-edged at the mention of his brother, making me wonder if there's something deeper he's not prepared to tell me. I leave it at that. I'm not in a position to satisfy my curiosity, after all.

"What about you, Magnus? Tell me about yourself."

He shrugs, his face unreadable. "Not much to tell. I'm New York born and raised. But I studied in Cambridge University."

"Why didn't you work for Grant Properties and continue the family business?"

He shrugs. "I refuse to live under my father's shadow." He pauses briefly. "My great-grandfather inspired me, so like him, I wanted to do things my way."

"What you've built *is* pretty impressive."

"Being a Grant didn't make it easier for me, believe it or not. Hard work, good people, and a bit of luck have brought me to where I am today." The pride in his voice is justified.

"I'm sure your parents are proud of you."

"I hope so. Well, enough about me," he hurriedly declares. "Let's talk about you. So far, all I know is that you're Texan. I picked that up from your accent, though it wasn't easy since you've been covering it up. You have a son who looks just like you and whom you're very protective of. And you're feisty as hell, which I find incredibly sexy. That's as far as I know."

He gives me a lopsided smile, and I chuckle to cover the nerves I'm suddenly feeling. Thank goodness the lighting is dimmed, otherwise he would've picked up the redness of my cheeks.

"Interesting assessment. Let's add more facts to what you know, okay? I moved to New York, as you know, about seven years ago. I'd like to think that I've adapted quite well. Part of my genius plan to do so is to remove my accent. But the drawl is hard to remove. Sometimes it's worse when I get anxious. But these are things you already know. "

He smiles to me, and I notice a sparkle in his eyes. "But I enjoy hearing the drawl. Maybe that's why I find that temper of yours stimulating."

Oh.

"Tell me about your family."

"Well, that's the difficult part. You see, I haven't had any contact with them since I moved, so I can only talk about my family up to that point."

His brows furrow. "So, you don't keep in touch with your parents at all?"

I shake my head. "No."

"May I ask why?" His voice is coaxing me to open up.

"It's complicated, Magnus." I close my eyes, shaking my head slowly and trying not to make my voice shake.

"How complicated?"

I exhale deeply. "Very. Look, my life isn't too far off from yours. My father is a successful businessman, and my mother runs the household and a charity here and there. Keeping up appearances is very important to them. When I realized that their reputation was more important to them than loving their daughter unconditionally, I upped and left."

He doesn't respond back, but regards me thoughtfully. "I'm sorry to hear that. But I'm sure they miss you terribly."

"I miss them too. But it's better this way. I've burned my bridges, and I have no plans of rebuilding in the near future," I sound harsh, bitter even. But the wounds are still so raw and painful.

He nods slightly, his eyes focused on me. "Maybe in time, you'll feel comfortable talking to me about it?"

I smile a little, grateful that he's not pushing me even though he knows there's more to my story. "I hope so. In time."

"I better check on the lamb. Excuse me." Then he gets up and heads back to the kitchen.

"Can I help you out at all?" I ask, about to stand up. But he holds his hand up to stop me.

"You're my guest, Isabelle, and I'm still trying to impress you." That makes me smile up at him as I sit back down.

Rosa had already taken the roast lamb from the oven, and it's now resting on a space above the stove. Magnus checks the lamb before slicing it into smaller cutlets. Once he has the pieces he wants, he starts to plate the lamb with what looks like potatoes and sauce.

Seeing him command the kitchen gets me all hot and bothered. There is nothing sexier than a man who can cook. It makes me wonder what else he's good at. Thoughts of how he's made me reach my climax so quickly come to mind. I just as quickly push it off my head as soon as I see him approach.

"Miss Morrison, your dinner is served. Roast rack of lamb with mint salsa verde, and smashed potatoes with truffle butter on the side." He carefully places the plate in front of me.

I chuckle involuntarily.

"What's so funny?" he asks with a curious look on his face.

Still grinning, I explain, "Sorry, this just reminds me of the time I served you at the restaurant. And now you're serving me. Full circle, huh?"

"Ah, the irony of the situation didn't escape me. I wanted to pay tribute to it. That's why I wanted our first date here, at my place. This time, I get to serve you."

Okay, my heart just skips a big beat right there. "Oh ... oh wow. I think this is the sweetest thing anyone has ever done for me. This, and you visiting me this morning." Is he always like this? I take a sip of my wine, feeling a little overwhelmed by all of his efforts. It all feels too good to be true. *He's* too good to be true.

"I've no doubt you would've been treated like a queen on your past relationships." There's an edge to Magnus's tone, but I can't answer back. The memory of my ex sends a cold chill down my spine. Yes, Cooper made me feel like the most precious thing on Earth ... until that moment when he decided to stop.

I focus my eyes on the meal, unable to look at Magnus at all. An awkward silence passes between us, and I know that if I don't speak up now, this date might end up in a disaster.

And I don't want this date to end. I shove the ugly thoughts away so I can focus on the beautiful man in front of me.

"Well, I only really had one serious boyfriend. After I had Ethan, I kind of avoided the whole dating scene, so this is quite an eye-opener for me." Magnus smiles warmly, and I smile with him. "Speaking of eye-opener, I have to say this is delicious, Magnus. You're a man of many talents."

I hope my little diversion steers the conversation away from my fucked-up past.

He breaks into a smile, then shrugs. "I love to cook, but I am a businessman first. That's who I am. Cooking just helps with the stress."

"No wonder so many women fall for you," I say, speaking my mind before I can stop it.

"Really? And how would you know that?" He smiles at me, his eyes gleaming wickedly in the candlelight. "Would you believe me if I told you that I can count with one hand, the number of women I've cooked for? And two of those women are my mother and my sister."

I look at him in disbelief. *Surely, that can't be true?*

"So I'm part of that handful of women?" I swallow hard. "I don't understand, why would you cook for me then? I mean, you could've taken me to Denny's and I would've been happy."

He laughs. "And that statement alone is the reason why I wanted you to have a homemade meal instead."

His laughter dies down, and he regards me thoughtfully. "And just so you know, regardless of what you see on TV or the social media, I haven't really been in a serious relationship in quite a while too. The media just tends to exaggerate."

I stare back at him blankly. What is he trying to say? Is he warning me not to expect anything serious? Maybe I'm putting too much into this whole date.

"You don't have to worry, Magnus. I'm not after a serious relationship either." I hear myself saying the words, but my chest is tightening up because I don't mean it. I turn my attention to my plate, hoping he won't see the hurt etched on my face.

Magnus stands up and comes around to my side, carefully removing the knife and fork off my hands, not realizing I've been gripping them too tightly. He takes my hand and stands me up so we are face-to-face. I hesitate to look at him because I know he'll see how I truly feel. But he raises one hand and cups the side of my face, willing me to look at him.

"If you think I'm doing all of this for something casual, then I'm afraid you've misunderstood me." I feel the heat in his stare spreading through my whole body.

"So what are you trying to say?" My voice is so soft, but my heart is beating so strongly that I can feel the blood rush in my ears.

"What I'm saying is that *casual* is not what I want when it comes to you. What I *want* is for you to be all mine—body, mind, the whole package. I'm selfish like that, Isabelle. What I want is to be that man who treats you like a queen."

Before I can respond, he dips his head down and touches his lips with mine. I kiss him back, deeply, and fervently, wanting him to see just how much I want the same thing. I want this man to be all mine too. I want to be the only one he kisses like this and the only one he touches like this. I finally realize I can't deny what I've been feeling all along. I'm willing to take my chances with Magnus.

"You don't need to treat me like a queen to have me, Magnus," I whisper against his mouth before looking him squarely in the eyes. "I think you've had me from the very beginning. I'm all yours."

"Oh, baby." He swoops me up and carries me off the deck, leaving our dinner behind. With my arms around his neck, our mouths still fused together, he takes me around the corner to a circular daybed, next to the outdoor hot tub.

There, we lie together, still kissing, our tongues tasting each other. His hands are now exploring every curve of my body, and I arch myself against him, needing the extra contact. I reach up to start unbuttoning his shirt, but he gently holds my wrist in place.

"Wait! I can't believe I'm doing this, but I have to stop you."

"What? Why?" I ask urgently, nibbling his jawline, my hands running up and down the length of his muscular torso.

He hisses, struggling to win his internal battle of wills. "It's our first date, Isabelle. I want to do this right."

"Then make love to me," I whisper in his ear, licking the edge of his lobe with the tip of my tongue before gently nipping the soft flesh with my teeth.

He growls, before gently pulling himself off of me to sit at the edge of the daybed. I frown in objection.

"I just need for you to be sure about this." He turns around to me, softening my furrowed brows with his thumb. I slowly lift myself up to sit next to him, with my arms wrapped around his waist. He turns his head to kiss my temple. Then he puts his forefinger on my chin and lifts my head, his blue eyes scorching my greens.

"You're very special to me, Isabelle. And believe me, I don't want you to feel anything but special." He kisses my forehead, then the tip of my nose.

"Then I want you to make love to me, Magnus. Please, if I wasn't ready before, I know I'm ready now," I whisper, my eyes pleading.

His eyes are darkening, the lust on his eyes becoming more obvious and intense. He buries his face in my hair.

"Why are you making it so hard for me to say no?" he says.

"I'll make it easy for you then. Say yes."

"Hmmm. Are you sure, baby?"

I answer by tracing the tip of my tongue against his lips. He answers back by kissing me with unbridled passion that it practically takes my breath away.

I suddenly feel Magnus's arms around me, and he lifts me up from the daybed, holding me by my ass as he carries me towards the stairs, with my legs wrapped around his waist.

"You keep sweeping me off my feet, Magnus." I giggle softly, my arms around his neck for support.

"I haven't even started, baby." His adrenalin must be pumping because it doesn't take us long before we're in his bedroom.

"What about Rosa? Um, she might hear us …"

He chuckles softly. "She was under strict instructions to go home right after the mains are served."

"Oh. I like a man who plans ahead."

"Good to know." He kisses me once again as he gently lays me on his bed. Then he stands up in front of me, his lustful eyes melting my core as they take me in from head to toe. He walks to his nightstand and lowers the blinds of his windows with his remote control. He then directs the remote control to what looks like a music player flushed on the wall. Music starts to surround the room. I know this … Portishead's "Glory Box."

Damn, this man knows how to set the tone.

"What about desert?" I ask coyly. "I wouldn't want to miss out on what you worked hard on."

He starts to take his shoes off, a smirk appearing on his face. "I'm sorry, but I only caught the last two words of what you said. And the answer is yes."

I lift myself up with my elbows to watch him as he stands in between my legs. He takes off my heels, his hands slowly caressing my thighs as they travel up to unbutton my jeans and unzip my fly. I lift my hips and bite my bottom lip as he slowly but deliberately take my jeans off. I move further on the bed, and I kneel on it, my eyes not leaving his. I take my blazer off, followed by my top, until only my lacy bra and panties are left.

"Your turn," I tell him, licking my lips in excitement.

The way his eyes roam all over my near-naked body makes me feel so hot. This man wants me, just as much as I want him.

He takes off every article of his clothing, making me salivate on his magnificent body. And all I can think of is one word: mine.

Then two other words come to mind. "So hard."

I must have blurted it out aloud, because he looks down on his well-endowed cock, looks back at me, and nods once with that damned sexy smirk of his.

I might've had a mini orgasm just then.

He joins me in bed, kneeling in front of me, and we are so close that our faces almost touch, but he doesn't kiss me. Instead, his right forefinger slowly traces a line from the side of my neck down to my sternum, to my cleavage.

"So sexy," his voice is low, as he takes off the front clasp of my bra. He lets out a growl at the sight of my breasts. He cups them both and gently strokes my nipples with his thumbs. The sensation makes my knees weak and I moan, leaning back until I'm sitting on my legs with my hands supporting me from behind.

He takes advantage of my position, and he swoops his head down to suckle on my right nipple. I gasp, as he blows on it slightly, the feeling of my wet nipple against the waft of cool breath, makes my already stiff nipple even more pronounced. He doesn't neglect my left nipple, giving it the same treatment.

"That feels so good," I sigh.

He licks and kisses his way to my neck, then his right hand cups my chin, gently directing my mouth to his. He devours me … my mouth, my tongue … all for him to enjoy.

"Tell me you're mine, Isabelle," he commands roughly against my mouth.

"I'm yours, Magnus. I'm yours ... please ... take ... me ...," I moan, arching my body up to him.

His lips travel downwards, and my breathing hitches. Magnus squeezes my breasts and twists my nipples as his tongue licks the space between my navel and the top of my pubic bone.

He straightens my legs so he can take my underwear off. Then he opens my legs wide and starts kissing my inner thighs. I gasp as soon as I feel his tongue claiming what's his.

"So sweet ... and all for me. All mine," he asserts coarsely, his tongue tracing delicious circles on my clitoris.

I grind my hips involuntarily, moaning loudly.

"I love to hear you moan for me." His voice is husky, almost animalistic. His thumb replaces his tongue, and I gyrate against it. My whole body is quivering and seeking an inevitable release.

"Oh my God," I whimper.

"You want to come, don't you? I want you to explode, baby." His words, his reverence of me, his expert fingers, and the way his tongue is darting in and out of my core, have opened the floodgates, and I come so hard my whole body trembles. I hold onto the pillows under me, needing something to grip as my body convulses with sheer pleasure.

He licks off all the aftermath, and the sensation of his expert tongue on my throbbing sex is delicious.

"That's it, baby. God, you taste wonderful."

As my body starts to relax, he moves on top of me completely, our faces only inches apart.

"Mmmm, I'll never get tired of seeing you like this." He kisses me, and I taste my sweet saltiness on him.

He slips his tongue inside my mouth, and I suck it enthusiastically. Then, feeling confident enough, I push him off and maneuver myself so he's now underneath me, straddling him by his waist. His hazy eyes widen with surprise at my boldness.

"What are you gonna do to me?" he whispers, and a smirk is starting to form.

"Shhh. I want you to watch me." I place my forefinger in his mouth, inserting it inside and moaning at the feel of his wet tongue flickering on my finger. Then I slowly pull it out, using the wetness to trace his skin in its downward exploration—his chin, to his neck, his muscular chest, and his sculpted abs. My finger finally stops just under his happy trail, and I shift my position so I'm kneeling in between his legs.

I raise my palm to my mouth, and I moisten it with my tongue. He groans when I wrap my moistened hand around his velvety smooth cock. He's so thick when he's hard, but I manage to grasp him firmly, moving my hand up and down his length. His glazed eyes watch my every movement, captivated. Yes, he's definitely enjoying this.

I notice a pearl-like bead on the tip of his cock, beckoning me for a taste. So I bend down to lick that sweet dew off of him.

"Yessss," he whispers with gritted teeth.

He continues to watch my every move, moaning again as I cover my mouth around him, sucking him, inch by inch, relaxing my throat so I can take him all. Then I pull up and do it all over again, increasing my tempo, until his hips are moving to the same beat.

"Oh, fuck, Isabelle. Come here," he growls and sits up, reaching for a condom from his bedside drawer then pulling me close. He pauses looking at the condom, then back to me. He seems hesitant, and I know right then he wants the same thing I do.

"Magnus, I take the pill. And I'm clean. I … haven't had sex in quite a while."

"Are you sure? I'm clean too, and I get checked regularly. But I want you to feel safe when you're with me."

"And I do. I feel safe with you," I answer without hesitation because it's the truth. So I take the condom from his hand, and I toss it back on the table.

"You … trust me?" he asks tentatively.

I nod, looking him straight in the eyes. "I want to feel all of *you* when you're inside of me, Magnus."

"My Isabelle …" He guides me and positions me so I'm underneath him, his whole body like a protective shield over me.

This is the moment where I need to be sure that he feels the same way I do. Though I'm not asking for love, I need to know if I have him as much as he has me. I cup his face so we're eye to eye. "I want to hear it from you too, Magnus. I want to hear you say that you are mine."

I never should have doubted him because I can see the answer I need, written all over his face.

"My Isabelle ... you've had me since the first time our hands touched." He kisses my lips tenderly, lovingly. "I am yours. So take what's yours."

I don't think I'll ever get sick of those words. My trembling lips lift into a smile. "Make love to me, Magnus."

Our lips fuse into one, with Magnus opening my legs wider in preparation for him. His fingers dip down to my soaking apex, whispering how ready I am for him in between kisses.

But as soon as I feel the tip of his cock enter me, a cold chill begins to spread all over my body. I shut down. My whole body goes rigid, and my eyes clamp shut. And then I begin to whimper helplessly, my hands resting on Magnus's shoulders close into fists.

All I can think of is *him*! *Cooper*!

"Isabelle? Baby, look at me." I can hear Magnus. I know it's him, but I'm still frozen and unwilling to move.

My fists push at his chest, but my eyes are still shut. God, I can't look at him. I'm too ashamed. Too damned ruined. I feel the tears flowing, and I can't even stop it.

"I'm sorry ... I ... I can't. Oh my God, why can't I do it?"

Magnus gets off of me and that's when I open my eyes, it's like fucking déjà vu because I see the look of confusion and bewilderment on his face. The same reaction he had the first time I freaked out. But now it's different. By the way he looks at me, he knows something's up. But I can't tell him. I can't because he won't want me anymore if I do.

I don't realize that I'm bundled up in a fetal position, my legs bent to cover the rest of my body and my face buried in my hands. I'm crying hysterically, rocking back and forth. Shame and disgust intermingle with anger. I can't believe that after all these years, Cooper still has the power to hurt me this much.

"For Christ's sake, what the fuck is wrong, Isabelle? I need to understand why you tell me you want me, then freak out the moment we ..." He raises his hands and growls out a curse word in agitation.

"I'm sorry. I … I thought I'm ready," I answer back shakily, too ashamed to even look at him.

"Ready? For crying out loud, you're not a virgin! You blow hot and cold. I mean, what the hell is—"

"I was raped!" I yell out in agony. I keep my eyes shut because I'm too afraid to see his reaction. But the cat's out of the bag now, and I know I can't hold anything back anymore.

"I was raped, in the most horrific way—to the point where I actually wished for death to take me. And now you know how disgusting I am. I didn't want to tell you … but now you know and I … oh, my God, I need to leave. I'm sorry for doing this to you, I … I'm sorry …." I shoot out of the bed, rambling on as I gather my things. I need to get out of here and out of his life. I don't deserve happiness with anyone, especially with this beautiful man.

Just then I feel his hand on my wrist, and I pause momentarily. His warm hand on my skin feels so good and comforting. But I don't deserve it one bit.

"Stop it. Don't run away again. Let's talk about this." Magnus's tone is gentle, and when I turn to look at him, I'm shocked to see that there's no ounce of judgment or disgust in his face. Nor is there pity. But I can see his jaw clenching, and I know he's angry on the inside … probably angry with me for keeping this scandalous information from him.

But then he wraps an arm around me, and with the other hand, he takes the clothes I picked up, off my hands and instead, lifts the sheets from his bed and ushers me under. I hesitate at first, but as soon as I lie down under the sheets, I can't help but feel somewhat comforted. He grabs his boxers and puts them on before sitting right beside me. Not under the sheets, but just at the edge of the bed so we are face-to- face. Finally, he switches the music off, and all we can hear are the sobs I'm so desperately trying to stop.

"Tell me what happened, Isabelle. Who did this to you?" He gently brushes off the strands of hair sticking on my face from all the crying. He's so gentle, which is contradictory to the hardness in his expression. Why will he want to talk about it when he's so obviously upset? He grabs some tissues off the box and wipes my damp face before positioning it over my nose, as if willing me to blow. It's an extremely caring gesture, but right now, I'm feeling mortified as it is. So I take the tissues from him and clean up after myself instead. Then with a deep breath, I close my eyes to gain my composure.

"He was supposed to be the love of my life. Well, at least back then I thought he was. Our parents were old friends, way before he and I were born. So it was sort of natural that we became close friends. It developed into something more in high school. Sure we dated other people but somehow we always ended up together. I thought I was very lucky to be with him. Everyone envied us in school, even called us the 'A-List' couple." I laugh, though there's no humor in it at all. "And I thought he loved me as much as I loved him because he didn't push me for sex. I wasn't ready yet at that time, and he was fine with it."

I pause, unsure if I should continue … if I even want to continue. But Magnus holds on to my hands firmly. Somehow, my hands so secure in his, help me, so I push on.

"When we got to our senior year, he started getting impatient. He would lash at me, then he'd apologize. Or he'd pick a fight about the stupidest things. Then I found out he started hanging out with those frat brothers from the college he was going to. They were trying to woo him into joining their brotherhood. You see, my ex comes from a powerful political family. So he was like fucking royalty in that ivy-league school he got accepted in. To be honest, he probably got in that university because of his last name and nothing more. One day I heard from my then best friend that he slept with a sorority chick he met through his new college buddies. So I confronted him about it, and he admitted to it. He apologized and begged for me to take him back. He said it was a mistake and that he was drunk, blah, blah, blah. But I was no fool. I knew he messed around before, and I was willing to forgive him then because I did love him. But I was going to college myself in Cali and I needed a clean slate. We were over a long time before we even realized it, I think. I've had enough, so I broke it off. He was so upset at first and called me every name in the book. It's not in his nature to accept failure or rejection, and I think I hurt his ego more than his heart."

Magnus listens intently. But the way he keeps clenching his jaw doesn't escape me. But I'm coming to that point in my story where I need more than just his hands holding mine.

"Magnus? Do you mind sliding under beside me? Please … I just need you to hold me, that's all."

The look of understanding in his face tugs at my heart and without a word, he gets under the sheets beside me, and we lie down in his bed together, with him holding me close, my head resting on his shoulder.

"How's this?" he asks soothingly.

"Better. So much better."

I take another deep breath.

"We kind of avoided each other up until graduation. I even saw him dating some of the girls from school. And as for me, I just wanted to finish my senior year in peace with no one holding me back. I was admitted at UCLA and was about to start a degree in business economics. It was an exciting time for me. Graduation was a nonevent, most of my friends practically left my side because I broke up with my poor ex, but I didn't care. He moved on as far as I was concerned, and so did I. College life was amazing. I met new friends, I dated a little, I enjoyed my major … in other words, life was good. Before I knew it, the Christmas holidays have arrived, and I was back in my hometown to spend time with my family."

I pause a little longer now, not quite sure if I want to continue. But I feel secure enough with Magnus's that I force myself to finish telling him the whole story.

"One day I saw my ex at my doorstep looking all contrite and sweet. Much like how I knew him growing up. He asked if we could at least move past our differences; after all, we were friends first. It was a convincing speech, and it surprised me in a good way because it was like, my old friend was back, you know what I mean? He invited me to their annual New Year's Eve party at their family's estate. Naturally, I accepted—our family never missed any of their New Year's parties. The party itself was fun, as always. After the fireworks, all the old folks went home, leaving us 'kids' to continue on. Of course, the party was full of booze, and like any respectable party girl, I drank and had fun. I mean, I'd be going back to college soon, so I intended to get wasted. Last thing I remembered was someone handing me another shot … I blacked out after that."

Magnus's hold on me tightens, and his lips touch the top of my head. He knows what's coming, and it's almost like he wants to protect me from it.

And that's when I spill whatever details I can remember about the rape. From the way he kept drugging me, to the way he kept me blindfolded so I couldn't technically identify him. And when he was through with me, how he held me captive for days until I had no more physical evidence to show. He did all of these, while alternating between telling me he loved me, and apologizing. As I recall all the sordid details, my tears return, and Magnus's shoulder is bearing the brunt. But I realize the tears are not from the memory of all the disgusting things Cooper did to me, but for the aftermath. I'm crying because of what I've become and for the innocent little angel who I hope *he'll* never come to know.

And after all the tears are shed and I'm completely dried out, Magnus continues to hold me closely, wrapping me in a full hug. I don't even realize the implications that my revelation will do to us. Now he'll see how damaged I am. How awful I'll be for his public image if we ever take things further. But without a word, he lifts the arm I've tucked between us, and locks it around his shoulder, making sure I won't let go. It's like he wants me to hold on to him, to make sure I won't let go and run.

Our silence is broken by the sound of his voice, cracked and full of emotion. "Who did this to you, Isabelle? Tell me who that guy is so I can make that son of a bitch pay for his crime. Is he in jail now being someone else's bitch?"

"You have no idea how much that thought makes me happy." I pause, exhaling aloud. "But he was never arrested. Last time I checked, he's running their family business."

"What? Who *the fuck* is he, Isabelle?" The quiet fury in his voice is unmistakable.

"Magnus, I purposely avoided mentioning his name because I'm trying to protect you. His father and uncle hold powerful government positions, and they have a *lot* of clout. His family pretty much owns the local police, for goodness sake. I told my parents what he did to me, but it was like talking to a brick wall. My father's company grew because of all the contracts given to them by my ex's family. To my mom and dad, our pairing was a match made in heaven. They loved him like their own fucking son. You know what he did at the time he was holding me captive? He actually fabricated a story, saying we agreed to get back together, and he whisked me off in Cancun or some shit like that. Then he said that on the way back, *I* got upset with *him* because I asked him to marry me, but he said we should wait. I mean, he fucking thought this through! And my parents ate it all up. They believed him and said flat out to me, that I should stop being so melodramatic because I was getting him in trouble over a misunderstanding. They even said that if I went to the authorities to report what I claimed to be a rape, they would disown me for bringing shame to the family. I knew then, I needed out. I was dying on the inside and if I stayed, I might as well be dead. So a few days after he brought me back home, I packed as much as I could, and left with whatever money I had saved. Thank goodness I had cash hidden away. I didn't bring any credit cards, for fear they would use it to trace me. I bought a one-way ticket to New York, using my second name, because I knew I could remain anonymous in this city. I didn't even bother dropping out of UCLA. I just wanted to disappear. But when I got here, I found out I was pregnant."

"And yet, you decided to keep Ethan. After all that had happened to you, you still decided to keep your baby. Most women would go the other route."

"I never contemplated an abortion. It wasn't Ethan's fault that his father turned out to be a monster. And I wanted to believe that at one point, we did love each other. My son is everything to me, and I love him with all my heart. He's the reason why I even bother to get up every morning."

Magnus tips my head up to meet his warm gaze. "You are a phenomenal woman, Isabelle."

I shake my head. "No, I'm not," I answer softly. "All I am is a survivor who's taking it one day at a time."

He doesn't respond back. Instead, he just looks at me with an unreadable expression. Then he dips his head to kiss my forehead. His lips linger on my skin, so soothing in it's tenderness that I close my eyes to savor the feeling.

He eventually pulls away, and we lay in silence with unanswered questions still hanging in the air.

"You know what bothers me though? Your family is wealthy enough so they must have the resources to find you. How come they haven't found you yet? Did they even try to look for you?"

I chew on my lip, deliberating whether or not I should admit to a big piece of the puzzle. If I do, he can easily find out who raped me if he looks hard enough. And I know he has the means to do so. But if I hold back, all I'm doing is showing him that I don't trust him, when in fact I do. I know in my heart he's a good man, and I've never felt safer with anyone than I do with him. But can I keep Magnus safe once I open Pandora's box?

There will never be a right or a wrong answer to this dilemma. So I'm doing what my heart dictates. I sit up, wrapping myself with the sheets, and I offer my hand out for a handshake to which he tentatively accepts.

"Hi, Magnus Grant. I don't think we've officially met. My name is Autumn Bridges, but you can call me Isabelle Morrison."

CHAPTER 10

For what seems like an eternity, Magnus remains silent with my hand still in his. The lack of reaction is starting to make me regret my decision to reveal my true identity.

I must have opened myself up to some hurt again.

"Say something ... please," I urge nervously.

But he doesn't answer straight away. Instead, he sits up, lifts my hand and kisses my knuckle. Then he touches my hair, tangling his fingers between the locks. But it's the way he's looking at me, like he truly sees *me*. There's no judgment in those blue eyes of his, only understanding.

"Just like your hair ... the color of autumn leaves."

"Yes," I sigh in relief. "I used to love my name. And I still do. There weren't a lot of girls named Autumn in Texas."

"Is this asshole so terrifying that you had to go through such an extreme measure to hide?"

"You have no idea," I reply, shaking my head. "I had to be anonymous. I didn't want to be found. If *he* ever caught wind back then that I was carrying his child, who knows what he could've done. I couldn't take that chance, Magnus. I just couldn't." Tears well up again, as I think about the terrible possibilities.

Magnus gathers me in his arms and crushes me against his body. But he feels stiff against me, and his heavy breathing betrays an anger he's unwilling to show me.

"I know it wasn't easy for you to open up about your past. That's why I'm thankful that you trusted me enough. But baby, you will never have to be afraid. I'm here now, and I promise I will never allow anything bad to happen to you or Ethan."

He pulls away slightly, and I instantly notice the hardness in his eyes, which is polar opposite to the gentleness of his voice. "You might not be ready to reveal his name right now, but in time, I hope you'll feel secure enough to tell me."

Nodding, I whisper, "Thank you." And I wrap my arms around his neck as my trembling lips find his. Magnus grazes his tongue over my mouth, and I let him in, allowing our tongues to communicate where words don't seem enough.

He's still here with me. After everything I've revealed to him, Magnus still wants me here, in his arms. And he's kissing me ... *really* kissing *me* ... the person who just revealed how broken she is. Magnus's arms are holding me safely while his lips continue to comfort me.

I never thought I'd ever end up with someone like him, and whether this lasts or not, all I know is right now, my heart is swelling with indescribable happiness. After seven years of being held captive by my own past, I'm finally free.

A rush of need for everything that is Magnus overwhelms my whole being. Before I know it, I'm pushing him back on the bed, my legs caging his hips. I'm fully naked, and I'm desperate for him to be, as well.

"Baby, are you sure?" he asks with shaky breath as I hastily take his boxers off. I stop for a second to admire his magnificent cock, already hard and thick, and all for me.

Mine.

I run my hands on his hard chest, down his sculpted abs, and back up again. "I've never been intimate with anyone in seven years because I was so afraid. Magnus, I know it's technically not true, and it may be a ridiculous notion, but would it be okay if I remember you as my first?" I ask with nervous uncertainty. I hear Magnus groan as I perch myself on top of him. He reaches up and cups my face and pulls me down, smashing our lips together. All the emotion between us seems to culminate in this kiss. Then with another groan, he pulls away, both of us panting with desire.

"Baby, it's not ridiculous at all. It's my honor to be your first. Technically or not, *this* should be what counts."

"Oh, Magnus." Overcome with feelings I can't fully describe, I bend down to kiss him once again. Then with one hand, I guide his magnificent cock to my wet opening. And as I sink down his hard length to accept him fully, I pause, not even realizing I was holding my breath. He's big, and I didn't realize how big until I feel my insides stretch almost painfully to accommodate his size.

Magnus holds me by the hips steadily, and holding my gaze just as steadily as well. "Breathe deeply, baby. It'll help."

So I breathe deeply, and I let myself go.

"Holy shit, we fit so perfectly," he groans out, still holding onto my hips as we begin to move together.

If I thought he felt big in my hands, he feels even more so inside of me. The slight discomfort I felt initially has now been replaced with pleasure, with every inch of him touching parts of me I never knew existed. I stare down at the man who has completely smashed all the walls I've put up. This man has singlehandedly given back to me something I thought I'd never have back—hope. Hope that I can trust another man again ... hope that I may even fall in love again.

Oh wow, did I say love? Where did that come from?

Magnus gently lifts me off and before I know it, I'm underneath him, completely engulfed by his large frame. I would stay here forever if I could. With our lust-filled eyes connected, he enters me once again. I gasp, my body still getting used to how he fills me up so completely. And with every stroke, with every kiss, with every feel of his mouth and his hands on my skin, Magnus is bringing me closer and closer to the edge.

"Your pussy's made for my cock, Isabelle. Tell me how this feels for you." His words and the way he nips my lobe afterwards tip me over. That is it for me.

"So good, Magnus! Oh, my God!" And I shatter into a million pieces, calling out his name over and over again until my throat feels dry and my voice is barely a whisper. Yet he continues his delicious thrusting and damn, the way he's looking at me right now ...

"Come for me again, baby." He opens me wider for him, raising my hips so I feel him deeper inside of me. I cry out when he hits *that* spot, and just as he does, his thumb finds my still sensitive clit, and he starts rubbing it in rhythm with his every thrust. I grab hold of the pillows underneath me, needing something to hold onto as I feel every single wave of pleasure overcome me.

"Magnus, I'm coming again. Oh, my God, I'm coming again!" I buckle underneath him, and he holds me steady, placing the same hand over my lower belly. I know he can feel my insides pulsating around his cock, and he squeezes his eyes shut like he's doing his best to hold back.

But that doesn't last long. He pulls back slowly before thrusting himself again inside my now overly slick passage.

"So beautiful when you come. You're. Gonna. Tear. Me. Apart!" His tempo intensifies, and now I'm holding onto his shoulders as every thrust becomes increasingly stronger. And with a growl reverberating from within him, Magnus reaches his climax and with such force that I feel every jerk of his cock as it fills me with his warm seed.

"Isabelle...," he murmurs, burying his head on the crook of my neck. He cradles my head with his hands while I wrap my legs and arms around him. We hold each other like this as we wait for our breathing to settle.

Who knew I could come more than once, with just the same intensity, in such a small space of time? Will it be like this with Magnus? I definitely won't mind testing this theory out with him over and over again.

After a short moment of silence and with him still inside of me, he lifts his head and kisses my forehead, my nose, and finally my waiting lips, staring down at me with a hazy smile on his face.

"I don't know why I waited so long. That was so good, maybe I should've done that years ago," I tease, biting my lip to keep me from giggling.

Small wrinkles form in between his brows. "Really? I doubt if you would've come so hard with anyone else. You waited this long because you were waiting for me ... to be your official first!" Magnus teases back.

"Oh, my God! You're lucky I find your arrogance hot," I answer back, nipping his chin.

"Hmmm, does that mean you're ready for round two?" He licks the side of my neck, making me giggle out loud.

When our laughter subsides, he gently slides off of me but gathers me close so I'm safely nestled in his arms. It's so warm and comfortable having him this close that my body finally succumbs to exhaustion and my eyelids become heavier.

I wrap my free arm over his chest, and he kisses my temple tenderly. I can feel my eyes getting heavier. But my mouth has a mind of its own.

"I really thought that after telling you everything, you'd be running me out the door by now."

"I'm not gonna lie and say that I'm not overcome by the need to break that punk's neck after the awful things he put you through."

He tips my chin up with his finger so he can look at me directly, and I can see the fierce sincerity in his eyes. "But I want you to remember that what happened to you wasn't your fault in any way, do you understand? This is all on him." I nod meekly, not saying a word.

We stare in each other's eyes for a few more moments before his expression alters and his sexy smirk slowly decides to make a welcome appearance.

"And by the way, even though Autumn is indeed a beautiful name, Isabelle is a *far* sexier name. You're a sensual woman, so your name should reflect as such."

I let out a small chuckle, "Actually, Isabelle is mine and my great-grandma's second name."

"Ah, then your great-grandma must've been a very sexy woman in her day."

"Magnus, ew!" I giggle, smacking him playfully on his chest and making him laugh as well. I've never laughed like this with another man in years, and gosh, it feels good.

"Where did Morrison come from?" he asks while lazily stroking my back.

"It's kind of embarrassing," I answer, shrugging. "I have a big crush on Jim Morrison, you know, the singer from The Doors. I know, I know he's dead and all, but the way he sings and the way he moves ...," I sigh dreamily.

"Hey, hey hey! I'm right here, you know. You're making me jealous of a dead guy!" He squeezes me playfully.

"You asked," I tease back.

"Hmm, and to think I used to love his music too. Used to," he grumpily responds.

After a few minutes of comfortable silence, I prop myself up with my elbow so I can gaze down on his handsome features.

"You're staring," he murmurs in a low voice.

I trace my finger on the bridge of his nose. "I'm just trying to store this into my memory, in case I woke up one day and realize it's all a dream."

Magnus cups my face, as his thumb caresses my cheek. "Our eyes are wide open, and I know that I've never seen or felt anything so clearly in my life. This is real. You made this real, Isabelle."

Oh.

"Talk like that can get you in trouble, Mister. What if you decide to move on, but I refuse to let you go?" I ask half-teasingly.

Magnus tucks a few strands of my hair behind my ear, as his eyes move from my lips to my eyes. "Was that meant to be a threat? Because frankly, I prefer that to be a promise." Then he pulls me down so our lips can meet.

After a deep and satisfying kiss, I lay my head on Magnus's chest with a smile on my face. I'm so close to slumber, and yet my heart still manages to skip a beat.

***

"Mmmm, damn! This apple crumble is to die for, Magnus. You have to give me the recipe. Ethan would love this!"

After sleeping for a couple of hours, Magnus wakes me up in the middle of the night, as he's feeling hungry. But his is a two-pronged hunger which, I must admit, pretty much reflects my own hunger as well. Once we've satisfied our hunger for each other, twice, I may add, we finally make our way back to Magnus's kitchen. We've just been through a roller coaster of emotions after my recent revelation. And add to the fact that Magnus and I have finally done the deed—three times so far and counting. No wonder I'm feeling wonderfully sore and pretty famished.

Magnus and I are finally eating the desert he prepared for our dinner date earlier. He's wearing a white shirt that hugs in the right places, and lounge pants that sit just under his pelvic bone. He looks yummier than the desert itself, and I'm doing my best not to stare and drool too much. I'm wearing one of his shirts which barely skims down my butt. It makes me a little self-conscious, but my fears seem unfounded, judging by the way Magnus keeps ogling me from my braless chest to my waist down.

"I'd be happy to make them for you anytime you want. I made some extra if you want some more?"

"No need to ask me twice," I respond, beaming at him.

"Where'd you learn to cook, anyway?" I ask as I finish off my second helping.

"My family had a personal chef, who used to cook the best meals. He got me interested in cooking, and I used to watch him in action. Once in a while, he'd let me help him. I learned a lot in that time that he was working at our family home."

"So does he still work in your family home?"

"He decided to open a restaurant with his son in Florida. Maybe I'll take you there some time."

Did he just make future plans with me? I don't know what to say, so I flash him a smile instead.

He gives me a smile back and raises his glass of Moscato. "To Chef Sammy."

I follow suit and raise my glass as well. "To Chef Sammy."

Magnus takes our empty plates and wine glasses and place them in the sink.

"Need help washing up?"

"Don't worry, Rosa will take care of these tomorrow," he says dismissively.

"C'mon, there aren't a lot of dishes or cutlery, anyway. They just need to go in the dishwasher. Here, I'll do it. It's the least I can do after your wonderful hospitality." I give him a wink as I walk around the large bench top where he's standing next to the sink. Feeling bold, I give his ass a squeeze, and he lets out a growl. His reaction makes me giggle.

As I'm rinsing off any excess food from the plates and cutlery, he helps stack them in the dishwasher, after I direct him which area of the trays they should go. Once we're done, he wraps his arms around me and playfully bites my neck, making me shriek.

"Oh shit!" I whisper, covering my mouth.

"Naughty girl. Lucky no one's at home except us," he growls at me. "Come, let's take a shower. I have this sudden urge to soap you."

But the way he's watching me with darkened eye, it tells me soaping is not what he's got in mind. "Soap me, huh? Lead the way," I answer, excited at the thought.

He holds my hand and takes me up the stairs, and I get more excited with every step. Back to his bedroom, he starts taking off his clothes, making my mouth water once again as I stare at every ripple of his muscles. I can't get enough of him naked. Magnus is like a beautiful sculpture, an expensive work of art.

"It gets me hard when you look at me like that," he says in husky tone, his mouth twitching into his sexy smirk.

My eyes widen, and my mouth gapes open. He walks towards me and in one swift move, he takes my shirt off, exposing my naked body.

I tilt my head to one side. "Now, are we going to have a shower or not?" I ask casually, acting unaffected by his carnal gaze.

I turn around, and I sway my hips a little more as I walk, knowing full well he's following my every move.

Inside the spacious shower, Magnus starts to soap my back, my breasts, and every sensitized part of my body. I feel his hardness against my buttocks while his hands seem to focus on my breasts, rubbing each pebbled nipple, tweaking it with his fingers until I cry out. The need to give him the same pleasure sees me putting soap on my hands and creating some lather. Then I reach behind me so I can close my soapy hands around his cock.

He groans out my name, appreciating the way I slide my slippery hands up and down his hard shaft. Then his soapy hands leave my breasts, sliding down to my inner thighs, as he pulls me under the shower.

The drops of water seem to escalate the sensations on my skin, and I moan, leaning my back against his chest, still stroking his cock with one hand and holding onto his neck with the other. His fingers move right to my sweet spot, rubbing up and down my folds until my knees feel like jelly.

"Oh, yes, right there," I breathe out as his fingers find my clitoris, taking me to the brink with slow but torturous circles.

My hand moves rhythmically over his cock, feeling him growing thicker and harder. It boggles my mind how easily he switches on, but this is Magnus. And I'm finding out, to my obvious delight, how incredibly virile he truly is.

And right now, this virile man's attention is focused solely on me ... all over me.

I flinch as soon as I feel two of his fingers inside my wet core. "Hmmm, you're still sore, baby, and yet so fucking wet inside," he whispers as he licks my neck, leaving fire in its trail.

He turns off the shower and before I know it, I'm being carried with my legs wrapped around his waist, with my arms coiled over his shoulders. Like magnets, our lips find each other, unwilling to separate, even as Magnus steps out of the shower, with one arm supporting me and with the other making a grab for the towel. He drapes the large, fluffy towel over me before padding back to his bedroom and laying me on the bed.

"Wrap this around you," he cocoons me inside the towel to stop me from feeling the chill. Then, he walks back to get a towel for himself.

But my desire for Magnus to see me ready for him overrules my common sense so I unwrap the towel and sit at the edge of the bed. I open my legs and hold my breasts just as he's walking back to the bedroom. He stops midway, dropping the towel he is using to dry off his hair.

"Fuck ... me," he exclaims in that gravelly tone that only makes my sex tightens with need. And the carnal hunger in his eyes never leave my body, making me whimper as he quickly closes our distance and kneels in between my opened legs.

"You just brought me to my knees again, woman," he hisses with gritted teeth, his voice so full of desire as he stares at my apex like a predator to its prey.

"What do you want me to do?" He finally lifts his head, and I can't miss the devilish glint on those stunning blue eyes.

He's waiting for my answer, and the longer he waits, the more the edges of his lips twitch up into a wicked smirk.

"Tell me exactly what you want me to do, Isabelle. Would you like me to lick your wet pussy?"

I hesitate, a little taken aback by the blunt question. But he's waiting for my answer. "Yes. Yes, please."

"Please ... what?" he asks in that low yet rough tone of his.

"Damn it, Magnus. Please ... just lick my pussy." There, I said it. God I feel so stupid. I cover my hot face with my hands.

But then Magnus gently pries my hands open. He tries to catch my eyes, and when I finally feel brave enough to stare back at him, I'm amazed at how the wickedness in those eyes are now replaced by tenderness ... with a heavy ounce of lust still intact.

"Don't be scared to tell me what you want, Isabelle. You are mine, and I will do anything to take care of what's mine." Then he softly kisses the palms of my hands before lacing his fingers with my own.

"Now watch me give you pleasure." Still locking my eyes with his, Magnus dips his head down and with slow precision, I watch his tongue give my pussy one ... slow ... stroke.

"Holy sh ... aahh!" I flip my head back in ecstasy, my chest heaving.

"Open you eyes and watch me, Isabelle. I'm far from done with you," Magnus's guttural command instantly draws me back to him.

He lets go of my hands so he can open my legs wider, making me sit even closer to the edge that I have to plant my hands to my side to stop me from falling off. He keeps me open for him, with his thumb drawing lazy circles on my ultrasensitive skin.

"You drive me crazy, woman," he growls before he dips his head once again, and I'm lost amidst a fog of licks, sucks, and nips.

The need for more friction has me gripping his head so I can gyrate against his tongue and the raspy stubble of his five o clock shadow. I'm so close, so damn close that when his fingers find my hardened nipples and tweaks them, I lose it.

"Magnus ... Magnus ... Magnus ...," I chant his name, losing it all over his expert mouth. I hear a low rumble emanating from deep within him, and it does things to me that I can't describe.

When I finally settle down, Magnus stands up, licking his mouth like a cat that just had its feed. He's so sexy like this. Smug and self-assured. So fucking sexy. My greedy eyes travel downwards from his glistening lips, to his defined pectorals, then his sculpted six-pack. It's a smorgasbord of lean muscles, and the sight makes my mouth water with a different kind of hunger. That's when I realize that right in front of me is the holy grail of body parts. It is glorious and equally as self-assured, and it's in full attention and is aimed towards me. I look up at the owner, and he knows I've been staring down at it. He must've seen the covetous look on my face, and I should feel embarrassed but I'm not, because he's looking at me the same way.

I don't have to ask. I wrap my hand around his magnificent manhood, gripping its long, thick length firmly, earning me a groan from its sexy-as-fuck owner.

"You have a beautiful cock," I say out aloud, gazing at it like it's a cold glass of water on a scorching summer day.

"Then wrap your beautiful mouth around it," he commands roughly. I open my mouth slowly and look up to him because I want to watch his reaction. My tongue comes out, and I ever so slowly lick the pearly bead from the tip of his cock, then my mouth closes in to suck out whatever's left.

"Yesssss!" Magnus hisses, slightly baring his teeth. His eyes are darkened and full of savage lust as he watches my every move, and I hope my lack of experience will make up for my enthusiasm. God, this man is doing me in, and I can't believe how turned on I am … again. I want him to fill me with himself, and my mouth is a good place to start. Magnus whispers my name as I take all of him in and pull out up to the head, sucking the tip and sliding down as far as I can take him. Even when I try to relax my throat, I still can't take his entire length. But he doesn't seem to mind, judging from the way he eases my hair away from my face and murmuring how beautiful I am. I feel a rush of confidence, finding a rhythm with the way I drag his cock in and out of my mouth. He begins to move with me in a slow grind. I cup his balls, feeling they go more rigid. I leave his cock for a moment and start licking each sac, mewing with satisfaction when I hear Magnus groaning with pleasure. I know he's close. I can feel it in my hands and in my mouth. Excitement bubbles inside of me, knowing what's coming next. I never thought I'd ever reach this point with another man, and yet here I am, about to make a sex god come in my mouth. I increase the tempo, sucking the head, licking the length underneath, fitting what I can in my mouth, until I feel his hands hold my head steady and his whole body goes rigid.

"I'm coming, baby. Are you ready?" Magnus asks with an unsteady voice, taking over by holding his cock firmly with his hand. I know he's doing his best to hold off, to make sure this is what I want. But I can see his self-control ebbing away.

I can't wait any longer myself. I show him how much I want him, how much I need *all* of him. I spread my hands all over his rock hard stomach, and looking up to him, I open my mouth right under his swollen tip.

"Don't look away, Isabelle. Holy … fuck!" And he comes in my mouth, his cock throbbing and his warm salty-sweetness coating my tongue and giving me an adrenaline rush unlike any other. When he's given me every last drop, I let it all slide down my throat.

Our eyes are locked the whole time, allowing me to see his vulnerability. It's empowering, and I feel my heart swell up with emotions unknown to me before Magnus.

I lick my lips, now holding his still-stiff cock. Magnus is breathing heavily, his hooded eyes still clouded with desire. Desire for me. Without a word, he bends down to lift me up, carrying me across the room with my legs around his waist. I hold onto his shoulders, our eyes never leaving each other and yet we're close enough that I feel his warm breath on my lips. I gasp when I feel the cool glass of the window against my back.

He bows down and oh so lightly traces my lips with the tip of his tongue, coaxing me to open them. As soon as I do, his tongue plunders my mouth. I let out a moan when he begins sucking my tongue as if mimicking my recent endeavor with his cock.

And speaking of the devil, and yes, it's very, very wicked indeed, his cock is still hard and poised so close to my opening. Like clockwork, my insides clench, and my hips begin to gyrate.

"I need you inside me, Magnus," I plead with him breathlessly, grazing his jaw with my teeth.

He groans audibly, moving his hips with me but not heeding my request. "You're sore, my little temptress. I can't risk hurting you further because I *will* fuck you hard."

I tangle my fingers through his hair, pulling at it to catch his attention. "Try me. I'm stronger than you think. Fuck me like you want to. I can take it." I lift myself up against the window, reaching between us, guiding his cock at my slick opening. Then I push my weight down and instantly get my fill. All. Of. Him. Magnus's eyes widen, and his mouth gapes open, mirroring my exact expression.

"Oh, sweet Jesus!" he roars out, but he isn't moving, looking to me as if asking if I'm okay.

I'm nodding like a crazy person. "Yes … yes … fuck … me!"

"Hold on, baby." I tighten my grip while he wraps his arm around my waist to hold me close. Then he places his other hand firmly against the glass and slams hard and fast inside of me. My breasts are squashed against his chest, my hard nipples rubbing against his skin.

"So good … so fucking good …," Magnus's guttural voice reverberates against my whole body as he licks and nips my neck and shoulders. I can't speak a word. All I can do is whimper, almost in tears because it feels too amazing … like it's a privilege given to a chosen few.

A sheen of sweat now cover our bodies, increasing with every exerted move. With the room all quiet, all I can hear are the slick sounds of our sweaty bodies, the sound of our crotches slapping with every thrust, mixed with our duet of moans and groans and murmurs of how ... fucking ... good ... this ... feels.

I know I won't last. He's so gloriously deep inside of me that he keeps hitting that spot, and I can't escape the way his pubic mound keeps rubbing against my engorged clit. I'm going ... going... "Aaaahhh!" Gone.

I latch on his shoulder with my mouth trying to muffle the sound of my screaming. A low rumble escapes from Magnus, but he doesn't stop thrusting, drawing out my climax until, with a growl and one last thrust, he's gone with me as well, filling me with his seed. He slows down eventually, as do our breathing. I don't even realize how far my back arched from the window. Then with him still inside of me, he carries me towards the bed. I lay my head on the crook of his neck and leave lazy kisses on his skin.

Magnus pulls out slowly and lays me on the bed. It makes me wince with pain a little, but I make sure not to show him. Then I watch as he walks to the bathroom, returning with a small wet towel. He eases my legs open gently.

"This might be a little cold, but it will help with the soreness." I squeak as soon as the cool towel touches my hot, but definitely sore opening. Magnus can't conceal the look of worry on his face so I have to put his worry to rest.

"That feels really good. Thank you." I rub his arm reassuringly and reach over to kiss his shoulder. He smiles back, and the tender moment makes my heart want to leap out. After a few moments, he does his sweet ritual of tidying me up.

"Thank you," I voice out softly, feeling weirdly shy all of a sudden. He gives me a lopsided smile, like *he's* feeling shy as well. Him ... shy? This guy is all kinds of amazing, and I have to pinch myself right now just to make sure he's not a figment of my imagination, or a book boyfriend from the novels I read. He tosses the small towel on his nightstand before lying in bed with me, pulling me towards him in a spooning position.

I can seriously live in these arms. I don't even care where, and as long as these arms are around me, nothing seems to matter.

"How are you feeling?" he whispers against my ear, nipping my lobe slightly.

I turn around to face him with a silly grin on my face. "Like I'm totally and utterly fucked." I raise my hand to smooth his hair back from his eyes.

"You'll still be sore when you wake up." He lifts my leg and sits it over his hips, caressing my thigh gently and leaving warm tingles in its wake.

"Hmmm, if you keep that up, I could personally guarantee that I won't be walking straight when I get up in the morning. Do you want that on your conscience, Mister?"

He chuckles, before planting a chaste but lingering kiss on my mouth.

"What am I going to do with you, beautiful temptress? Strike that … *my* beautiful temptress."

"Letting me rest in your arms would be great," I answer, unable to hide the slight awkwardness in my voice. It just occurs to me that he hasn't mentioned whether or not he wants me to sleep over.

"That was my plan all along … seducing you until you have no other choice but to want to *be* in my arms," he answers with that sexy smirk of his.

"Is it now?" I murmur with a smile.

"I had a few surprises on the way, yes. But it all worked out in the end." Magnus pulls me in a little tighter before kissing my forehead.

The smile I had on my face is gone and my heart drops. I brace myself up with one elbow and lay a hand on his chest. "Magnus, I'm sorry—"

"Shh. Hey …," he interrupts, placing his forefinger on my lips before using the same hand to cup my face. "I know where you're going with this, and there is nothing … *nothing* for you to be sorry about. What happened to you was a huge injustice, and I still think that fucker should pay for his crime. But you came out of it stronger and more resilient. If anything, I'm sorry that he's not in jail for it. And if you let me, I'll make sure he pays—"

Now it's my turn to interrupt him. His words are killing me in the most beautiful way, and I have to stop it. I turn to his hand and plant a kiss on his palm, closing my eyes, because the tears are beginning to well up. His breath hitches with my gesture. He slides his hand to the back of my head, and he pulls me down so my lips will kiss him instead.

This kiss is passionate, yes, but oh, so different from any other kiss we've shared before. My eyes are still closed, and I feel every flicker of our tongues, every tug on my lips, and every way Magnus expresses that he cares. I feel it *all* in this kiss. And I think I may have forgotten how to breathe.

"Open your eyes, Isabelle," he urges with an unsteady voice. I open my eyes, slowly, just as our foreheads touch.

"He will never harm you again. I'll make it my personal mission that you and Ethan will be kept safe. "

Oh. This man is too much … too good to be true. I simply can't allow him to take on this obligation. "Magnus, you're trying to take on a lot of my personal baggage. I can't allow you to do that. You don't have to take care of us, I can—"

"Okay, would you like me to bring out my shushing finger again, my stubborn temptress?" He raises his forefinger at me, simultaneous with his brow in a very authoritative way.

Shit. Why do I find it sexy when he's bossy like this?

Without thinking, I lightly nip the errant finger, holding his hand so he can't take it away. He makes an indignant sound which turns into a hiss as soon as my mouth closes, and I begin to suck my way down his finger. I finish by kissing the now moistened finger, which he then slowly drags down my lower lip, my chin, and in between my breasts, leaving a hot trail of my skin.

A rumbling escapes his throat as we stare at each other with heated intensity. I wait with bated breath for his next move, but he keeps still. Instead, he kisses me gently before positioning me back in the crook of his arm.

"You need your rest, naughty girl. Sweet dreams."

"You too," I murmur with disappointment. But as he presses his lips on my temple, and I hear his heartbeat slow down into a steadier pace, my eyelids become heavier. So I close my eyes and let myself drift off into a thankfully, dreamless sleep.

I open my eyes just as the sunlight begins streaming through the windows. I'm a little disoriented, squinting as I look around the light-soaked room. A smile rises from my lips when I realize I'm still in Magnus's room. God, it feels so good in his bed that getting up is almost painful. I grab the duvet and inhale deeply, loving how the sheets smell of laundry soap and Magnus. I just want to surround myself in all things Magnus.

It would've been better if he's in bed with me though, but he's not. I call out his name, but there's no answer so he must've left the bedroom. I check the time. *Shit*, it's almost seven. I should head back home in case Ethan wakes up looking for me. I jump out of bed and head to the bathroom. There's no time for a shower, so I wash my face instead. That's when I notice that Magnus left a new toothbrush, still in its packaging, next to his toothpaste. I can't help but smile. Yes, it's a tad on the presumptuous side, but it's a sweet act, nonetheless.

After pulling my hair up in a loose bun and dressing in last night's clothes, I'm good to go. I grab my purse and make my way downstairs, holding both my purse and shoes with one hand while sending a quick text to Michelle to let her know I'll be home soon. I scan Magnus's vast living space, but he's not around. Then I surmise he may be in his study. So I walk past the kitchen to the room behind it. The door is slightly closed, but as I'm about to knock, I hear his voice. He sounds pissed.

"No. I need you to confirm this for me. If my suspicions are true, then I need to fix it as soon as possible. (*pause*) I don't care how you do it, and how much it's going to cost. Get. It. Done. Good. Call me tomorrow." Then I hear what sounds like a hard object being tossed on the desk.

What was that about? Obviously something or someone's riled him up. I inwardly count to ten before knocking on the door and peeking in.

"Hey," I greet him with a fixed smile on my face.

He looks up and his frown disappears. "Hey yourself, beautiful. Good morning." He gives me a heart-stopping smile before waving for me to get inside. As soon as I do, he pushes his chair away from his desk and pats a spot on his desk that's right in front of him, which, I'm assuming he'd like me to sit. I humor him, leaving my shoes and purse on a chair by the door before parking my butt where he wants me. As soon as I'm seated, he closes our gap, opening my legs so he's in between, while his hands slide along the length of my jean clad thighs. Even with the thick denim material, I can still feel the warmth of his touch. It instantly puts me at ease.

"You weren't there when I woke up," I tell him with a small pout, brushing a few strays of his hair back.

"Sorry, baby. If I had a choice, I would've stayed in bed with you and your sexy-ass naked body. I just had some work calls to make. Speaking of naked, why are you so overdressed?" He looks at me with a playful scowl. My gaze moves downwards to his bare chest, staring a little too long than normal. I also notice he's only wearing boxers. And they leave nothing to the imagination. Dirty thoughts of Magnus instantly fill my head, and I'm sure he can see the redness of my cheeks. I can't believe that after what we've done last night, he still manages to make me blush.

I ignore his question, letting my curiosity win out. "Magnus, that call you just had. That wasn't about what I told you last night, is it?"

He just stares at me with contemplative eyes. Is he debating whether he'd tell me the truth, or whether he'd tell me at all?

"Were you listening in on my calls?" he asks softly. I can't tell if he's angry or curious.

"I'm sorry. I just overheard by mistake. I won't do it again if it upsets you," I answer defensively.

He chuckles. "It's okay, baby." Then in a more somber expression, he continues, "You've opened yourself up to me. I've no plans of hiding anything from you either."

Then his expression turns wicked. "But I won't tell you what it is about if you don't take off these damned jeans of yours."

"But I can't take them off. I only came over here to let you know that I'm going home."

"What? You're leaving just like that?" His scowl is back, and this time it's no longer playful.

"Baby, Ethan might freak out if I'm not there. We always have breakfast together. It's kind of an unwritten rule."

His eyes widen, and his wicked smirk makes an appearance. "Hmmm, you just called me baby. I like it. A lot." His hands travel from my thighs, sliding up to my waist. His thumbs are now caressing me just under my breasts. "Well, I'm taking you home. There's no way I'm letting your gorgeous ass go home alone. We can all have breakfast together. I'll help cook!"

I stare at him gobsmacked. "You *want* to have breakfast with me and Ethan? Michelle will be there too."

He stands up and leaves feathery kisses on my lips, my cheeks, and my jawline, sending wonderful tingles all over. "Why wouldn't I want to spend time with my girlfriend and her family?"

Girlfriend! "Um, sorry? I thought I heard you say I'm your girlfriend?"

"Well, aren't you all mine?" His light kisses transform into licks and nibbles.

"I am. In that case, that makes *you* my boyfriend," I answer, wrapping my arms around his neck.

"You bet your luscious ass I am," Magnus whispers roughly before he smashes his mouth against mine, squeezing my ass tightly with both of his hands. A moan comes out of me as I let his tongue in, letting it have its way. Hmmm, I'm kissing my boyfriend ... *my boyfriend, Magnus Grant!*

"You seem fixated with my ass," I whisper against his lips.

He pulls away and shows off his sexy smirk. "You are the sexiest, most drop-dead gorgeous woman I've ever seen. And right now, I'm this close to ripping your jeans off and taking you right here." He gives me one last panty-wetting kiss before pulling away with a growl.

"Give me ten minutes. Oh, and yes, I'm fixated on your sexy ass because it's mine!" And with an air kiss, he jogs out of his own study, leaving me turned on like the giant New Years Eve ball in Times Square.

And it's only after a few moments to myself do I realize that he hasn't told me what that phone call was about.

I'm admiring how Magnus looks effortlessly handsome in his gray T-shirt, slim, navy chinos, leather lace up boots, and pea coat. This man can carry whatever clothing he wears. But naked Magnus will always be my favorite. I giggle like an idiot on the inside.

We're holding hands on the way down to the underground parking where his cars are waiting. No Alex today, I assume. Magnus picks the Panamera this time.

I roll my eyes at him as soon as he disarms the car. "Seriously, Magnus, are all these cars yours?" I sweep my arm across the garage full of expensive-looking motor vehicles.

He shakes his head and chuckles while gallantly opening the car door for me. "No, I house my car collection upstate."

"Of course you do, silly of me to ask," I answer back sarcastically before sitting down. He laughs as he closes the door, and I roll my eyes once again.

"I thought high-end cars are supposed to impress women?" he asks with humor in his eyes.

"Is that right? Well, looks like I didn't get the memo," I say and Magnus lets out a hearty, infectious laugh, making me laugh with him as well.

It's funny how the little things Magnus does, always seem to overshadow his bigger gestures. While driving, Magnus reaches over and holds my hand or rests his hand on my thigh. It's almost like he can't go for too long without touching me, and it leaves me feeling cherished.

"I have to be out of town this week. I'm flying out on Wednesday, but I'll be back on Friday … earlier if it all goes well."

"Oh … okay," I answer softly, looking out the window to hide my disappointment.

"I just need to meet with my staff on our West Coast offices. There are some urgent matters that I personally need to deal with."

"Will you be going alone?" I ask, curiously.

"I'll be flying with Alex and Denise on my jet." He gives me a sidelong glance. "I'd love for you to come with me. How about it?"

"You know I can't. Of course, there's Ethan, then I'm starting my new job. I know it's your company, but it's not going to sit right with other people." I let out a big sigh. This is going to get so complicated, so fast. And it's going to get even more complicated after what I'm about to ask from him.

"Magnus, can I ask you a favor? Can we keep our relationship … quiet? At least until I've paid my dues and proven my worth to your company?"

The rays of the sun illuminate his eyes to an almost icy blue. He looks straight ahead, as if reflecting on what I just said. But the way his jaw is clenching confirms that he is definitely not happy with my request.

"Normally, I would say no because my ego is taking a hitting right now. But I completely respect your work ethics and your values. I also don't want to set a bad precedent within the company, so for now, we'll keep it between us. But my mother is hosting a fundraiser next Saturday for an arts charity she supports. It's going to be at The Lincoln Center. I'd like it, if we attend the event together."

I feel nervous when I realize what the fundraiser entails. "High profile fundraisers are usually covered by the press, aren't they? I want to be there with you, Magnus. I really do. But you also know I'm trying to remain hidden, right?"

He nods, stealing a glance at me. "I do. We'll skip the red carpet and go through the side entrance. Trust me, the last thing I want is to put you and Ethan in harm's way. If only you could tell me who this bastard is so I could stop him from making your life, hell."

I chew on my lip to stop myself from speaking out. Thankfully by now, we've reached my place. He puts the car on park, and with my resolve intact, I turn towards him, holding onto his hand firmly.

"You're very sweet, and I know you only mean well. But I want to protect you too, just as much as you want to protect me and Ethan."

Magnus raises our linked hands and plants a kiss on my palm. "You're driving me insane, Isabelle," he whispers against my skin.

I give him a lopsided smile. "That makes the two of us."

With a small chuckle, Magnus straightens up. "C'mon. Our breakfast won't cook by itself!"

Inside the apartment, it's surprisingly quiet even for a Sunday morning. I leave Magnus in the living room so he can deal with some work e-mails while I check on Ethan. He's still asleep on a spare mattress on the floor while Tasha is sleeping on Ethan's bed. I smile at their serene faces before quietly padding away to the kitchen where Magnus joins me.

"So ... what are we cooking this morning?" Magnus speaks softly so as not to wake anyone. He wraps his arms around my waist, bending down so he can leave a lingering kiss on the curve of my neck. It's a sensitive spot for me, and I can't help but bite my lip because I now feel hot all over.

"Hmmm," I look around the kitchen taking him by the hand. "I'm thinking stuffed French toast with crispy maple bacon on the side." I turn to face him, with my hands slipping inside his gray T-shirt and up his naked back.

"If you continue to do that, the only thing I'll be stuffing *won't* be French toast," he whispers low, the beginnings of a smirk on his face.

"Pervert!" I answer with a coy smile, half-wanting him to make true to his threat but knowing now is definitely not the right time. I remove my hands off his back, my face feeling flush.

"You'd have to help me prep and clean up, okay?" I tell him firmly while trying to keep a straight face.

"Yes, ma'am," he answers before giving me a soft kiss, a smile lighting up his handsome face.

We're in the middle of cooking breakfast when Michelle and Nathan greet us in the kitchen. Michelle is initially surprised to see Magnus, who's currently chopping some fruits. She's by my side in no time.

"Did he sleep over? I didn't hear you guys come in," my obviously intrigued friend asks.

"No, I slept over at his place. We just got home, and since everyone's still sleeping, I thought I'd surprise you guys with breakfast."

Michelle picks up a piece of chopped strawberries and pops it in her mouth. "I never say no to food." Then she walks over and whispers to me. "Dish ... later."

"Ditto ... later," I whisper back before we give each other a discreet high-five.

Magnus and Nathan are in the living room watching ESPN and getting to know each other. Michelle has earlier shooed Magnus away from the kitchen, and she and I are left to finish preparing breakfast and making coffees.

Not long after, we hear two pairs of footsteps running from the hallway towards the kitchen. Ethan and Tasha are both awake and excited. Ethan heads straight to me, giving me a big kiss and a hug.

"Good morning, honey! How was your little slumber party with Tasha?"

"It was good. Nathan read us both a story. I'm not used to having a daddy read me a bedtime story. It was cool!"

My heart tightens at Ethan's innocent observation. But I know in my heart that Ethan is a lot better off without his real father.

Just then, I see his face light up when he looks past me.

"Magnus!" Ethan yells.

Magnus is standing behind me, his right hand up and ready for Ethan's jumping high-five which my son eagerly gives. Ethan laughs when Magnus winces and shakes his hand in mock pain.

"Still as strong as last night. Well done, buddy!" Magnus winces.

Ethan responds by beaming at him.

"Alright," I interrupt their heartwarming exchange. "Breakfast is almost ready, so please set the tables, both of you."

"C'mon, buddy, you want to help me out?" Magnus happily asks my son.

"Ok." Ethan shrugs. Magnus looks back to me and gives me a wink and a big smile.

"Thanks, boys!" I yell back, and a picture flashes in my head of what it would be like, if Magnus, Ethan, and I were living in domestic bliss … like one big, happy family.

I shake my head. *Get a hold of yourself, Billie! Don't get any weird ideas.*

I arrange each plate with stuffed French toast, bacon, and some chopped berries before dusting the top with icing sugar. Michelle brings the finished plates to the dining room.

Everyone seems impressed with breakfast, as I hear them commenting appreciatively. We're all munching away when Magnus leans over to me.

"I think this would have to be my favorite breakfast. But I think it'd taste better if I'm eating it off your naked body."

I almost choke on a piece of bread. "Magnus! There are children at the table?" I reprimand him in the most inconspicuous way possible, looking around the table to make sure no one hears. Luckily they all seem pretty oblivious to our exchange.

His phone must have vibrated because he frowns and takes it out of his pocket. He excuses himself courteously before standing up and going to my room for privacy.

Michelle follows Magnus with her eyes then looks at me with raised eyebrows.

"So what are your plans today, Michelle?" I ask her pointedly, making it known that I caught her reaction.

"Well, Nathan will be taking Tasha to her mom's first, then he and I will be heading over to MoMA to check out that exhibition I told you about previously." She looks over at Nathan who gives her a wink. It makes me happy to see my good friend connect with someone like Nathan.

"What about you, Billie? You have a date with Ethan, right?" Michelle reminds me with raised brows.

"Of course! Where are we going again, Ethan?" I look over at my son who's busy eating his bacon.

He chews the food before answering, "Central Park Zoo, yeah!" My boy is so excited he pumps his fist in the air.

"Is Magnus going as well?" Michelle asks. *What are you doing Michelle?* I try to ask her with my eyes, shaking my head slightly, but she ignores me.

"Oh, well, Magnus is only staying for breakfast. I'm sure he'll have other things to do today."

Ethan walks around the table and tugs my sleeve.

"Mom, could Magnus come to the zoo with us? It'll be fun with him. Please?" Ethan asks with pleading eyes.

Please don't look at me like that, Ethan. My heart melts.

"Well, I can ask him, but I'm not sure he'll say yes. Magnus must have been to the zoo a lot of times, buddy," I explain as I playfully ruffle his hair.

"Could you ask him now? Please, Mom?" Gosh, I am a *sucker* for those big green eyes.

"Finish your breakfast first, then I'll ask him." And without uttering a word, Ethan sits back down and eats the rest of his breakfast, just in time as Magnus returns from his phone call.

He looks preoccupied, with small wrinkles occupying the space between his brows. It makes me wonder again, what the phone call was about. I lean towards him as soon as he sits back down.

"Everything okay?" I whisper, looking at him with concern.

"Yeah, that was one of my guys. Looks like we're visiting our West Coast office sooner than planned."

"When are you flying out?"

"Tomorrow." He looks at me and notices my now downcast expression.

"Don't worry, I'll be back Wednesday at the latest, okay?" he reassures me softly, brushing my hair back, and not realizing our intimate display is, well, on display.

I nod, forcing a small smile to appease him. Just knowing I'm on borrowed time before he flies out, makes my chest feel heavy.

After breakfast, Michelle and Nathan offer to wash up while Ethan and Tasha move on to the living room to play, leaving Magnus and me sitting on the couch, watching over the kids.

I glance over at Magnus and notice a tender smile etched on his face as he watches the kids play. He's been so nice and good with Ethan so far, and Ethan seems to be taken by him. It makes me wonder about his thoughts on fatherhood though. But I stop myself immediately. It's way, *way* too early to think about such things.

He must have felt my eyes on him. He turns to me and squeezes my thigh.

"Ethan likes you, you know. He wants you to come with us to the zoo today."

"He does?" He grins.

"I told him I'd ask you but you don't have to, there's no obligation for you to join us or anything."

"Isabelle, it's not an obligation if I want to go," he answers, squeezing my thigh again.

"Are you sure?" I ask again.

"Would *you* like me to go with you?" he asks curiously.

"Of course, I do. But are you sure you're ready to do the family thing? I don't want to rush you," I answer, looking uncertain.

Magnus looks at me intently, his blue eyes radiant and hypnotic. He checks to see if the kids are watching before he leans forward and gives me a chaste kiss. Then he stands up and walks over to where Ethan and Tasha are playing, sitting down next to my son before starting a conversation with him. I try to listen in, but the cartoons on the TV makes it impossible to hear what they're talking about.

After a short while, Magnus and Ethan give each other a fist bump before Ethan resumes playing with Tasha. Magnus stands up and walks back to sit next to me, a satisfied smile on his face.

"So what was that about?" I ask curiously.

"Oh, nothing really. I just asked Ethan if I can go with him and his mom to Central Park Zoo, and he said yes," he answers nonchalantly, shrugging his shoulders like its nothing.

Nathan and Michelle emerge from the kitchen, fetching Tasha before saying their good-byes.

"We have to stop by my apartment before we head to the zoo," Magnus wraps an arm around my waist, lightly tracing circles over my shirt and sending delicious tingles to every part of my body.

"Sure, no problem," I answer breathlessly. I excuse myself from Magnus so I can pick the clothes Ethan will be wearing today. I need the distance from Magnus while my son is around. After all, the last thing I want is for my son to witness me, making out with a man he just met.

"Ethan, sweetheart, I've laid out the clothes you'll be wearing, okay?" I call out to Ethan from his bedroom, trying to tidy up the clutter from last night's sleepover.

"Yes, Mom. I'm almost done packing up," Ethan yells out from the living room.

"You've raised a good kid there." Magnus has followed me and is now leaning by the doorframe.

"I hope so. It's not easy, but Ethan's worth it," I answer wistfully.

Magnus walks inside and picks up a framed picture of Ethan with me, which was taken from his first birthday. I'm about to tell him a funny story about the picture, but I stop when I notice the sadness in his eyes. It makes me want to hug him and make it all better.

I'm wondering what brought about that reaction.

But in an instant, he closes his eyes and lets out a deep exhale. And the look is gone as he puts the picture back on the table without saying a word.

"Are you okay?" I ask gently, placing my hand on his shoulder.

"Yeah, yeah, of course. Great photo," he answers distractedly.

So he's not going to tell me what that's all about. I feel a pang of hurt with Magnus holding back so much about him, when I pretty much opened the floodgate that is my life. Are his wounds too fresh that they still hurt too much to talk about? My heart feels heavy for him, and I know I care enough for this man to overlook his trust issues. But he needs to realize I'm here for him as much as he is for me. I turn him so he's facing me. Then I wrap my arms around his neck and pull him close, my mouth by his ear.

"When you're ready, please promise me you'll open up. You know pretty much everything about me. I hope you'll trust me enough to share yourself with me too."

He nods, brushing his knuckles against my cheek. "I know and I'm grateful for your trust. Sometimes I feel I don't deserve it. But just give me a little time, and I promise I'll tell you everything. "

I press a kiss on his cheek, smiling warmly at him and not letting go until he finally smiles back.

"See, now *that* is a gorgeous smile," I tell him softly.

His smile widens. "Thank you. Have I mentioned recently how amazing you are?" he whispers as he stares deeply into my eyes. His eyes seem to convey gratitude he can't express with words, and the way my body warms with them, leaves me breathless.

"No, but just tell me anyway if you're not sure." That makes him laugh out aloud. It's a beautiful sound, so I join in as well.

I press both of my hands against his chest, patting its hardness and pretending it's not turning me on. "Good, so are you okay to wait for us while we get ready? I need a good shower. I smell like fried batter and bacon grease." I pull away, but when I start walking off, he grabs me by the arm and pulls me back against his hard torso, holding me by my waist.

"Hmmm, can I join you?" he asks, wickedly grinding his crotch against my belly. "I just pictured you naked right then, and look what happened."

Oh, hot damn, he's hard already. Sweet Jesus, give me strength!

I playfully slap him on the chest before pushing myself off his clutches.

"Magnus! This is my son's room, and I can hear him coming back!" I whisper with gritted teeth, trying to sound defiant but failing miserably.

He raises his hand in fake surrender. "Okay, okay. I'll watch CNBC while I wait. Hearing how the world market's going is like having a cold shower, anyway."

Just in time, Ethan is back in his room, with Magnus giving him a fist bump as he walks out.

"Have fun with your news," I call out to him laughingly before helping Ethan with his clothes so I can have that shower.

Once he's done and ready, Ethan marches back out to join Magnus. I head straight to my bedroom, when I hear my phone beep from my jeans pocket.

'Need help out of those clothes?-M' Magnus! I roll my eyes out before replying. *'Thanks, but somehow I don't think you'll be any help at all. Nice try though.'* I hit *Send* before getting ready for a shower. But then an idea hits me as I pass by my full-length mirror.

Feeling brave and a little giddy, I pose in front of it, placing my auburn hair over one shoulder, covering my face with the phone, positioning my arm so it's just covering my nipples, and angling my thigh so it crosses over my crotch. Once I'm satisfied, I hit the camera button. Inspecting the photo, it makes me look like a sexy '50s pinup girl … I like it!

I attach it on a new message for Magnus (double-checking to make sure I'm only sending the message to him), then I leave a caption: *'While you're waiting …'* and hit *Send*, giggling before I delete the photographic evidence off my phone. Oh well, screw the consequences. If this thing goes viral, at least my face is covered.

And as soon as I hear a loud groan from outside, I laugh out aloud. I laugh even louder when I hear Ethan asking him to see what's in his phone.

Grinning alone like an idiot, I finally hit the showers.

Once done, I decide on my printed skinny pants, black, loose, off-the-shoulder sweater, and a stretchy camisole underneath. I pull my hair back into a ponytail and forego my usual makeup, only opting on some lip gloss. After putting my comfortable boots on, I grab my purse and head out.

I stop short before calling out the boys. In the living room, Ethan and Magnus are on the floor, playing with Ethan's action figures together. They don't hear me walking in, giving me a chance to stand by the wall, and discreetly watch them play. I can't wipe the smile off my face, seeing how comfortable they are in each other's company.

I try my best to be both mom and dad for my son. But I notice how he looks longingly at Nathan and the other daddies from his school. And now I see that same look directed at Magnus.

And I know right there and then, that if things don't work between Magnus and me, it will hurt him as much as it will hurt me.

I blink back the tears furiously and hastily compose myself.

"Okay, boys, ready to go?"

"Whoa, this is like Batman's car!" Buckled up and on the way to our pit stop at Magnus's, Ethan looks in awe of the Panamera, which worries me, since he keeps touching and pushing on things.

"Honey, please keep your hands on your lap, okay?" I instruct Ethan, which he thankfully obeys. I glance embarrassingly at Magnus, who has the same preoccupied look on his face that he had in Ethan's room. I resist the urge to ask him again. Instead, I reach out and hold his hand that's resting on the gears. It was enough to come back from his state, and he turns his head briefly to give me a warm smile.

"Are we going to the zoo now, Magnus?" Ethan asks while looking out the window.

"Not yet, buddy. I just need to stop over at my place, okay?" he answers, looking at his rear view mirror before turning to me.

"I have a couple of things to sort out, so I'll be in my office for about half an hour or so. Then we're switching cars. Alex will be driving then."

I turn to Magnus with concern. "Magnus, seriously, I don't want to take up your time. If you have work to do ..."

"I want to spend this time with you and Ethan. Like I said, I'll only be about half an hour." He turns to the corner, and we're at his building, waiting for the underground garage door to open. We make our way up his penthouse, and as the elevator doors open, Alex is already waiting for us at the foyer.

"Good morning, Mr. Grant, Ms. Morrison," nodding to both of us, and bending down in front of Ethan.

"And you must be Ethan. How are you?" he asks Ethan in a kind voice.

"I'm okay," Ethan answers while shuffling his feet.

Magnus speaks with Alex before he starts walking again, and we follow after him. "Okay, so I'll just be in my office, make yourselves at home ... by all means, of course. If you want anything to eat or drink, Rosa is here to help out, okay?" He gives me a quick kiss on the lips, only lingering slightly, before leaving us with Alex.

"I'll just take Ethan to the balcony. I'm sure he'll enjoy seeing the views. Will that be okay?" I ask Alex, breaking the awkward silence.

"Oh, of course, ma'am. Like what Mr. Grant said, make yourselves at home," he answers kindly.

I hold Ethan's hand, and I take him down the hallway, past the dining room, the various living spaces, before opening the balcony doors and walking outside.

"Wow! Mom, we are so high up, I can see the tops of buildings everywhere!" Ethan exclaims in awe. I can't really blame him. This *is* an impressive penthouse.

I suddenly blush when I recall what Magnus and I have gotten up to in here last night. I turn away from Ethan, hoping he won't notice my crimson cheeks.

Then Ethan starts walking around the whole stretch of the balcony, which almost wraps around the whole apartment. Then he starts to run while I follow, only to stop next to the swimming pool and hot tub. He jumps on the daybed, and I try not to react as it's the same one Magnus and I were making out in, just a number of hours ago. Then Ethan lies down with his arms at the back of his head like he owns the place.

And maybe if the circumstances were different, he'd be enjoying a life like this back home. Home ... who am I kidding? New York *is* my home.

"I wish we lived here, Mom," he contemplates.

My stomach dips. "Honey, we have a nice home, and what about Michelle? We can't leave her in Brooklyn," I explain.

"But she can stay with Nathan and Tasha and we can live here. Or she can stay with us too. We can just ask Magnus, right?" Ethan insists. It's funny how a child can look at things so simply, not knowing how nothing is as straightforward as we want them to be.

"Maybe if we save our money, we can afford to live in something like this," I explain, wanting to end the conversation.

"Yeah, okay," he concedes, satisfied with my compromise.

In my peripheral vision, I notice a figure walking towards us. It's Rosa wearing her big, warm smile, holding a tray with milk and cookies, and a small pot of tea.

"Good morning, Isabelle." She nods at me with her smile, thankfully no hint of awareness of the events from last night.

"Hello, Rosa," I answer, delighted to see her welcoming face. "This is my son, Ethan." Rosa smiles and extends her hand to Ethan.

"Thanks again for helping Magnus out last night," I continue, still blushing.

"Think nothing of it. Magnus wanted to impress *you*, and I just helped a little," she answers. "Between you and me, it's been quite a while since Magnus brought someone to his home for dinner. And he doesn't cook for just anyone," she adds with a wink and a grin.

Oh. I remember Magnus mentioning this last night but with Rosa confirming, I'm now rendered speechless.

"Wow, choc chip cookies!" Ethan exclaims excitedly while clapping his hands. I inwardly thank my son for the interruption.

Ethan looks up at Rosa. "Thank you, lady," he says shyly.

She bends her knees so she is almost the same level as Ethan. "I hope you enjoy the milk and cookies, Ethan. And if you want some more, just ask, okay?" she informs him sweetly.

"You're very kind to do this, Rosa. We really appreciate it," I tell her honestly.

"It's no trouble, Isabelle. Your son is adorable." She gives Ethan a small wave and with a kind nod to me, she returns back inside.

I pour myself a cup of tea, the fragrance of jasmine and green tea soothing my senses. The chocolate chips cookies are still warm, with the chocolate chips melting in my mouth.

Ethan is chewing his cookie with a contented look on his face. I take this opportunity to sit next to him, wrap my arm around his shoulder, and have a little chat with him.

"I'm happy that you and Magnus are getting along well."

"He's funny, Mommy. Are you going to see him all the time?" He looks at me with his big green eyes.

"I sure hope so. Would it be okay if I do?"

Ethan nods. "Yup ... and is he going to be my daddy?" he asks eagerly yet innocently.

His question leaves me dumbfounded and speechless. I never even entertain the idea of Ethan looking to Magnus as father material. I carefully think about the next words I'll say.

"Honey, right now, Magnus is Mommy's special friend, okay?" I answer firmly, giving him a squeeze.

"Oh, okay." My heart breaks at the look of disappointment in his face. "But I think he'd be a cool dad," he adds.

Before I get a chance to answer, Magnus is already walking towards us.

"There you are. So, are we ready for the zoo?" he asks, looking straight at Ethan, who jumps out of my arms and off the daybed.

He pats Ethan on the shoulder to get his attention. "Ethan, why don't you go and see Rosa. I think she packed you more cookies."

"Yay!" And off goes my little cookie monster of a son.

Magnus offers his hand to help me off the daybed. The warmth of his hand with mine never fails to make me go all tingly.

"Thank you. Did you fix whatever needs fixing?" I ask, leaning against his body as his hand drops to my waist.

"I did. And I didn't want to let my girlfriend wait for too long," he murmurs against my ear. Good thing I have him to lean on since my legs have turned to jelly.

"Ah, I'm sure your girlfriend appreciates it and will show her boyfriend just how much, tonight," I answer back with a coy smile.

I hear him growl under his breath, making my insides tighten. "Does it involve more pictures?"

I turn to face him, my breasts pressed against his chest. With my fingers, I start drawing lazy circles on his hard pectorals. "I don't know. I'm thinking, nothing says 'thank you' than a live show."

And that's when I look up and see his eyes turn from wicked to hungry in one second. He's so hungry for me. And God, I'm so hungry for him! But before he can reply, he looks up and his expression switches back to wholesome.

"Yay, I got cookies!" Ethan shouts out.

"Awesome," Magnus replies half-heartedly, making me giggle.

Magnus pulls away and discreetly adjusts his crotch. Oh dear, I got him hard!

He glances over to me wearily. All I can do is bite my lip to stop myself from laughing. Luckily, he finds humor in it and chuckles softly.

"Okay, time to go to the zoo," Ethan yells out, thankfully oblivious to what just transpired between Magnus and me.

I hold Ethan's hand with mine, and we follow Magnus out. Alex is waiting for us by the Cayenne. He opens the door for us, letting Ethan in first, then myself. Magnus goes around the SUV and sits at the other end, so Ethan is between us. After I buckle Ethan's seat belt, Magnus gives my son's hair a little ruffle, which makes him giggle. I take in their little exchange, my heart fluttering with immeasurable happiness.

CHAPTER 11

Alex drops us off near the arched entrance of the zoo. I'm just about to line up to pay for the entrance fees, when a lady wearing the park employees' uniform approaches us.

"Hello, Mr. Grant. I'm Cynthia, and I will be your zoo guide today." She is bubbly and flirty with Magnus which makes me a little uncomfortable. But trust Magnus to make me feel better by reaching out to hold my hand.

"Hello, Cynthia. Thank you for the welcome. This lovely lady standing next to me is my girlfriend, Isabelle, and the little man next to her is Ethan."

Girlfriend. I don't think I can ever get sick of that word.

Cynthia's flirty smile falters, and she replaces it with an even bigger smile. It's fake, but at least she's trying.

"Hello, Ms. Morrison, and hello there, Ethan!" She bends down in front of my son and produces a baseball cap with a Central Park Zoo logo on it.

"Here you go, now you have to wear this while you're here. Then later on, you will get to feed some of the animals. How does that sound?"

"Cool!" Ethan remarks, thanks Cynthia, and wears the cap. He's excited but a little overwhelmed by the attention, and I can totally relate with him.

"What's going on, Magnus?" I whisper discreetly.

"I give a substantial donation to the zoo every year, and with that comes a few perks, including VIP privileges," he whispers back with a smug look on his face.

"Oh, I see," I reply with my brows raised. "Well, I hope you continue to do so because children love this zoo." I lean towards Magnus, and I give him a little nudge on the shoulder. "Oh, and thanks for the free pass, boss," I add with a flutter of my eyelashes.

He squeezes my hand as our eyes hold each other steady, and for a moment, we get lost in each other's gaze.

"So if everyone's ready, we should head in," Cynthia interrupts with a slight disapproval on her face—mostly directed at me.

I respond with a sweet smile. "Thank you, Cynthia, after you."

Our day at the zoo turns out so wonderfully. Cynthia regains her professionalism and gives us a very informative tour. Ethan is able to feed some of the animals, an opportunity only reserved to a chosen few.

Although Magnus is on the phone on a few occasions, which I understand since he's very hands-on with his company, he still manages to find my hand … or my waist to hold on to.

We're at the gift shop on our way out, but before we can leave, Ethan insists on a monkey mask, which I get for him after waving off Magnus's insistence at paying for it.

Ethan is walking ahead, wearing his new acquisition, while an unusually quiet Magnus and I are walking together hand-in-hand.

Finally finding his voice, he speaks to me in a low tone. "Isabelle, you're my girlfriend, so you don't need to spend your own money. It won't sit right with me if I can't take care of you," Magnus insists, not used to getting no for an answer.

"And it wouldn't sit right with *me* if you pay for everything." From the scowl on his face, he still isn't convinced.

I move his arm so it's now wrapped around my shoulder, and he instantly pulls me close. "Look, how about if I put it this way—I work for Grant Corp so, technically, the money I earn still comes from you."

"That's different."

I sigh. I can't believe he's blowing this out of proportion. I've been taking care of both myself and Ethan so this shouldn't be a big deal.

"Well, Mr. Grant, you just have to suck it up. Stop acting like a brat and accept that I'm not the dependent type."

He looks stunned and turns to face me, making me fully aware of our height difference which is over a foot to be exact.

"No woman has *ever* spoken to me like that. Ever."

My heartbeat quickens, and I'm lost for words. Did I just offend him? I think I did.

He leans down, so his mouth is close to my ear. "And no woman has ever gotten me so turned on after speaking to me like that. Ever. Just be glad we're in a public place and Ethan's with us. Otherwise, I would've fucked that sassy little mouth of yours."

Oh … oh my!

He grazes my cheek with his lips as he pulls away, before taking a firm hold of my hand so we can catch up to Ethan.

Still too flustered to speak, we leave the zoo in silence. Until Ethan, still wearing his monkey mask, tells us that he's hungry and wants lunch.

Magnus chuckles. "C'mon then, lets go get something to eat. How do you feel about a cheeseburger and a chocolate ice cream shake?"

"Ahem, excuse me, I'm his mother? Don't I get a say on this?" I speak up, finally gaining some composure.

"Mom, I want a cheeseburger and a chocolate shake! Please, please, please?"

"Okay, if that's what you want," I reply, looking up at Magnus and shaking my head.

We walk out of the park and cross the road towards Magnus's ride.

"So, Shake Shack for lunch? My treat." Magnus looks at me pointedly before instructing Alex where to go.

I know I have to come to terms with the reality that being with Magnus would mean letting go of some of the independence I've been accustomed to. I must admit though, as much as I want to fight it, it feels nice to be with someone who seems to genuinely want to care for us.

"Of course, your treat," I answer softly.

Shake Shack at Madison Square Park is packed as usual. I line up right at the end, ready to tell Magnus and Ethan to grab a seat, when Magnus tells us to go with him instead. We walk past the long line of customers and straight to the back of the shop. He speaks to the manager, who appears to be someone he knows. Then Magnus asks us what we'd like, which he relays to the store manager. After a good-natured handshake between them, Magnus, Ethan, and my confused self, are ushered to our seats.

"Okay, what just happened? We just skipped the line. You know the manager?"

"I know Danny, the guy who owns this establishment. I'm just calling in one of the many favors he owes me."

I just stare at him, still confused, with Ethan completely oblivious to what's going on.

Magnus leans over and whispers in my ear, "And you'll be pleased to know, I didn't have to pay a single cent. So you get to keep your independence, and I get to not act like a brat."

Oh, he's teasing me now? Well two can play that game.

"Good boy, maybe if you keep this up, you get to collect your prize later."

He lets out a deep growl against my ear. Magnus is a growler, I've come to realize, and I like it. I like it a lot. He's so primal behind those power suits and public persona that I love to explore that other side of him further.

After our late lunch, we all move on to the nearby playground so Ethan can burn off some of his excess energy. Magnus and I find an empty bench by the swings so we can watch Ethan play. Magnus has bought us coffees, and we sit together in comfortable silence, his arm around my shoulder. Once in a while, I notice women pass by trying to capture his attention, by walking sexily in front of us, smiling, giggling ... even blatantly staring. And they don't seem to care that I'm sitting right next to him. But Magnus seems unaware of it all; even boosting my self-confidence by nuzzling my neck or giving me light kisses on the lips. The simple intimacy of his gestures makes me feel cherished and wanted ... something I never thought I'd ever feel again. Come to think of it, it's something I have never actually felt before. I wrap my arms around his waist, and I smile as he tightens his hold on me, as well.

"Thank you for today. Ethan is having the most wonderful time," I look up to him with a grateful smile on my face.

"And are you having a wonderful time, as well?" he asks, looking down at me, studying my face. The intensity of his blue eyes is sending warm tingles all over my body.

"You took time from your day to spend it with us. Baby, you are so getting lucky tonight," I whisper back. I lift my head to kiss him on the cheek, but he holds my chin with his forefinger and thumb, his striking blue eyes locked on to mine.

I close my eyes, waiting for his lips to touch mine. The anticipation is making my heartbeat even faster.

"Ewww!"

My eyes burst open and right in front of us is Ethan with a disgusted look on his face. He's even fake gagging.

Magnus closes his eyes in frustration, still holding on to my chin. But he suddenly chuckles, and I can't help but join in.

"Were you just about to kiss my mom, Magnus?" Ethan isn't in a laughing mood as he focuses on Magnus.

Magnus tries to keep a straight face. "Um, yes. I was just about to give your mom a kiss. I hope that's okay with you?"

Ethan looks at me seriously. "Did Magnus ask permission, Mom?"

"Ethan, it's okay. Magnus has my permission." Why is Ethan so overprotective all of a sudden?

Ethan looks at both of us, and then shrugs his shoulders. "Okay, I just don't want Mommy to cry, that's all."

What? My face drops, and I reach out for Ethan's hand. "Honey, what do you mean? Of course, I won't cry."

Ethan fixes his eyes on the ground. "'Cos sometimes I hear you cry in your room, and I keep asking Michelle why. But all she says is it's 'cos a boy kissed you, and you didn't give him permission."

I gasp, my heart breaking for my son as I pull him in my arms. All this time, I never realized Ethan could hear me from my bedroom. God, how could I have been so oblivious?

"Baby, I'm so sorry you had to hear Mommy cry. I was just having bad dreams, that's all."

"But is it true, Mommy? Did another boy make you cry?"

I'm not sure if I want to strangle Michelle or hug her at how she's explained my awful dreams to Ethan. But he needs answers straight from me.

"Ethan, it's true. But that was a long, long time ago and ... well ..." I glance over at Magnus, whose stunned expression has now hardened, his jaw clenching tightly. He catches my eye, and his face is impassive, even when I produce a smile. "Mommy's very happy now. And I'm going to make sure my bad dreams will go away for good, okay?"

"Okay. But don't worry, Mommy. I'll protect you from your bad dreams." His voice is muffled because he's hugging me just as tightly as I do him, which is just as well, so he won't see the tears in my eyes.

Ethan doesn't need to feel like he has to be responsible for me. *I'm* the one who needs to protect *him*. I resolve to book an appointment with Dr. Mitchell first thing tomorrow. I need to continue going to therapy. I need to be better for both of us.

Magnus doesn't utter a word. But the way he's moving his hand up and down my back is comforting and speaks volumes.

" I think it's time we head home," I suggest.

"Come on, I know where Alex is parked." Magnus presses his hand on my back towards the car.

"Okay."

When we approach the SUV, Magnus speaks with Alex before taking his seat next to us.

"Alex will drop you off first. I have to get back home after so I can pack for the trip."

"Oh, okay. So are you staying over?" I ask, getting excited at the possibility that he's staying for the night.

He smiles down at me before whispering, "If that's what you want, then you bet your sexy ass, I will."

"It's what I want, thank you." I try to sound nonchalant, trying not to show how happy his answer made me.

In the car, I send Michelle a text message that we're on our way. However, she's left me a message first, from about a couple of hours ago, saying that she's having dinner at Nathan's and will be home late. I guess our talk can wait until tomorrow. I'm still pissed that she took it upon herself to explain something like this to Ethan, when it should have come from me, his own mother. Good intentions notwithstanding.

Ethan has fallen asleep beside me en route to our place. I sneak a look at Magnus, and he's text messaging someone with a small frown on his face. He must have felt my eyes on him, and he looks up to me, his frown leaving his face.

"Hey," he says softly, giving me a smile that doesn't quite reach his eyes.

"Everything okay?" I ask gently, reaching out from behind and laying a hand on his shoulder.

"Yeah. Issues … you know how it is," he answers, looking a little distracted. "But it's okay, it's not that big a deal." He holds my hand in his, massaging my knuckles with his thumb. I try to gain comfort from his touch, but it's proving difficult when he's withdrawn like this.

Is he beginning to realize that I'm more troubled than he thought I was? The idea worries me as we head home in silence.

After Magnus drops us off at the apartment, a still sleepy Ethan heads straight to his bedroom to get more sleep. I decide, based on what's in the fridge and pantry, that beef stroganoff with pasta is what I'm cooking for dinner.

After over a couple of hours, Magnus still hasn't shown up. I have already finished cooking and cleaning up the pots and pans, just to give him a chance to get here. I try calling him twice, but my calls just go to the voicemail. On a last ditch effort, I send him a text message asking if he's still coming over ... and if he cannot, to at least let me know.

No response back.

"Mom, I'm hungry." Ethan, who has been awake in the last hour or so, comes walking purposefully from watching TV in the living room.

"Dinner should be ready soon. Have you finished your homework?"

"All done," he quickly answers. "Is Magnus coming over for dinner?" Ethan asks looking at me expectantly.

"I'm not sure, honey," I shrug, hoping he won't notice my disappointment.

We're set up at the breakfast table, a normal occurrence when it's just the two of us eating. Ethan decides to break the silence. Looking at me worriedly, he asks, "Mom, is Magnus angry at me because he didn't get to kiss you earlier? I'm sorry, Mommy."

I literally feel my chest tighten. How Ethan stayed so strong even after hearing me go through the aftermath of my hellish past is beyond me. But he's been hurting, and I didn't even know it. I should've seen it coming, but I've been so caught up with trying to fix myself that I failed to see that my son is breaking as well.

"You know what, Ethan, it's not your fault, and never ever think that it is, okay?" I reach out to hold him close. "But honey, next time, if something's troubling you, no matter what it is and no matter who it's about, I want you to know that you can always come to me, and I will listen and I will understand, okay? Mommy loves you very much, and I will always, *always* be here for you. We're a team, remember?"

I give him a smile, hoping my glistening eyes don't give myself away. He nods and gives me a lopsided smile back, lighting up his face entirely.

"Okay, now who's ready for some pasta?"

After dinner, I help Ethan have a quick shower, brush his teeth, and put his pajamas on so he can go to bed. After one story and a warm cuddle later, Ethan is fast asleep.

In between sips of wine and soaping the dishes, my phone rings. It's Magnus … probably cancelling tonight. My mouth forms a thin line as I press the *Accept* button.

"Yes?" I snap.

"Steady there, gorgeous. I'm outside. Please buzz me in."

"No, don't bother coming up. It's late and Ethan's asleep and I'm tired, so …"

"Look, I know I'm late, and I'm sorry. Please just let me in."

How dare he sound annoyed! I grit my teeth, lowering my voice so Ethan won't wake up. "Listen here, Mister! I had to convince my son that it wasn't his fault you didn't show up."

"What? Why would he think that?" He sighs audibly. "Isabelle, could we at least talk face-to-face so I can explain? I'm not going back home so you might as well open the damn door."

The sudden change in his tone pushes me to rethink my stance.

"Fine. Come in," I quip.

"Thank you," he answers, sounding relieved.

Once Magnus is in the apartment, I turn to lock our apartment door again, not realizing he's standing so close. My breath hitches when I turn around, and he's inches away.

"Look, Ethan's already in bed. He thought you didn't show up because he was protecting me." I try to move past him, but he walks even closer, forcing me back until I'm against the door.

Our bodies are now touching. He tips my chin up so I can look at him face-to-face. And I melt. I melt under his blue-eyed gaze and the want that's written all over it.

"I didn't realize I hurt his feelings. I'm truly sorry about that," Magnus whispers.

"Don't sweat it. Not your fault," I answer, cursing myself for my shaky tone.

"So do I have permission to kiss you, Miss Isabelle Morrison?" he asks, staring intently at my parted lips.

My eyes are set on his lips as well when I answer, "You've had my permission since the first time I saw you."

"Baby," he murmurs as he dips his head to meet my mouth.

But he still has some explaining to do. He can't distract me like this. I loosen my grip on his hair and quickly push away from him before our lips even touch. He exhales deeply and rakes back his hair in frustration.

"Why didn't you bother texting me at least?" I ask, planting myself on the couch.

"I received a text message from an ex, and she said she needed to talk. I didn't think much of it, I even deleted her text." Magnus sits beside me. "When I got to my building, she was at the lobby waiting for me to show up."

I stare at him, wide-eyed and dumbfounded. Seriously, is he telling me that he prioritized his ex over me? I purse my lips and slowly move further from him and closer to the other end of the couch. I might just slap him in the face if I didn't put that distance between us.

"Isabelle. It wasn't like that. She's an ex, but she's a family friend as well, and we've kept in touch."

I'm horrified now, and it must be written all over my face. "I don't think I want to hear anymore. I think I know where this is leading so …"

"No. You don't know the whole story, Isabelle, so please … just hear me out." The desperate look on his face tugs at my heart, and as angry as I am, I know I should pay heed to what he has to say. Then I'll decide if I should kick his ass to the curb or not.

"Fine. Talk," I demand.

"Thank you," he responds, raking his hair haphazardly. "Five years ago, I thought I married the love of my life." He tries to read my reaction, but I'm too shocked that all I can manage is blink. Fucking married? That wasn't what I was expecting at all!

"Tell me about her," I reply, my voice sounding surprisingly calm.

"Her name is Martine Harper. Our story started out pretty much like yours. We were family friends who became high school sweethearts. We were in love. At least I thought we were. It was just inevitable that we became involved, you know? After high school we decided to go to Cambridge together so we could get away from our families. We made the most of our independence as well as the hefty allowances our parents gave us. We drank and experimented with drugs. Whatever we assumed was cool and excessive, we tried them. How we managed to stay afloat during our college days is beyond me. When we were in our final year, I thought she was it for me. I proposed marriage, and she accepted. She found a ring she really wanted, and just like that, we're engaged. But I've convinced her to wait until after we graduated to tell our parents."

Okay, so he had a wild childhood just like any entitled rich kid. I was in the same boat, so I can totally relate. What's weird though, is the jealousy I'm feeling towards this Martine Harper. Magnus wanted to live the rest of his life with her, and the thought of it is eating me alive. But I say nothing, somehow needing to hear the rest of his story out.

"We got married after a year. It was all over the society pages. Just like how Martine wanted." He sneers at the end, and a little spark of hope lights up within me.

"By then, I've started my own business and putting in a lot of hours into it. Martine didn't seem to mind since she was also busy with her career in her father's company. This means that although we were still intimate, they were becoming few and far between."

Magnus must have noticed me cringe. It's way too much information for me to handle. He utters an apology before reaching for my hand and kissing it. But I pull my hand away, ignoring his apologetic expression. I may have asked for his honesty, but imagining Magnus in the arms of another woman, let alone a childhood sweetheart, is not good for my insecurities at all.

He sighs aloud, "Then Martine fell pregnant on our third year of marriage."

I think I'm going to faint. "You … you have a child?"

He stares at me, unblinking. "Please … just let me finish the story. She knew, but she never told me. Apparently, she was going to get it aborted, anyway, because she thought it … inconvenient. She never liked children, and I hoped she would change her mind once we're married." I note the bitterness in his voice as he continues. "I found out about the baby too late. One night we were having our usual dinner and drinks with friends. Before we left, we had a fight about … God, I don't even remember what it was about. Then she started flirting with the bartender to piss me off. The fight continued in the car on the way home. We were both drunk by then but I thought I could handle it. She tried to grab the wheel, saying I drove like her grandma. We swerved and hit a light post."

His voice gets shaky, as he looks on the ground, not wanting for me to see his face.

"I got out of it with only minor cuts and bruises. Martine broke some ribs and had a concussion, but she was given the all clear. Only that was when the doctor told me that Martine was pregnant."

I reach over instinctively to hold his hands which are both clenched into fists. He softens them and tangles my hand into one of his. We're both staring at our linked hands when he continues.

"Unfortunately, the baby ... my baby ... didn't make it. When I confronted Martine and asked why she never told me, she started crying her eyes out, apologizing and begging for forgiveness. She said she wasn't sure if she wanted to keep the baby or not. That's why she couldn't tell me. Like I didn't even have a fucking say on the whole thing. If she was selfish enough to hide her pregnancy from me, what else could she be hiding? And the way she drank alcohol, like she didn't have a care in the world ..." He sighs, tightening his grip on my hand, "Losing the baby shattered me. I couldn't be with her after that," his voice cracks at the end. Five years on and he's still broken up about it.

And I know how hard it is to pick up the pieces.

I slide closer to him and wrap my arms around his waist. But he lifts me up and holds me on his lap. I let his head press against my chest, and he closes his eyes, inhaling deeply, his hold tightening on me when he exhales.

I press my lips on his temple, closing my eyes to stop my tears from falling. "I'm so sorry this happened to you, Magnus. I can't even imagine how that must have felt. And you ... I don't know what to say." I feel so much anger towards the woman who did this to Magnus. How can someone be that irresponsible and so selfish? How could she do that to the person she promised to love forever?

"I filed for divorce straight after. It was a quick settlement and thankfully, she didn't put up a fight. We had a prenup after all. When it was all finalized, I regrouped and realized I needed to do something more fulfilling to fill the void. I thought throwing myself into my work would be enough to distract me from the sense of loss, but it didn't. I have friends involved in building schools in underprivileged countries. So with their help and my own money, I set up a foundation, flew to Tanzania and helped build a small primary school for disadvantaged children. Helping those kids felt like more of a blessing to me, I think. They kept me grounded. I'm hoping to build another school soon."

Of course ... I remember the photograph I saw hanging near his office. It's the one where he's laughing and surrounded by equally happy kids. The building behind it must be the school he's talking about.

He's incredible. I think I've just fallen for him even more.

"Magnus, what you did made so many children happy. You could've gone the other way, but you used your bad experience and did something positive. I'm proud of you."

"And now you know why I called you phenomenal. You love your son unconditionally, regardless of the circumstances. I'm the one who is proud of you." Magnus brushes his fingers tenderly on cheek. I feel so overcome by my feelings for him, that I throw my arms around his neck and pull him towards me so I can give him a deep, slow kiss. He spreads his hands on my back and moans softly against my mouth. I want to tell him with my kiss how much I want to take his pain away ... how much I care for him.

I open my eyes to meet his, and my heart tugs at how they still look a little lost. "You're an amazing human being, Magnus Grant. You just impress me every single day."

He cups my face with his hands, then he shakes his head, his eyes looking away. "No, I'm not, Isabelle. I wish I were."

"Let's just agree to disagree, okay?" I offer him a smile. He nods, but his eyes still seem troubled.

"So Martine was waiting for you at your place. She's obviously been there before. What did she want?" I ask, trying hard not to sound jealous even though the vile thoughts of them together are still in my head.

"Since the divorce, she moved back to the UK to set up a branch of their family's finance company. But this afternoon while we were both in the car from the zoo, she sent me a text message to let me know that she's coming back to live in New York." He hesitates, and his hesitation is making me nervous.

"And?" I whisper.

"She made it clear that wants me back," he answers softly.

Shit ... I think I just felt my heart break. "Oh. Okay," I reply, trying to hold the bile that's rising up from my stomach. I feel like I want to throw up. I try to dislodge myself from Magnus. But he refuses to let me go.

"Don't, Isabelle," he says firmly. "Please don't jump into conclusions."

"I don't understand, Magnus. So are ... are you getting back together with her?" I can't look at him directly because I know I'm getting teary. But he turns me to him, and I have no escape from the heat of his gaze.

"Martine and I have a lot of history, and even after the divorce, we agreed to be friends and to keep in touch. Just because our marriage didn't work out, doesn't mean we can't be at least civil with each other."

I can't let him finish. Is he serious? I push myself away from his arms and so I can distance myself from him. He's scowling at me, but I don't care. I don't want him to see the pain in my face, or the tears welling up in my eyes. Why did he have to come all this way, only to break up with me?

I stand by the window, needing to look elsewhere but at him, hugging myself in desperate need for protection. "So you *do* want to get back with her, is that it?"

"Isabelle, will you come here and stop jumping into conclusions?" I shake my head 'no.' He rakes his hair back once again. "What I'm saying is, I heard her out, and then I. Told. Her. To. Leave. Immediately."

My breath hitches, and he doesn't wait for me to walk back to him. The next thing I know, he's standing right behind me. He turns me to face him, cupping my face with his large hands and tipping my head up. My moist eyes and trembling lips are now in full show.

"I told her there's no romantic future between us anymore because I'm crazy about this amazing woman I'm seeing."

"You are? Who is she?" I ask in a broken voice.

His thumb brushes the stray tear that has fallen from my eye. "She's standing in front of a very lucky man right now."

My heart is exploding like tiny fireworks. "How … how lucky does he think he is?" I ask, my shaky hands making their way up on his broad shoulders.

"Luckier than he deserves." He presses his lips on my forehead, and my tears start to fall freely.

"Oh, baby, don't cry," he whispers softly. "This is where I want to be, Isabelle."

"But why did it take you so long to get here?"

"Because she refused to leave at once. When she finally did, I got held up with work shit. But the whole time I was away, all I could think about was you. I don't even know how I'll cope when I fly out."

The sincerity in his eyes makes it so easy for me to forget about the pain I just felt. How he gets me to jump from one extreme emotion to the next is beyond me, but right now, it feels so worth it.

I'm falling for Magnus Grant. And I'm falling *hard*.

"I don't know what to say."

He lowers his head again, his eyes intent on my lips. "How about, kiss me, Magnus."

"Kiss me, Magnus."

His mouth plunges onto mine, and I take him like a person deprived of oxygen. I grip the back of his head, pulling him into a deeper kiss, his tongue meeting mine as they dance so sweetly together.

Before I know it, I'm lifted off of my feet, something I've found Magnus likes to do. But this time, he's cradling me close.

"I need you so much, Isabelle," he murmurs as he nibbles the curve between my neck and shoulder. His left hand is underneath my sweater, and I sigh as I feel him graze my naked skin underneath.

"Not here," I whisper, needing the privacy of my own room.

He carries me there, my mouth hot on his neck while he locks the bedroom door behind us. He puts me back on my feet, and I quickly take my shoes off, while Magnus takes off his jacket and shirt. I lick my lips at the sight of his sculptured body. Before I can stop myself, I start licking his six-pack, feeling each square outline with my tongue. He moans and closes his eyes.

"You like that?" I ask against his skin, grazing my teeth against his stomach muscles. When I pull away, he frowns in protest.

"Take off your pants," I command, breathlessly.

He smirks that sexy smirk of his as he unbuckles his belt, and kicks off his shoes. Then he takes off his pants, leaving only his blue boxer briefs on. The sight of the large outline formed on his underwear leaves me panting.

"Your turn," he holds me by the hips and pulls me against him, so I can feel his burgeoning hardness against my belly.

I take off my sweater, pressing my naked breasts against his bare chest. Then I lift my arms around his neck, pulling him in for a kiss. I explore his mouth with my tongue, tasting him, loving how he feels against me.

"Hmmm, no bra ... very good," his hands caress my back, sending tingles on my naked flesh.

With my free hands, I push down at my leggings, shimmying until I can pull my feet out.

I let out a small shriek when he suddenly lifts me from my legs and practically throws me on my bed. We kiss hungrily, like animals in their primal state. I wrap my legs around his waist, pulling his hips down so I feel his hardness against my apex. I slowly move my hips against him and the friction of his cock and my pussy between the thin materials of our underwears makes us both moan with pleasure, and yearning for more.

"I need you now, Magnus," I whisper against his ear as he kisses my neck.

He lifts his head and looks me in the eyes. "How much do you need me?" he asks, pulling himself away from my neck to look me in the eyes again.

"Like I need air to breathe." I hold his gaze, and he groans as he kisses me hungrily, his tongue stroking mine.

"You have no idea what you do to me. And I plan to show you every day, so don't let me go," he mumbles against my lips.

His words should scare me. But all I feel right now is something deeper than I've ever expected or wanted. I need to taste him. I need him to feel as good as he's letting me feel right now.

"I want you in my mouth," I whisper as I writhe my hands down so I can tug on his underwear. My eyes widen appreciatively at his waiting hardness.

"You are so pushy, woman," he chuckles softly, but his eyes are clouded with lust. "You won't be needing this anymore either." I gasp when he rips off my panties in one swift move.

"Come here." I stare at Magnus with hunger, lying on my back and motioning him to straddle me between my chest.

He looks at me with uncertainty, but as soon as I grip his impressive cock with a firm hand, he knows I'm serious. He positions himself so his commanding manhood is just inches away from my face.

I lick my lips, stroking his length with my eager hand. Then I drag my tongue on his head. He moans, putting his hands on the wall above the headboard and tilting his head back, whispering my name as my mouth engulfs his cock. I place my own hands over his firm buttocks and pull him towards me slowly. He picks up the rhythm and starts to grind his hips, his cock moving in and out of my slick mouth.

"Isabelle, what are you doing to me?" he mumbles, his head up, like he's talking to the ceiling.

Just then, I feel his hand reach down my pussy. His fingers find my clit, drawing circles around the now sensitized area. I groan, bending my knees and lifting my hips, wanting more of his touch. And he obliges, getting me closer to orgasm with his skilful hands.

"Isabelle, I'm going to come, baby." I feel his body tense up, while his fingers continue their invasion inside my core. He finds my G-spot and flicks his fingers inside until I can't take it anymore. Oh my God, I'm coming too!

My climax comes in waves from my belly to my core, tightening around his soaking fingers. Magnus stills, and with a deep guttural moan, he shoots himself inside my mouth.

"Fucking wow!" he exclaims shakily while my hand gently massages his still hard cock.

When I finally let him go, he shifts his position so he's lying on top of me. He wants me to watch as he sucks on each finger still coated with my orgasm.

"Mmmm," he murmurs, and my cheeks redden at the sight.

"And yet she still blushes. You are unbelievable, my beautiful temptress." Tittering from embarrassment, I try to hide my face with both hands, but Magnus still manages to kiss the tip of my nose. I muffle a squeal when he dips his head at the crook of my neck and leaves kisses on the most sensitive part, before his mouth heads downwards to my heaving breasts.

I arch my back, gripping the pillows underneath me. My whole body is still sensitive from that orgasm, so I feel every kiss, lick, and scrape from his stubble. He squeezes my breasts as his mouth makes its downward path, his tongue licking patterns on my skin, down to my navel, towards my now throbbing pussy.

"Magnus ...," I bite my lip at the moment his tongue meets my swollen clit.

"I'm here, baby," he answers, his voice muffled as he continues to pleasure me. But I need more of him. I need to have *that* connection with him.

"Please, I need you ... inside."

With that smouldering stare, he rises up and aligns himself above me. I raise my legs over his waist as he enters me oh, so slowly. He wants me to feel every ... inch ... of ... him. I hold onto his back, loving every sculpted sinew. God, I just love every single part of this man.

Love. I look into Magnus's eyes, and I'm beginning to see him in a new light. I love how his kisses make me swoon, I love how his skin feels against mine, I love how he makes me feel so beautiful, and I love how he fits so perfectly inside of me. But most of all, I love that how, in the short amount of time I've spent with him, I am like my old self again. How can someone make me feel this much in a matter of weeks? But the answer to the question has been there, even before I realized it—I love him. *I am in love with Mr. Magnus Grant!*

But I can't tell him. Why? I'm afraid. I'm afraid that he might not feel the same. What if this is purely physical for Magnus? That how I feel is completely one-sided? What I need to do right now is to stop overthinking this and to just enjoy this moment.

And enjoy it, I will.

I fist my hands in his hair and push him down, kissing him ferociously. He moans against my mouth and while inside of me, shifts our positions so I'm now on top. *Oh God, this is amazing!* I grind my hips against his, feeling his girth stretch me inside. His hands wander all over my body, caressing me with his fingers.

"Tell me you're mine, Isabelle." He looks up at me with so much reverence in his eyes that my heart inflates.

I place his hands on my breasts, and I squeeze them for him. "I'm yours, Magnus … always." I pant.

I arch my back as I grind my hips over him, leaning backwards and holding on to his thighs. He finds my clit and rubs it furiously with his thumb, making me bite my lower lip to stop me from screaming out his name and waking up the neighborhood.

"You ... are ... so … beautiful," he moans roughly with every thrust. "All … mine."

"Yes, Magnus, … yesss!" I come with such a force that blood rushes to my head and my whole body spasms.

With a few final thrusts, Magnus roars out my name as he comes and empties himself inside of me.

Still panting, I slump over his chest, hearing his strong heartbeat against my ear.

After a few minutes, he gently lifts me off and positions me right beside him. He grabs some tissues and gently tidies me first before himself. Then he lifts the duvet and pulls it up to cover us both. I turn to face him, touching his handsome face, running my fingers through his soft dark hair.

He reaches for my hand and covers it with his own, moving it over his chest. I feel his heart beating, fast and strong, until it starts to slow down. But my heart is still racing because his eyes are fixated on me. It makes me wonder if there's love for me behind those blue eyes. I know that one day soon, I have to tell him how I feel, but I'd risk scaring him off. Yes, I know he wants me … all of me. But wanting is different from loving.

I set these worrying thoughts aside. Right now, my entire body feels like lead, and I can't help how happy it makes me.

I didn't realize my eyes have fallen shut until I feel my head on Magnus's chest and his arm holding me tight.

"It appears I might've worn you out. Hope you have sweet dreams, beautiful."

I nod slowly. "Okay," I murmur, "Magnus?"

"Hmmm?"

"I'll really miss you when you go," I mumble, barely speaking comprehensively.

He sighs. "So will I, very much. Now sleep, my Isabelle. You'll need your energy for your new job tomorrow," he kisses my temple gently.

"Mmm, okay … love you." And I am out like a light.

CHAPTER 12

I feel a warm glow illuminate my bedroom as I wake up the next morning. I try to recall what had happened before I slept, and I grin stupidly as soon as I remember. Then a cold chill runs through my spine. *Oh shit, did I just tell Magnus I love him? Whatever happened to restraint, Billie?*

I turn to where Magnus was lying beside me, only to find he's no longer there. *He bailed on me! I must have scared him off!*

My heartbeat races nervously as I sit up and look around my room, and feel relief when I see his iPad on my study table, with his shirt draped on the chair beside it. I hear footsteps on the hallway approaching, then my door opens, and it's Magnus, shirtless with only his pants on, two cups of coffee in his hands.

My breathing quickens, and I know it's not just at the sight of him, or the memory of our mind-blowing sex last night. It's because of what I said *after* that mind-blowing sex.

"Good morning, beautiful," he greets me in a quiet voice, closing the bedroom door behind him. The light coming from the window is showing every detail of his sculpted torso.

"Good morning," I reply shyly, a blush creeping up on my cheeks. "You're up early. I thought … I thought …"

Smiling gently at me, he ignores my stuttering, his expression placid, like I never uttered something so terribly embarrassing last night before I fell asleep.

Maybe I didn't say it out loud. Maybe I said it in my dreams.

But there's something about the way he's looking at me. Like he's waiting for me to say something. Yup. I definitely said it. Great.

When I refuse to speak up, he shrugs slightly. "Sorry I got up earlier. I had to deal with some work issues. It never ends, as you can imagine. I hope you don't mind if I took the liberty and made us coffee." He sits on the edge of the bed beside me, and he places my cup on the nightstand.

"Um, thanks, Magnus. So … issues in your West Coast office?" I ask, sounding like an idiot and feeling like I'm walking on eggshells.

"Sydney … in Australia. I had a recent acquisition there, and I'm just clarifying some legalities with my lawyers," he explains.

All this small talk is driving me crazy. We both know we have to talk about the proverbial elephant in the room.

"Magnus, I wanted to talk to you about last night ..." I tuck strands of my hair behind my ear, trying to think of the right words to say without messing it up.

He doesn't say a word, and his expression softens. He reaches out to hold my hand in his, and the butterflies in my stomach go ballistic.

"I'm ... I'm sorry to put you on the spot like that," I croak, losing my voice all of a sudden.

I look into his expression. His blue eyes seem to bore a hole through me, and I feel so exposed. It doesn't help that I'm still naked either. I raise the duvet up to my neck in a lame attempt to be discreet.

He reaches to cup my face into his hand, and I close my eyes, unable to look at him. Then I feel the bed shift and his lips are on mine; softly at first, but the kiss deepens. I hear him put his cup of coffee on my nightstand, and he places his other hand on my back to hold me steady. I gasp at his warm hand caressing my bare skin.

He pulls me closer, and I wrap my arms around his neck. The duvet falls, revealing my breasts. I press them against his bare chest, the memories of my last words from last night momentarily replaced by my need to feel his skin on mine.

But he pauses and pulls away, but not entirely letting me go.

"Isabelle, sometimes we say things out of compulsion. Did you mean what you said last night?" He lifts my face, forcing me to look up at him. I try to search him for clues so I know how to answer him. But he's not giving anything away.

Maybe he's giving me a way out. Or maybe he thinks I'm jumping the gun ... that even though he's sexually attracted to me, he doesn't see me *that way*. But I'm feeling selfish. I'm just not ready to let go of him yet. And I have a feeling I'm never going to be ready to lose Magnus at all.

"Sorry, Magnus. It's a reflex thing for me ... you know, I tell it to my son when he has nightmares in the middle of the night and sleeps here with me." I look away after explaining my half-truth.

"Can you look me in the eyes and tell me you mean that?" His voice is quite calm and controlled. I wish I knew what he's feeling.

I brace myself and look him squarely in the eyes, hoping my gaze won't falter.

"I'm sorry if I put you on the spot. And you're right. We say things out of compulsion. I mean, we've only started seeing each other. Plus, it was pretty emotional last night and exhaustion caught up with me, so I couldn't control my words." It isn't a complete lie, but I still feel like digging myself a hole and jumping in it.

Judging from the worry lines that form in between his brows, I might have managed to make things worse. Surely, he should be thrilled that I'm not pressuring him to say the *L* word back? But those lines disappear as his eyes follow his fingers gliding up my bare arms, stopping once again at the back of my neck.

"I care about you, Isabelle. I care about you more than you can imagine. And I know these feelings I have for you is stronger than I've ever felt with *anyone*. But I'm glad you agree that it's too early for us to say it. I want you to reserve judgment until you're truly sure it's me you want."

I don't deserve this man. I nod feebly, my eyes focused on his mouth. "I care about you a lot too. Thank you for not freaking out and running away."

Magnus pulls away and regards me thoughtfully. "Now why would I run away from you? I'm not going anywhere, baby," he says, smirking that wicked smirk of his.

"Not going anywhere, huh? Aren't you flying away today?" I ask teasingly.

"Say the word and I'll stay," he responds back, before nipping at my lower lip, sending delicious shivers down my spine.

"I won't take you away from your work. But kiss me now before I change my mind an—"

Before I can finish, his mouth descends onto mine. The forcefulness is almost painful because I know now, that there's true emotion behind it. I open my mouth slightly, coaxing his tongue to invade my mouth. He tastes of coffee mixed with mint. Yummy. I lightly suck at the tip of his tongue, and hear a groan rumble from his throat. His mouth starts to relax, and his kiss turns from rough to soft, to erotic, in a matter of seconds. It's the type of kiss that makes my core tighten and my crevice wet with want.

His hands gently squeezes my naked breasts, and I sigh against his mouth as soon as he tweaks my burgeoning nipples. He starts to ease himself down, making me lie back on the bed. His mouth relieves his fingers, suckling on my puckered nipples with gusto. I arch my back, wanting his mouth and his hands to do more.

But then he stops what he's doing and lifts his head from my chest, with a frown creasing his forehead. He grabs his phone from his back pocket and lifts himself off me in a huff. The cool air I feel on my skin when we separate makes me whimper in protest. He glances at me with an apologetic look before opening the text message on his phone.

"It's Alex. He dropped me off last night but I left my overnight bag in the car. I better meet him downstairs so I can change." He stands up, and I do the same, with my naked body in full view as I fetch my robe hanging by the door.

"Or we can just let him wait a little while," he intercepts and pulls me against him before I can even reach my goal.

I slap his hand away. "Ethan will be awake shortly! Go see Alex now!" I command lightheartedly. I quickly grab the robe and cover myself up.

"Hmm, bossy." He smirks at me, and turns to leave. But halfway through, he pauses, and looks back to me with a somber look in his eyes.

"Isabelle, I just want you to know … I don't want us *to let it go* or to *forget about it,* okay? I mean it when I say I just want you to be sure." And then he's out the door, leaving me standing with my mouth agape.

I head to my bathroom to brush my teeth, realizing all too late that I've been making out with Magnus with morning breath. Ugh, not again. I also try to convince myself that I've just dodged a bullet, and that it's incredibly presumptuous of me to think that Magnus would love me back after only knowing me for such a short period of time. And if things don't work out between us, at least I spared myself the humiliation that comes with the impression of an unrequited love.

But who am I kidding? As much as he tells me he cares for me and has strong feelings for me, it hurts that he doesn't want to voice it out. And yes, I do love him. And I will accept whatever part of himself he wants to share with me. But I know I need to protect myself too, at least for Ethan's sake.

The door opens behind me, and I feel little arms wrap around my waist.

"Good morning, Ethan!" I bend down so I can give him a big cuddle back.

"Good morning, Mommy! Where's Magnus? I heard his voice when I woke up. Is he gone? Did I miss him?" he asks curiously, with a tinge of worry in his eyes.

"No, sweetie. He just stepped out to get something from Alex. You remember Alex, right?"

Ethan looks puzzled, before nodding eventually.

"So how about you start getting ready for school, huh?" I suggest before kissing the top of his head.

"Awww … Aaalriiight," he complains dramatically before dragging his feet out the door.

I wander out of my room, heading towards the front window. I see Alex and Magnus talking next to his SUV. They must sense my eyes on them because they both look up, with Magnus giving me a small wave. I feel a blush come up to my cheeks at being caught out, but I give them a wave back before heading back to my room to get my cell. Michelle didn't come home last night, and although I'm sure she slept over at Nathan's I still need to make sure she's okay.

There are two missed calls and a message on my phone, all from Michelle. I open the message. *'Answer your damn phone, girl! I'm staying over at Nathan's but I'll be back early tomorrow. I'll pick up Ethan in the afternoon. Good luck today!!!! XXXOOO PS: Catch up later!!! ☺'*

I can't help but smile to myself. Both Michelle and I seem to have found someone pretty special around the same time.

I quickly check on Ethan, who is busy brushing his teeth. I step into his room to lay out the clothes he'll be wearing in school today before heading back to my own room. I decide on my black shift dress with a light emerald cardigan, knowing how the color seems to suit my skin tone, hair, and eyes. I lay my clothes on the bed which I have now made up, feeling conscious of what just transpired here last night.

Magnus opens the door with a carry-on luggage, presumably his change of clothes.

"Do you mind if I use your shower?" he smiles sheepishly.

"Go ahead. I'll prepare us some breakfast. Eggs and toast okay?" I ask, needing to leave the room in a hurry. The thought of Magnus being naked in my shower is too hot to handle.

But as I walk past him, Magnus wraps his arm around my waist. "Care to join me?" he whispers in my ear, and his voice seem to head straight to my core.

"Ethan's awake," I whisper back, "and he's looking for you. He's in his room now, getting ready for school."

His face lights up. "Really? He's looking for me? I better make sure to clear the air between us."

"Sounds good. Use that charm of yours because for some reason it seems to work for me." I giggle at his fake indignation before wrapping my arms around him and giving him a soft kiss. I quickly disentangle myself before our urges get the better of us.

At the kitchen, I decide on preparing something simple— scrambled eggs with chives on toast for me and Magnus, and a cheesy version for Ethan. I have to keep it simple this morning since I don't intend to be late on the first day of my new role.

Ethan is first in the kitchen, and he greets me with another kiss and sits at the breakfast table, happily eating his cheesy eggs on toast while I pack his lunch.

Magnus follows not long after, and I double take, like a love-struck teen, at how handsome he looks in his navy blue suit, crisp white shirt, no tie, and tan oxfords. His hair is neat and slick but still unruly enough that it looks like he ran his fingers through them. He sees me gaping at him and winks at me, a smirk fixed on his face.

"Your eggs are amazing, Isabelle," Magnus tells me as the three of us are eating the last morsels of breakfast on our plates.

"I love it when Mommy cooks me breakfast," Ethan adds.

"I love it too. I hope I get to eat her breakfast every day," Magnus replies back, but his eyes are on me. Thankfully, Ethan doesn't understand Magnus's double entendre. But I can't help how my heart swells knowing Magnus wants to be with me ... with *us*.

"I have to get ready for work. Just leave the dishes in the sink, and I'll clean them later." Then I hurry off to my room to shower and get dressed.

After the shower, I dress carefully, keeping my fingers crossed that I look the part of an assistant to the CFO. Satisfied with my appearance, I pick up my purse and head back out to see Magnus and Ethan still sitting by the breakfast table. They've cleaned up, bless their hearts, and are laughing out loud at a video from Magnus's iPad. They both look up, and as soon as I see Magnus checking me out from head to toe with a look of ownership in those blue eyes, I know for sure that not only do I look good right now, but that the person I love desires me as much as I desire him.

"Mom, Magnus said he wants to take me to school," Ethan announces eagerly as he runs back to his room to get his backpack.

What? He's really taken on this whole family thing. "Honey, *I'm* taking you to school. Magnus, you don't have to do that. Aren't you supposed to be flying to San Francisco this morning? What time's your flight?"

Magnus gets off his seat and walks to me. "Baby, I'll take any excuse to spend a little more time with you. Plus Ethan asked me, and I want to do it for him. So, is it okay?"

How can I say no to that? "Okay … yes."

"Oh, and I'm taking you to work before I fly out." With a grin, he kisses me gently on the cheek and walks ahead, not giving me a chance to protest.

We're all inside Magnus's SUV en route to Ethan's school. It's a very short car ride since the school is only a few blocks away. As soon as we reach our destination, Ethan asks Magnus if he could take him all the way to his classroom. Magnus checks with me if it's okay, and I answer with a shrug and a resigned smile.

It feels weird walking up the steps of Ethan's school with another man, even weirder that mothers and nannies are staring at him like wolves eyeing fresh meat. I actually feel like slapping their gaping mouths, but I can't blame them either. Magnus is indeed, one hot piece of meat. But he's my piece of meat, not theirs!

After kissing Ethan good-bye, we return to the car in silence, aware of the continued stares we're copping. One father comes up to Magnus, shakes his hand, and praises him for his philanthropic efforts. Magnus takes it all in stride and shows humility by saying he's only part of a bigger team of people who help out. Seriously, is this man for real?

Just watching him look so commanding in his presence, and yet so modest in his interactions makes me feel proud to know him. I still can't believe this man is interested in me, and has grown fond of Ethan. I have to pinch myself to make sure I'm not dreaming.

Ouch. Okay, so I'm not. Like he said before. This is happening and now I have a big smile on my face.

"What's with the big smile, baby?" he asks, holding my hand in his as we step inside the Cayenne.

"Nothing. I just can't believe it," I answer, shrugging.

"Believe what?" he queries, rubbing his thumb over my knuckles.

"That Magnus Grant is not too big for his boots to take my son to school."

He chuckles. "It's something new to me. But I'm happy I did it, and I'd like to do that often if that's okay with you."

"Why? I mean, all the attention you were getting …"

He shrugs. "I've gotten used to it. It kind of comes with the territory. But I generally still maintain a low profile. I'm no rock star or Hollywood actor."

"You're hot enough to give any Hollywood stud a run for their money," I tease, but still being completely honest.

He scowls at me. "Isabelle, you're mine now. I don't want you looking at other *studs*. I've never been the jealous type, nor am I ever the violent type, but just the thought you lusting over other guys makes me feel like smashing something."

I stare at him, gobsmacked. "Seriously, where is this hostility coming from? I *am* yours. I'm not lusting over anyone else *but* you." I lean over and move my head closer so only Magnus can hear. "You're so fucking hot, just thinking about you gets me so wet."

"God, I love your dirty mouth," he roughly whispers back.

Did he just reference my mouth with the *L* word? I choose not to speak up about it.

"So … I'm still hot even if I'm not too big in my boots?" he cups my face and gives me a tender kiss. As I pull back, I look into his blue eyes, and I give him a coy smile.

"There is nothing *small* about you, Mr. Magnus Grant," I add, batting my eyelids.

He grabs my hand and places it over his hardened appendage. *Fuck me, everything is definitely big on this man!*

"Magnus, we're not exactly alone," I warn him in a low tone, but gripping his cock over his trousers and stroking its length is enough to make even me, forget.

He nips at my earlobe. "Just wait until I get back, my little temptress. I'll give you all the hardness you can handle."

Oh dear, I think I convulse a little. "Sounds like a threat. I can't wait," I add with a wink.

He laughs out aloud, and I join in. Then he lifts my wayward hand and kisses my palm. And just like that, I switch from lusty to swoony in no time at all.

Magnus talks about his family for the rest of the trip to work and how he's looking forward to introducing me to them at the charity event on Saturday. He picks up on my apprehension and assures me that there's nothing to be scared about. I smile back at Magnus, nodding my head in agreement. But in the back of my head, being a runaway, single mom from Brooklyn doesn't exactly present me in a good light, especially with a wealthy family like the Grants. I should know because my parents are pretentious snobs, and they only wanted me to date boys who come from the same social hierarchy.

By now, we're close to Grant Corp's building. "Um, Magnus, is it okay if you drop me off a block away from your building?"

"Why?" he asks, a frown on his face evident. "You don't want to be seen getting out of my car?"

"Yes. People talk. Magnus, I'm not prepared for people to think I got ahead because I'm humping the CEO."

"I don't give a flying fuck what they think of our relationship, but I sure hope that's not how you truly see this." He points to both of us with a huge frown on his face.

Shaking my head, I answer back softly, my cheeks blushing. "No, ... of course not. You know how I feel about us, Magnus."

His expression relaxes, and he brushes his thumb against my heated cheek. "You're very special to me, Isabelle. Don't let anybody else to tell you otherwise." Smiling, he continues, "I can't wait until I'm able to show you off to everyone."

"Magnus ... what if my ex—"

"No," he interrupts me firmly. "He doesn't deserve to be in that beautiful mind of yours. I will never let anything bad happen to you and Ethan. He'd have to go through me first."

I swiftly wrap my arms around his neck, and I cling to him with my head on his chest. He holds me tightly against him, and I know without a doubt he'll do anything to keep us safe. This man is too much. Still clinging to each other, Magnus instructs Alex to drop me off as per my request, and after a few minutes, Alex parks the car exactly a block away. He gets out, allowing us some privacy.

My heart drops. This is it. I won't be seeing Magnus for two long days. I'm hating it already.

"Call me as soon as you get there, okay?"

"I will," he answers sincerely. "Keep your phone close to you."

He leans over, then presses his mouth on mine. Our kiss is soft and chaste at first, but progresses to something deeper, with a sense of yearning and sadness at the prospect of being apart.

Exhaling deeply, Magnus pulls away, hesitant as I am to let go. "I'll call you and text you. Make sure you have your phone close to you at all times, okay?" he reminds me once more.

"Yes, boss! I heard you the first time," I tease softly, trying to be funny but actually feeling miserable on the inside.

"I'm serious." His face is stern, making me realize he's not kidding around.

"I *will*. Can I get in touch with you too?" I ask hopefully.

"I'll be quite busy, but Denise knows to put you through."

"Okay." I pause, trying to hold my composure. I know I'll see him again soon, so why am I still so down?

"I'll miss you, Magnus."

"I'll miss you too, baby. I still want you to come with me. Just say the word, and I'll let Charles know."

I shake my head sadly. "You know I can't."

He nods regrettably then plants a kiss on my temple.

"Take care, my sweet Isabelle." He's so genuine, and so beautiful in his show of affection that I melt right in front of him.

"You too, my big boss man." I say as I kiss him tenderly before opening the car door. I notice Alex is waiting by the side.

"Good luck today, baby."

A thought strikes me as I am getting off the car.

"Do *not* meddle," I remind him, my forefinger firmly pointing at Magnus.

He gives me a smirk. "Sure."

Now I know he surely will.

I roll my eyes at him. "I'm serious," I reply.

All he gives me is that sexy smirk of his and a brief shrug of his shoulders. I shake my head and roll my eyes before letting Alex close the door. But inside, my heart is fluttering.

"Take care of him, Alex," I remind him softly.

"I always do, Ms. Morrison. Have a good day." He nods to me before coming around to the driver's seat.

I wave good-bye as they drive off. Checking my watch, I have less than ten minutes to go before work time starts, so I walk briskly towards Grant Corp, looking around and hoping no one has seen me get out of Magnus's car.

I make it to the office on time, and thankfully, Mr. Dune is not in his office yet as I walk past to reach my desk. I let out a small gasp when I see a gorgeous bouquet of white roses and light pink peonies in a crystal vase. How'd he know they're my favorite flowers? I open the card that comes with the flowers, and I smile at the handwritten message. *'I miss you already, Isabelle. Good luck today. I'm sure you'll do a great job. Yours, M.'*

I can't help but smile giddily at this sweet gesture, and I keep the card in my purse, before taking my phone out to send Magnus a message. *'Thank you for the flowers! They are beautiful, and I'll think of you always when I look at them.'*

My phone rings in less than a minute, and I let out a small curse before muting the volume.

"Hello?" I answer in a soft tone.

"Glad you liked the flowers, baby."

"Love them. Thank you. How'd you know those two are my favorite flowers? And who brought them to my desk?"

"My woman has so many questions. You had a small vase of three roses and two peonies on your coffee table. And the answer to your second question is Denise. "

"Oh, you're good. But wait, so Denise knows about us? What if people find out it's from you?"

"She's my EA. She signed a Non-Disclosure Agreement before I hired her. But she's not going to say anything because she knows I trust her, NDA or not. And so what if people find out? Maybe it would keep all the other men from hovering around you."

I roll my eyes even if Magnus can't see me. "Men don't *hover* around me. You're being paranoid."

"You may not see it happening but I do. I'm this close to marking you permanently to keep them all away."

"Marking me?" Why does the thought of him staking his claim on me suddenly sound extremely appealing?

"Mm-hmm. You are mine, Isabelle. Your mouth, your skin, your breasts, your pussy … everything."

Oh, dear God. His husky tone makes me cross my legs to stop my core from throbbing.

"Is there any part of me I can keep to myself?" I ask in a whisper, hoping no one can pick up on how turned on I am.

"Of course. Me. You can keep me. And your mind because I love how you think."

Oh. Damn. He's. Good.

"So I can keep you, can I?" I ask coyly.

He chuckles softly, and I picture him wearing that sexy smirk of his. I wish I can see it right now.

"My mouth, my skin, my mind, my hands, my cock ... everything." His deliberate sensual tone while enunciating every word makes me clutch my legs tighter.

"On that note," he continues, "I better hang up now because I'm picturing you naked, and it's beginning to feel uncomfortable underneath my trousers. I'll see you soon, Isabelle."

"Okay. Talk to you later."

And we hang up, with me still feeling giddy and extremely horny. I don't know if I can last so long without Magnus. What if he gets distracted with all those damn West Coast women parading in front of him? Assuming he's going to Cali anyway. But who cares? Women flock to him no matter where he is.

Doing my best to push the depressing thought out of my head, I log on to my laptop to start work. That's when I notice Mr. Dune approaching.

"Good morning, Mr. Dune. Is there anything I can get for you?" I ask as I catch up to him.

He turns to me with a kind smile. "Yes, coffee please, black with two sugars. And come to my office so we can discuss my schedule as well as your everyday responsibilities."

"Sure thing." I give him a brief nod before making my way to the kitchen.

I begin making Mr. Dune's coffee, trying to ease the nervous tension fluttering inside of me. It's actually a good thing that Magnus isn't around so I can focus on my new job without any distractions.

Mr. Dune looks up from his computer screen as I place his coffee on his table and sit across from him, complete with the tablet provided to use for meetings and note-taking.

"Thank you, Isabelle, and by the way, welcome to my team!" He reaches out to shake my hand which I subtly but quickly take back. I guess I'm still uncomfortable with other men touching me, but I note that Mr. Dune's touch, though it makes me feel uncomfortable, it'st not to the point of nausea. That's a good thing. Thankfully, Mr. Dune doesn't seem to notice my reaction.

"Thanks, Mr. Dune. And please ... call me Billie."

His smile is sincere and his expression open, making me feel at ease with him. "Billie it is. And Mr. Dune makes me sound way too old. Call me Charles, by all means. In fact, I insist on it. How was your weekend? Good?"

"I had an amazing weekend. And you?" 'Good' cannot even describe the weekend I just had.

"My wife Caroline and I spent the weekend up at Martha's Vineyard. You've been there? It's beautiful, we love it over there," he answers with a a sigh and a warm smile.

"Look, I honestly never had the need for an assistant, but with Grant Corp continually growing, I was getting swamped. So I knew it was a great idea when Magnus suggested I hire you. And after checking your qualifications, it was an easy decision for me."

"Thank you, Charles. I know how great this opportunity is, and I'm willing to work my hardest."

He nods, his expression showing a trace of uncertainty. "But I have to let you know, I do take on a lot, so you have to help me prioritize."

"Well, that's what I'm here for," I answer with a smile.

My first meeting with Charles has gone well. He is quite a charming man and a self-confessed finance geek. He knows a lot about the business and the ways to keep it cost-efficient. Unfortunately, he does like to take on everything, so it's up to me to manage issues that do not require his hands-on approach. It's a demanding role, but I look forward to learning more under his tutelage.

Half an hour before lunch, my phone rings.

"Good morning, Mr. Dune's office, how can I help you?"

"Hi, Billie, it's Boyd."

Shoot. I haven't even spoken to him or Jess and Marla since Friday! So much has happened since then, I can't believe it has only been two days.

"Oh ... hi, Boyd. Hey, I'm so sorry for leaving you guys at Cirque last Friday."

"Nah, it's cool. We left pretty much after you did and moved on to another club. Hope everything's okay?"

"Um yeah, everything's okay. Though I'd still like to make it up to you guys soon."

"Well, it's your first day at your new job. Are you okay to join us for lunch today at twelve, and we can catch up?"

"I'd have to check with Charles, but otherwise, sure! Meet you guys at the lobby?"

"Whoa, first name basis with the big boss, cool! Okay. See you then! Oh, and Billie?"

"Yes?"

"I miss ... I mean, we miss you down here."

Goodness, this could end up being one awkward lunch.

"Same here. See you all then!"

I check with Charles about my lunch hours, before finishing up some correspondence. By twelve noon, I am ready for my break. I give Charles a heads up before heading out.

At the lobby, I'm relieved to see Jess and Marla with Boyd already there. We give each other brief hugs, with me gently pulling away from Boyd's lingering arm.

Marla holds me by the shoulder. "What happened to you last Friday? C'mon, you were saved by Mr. Grant himself! I can't get over how hot he was knocking that loser out cold."

Oh ... I forgot they witnessed that. That incident feels like aeons ago. "It's his club and we're his employees, Marla. He probably feels responsible for us. Plus that creep was major douche, so I'm glad Mag ... Mr. Grant took care of him," I reply, shrugging my shoulders, and hoping they didn't notice the little slip-up. "So where are we having lunch?"

"Let's go to that Mexican café at West Forty-sixth," Marla suggests.

We all nod in agreement and make the short journey to the bustling eatery. We luckily get a table and order something quick and easy. I resist my friends' offer to have sangria. I need a clear head to do my job right.

"Too bad you missed out on the rest of the night though," Marla adds as she sits down next to me. "But seriously, how hot did Mr. Grant look with that model, Sofia Meier? I mean, they were all over each other!"

I feel the color leave my face. Did they really see them as a couple? And what did Marla mean about them being all over each other? *No, Billie. Stop doubting Magnus. He said, Sofia plays for the other team, remember?*

"I didn't notice them making out or anything," I answer, trying to sound nonchalant.

"Well, Sofia had her hand on his leg, and Magnus was whispering something to her, and she started giggling. I thought they might've left together, but Sofia left alone because Mr. Grant decided he's going to be Billie's white knight. He left soon after though, so I guess he must've caught up with her.

"Do … do you know if they're really together?" I ask, hoping they don't notice the crack in my voice.

"Well, they never confirmed anything. But the way they were acting the other night, I think we can draw our own conclusions," Marla answers, shrugging her shoulders.

"He's a player. It's a well-documented fact," Boyd adds straightforwardly.

Their words are like daggers to my heart. What if Magnus was not entirely forthcoming with me? Just thinking about him with another girl makes me feel violently ill.

Now I have to deal with Sofia, Martine, and goodness knows who else! I'm way over my head here. Maybe I shouldn't have rushed into a relationship with Magnus just because he's the first guy in seven years who actually makes me feel normal again.

Who am I kidding? I'm in love with Magnus whether I like it or not.

My shoulders slump, and I put my food back on the plate. I'm not feeling hungry anymore.

"So, Billie, how's your new job going?" Jess interrupts, thankfully.

They are eager to find out about my new job, so I compose myself, and I give them a rundown of what I did today. Thankfully, our lunch break is almost up, and we start heading back to the office.

"Are you okay, Billie? We seem to have lost you there for a second," Boyd says in a gentle tone, lightly touching my shoulder to get my attention.

I move like I'm adjusting the strap of my shoulder bag, effectively removing his hand off my shoulder. "Yeah, yeah, I'm okay. I just need to mentally prepare for the afternoon."

"Well, I'm here if you need to talk, okay?"

I am touched by his genuine concern. "Thank you, Boyd. You're very sweet. But I'm okay," I reply with a smile.

Jess and Marla are walking a couple of steps ahead of Boyd and myself. As we enter our office building, I can see a slight frown on her face, and I know I have to clear the air out about Boyd.

"Jess, can I talk to you for a second?" I whisper discreetly.

"Sure," she answers softly, tucking her hair behind her right ear. And we let Marla and Boyd walk ahead of us towards the elevators.

"So how are things between you and Boyd?"

"What do you mean?" she asks, her face turning to crimson.

"I just want to let you know that I'm, well, dating someone at the moment, and even if I wasn't, I just want to reassure you that I am in no way interested in Boyd, except as a friend."

"You're not?" Her face lights up, and it makes me smile. "And this guy you're seeing, do we get to meet him soon?"

I blush at her words. "It's still in its early stages, so I can't say much yet. I suppose we'll see what happens, right?" She smiles and nods in response.

Back at my desk, I'm finishing a letter for Charles when my cell phone vibrates. It's Magnus. My heartbeat increases as I pick it up and press the *Answer* button.

"Hey."

"Hey."

His low, husky voice sends thrills up and down my spine.

"So, how was your flight?"

"Lonely. I miss you, baby."

"You have no idea how much I miss you too." I answer back breathlessly.

"How's your first day as Charles's assistant? You'll tell me if he makes you work too hard, right?"

"I've learned so much in one day. Charles hasn't been hard on me at all. Oh, and no, you can't interfere with my job. It's bad enough you're my boss's boss, so you have to let me do my own thing," I insist in a hushed tone, in case someone overhears me. Then that niggling thought I pushed away earlier is back. "Magnus, I want to ask you something, and I want you to tell me the truth."

"Okay, this sounds serious," I think I hear humor in his voice.

This makes me hesitate. Do I really want to ask Magnus about Sofia again? What if it ends up in another argument? Damn it, all I really want is his arms around me right now.

"Actually, come to think about it, it's not that important. I'm just glad you arrived safely, and I got to hear your voice."

There is a pause. "Hmm, Isabelle, I thought we're going to be honest with each other?"

"Then we'll talk about it when you get back ... no, actually, okay, I have to ask you, otherwise it'll bother me until you get back."

"What's on your mind?"

"I just wanted to know, are we really together ... exclusively?"

He sniffs, and his voice is cold when he answers, "I thought I made myself perfectly clear on this subject. Why? Is Boyd asking you out? Do you want to go out with him?"

"No, don't be silly. I'm concerned about you, about us. I mean, there's Sofia, and now Martine's back ... I just need to know. Am I the only one you're seeing? You know, for right now ... I mean ... shit!" I blubber out. "I'm so not good at this!"

He doesn't answer. Oh no, did he hang up?

"Magnus, are you still there. Hello?"

"Baby, I don't know whether I should laugh or put you on my knees, spank you, or fuck you senseless until you realize that there's no one *but* you."

Oh, what now? "Why would you want to spank me? I'm not a child! And that would hurt."

"Hmmm, on the contrary, my sweet Isabelle. Pleasure and pain always go well together."

How did our conversation get from zero to dirty in ten seconds? What's even more curious is how turned on I am at the thought of Magnus spanking me.

"I understand we've only known each other for a short period of time, but this is real, Isabelle. There's no one else." He sounds serious, and I believe him.

"Okay ... Thank you. It's just that I miss you so much already. Is that even normal? I mean, you know, missing you this much?" I ask him softly.

"I feel the same way, my temptress. I miss you so much, it's driving me insane."

"Well, I'll be here when you get back," I answer softly.

"That's something to look forward to. I have to go, baby. I'll talk to you later?"

"Okay."

There's a pause, as if both of us are waiting for the other to say something first.

"Hang up," I start.

He chuckles softly. "Ladies first." *Are we seriously doing this?* I giggle inwardly.

"Who says I'm a lady?" I tease.

"I can't wait to be inside you again."

"Magnus!" I whisper harshly, trying not to show how thrilled that makes me. Why does he keep throwing me off like this?

"Good-bye, Mr. Grant!" I whisper through gritted teeth.

I can hear his low chuckle.

"Bye, baby."

Then we both hang up.

I stare at my phone, willing it to ring again.

But a ping on my laptop shows I have a meeting to go to with Charles in half an hour. So I compose myself and try not to look too flushed. I still need to finish a letter and organize the paperwork needed for the upcoming meeting with the sales managers.

Today's tasks make the day fly by, and before I know it, it's time for me to leave. I politely decline an invitation by Marla for drinks, but we make plans to catch up closer to the end of the week. I'm too tired, and I want to see Ethan.

I *am,* however, disappointed that Magnus hasn't called me again nor has he sent any messages. I have to put it down to how busy he must be in … come to think of it, I don't even know where Magnus is. I can't believe I never bothered to ask! However, the night is still young. Hopefully, we can talk later.

On my way home, I notice a young loved-up couple so lost in each other that they seem to forget everyone else while they kiss and hold each other so intimately. It makes me think of Magnus and myself and how our situation can't allow for such open displays of amorous affection.

But I know that's a load of crap. I shouldn't really complain when I'm the one who imposed the ban.

I check my phone again while walking home, just in case I missed his call. Nothing. So before I can think twice, I'm pressing *Call* against his name. Denise answers.

"Oh, hi, Denise."

"Hello, Billie. Would you like to speak with Magnus?" Denise replies in her friendly but professional tone.

"Um yes, is he available?"

"He is just about to finish up on his meeting, but I can hand him the phone now if you want?"

I'm tempted to say yes. I miss him so damn much. But I decide to just wait. I don't really want to interrupt his work like a clingy girlfriend.

"Oh no, it's okay, Denise. Just let him know I called if that's okay?"

"Of course, dear."

"Thanks, … Bye." And then I hang up.

Ethan's face lights up when he sees me come in the apartment, but a look of disappointment crosses his face when he sees it's just me.

"Where's Magnus?" he asks with his brows furrowed.

I crouch down to give him a kiss on top of his head. "Oh geez, thanks for the awesome welcome." I tickle his ribs, making him scream with laughter.

"Well, Magnus is on a business trip. He'll be back hopefully by Wednesday. *Oh shoot, I forgot to ask Denise where they are.*

"Oh, okay." He nods, seemingly satisfied with my explanation.

"Ethan's been ranting and raving about Magnus," I hear Michelle's voice as she comes out from the kitchen.

I walk over to her to give her a hug.

"How are you Miss Thang?" I ask her, noticing her glow. "Someone's had a lot of loving last night!" I whisper, nudging her with my elbow.

"And you didn't? Pfft!" Michelle rolls her eyes at me, and we giggle together.

"What's so funny?" Ethan asks with a look of puzzlement on his face.

"Um nothing, honey, just happy to see Michelle again."

We prepare our dinner together, with Ethan setting the table, Michelle cooking the main dish, and I'm preparing the salad.

While eating, Ethan starts talking about his zoo day with Magnus and that he's really happy that Magnus isn't angry with him at all. Michelle is concerned and looks at me questioningly. I mouth 'later' at her. I still needed to talk to her about what she told Ethan.

After dinner and homework, Ethan is ready for bed. Once he's tucked in bed, I join Michelle in the living room. A glass of merlot is waiting for me.

"Okay, dish! So you and Magnus are getting serious, huh?" Michelle is wide-eyed and ready for gossip.

I take a long sip of my wine before answering, "Pretty serious, I think. But we're still getting to know each other." I let out a sigh. "Sometimes, I think he's out of my league ... you know what I mean?"

"Please, baby girl. Your family's moneyed. It's your choice not to be. You don't wanna have anything to do with it, and I totally support you for that."

"I know, but ... never mind," I hesitate, shaking my head and unable to look Michelle in the eyes.

"But ...? Wait!" Michelle points an accusing finger at me. "Oh. My. God. You love him, don't you? You love Magnus Grant!"

"Shhh! Ethan's asleep!" Rolling my eyes, I continue, "I don't know. Actually, yes, I think I do. I feel like a giddy schoolgirl when he looks at me. I get these jealous streaks when there's other women involved. I don't think I even felt like this with ..." I drift off, and Michelle reaches for my hand and squeezes it. "Michelle, I can't even describe how safe I feel when I'm around him. And it's scaring that shit out of me because I've only known him a short time. What if he changes his mind about me? And the women! Oh, my God, Michelle! How can I even compete with the beautiful women he's been with? I don't know what I'll do if Magnus decides to leave me for another woman. And then there's my son! Ethan will be devastated."

"Okay, calm down. You're jumping the gun here. How does Magnus feel about Ethan?"

"They adore each other."

"And how does Magnus feel about you?"

I shake my head. "I don't know if he's there yet. But he told me he cares about me."

"So he says he cares about you, but I've seen how he looks at you, and girl, that man is in love with you. Maybe he's just finding the right time to tell you."

I don't reply back. Magnus told me to be sure that it's really him I want. Maybe he's telling that to himself as well.

Michelle holds my hands and looks at me intently. "You're overanalyzing this, so stop. I know it's a big jump for you, and there are things that happen in relationships that are scary. Your self-esteem could even take a hitting, but it's *all* worth it."

I nod, her positive words sinking in and making me smile.

Then her eyes widen with excitement. "Holy shit, Billie, you know what this means, right? Double date!"

"Oh, wow, I never thought of that! We should definitely do it."

She stands up. "Okay, I'll check with Nathan when he's free and you check with Magnus, okay?" She starts to stand up, but I hold on to her arm, urging her to sit back down.

"Michelle, there's another thing I wanted to talk to you about," I start somberly. "Remember Ethan mentioning how he's happy that Magnus isn't mad at him? Well, it's because he caught us about to kiss while we were at the park, and he told Magnus to make sure that he asked for my permission. And when I asked him what brought that on, he said he hears me cry in my room. But he never came to me about it. He asked you first. Why have you never told me that he could hear me?"

The smile on Michelle's face disappears. "I'm sorry that I put you on the spot, Billie. But how did you feel when you found out?" Michelle asks me solemnly.

"Awful ... and extremely guilty."

"Exactly. See, you don't need the extra baggage. I helped him the best I could, honey. But I'm sorry if I overstepped the line."

I shake my head. "No, you're right. I just don't want him to be afraid to come to me."

"I did ask him why he didn't come to you first. You know what he said? He said he didn't wanna ask you because he didn't want you to cry again."

Tears spring up from my eyes. My poor baby, he shouldn't feel this way at all. He shouldn't worry about his mommy. It should be the other way around.

"I'm booking an appointment tomorrow to see Dr. Mitchell," I tell her with finality. There's no doubt about it, I need to go back to therapy. My nightmares are back, plus these new emotions springing up because of Magnus are definitely something I need to talk to a professional about.

"Good for you, Billie. It's going to be for the best," she beams at me.

"I know," I reply, laying my head on her shoulder.

Happy with our talk, we agree to watch the late news together while finishing our wine. I subconsciously wish that I'd see Magnus on TV. I feel a dull ache in my chest from missing him so much.

I check the time. It's almost twelve midnight and still no call from him. Maybe he's too busy. I decide against picking up the phone. I left him a message with Denise already. If he wants to call me, he should have done so by now.

Feeling tired, I give Michelle a goodnight kiss on the cheek before checking on Ethan and heading to my bedroom. I take a quick shower before I change into my favorite but scruffy-looking nightshirt. I check my cell phone, and my heart skips a beat when there's a missed call and an incoming message from Magnus. *'It's been a long day, and I'm tired, but we've managed to resolve the issues. I miss you, baby. I'll see you soon.* M.'

Feeling excited that he's free, I try calling him back, wanting to hear his voice, but both attempts go straight to his voicemail. I hang up before the beep. I don't want to leave a message. I want to talk to him. I lie down on my bed, but my eyes refuse to close. I can't sleep. I just need to have that connection with him, to know that he's reading something from me that'll hopefully give him a smile. I pick up the phone again so I can text him back. *'I'm in bed about to sleep. I miss you so much too. Goodnight my big boss man. XO'*

I stare at my phone after I press *Send*, hoping he answers back, but I give up after a while. I place my phone back on the nightstand and bury myself under the covers to force myself to sleep.

I wake up with a jolt. *What the hell?* It's my phone buzzing. I scramble to get my phone, jumping up when I see Magnus's name flashing on the screen.

"Hello?" I whisper, clutching the duvet against my chest, feeling my heart racing.

"Isabelle," he answers, relief evident in his voice. "I've been trying to call you."

"Do you know what time it is in here?" I ask, rubbing my eyes.

"I'm sorry, baby. I couldn't wait anymore. I have something sent for you, and I need you to buzz my guy in, okay?"

"What? At this hour? Oh, Magnus, who would deliver anything at this time?" I sigh aloud, slowly swinging my legs off my bed.

"Just trust me, baby, and don't hang up," he insists.

"Fine. Just a sec," I answer back, rolling my eyes and tucking the phone in the crook of my neck, so I can wear my robe.

I'm mentally kicking myself for not checking through our window before buzzing the delivery guy though. But it's such an odd hour that he probably got one of his minions or whoever to send it. And he did say to trust him. "What did you send me at two in the morning?" I ask. But as soon as I swing the door open, my mouth gapes, and I almost drop the phone.

"Me," Magnus answers … right in front of me. He's carrying his overnight bag in one hand and hanging up his phone with the other.

"Magnus!" I'm beaming, my heart thumping so loudly with joy that I'm certain he can hear it. Without thinking, I jump up to him, catching him by surprise, and wrapping my legs around his waist. I cling to him for dear life as we kiss like we've been apart for years, and not just a day.

He walks inside my apartment and locks the door as quietly as he can with his free hand.

"I … missed ... you ... so … much," I tell Magnus in between kisses, holding his face with my two hands. "Wait, how did you get here? Did Alex drop you off?" I ask, his handsome face still in my hands.

He nods, his eyes hungrily focused on my mouth. "I know I should've waited until the next day to see you, but when I saw your missed calls and your message, fuck, baby, I just wanted to be in the same bed with you."

In a few strides, he manages to take me to my room, lock the bedroom door, and lay me down the bed while still kissing the breath out of me. My robe gets undone while I was being carried, and now I'm feeling self-conscious of my ratty old nightshirt. Having Magnus appear like he did was not something I'd have anticipated … ever.

But he doesn't seem to care. He devours me with his eyes from head to toe, leaving delicious tingles in its wake. "I missed you, beautiful," he whispers, his voice full of longing.

Before I know it, he's taken off his shoes and socks, and he's on top of me. Holding me by the back of my neck, he deepens the kiss, our tongues entwining with each other in a sensual dance.

I pull away, catching my breath. "Wait, I thought you weren't coming back 'til Wednesday. Is everything fixed now?"

"I took care of issues that personally needed my attention in half a day. The rest, I left with my 2IC to finalize." His hands are on my legs, making their way underneath my nightshirt.

All the butterflies begin fluttering wildly in my stomach when he stops just below my breasts.

"Aren't you tired? Would you like me to get you something?" I ask, my breath too heavy with need for him.

Magnus gives me that sexy smirk. "No ... on both questions. I just want you."

"Good answer," I let my hand travel up to the back of his head. "You've no idea how happy I am that you're here."

"Then show me," he growls, his eyes hungry.

With a moan, I push his head down, smashing our lips together. I let out a gasp when I feel his hands on my naked breasts, squeezing them, making my nipples pebble in his touch.

At this moment, I know I need to see all of him. I push him off and on his back before straddling him between my legs.

I pause to admire him, as he lies down underneath me. His eyes are like a sea of dark pools, and they are honed on me and waiting for my next move. He's still wearing his crisp, white button-down shirt, now with two buttons undone, exposing a smattering of his chest hair. His hair, which was styled this morning, is now a gorgeous mess from running both our fingers through it. His big, strong hands are on my hips, holding me firmly.

I slowly unbutton his shirt, my eyes hungrily fixed on him. He exhales loudly as my hands skim over his naked chest, feeling every hard sinew. I remove my own nightshirt, exposing my breasts and leaving me with only my panties on.

"I missed you so much, it was driving me insane," I murmur as I bend down to leave a trail of kisses from his lips down to his neck, my nipples grazing his torso.

Magnus lifts his head and inhales my neck, and I moan when I feel his wet tongue follow the curve between my shoulder and neck. "All day, I've been thinking about your face, and your scent, and your sweet fucking taste." He fists my hair and nudges my head down so he can lick my lips. But I catch his wicked tongue, and I suck it like I would his cock.

And oh my, how hard does his cock feel against my moistened crotch. I can't help but grind my sex against his own, the thin materials of our clothing becoming a frustrating barrier that I want to get rid of.

He sits up to remove his shirt, and in my impatience, I move downwards so I can unbuckle his belt and pull off his gray trousers. Feeling bold, I stand over him and shimmy off of my panties, my eyes never leaving his smouldering blues.

"Your turn," I command, and he complies with a crooked smile, deftly removing his black boxer briefs and showing me what I've longed to see.

Magnus grabs me by my wrist and pulls me back on top of him, kissing me hungrily. In one swift move, he's on top and in between my legs, our naked bodies forming a single unit.

"I have to be inside you, Isabelle. I need to feel your perfect pussy around my cock."

His fingers glide over my crevice, and hisses a 'yes' because I'm slick and ready. Then he slides the same moist fingertips over my lips. But before I can even taste myself, his mouth is over mine as he licks and sucks my already swollen mouth.

"Every part of you is so fucking sweet." And in one big thrust, Magnus fills me utterly and completely. He doesn't move at once, but he just stares into my eyes. I notice awe in those darkened blues but there's also torment. Why does he feel tormented? Isn't he happy like I am since we're together now?

"Baby, what's wrong?" I graze my thumb on the slight wrinkling between his brows, trying to smoothen them out.

In one blink, whatever anguish I saw in those eyes is gone. Now all I see is lust. Pure. Unadulterated. Lust. For me.

He pulls his hips back and thrusts back in, making us moan in unison. He continues over and over again, gaining momentum and taking my breath away.

We make love like our lives depended on it, communicating all our unsaid feelings for each other through our touch and our kisses. Our climax is simultaneous and primal, leaving us both exhausted but satiated in each other's arms.

CHAPTER 13

"Are you staying?" My fingers are tracing the ridges of his torso with my head perched on the crook of his shoulder.

"Would you like me to stay?" Magnus sleepily asks, stroking my hair slowly.

"Yes."

"Then I'm not leaving this bed." And he kisses the top of my head so we can both surrender to slumber.

"Mommy! Wake up, Mommy!" I stir up to Ethan's knocking at my bedroom door.

"Oh, shit," I whisper with a jerk. I turn around, and Magnus is still in deep sleep … naked, with his arm possessively around my bare waist. I smile at the serenity of his handsome face. It takes a lot of my self-control to stop myself from touching his stubbled cheek and kissing him.

"Mommy, open the door!"

Oops, I almost forgot my son's knocking! I do my best not to wake Magnus up, knowing he's still tired from the flight and from … well ... I bite my lower lip at the memory of our lovemaking few hours ago. To call it amazing is understating it.

I carefully remove his muscular arm off my waist, and I get off the bed, covering him with the duvet until he's decent, before hastily putting on my underwear and nightclothes. I tiptoe towards the door, opening it a crack.

"Mommy, why do you have the door locked? You never lock your door," Ethan reprimands me, his face in a frown as he tries to get inside.

I put my forefinger up to my lips, motioning him to be quiet, and I walk out of the room with him, closing the door softly.

"Sorry, baby, but I locked the room because Magnus is inside sleeping. He's very tired from his business trip."

Ethan's eyes light up at the news. "Magnus is here? Yay!"

I put my forefinger up my lips again. "We have to keep quiet so he can sleep, okay?"

Ethan nods. "Okay, but can I see him later? Can he take me to school?"

I bend down to his level, my voice soft but firm. "Honey, I don't think—"

"Sure, buddy. Your mom and I will take you," Magnus interrupts, making me jump. I swiftly turn around at his direction. I didn't hear him get up or open the bedroom door.

He has a big smile on his face, he put his trousers on haphazardly, and has yet to button his shirt. But damn, he looks mighty fine, even when unkempt.

"Magnus!" Ethan screams, and he runs towards Magnus to give him a big hug, almost throwing him off-balance.

"Whoa, easy there, buddy!" he says with a laugh. I notice how his expression always softens at the sight of my son, but his eyes still betray some sadness. It breaks my own heart every time, knowing why it was put in there in the first place.

Magnus sneaks a glance at me, and I give him a reassuring smile.

"Would you like to wake Michelle up, honey?" I ask Ethan, who beams at Magnus before making his way towards Michelle's room to wake her up.

Magnus walks over and gives me a chaste kiss, before squeezing my ass cheek and making me squeal.

"Morning, sexy," he growls in my ear.

He pulls me back inside my room, and he shows me in the quickest way he can, how sexy he truly thinks of me.

After breakfast, we all prepare to head out, with Alex already waiting for us outside next to the Cayenne. Magnus looks great in his gray suit, a fresh, white button-down shirt, a striped tie, and black oxfords. I decide to wear a simple black midi dress with a chunky red necklace.

We drop off Ethan at school, and like before, I notice parents and teachers giving Magnus gaping glances. It makes me a little uncomfortable, knowing this is the sort of thing I have to deal with every time I'm with him. But he seems so used to it that he just takes it all in stride.

The car ride to work is quiet. Magnus is busy writing an e-mail on his iPad but once in a while, he holds my hand or squeeze my leg, making me feel cherished.

And at this moment, I know that I will not care less if people find out about our relationship. Even if Magnus never professed his love for me, I am still his as he is mine.

We're at the stoplight a few blocks away from Grant Corp, when Magnus turns to me. "Would you like Alex to drop you off at the same block?"

I turn to Magnus, startled by his question but even more so at the way his jaw is clenching. Like he's anticipating that I'll say yes.

"No, we can get off together."

"So you're finally proud to show me off?" he teases with a cocked brow and a silly grin on his face.

I reciprocate with a big smile of my own. "Actually I want *you* to show me off!" I laugh, jabbing his chest with my forefinger.

"Anytime, baby, anytime." And he ducks his head and kisses me. Then he nibbles my neck until his mouth touches my ear. "And for the record, I love getting off with you too."

Oh. My. God.

I'm still blushing from Magnus's last comment when Alex stops in front of Grant Corp. He gets off the car and walks around to wait at the sidewalk. I hurriedly straighten myself up, hoping I don't look like I just had a make out session with the big boss man himself.

I steal a glance at Magnus, who's looking at me with amusement. That's when I notice a small smear of lipstick at the corner of his lips! I lift my forefinger to quickly wipe it off, but he catches my hand and kisses the tip of it instead.

"Uh-uh. Leave it, Isabelle." He tangles our fingers together in an attempt to stop me. Not that I'm complaining, anyway ... I love how his hands engulf my own.

"But people will see—"

"That I've been marked by my woman? Good! I want everyone to know who owns these lips." He smiles against my knuckles as he presses his lips softly.

Oh holy hell.

Magnus unlocks the door so Alex can open it, with Magnus still holding my hand possessively.

"You ready?" he asks, his voice soft and comforting.

No, I'm not! I suddenly realize. But looking at Magnus and how proud he seems to show me off, all of my anxiety just ebbs away. "Oh, screw it. I'm done hiding. At least, I'm not hiding what we have, Magnus."

He rewards me with a drop-dead gorgeous smile that shows how happy he is with my answer.

"But … we still have to keep it professional," I remind him firmly before he gets off. He pulls me towards him and helps me off the car. I look around me, still conscious of how this may appear with the rest of the Grant Corp staff.

He dips his head, and I notice a few people looking and whispering at each other. "I'll keep it professional. But not in my office."

"Magnus," I hiss with gritted teeth.

"My office, my rules." And with our hands still linked, he leads me inside his building.

"Good morning," Magnus greets the whole front desk staff, unaffected by their stunned expressions at the sight of us together.

People are starting to greet Magnus, and he greets them back politely. I try to place some distance between us, hoping I can blend into the background. I don't think I'll ever be ready for the kind of attention he gets. I try to let go of his hand, but he refuses to loosen his hold.

Thankfully, he was forced to let go when an acquaintance offers his hand in a handshake, which he gruffly accepts. I step inside the elevator as soon as it opens, leaving Magnus to continue his conversation with the other suit. I see him seek for me, and he frowns when he sees me inside at the far end. I give him a wicked smile and shrug my shoulders as the doors close, leaving him behind.

Finally reaching my desk, I notice a few odd glances go my way. *Geez, news really do travel fast around here.* Just then, my desk phone starts to ring. It's Marla.

"Hey, Marla. Good morning."

"Oh, my God. Wait, I'll conference you."

Before I can utter a word, I'm put on hold for a second as Marla tries to connect me with whom I assume is Jess.

"Billie? You there?" Marla asks.

"Yes," I reply exasperatedly. "What's up?"

"Is it true?" It's Jessica's voice.

I can feel my hand feeling clammy all of a sudden, and my heart beating nervously. I know what they're going to ask.

"About?" I ask, stalling.

"A couple of people saw you get out of Mr. Grant's car!" Jessica exclaims.

"Oh, and apparently he helped you out of the car, and you were holding hands … with Mr. Grant. Fucking holding hands, Billie!" Marla squeals.

"Shhh! Marla!" I whisper harshly.

"Sorry, I got excited. Are you two dating? When did this even happen?" Marla asks persistently.

Damn it. Here comes the shit storm.

"Well?" Marla persists.

"It's all new … so new there's really nothing to talk about," I explain unconvincingly, wishing the floor just swallows me up.

"Bullshit! You're lying!" Marla concludes a little too loudly for my liking.

Jess shushes Marla before speaking with me.

"Billie," she starts softly, "it is kind of a big deal. He's Magnus Grant, the owner of the company, and you work for him. I mean, sure, we joke about it, but this sort of fraternizing might get you both in hot water. I especially don't want you to get the short end of the stick either. Just be careful, okay?"

I know … I know. Maybe coming out as a couple isn't such a good idea after all.

"I appreciate your concern, but we both know how risky this could be … Look, I have to go. Talk soon." And I hang up like the phone is on fire.

The rest of the morning flies by, and I barely notice that it's lunchtime as I'm doing my finishing touches on a PowerPoint presentation for Charles's meeting. I make it a point to keep myself busy because if I don't, I'll only be thinking about Magnus, and it's very distracting. I jump when I hear my phone ring, and I quickly pick it up.

"Good afternoon. Mr. Dune's office."

"I miss you," the low, sexy voice at the other end sends my nerves into overdrive.

"Hey … you," I answer back awkwardly while looking around me. I don't even know how I'll refer to him when he calls or speaks to me at work.

"Hey, you? Hmm, we need to work on that. How about you come upstairs, Isabelle? I need to kiss you, or I'm going to go insane. And then after, we'll have lunch and we'll discuss this 'hey you' situation. Then after that, I can have you for desert."

Holy shit, what did he just say?

"Well, I *am* hungry," I tease.

His voice is thick and rough, like a man whose need has to be satiated. "For what, baby? Tell me what you're hungry for,"

That's an easy one. "For you. Always you." I hear his breathing hitch, getting me even more excited. "I'll be there shortly."

"Hurry." And we both hang up.

Upstairs, Denise just waves me in with a knowing smile. I can't figure out whether to smile back or be embarrassed.

I raise my hand to knock on Magnus's door but before I can, the door opens, and he pulls me in, making me gasp in surprise. He slams the door behind me and lifts me up against the wall next to it so my dress hitches up to my hips, and my legs are wrapped around his waist.

"Finally." Then he slams his mouth on me like a predator feeding on a willing prey. He grinds his hips, and I feel how much he really, really wants me. I'm absolutely breathless against his lips and the way his tongue draws me into submission. Then I feel his hand sweep over the thin cotton covering my sex.

"Baby, you're warm and wet. Tell me whose this is?"

I look him straight in the eyes, his pupils dilated with lust. "Only yours."

"Only mine." He buries his head against my neck, inhaling me and leaving soft kisses against my skin.

Then I hear a rip as he tears the delicate material of my panties. But I don't care. Right now I need to feel him inside of me. His mouth is on me, as I hear his zipper slide downwards. I breathe in deeply, trying to prepare for what comes next …

"Oh, my God, Magnus!" I whimper, and he pauses so I can stretch to his size.

"What do you want, Isabelle?" he asks, our foreheads touching and his breathing warm and delicious against my mouth.

"I want you to fuck me," I plead, feeling my insides throbbing to the point of convulsing.

"Is this what you want?" And he thrusts, hard and fast. I hold on to him for dear life as the force of his every push hits me in that spot. It doesn't take long and I see stars, so I keep my eyes shut, hoping to gain some control.

"Open your eyes and let go, baby," he commands softly. And so I do. I open my eyes and look straight into his, and I see how he sees *me*.

God, and how *he's* coming undone for me.

"Magnus ..." He's too much, too beautiful, too good to be true, and he's making me come so ... damn ... hard! With a guttural growl, he follows soon after, filling me with his seed as he presses his lips against mine, thrusting his tongue in rhythm with every stroke of his hips.

Magnus still has me leaning against the wall as we try to catch our breath, with him still inside of me. The silence is broken when my stomach decides to make its hunger known.

"Hungry?" a chuckling Magnus asks.

Biting my lip to mask my embarrassed smile, I nod my head in agreement.

"Then I better get you fed, my hungry little temptress."

And after he cleans me up in that caring way he does, he leads me to the table by the window where our lunch is waiting. I titter as he pulls me onto his lap instead of the seat across from him. But as soon as I see the assortment of sushi and sashimi laid on a tray, I hear my stomach grumble again. I try to grab one of the chopsticks, but Magnus beats me to it.

"Uh-uh. I'm feeding you, remember?" he playfully reminds me before clinching a piece of salmon nigiri and dipping it in soy sauce.

"Open," he commands, and I do so willingly. The salmon is fresh and the sushi rice, soft and fluffy. A moan slips from my mouth as I'm chewing, mostly because it's so delicious, but also because Magnus feeding me is such a turn on.

"Good?" he asks in a low voice. He's staring at my mouth while I'm chewing, and I nod before brushing my lips against his.

"Hmmm. I never thought I'd get so hard watching someone eat raw fish and rice," he murmurs against my ear, and I believe him since I can feel him under my ass. I try to cross my legs tightly. With Magnus destroying my underwear, I cannot afford to mess my skirt.

He wraps me tightly in his arms and slides his tongue across my mouth as if to taste me. I reciprocate by feeding him sushi with my own hand, then sliding my own tongue across his mouth. So engrossed are we with our feeding and licking that we didn't hear the commotion from outside Magnus's office.

The door swings open, startling us both. I'm still on Magnus's lap when in comes a woman, looking svelte and glamorous in a navy blue tailored skirt and a white silky top, with a few top buttons open, showing off strands of pearls on her tanned chest. Her heels, which has to be Laboutins, emphasizes her long legs.

The expression on her face changes from mirth to surprise to displeasure at the sight of Magnus locked in an embrace with me. In the meantime, my expression is probably stuck on shock.

I try to pull away from Magnus, suddenly feeling intimidated by this woman's presence. But Magnus refuses to let me go.

"Magnus, please. Keep it professional, remember?" I whisper, and thankfully he accedes and we both stand up, with me all flushed and Magnus surprisingly collected.

"Well, well, what do we have here?" The svelte-looking woman purposely strides towards the minibar, helping herself to a drink, her eyes coldly scanning me from head to foot. She is obviously familiar with his office and knows where everything is.

I notice Denise is standing by the doorway, looking panicked and a little afraid. Magnus nods to her, still poker-faced, and she takes this as a signal and leaves the office.

"Martine, I'm sure you've heard the concept of knocking. Maybe you should start practicing it," Magnus tells her in a cool and detached voice.

Martine. I might as well throw in the towel now. I cast a tentative glance at Magnus, trying to gauge if she's an expected or an unwelcome visitor.

"Sorry, babe. I know our meeting isn't until one, but I thought I'd surprise you. Well, it looks like the surprise is on me." Martine looks towards me with a cocked brow.

Did she just call Magnus, 'Babe?' Really? Heat rises up inside of me, suddenly feeling proprietary over the man beside me.

"It shouldn't be surprising since I've spoken about Isabelle with you." Magnus tangles my hand firmly in his as he closes our distance with his former childhood sweetheart.

"But you're right. Introductions are in order. Martine, I'd like you to meet *my* girlfriend, Isabelle Morrison. Isabelle, this is Martine Harper, a family friend."

"Family friend? Cute touch. And you forgot to mention ex-wife and future business partner. Hello, … pleasure." She offers her hand out for a handshake, but she chooses to offer the hand that forces me to let go of Magnus. I notice Magnus's jaw clench at her act.

Her hands are soft, and her nails are manicured to perfection. I haven't even been in a nail salon in years.

"It's nice to meet you too," I reply, trying to stand my full height though still falling short.

"Well, as you can see, my girlfriend and I are not done with our lunch yet. Denise will take you to the meeting room. If you'd like some coffee or tea, she'll be happy to assist you." Magnus escorts Martine out of his office before she can protest. Thankfully, Denise is waiting outside, and she leads her down the hallway.

Magnus closes the door behind him, and we are by ourselves again.

"Wow, that was … pretty awkward," I speak out softly, not wanting her to hear us.

"Sorry about that, she can be very pushy when she wants to be." Magnus walks towards me, placing his hands on my hips. "Now where were we?"

"Look," I gently take his hands off. "I have to go. Lunch break is almost over, anyway." I start walking away from him, but he goes for my hand. The way his touch wreaks havoc to my insides is undeniable, that it makes me suck my breath in.

"Please stay," he urges in a soft tone. "Martine's just here to discuss a business proposal, that's all."

I know Magnus is trying to clear the air, but I can feel the weight of history between them like a truckload of cement, and I feel disconcerted by how obvious Martine's feelings are for Magnus. I can't compete with her. She's on a different level altogether. I feel a dull ache in my chest because the truth hits me—*I'm jealous. So jealous it literally hurts.*

"So you're doing business with her? Then I shouldn't be around for that." I firmly pull out of Magnus's grip. "Thank you for the lunch. It was … interesting." I move closer to give him a chaste kiss on the cheek, sadly knowing our moment is definitely gone.

He turns his head, and I feel his warm lips against my cheek. "I'm taking you home tonight."

"Don't worry about it. I don't know what time I'm finishing up, anyway."

"I'm not offering, Isabelle. I *am* taking you home tonight." He pulls away slightly, and I can see that he's serious.

I turn and look away, trying to sound detached. "Whatever. Just do what you want."

I start walking towards the door, just as I hear him curse sharply under his breath. I resist turning back, continuing out of his office instead. A little part of me is hoping he'll call out my name, but sadly, it doesn't happen.

I head straight down the hallway, past the meeting room where Martine's waiting. I hear her speaking with someone on the phone, letting out a melodic laugh, intentionally ignoring me as I pass by.

Denise gives me an apologetic smile as she sees me walking towards the doors.

"Sorry about that, Billie. Ms. Harper's not the type to take instructions from a lowly assistant. Her words, I swear," she whispers, rolling her eyes and pursing her lips.

"It's okay, I was about to leave myself," I shrug, trying to sound unaffected.

"Billie, please don't think I'm being brash, but I can see that Magnus really cares for you. Don't let his ex intimidate you, okay?"

Her words surprise me. Am I that transparent, or does Magnus talk about me with Denise? "Thanks, Denise. I appreciate that." I offer her a small smile. "I have to go now." I give her a small wave and head out to the elevator.

Back at my desk, my thoughts revert to the events that happened earlier, and I struggle with the conflicting feelings inside of me. Have I fallen for Magnus too fast? What if he doesn't feel as strongly as I do and now that she's back, decides to go back to Miss First Love? It makes me angry, mostly towards myself because I let him in so quickly. But I can't blame him either. He never said he loved me, so I really have nothing of his to hold on to.

I need to talk to Michelle. She understands me, and she gives me the best advice. But her relationship with Nathan is so new that I don't want to mess that up with my insecurities.

Then a thought occurs to me. I haven't booked my session with Dr. Mitchell yet! She's helped me before, and she can help me again.

Luckily, her phone number is still in my contacts list. I call up her practice, and the receptionist answers. Unfortunately, she tells me there's no availability any other day this week. But there was a cancellation for an appointment at five-thirty. I take this afternoon's appointment, knowing the sooner I talk to Dr. Mitchell, the better.

The next person I call is Michelle to let her know about my session with Dr. Mitchell tonight. She sounds enthused and assures me that I shouldn't worry about Ethan tonight. It's more important that I continue with my therapy.

I busy myself with work for the rest of the day, making sure I'm done by five o'clock so I can make it to my appointment. I decide against telling Magnus about my session with Dr. Mitchell. I can't face him right now. I'm still unsure about how I feel with him, not telling me about his business deals with Martine.

I'm in the subway when my phone rings. It's Magnus, of course. I press *Decline*, placing my phone back in my purse. After a minute or so, I hear it buzz, and I frown after reading his text message. '*Answer your phone, Isabelle! Where are you?*'

I put my phone on silent. Maybe Mr. Bossy will get the message and leave me alone if I ignore him.

I get off at my stop and walk the next block to Dr. Mitchell's clinic. Inside, the receptionist gives me a smile and confirms my appointment. I still have five minutes to spare before my session, so I use this time to collect my thoughts about what I should discuss with Dr. Mitchell.

"Billie? Long time no see. Come on inside, please." Dr. Mitchell is waiting for me by the doorway, her gentle tone welcoming and pleasant. I stand up, giving her a smile as I walk inside her office. It *has* been awhile, and I didn't think I'd want to come back here again.

"Hello, Dr. Mitchell. It's nice to see you again." I sit on my usual spot on the couch. I survey the room, and except for the lamp and some new fixtures, her office still looks pretty much the same.

"And it's nice to see *you* again. Although I must admit, I'm quite surprised when I saw your name today." She takes a seat on her armchair and takes her notebook and pen. "So how have you been since our last session? That was two years ago, wasn't it?"

"Yeah. It's been up and down. I wanted to continue to see you, but money was tight ..."

Dr. Mitchell nods, her face kind. "Well, you're here now. So tell me, what brought you here?"

"My nightmares have come back. I mean, I used to have them on and off before and could only remember some bits and pieces, but recently, they've gotten a lot worse. I thought I got rid of them." My heart starts to beat as I relive those awful dreams—those flashbacks I'd give anything to get rid of.

"Like I told you before, we can never guarantee that your nightmares will never resurface. Sometimes, all it takes is a certain trigger to relive those memories. Do you remember any significant events that happened prior to the recurrence?"

My heart starts to thud when I realize what the parallel event was.

"I met a man around that time," I answered softly.

Dr. Mitchell nods as she begins writing on her tablet. "Is this person still around?"

"Yes."

"In our past sessions, you told me that a man's touch made you nauseous, and we were trying to work on that before you stopped coming for your sessions. The trauma you've experienced years ago resonated in your anxiety to start new relationships." She pauses.

"Tell me, how does this new man make you feel? Do you feel the same kind of nauseous feelings when he touches you?"

"No, he makes me feel ... different."

"In what way?"

"I like it when he touches me. He makes me feel good ... safe." I feel myself blush bright pink.

"So what makes him different from the other men who made you uncomfortable?"

"I don't know. He just is." I've forgotten how it feels like an interrogation in here sometimes.

"Okay," she takes down notes and continues, "so when did your dreams start to intensify? Was it before or after you've met this new person?"

"It got more vivid after we … um … kissed." I shift from my seat, starting to feel uncomfortable.

Dr. Mitchell raises her brows and nods, but her face doesn't give much away.

"I see. Do you feel that your bad dreams have a link to your current relationship?"

"I can't honestly classify what I have with this guy as a relationship. To be honest, I'm confused most of the time."

Dr. Mitchell taps her pen on her chin and regards me thoughtfully. But she doesn't say a word.

So I continue, "I just want my nightmares to go away permanently, Dr. Mitchell. My son has been hearing me cry, and it's distressing him, as well."

She nods with an intent look on her face. "Would you like to tell me what you remember?"

I finish my session feeling a little lighter than when I came in. But when I open the door to leave Dr. Mitchell's practice, I stop dead on my tracks halfway down the steps. The last person I want to see right now is standing outside, staring at me with a big frown on his face. But it's the way his expression quickly changes to relief the moment he sees me that throws me off-balance.

"Magnus? How the hell did you find me?" I ask, bewildered.

He's in front of me in seconds. "You had me worried sick, Isabelle. I had to call your house. Luckily, Michelle was there to tell me where you are. Why weren't you answering your calls? And why didn't you even tell me you went to see your therapist?"

I can't do this with him right now. He's treating me like a fucking child! I'm a grown woman, for goodness sake! I have been through a barrage of questions with Dr. Mitchell, and I'm not about to go through another interrogation with Magnus.

I shake my head and brush past him. But he goes after me, his long strides catching up to mine with no effort at all.

"Isabelle, wait!"

"I can't deal with you right now. Please. I just need some space!" I say out aloud, quickening my pace.

"Is that what you want? space? Is that what your therapist told you?"

I stop walking, turning towards him. He looks at me with a wounded look in his eyes, and my heart drops. The last thing I want is to hurt him, even though I'm hurting right now, as well.

"No." I run my fingers through my hair in frustration. "I'm just tired, Magnus. And I just want to go home." I cover my eyes with my hand, trying to hide the tears that threaten to betray my stance.

"Then let me take you home," he insists gently as he reaches up to hook loose strands of hair behind my ear. The slight contact with his fingers sends currents of electricity through me. Just like his touch always does.

My head is down, unable to look at him because my tears can't be stopped. "Why are you doing this? I am so fucking damaged, Magnus. You deserve better, someone strong like Martine, in fact," I whisper out, my voice trembling.

"We are not talking about this again. I *want*. To *be*. With *you*. So talking yourself down like this hurts me, as well." He pulls me in his arms and embraces me. My tears are making his expensive shirt moist, so I try to push away. But he won't let go.

I feel his warm mouth against my ear, "C'mon, people are starting to look at us, and they're probably thinking I'm being a complete asshole to you," he whispers.

What he said makes me chuckle. "Well, you are, sometimes," I tease him softly.

He lets out a small laugh, pulling me closer as he walks me back to his car. He opens the door for me and kisses the top of my head before he helps me in. He leans over to his glove box and quietly hands me some tissues, which I use to tidy up my face.

We drive back to my place in silence. Once in a while, Magnus reaches out for my hand, lacing his fingers with mine, and making me feel all sorts of tingly inside.

"Would you like me to come up with you, or do you still need your space tonight?" he asks as he parks the car near my apartment.

"I think, that considering the circumstances, it's best if you go home. I'll be okay."

I see the disappointment in his eyes, but he nods in acknowledgment. "Okay, space it is."

I raise my hand to touch his cheek, and he leans to kiss the palm of my hand. As I feel my heartbeat quickens at his gesture, it makes me wonder if I'll regret my decision to not let him stay. I probably will. But I think we both need this space. We're too intense together and maybe tonight, we just need to take a little breather. I give him a tender kiss on the lips which he returns with equal ardor. But before our kiss gets any deeper, I pull away. He lets out a big sigh at my sudden retreat.

"Goodnight, Magnus. And thank you for finding me and taking me home."

"And I'd do it all over again. Goodnight, my temptress."

I close his car door and make my way to my apartment building, knowing he's watching my every move until I get inside. Once I'm inside the building, he drives off, and I suddenly feel emptiness inside of me.

Ethan has just changed to his pj's, and his face lights up as soon as he sees me walk in.

"Mommy!" He runs to give me the best welcome any mom can ask for.

"You're late!" he reprimands with a cute little frown on his face.

"I'm so sorry, baby. Mommy just had to take care of stuff."

"So it's taken care of?" his question makes me smile. If only it were that simple.

"It will be, baby." And I give him another hug and a kiss.

CHAPTER 14

I wake up the next morning in cold sweat, breathing heavily and clutching my duvet. I check the time, and it's only two o'clock. My hands are shaky, and my legs are wobbly as I try to reach for my notebook. It's happened again.

I remember the fear when I woke up after blacking out, the uncertainty at what happened, and the pain I felt, after *he* took what I've held precious in my teenage life. He took my virginity, and he violated parts of my body that were supposed to be taboo. It hurt so much that I cried out from the pain, both physical and emotional. I remember hearing him come back in the room where he held me captive, and I know for sure it was Cooper. He sounded high or drunk, but I recognize his voice from anywhere. It was the same tone of voice he had when he felt the need to remind me who was boss throughout our relationship. And God, he was aggressive … and so damned cruel. I remember how he tried to cover my nose and my mouth at one point during a fight and how he punched my stomach when I tried to fight back or got all bitchy towards him.

I remember them all. And after all these years, that episode in my life still leaves me angry, abandoned, and alone. I never told anyone because he told me he loved me, and he needed to do it because he wanted me to be perfect so we can get married. And I believed every fucking word he said. Until he took it so far that he finally broke me. That was when I knew I had to run as far away as I could go.

As I write down the details that Dr. Mitchell needs, I remember how Cooper vehemently denied that he did it. And no one believed me, not my family, nor my friends. After all, he was supposed to be my boyfriend. And he was supposed to be a God-fearing son of a mayor while I was the spoiled, attention-seeking daughter of a construction magnate. I had no proof, except for Ethan. But by then, I've ran away and only found out I was pregnant afterwards. The last thing I want is for him or his family to know about my son. My son will not go through the trauma of knowing that his father was abusive and a rapist.

I'm unable to sleep after I finish writing. I check the time, it's one-thirty. Great. I pad to the kitchen to make myself some chamomile tea.

Back in the bedroom, I grab my cell phone, in two minds, while staring at Magnus's name in my contacts list. I want to talk to him so badly, to tell him to come over. But I can't be that selfish especially after I refused his offer for him to stay with me.

Still wanting that connection with him, I resort to sending him a text message instead. At least he can read it later this morning. *'Hey. Couldn't sleep. Sorry if I woke you up. Just have you in my thoughts and I hope you're having sweet dreams .... XO, Your Isabelle.'*

I finish my tea and lie down in my bed, staring at the ceiling, until the lull inside the room soothes me down, and I close my eyes in pursuit of slumber.

Buzz! Buzz! My eyes shoot up when I hear my phone vibrates. My heart leaps when I see Magnus's name flashing on the screen. *'I miss you baby, more than you know. Your M.'*

His message makes my heart flutter. *Your M.* I still have a smile on my face as my now sleepy eyes close, and I drift off in a thankfully dreamless sleep.

***

Work is crazy today, and even Magnus is scarce. Except for a short message or two on my cell phone to check on me, he is too busy to even get a hold to. By the end of the day, he gives me a call to say he's sorry he can't take me home today, but Alex will drive me home instead. He also reminds me about the charity event this Saturday. I say yes on both, but I can't help the nervousness I feel at meeting the Grant family for the first time.

It's a quiet night at home. The three of us—Michelle, Ethan, and myself, discuss Ethan's upcoming birthday party which will be in a few weeks' time. We decide to have his party at home to save money, but I reassure Ethan that I'm planning a number of fun games to keep his guests entertained. His good friends from school are coming, so it should be a good day for everyone.

Before going to bed, I do a quick check on my cell phone. My heart dips when there are still no messages or phone calls from Magnus. *What happened to him?* Is he still giving me the space I want? I decide to call him, and my heart jumps when I hear his voice on the other line. But I can barely hear him from the loud music in the background.

"Hello? Magnus?" I ask aloud, but not too loud so as not to wake my already sleeping son.

"Isabelle? Hey, is everything okay?" he asks, sounding somehow distracted.

"I'm okay. Where are you?"

"I'm at Cirque. We're entertaining some potential business partners," he answers, sounding a little on edge.

"Okay, then I won't keep you. I just got worried that I didn't hear from you, that's all," I explain with a tinge of sadness, hating myself a little for sounding clingy.

"I'm sorry, Isabelle. I've just been busy with work. I'll call you later, okay?" He sounds sincere, and it makes me feel a touch better.

Then I hear a woman's haughty yet regrettably familiar voice in the background, interrupts, "Who's that, babe? Is that the little slut from your office calling you?" The remark was immediately followed by Magnus's muffled chastising words, possibly directed towards the source of the bitchy remark.

Little slut? What the fuck is going on? Is Martine the supposed guest he's entertaining?

It takes a lot for me not to march my angry ass to Cirque and slap the pretty out of that woman. But she's not worth it. And if this *thing* I have with Magnus ends, and after this call it might as well be, I'd like for it to end, while holding on to whatever dignity I have left.

"Isabelle, I'm sorry." Magnus's voice is a mix of anger and remorse. But I can't let him continue. I can't stand to hear any more of his excuses.

"Yeah, well, I'm sorry too. It looks like you've got your hands full. Don't let this little slut keep you, ever again. Good-bye." And I hang up, with my heart ripping off my chest.

Stupid! Stupid! Stupid! Why did I even think I have a chance with him?

The dam is broken, and my tears are pouring down my face, my sobs becoming uncontrollable. I feel like such a fool, believing that he truly cares for me and that he'll keep me safe. But he's the same as all the other rich, entitled douchebags I've known.

I punch at my pillows and bury my face in them. Why am I so fucking gullible? I opened up to him, trusted him, and even fell for him. And just when I asked for some space to work on my issues, he's off with his ex, Martine.

Hah! Family friend, my ass!

My whole body is shaking with anger and betrayal, and I completely lose it, crying my heart out on my pillow, muffling the sound so Ethan doesn't hear me.

My phone vibrates again, and it's Magnus. I press *Decline*. He rings again after a minute, and I decline again, eventually switching off my phone altogether, before closing my eyes and hoping sleep just takes over.

Half of me never want to return to Grant Corp. Maybe I just won't. I can't bear to go inside his building. I'll fake a sickness. I need to be away from Magnus and everything that will remind me of him. But who am I kidding? I need this job. My immediate boss is good to me. Plus, I need the money so I can see Dr. Mitchell again. This is exactly why I should have kept away from Magnus. I'm such a fool!

I am lying in my bed for God knows how long, unable to sleep, my head throbbing with what promises to be a massive migraine. It's an unwelcome side effect for too much crying ... something I've gotten used to in the past years. After downing a dose of ibuprofen, I throw my head back onto the pillow.

It's barely half an hour after I lie down when I hear knocking on my bedroom door.

Michelle! Just leave me alone, please!

I get up once more, and I open the door, and Michelle is staring at me with her phone up, a displeased expression on her face.

"I'm sorry, but Magnus is calling me, yet *again*, and asking for you. I mean what the fuck? Why can't he call you?"

"Because I switched off my phone. I refuse to talk to him. Just hang up."

"Look, I don't know what he's done to you but deal with him or I will have to." She shoves her cell phone in my hand before she heads back to her bedroom. I stare at the phone for a second, trying to regain some bravado before pressing the *Hold* button.

"What do you want, Magnus? Was I not clear when I said good-bye?"

"Isabelle, you're overreacting. Look I'm just outside, please just let me in."

Shaking my head, I pad down the hallway to our front window, and I see Magnus looking up at me with a despairing look in his eyes. I can't help the tugging in my heart. How can I still have the urge to comfort him after what he's done?

"Please, Isabelle, let me in," he asks softly on the phone.

"No, I'm not letting you in. I'm coming outside," I reply before hanging up.

I retrieve my robe and wear it over my nightdress, before grabbing my keys and heading out. I check myself at the mirror next to the door. I look haggard, but I don't care. I just want this over and done with.

I open the main door to see Magnus, looking handsome as always, in his tight blue jeans and black button-down shirt with sleeves rolled up, showing his muscular arms. Both of his hands are in his jeans pockets. For such a powerful man, he looks lost, almost vulnerable. But my armor is up, and I try to do my best to appear unaffected by his presence.

"Well, I'm here now. You have five minutes before I go back upstairs." I cross my arms in front of me, reinforcing the barrier between us.

"Thank you for seeing me. I'm sorry you're upset, but Isabelle, you're overreacting."

What the? My eyes widen in indignation, "*I'm* overreacting? Maybe I'll just give you two minutes to explain, before I slam the door on your face so I can go back up."

"Don't do this. I was at the club with Martine, yes. But please believe me when I say we were entertaining prospective partners for a joint venture, that's it."

"Oh, that's right. You and Martine are 'business partners' now. Well, congrats to both of you," I answer sarcastically.

"I'm being honest with you. And I don't understand why you're getting upset. If it's because of what she said, I told her never to talk about you like that again or our business partnership is over. And anyway, didn't you ask me to give you space?"

"I …," I look up to him with wide eyes, shaking my head as I try to squeeze more words out but to no avail. Of course, he's right. *I* asked for space. And if he's being honest with me, then I should give him a chance.

"I'm sorry, you're right, Magnus. It's just that when I heard Martine's voice, I knew I just … I don't stand a chance with her," I sigh resignedly.

He raises his hand to cup my face, and I can't help but close my eyes. I need his touch. I haven't realized how much I miss it until now. "Baby, you have it the other way around."

I slowly open my eyes to look at his and my heart tightens at the way he's looking at me.

"You're worth fighting for, Isabelle. When will you ever realize that?"

"I'm sorry, Magnus. But … with me, and my brand of crazy, I just … I don't know how we can both survive this."

"We'll survive if we help each other heal … and until you feel ready, I'll fight for both of us. I'm not going anywhere," he whispers, coming close and burying his head in my hair and pressing his warm lips on my neck. Without warning, my lips start to tremble, and I call his name out breathlessly. He lifts his head, and his eyes seem to bore into mine, my eyes mirroring his.

"I'm going to kiss you now." And before I can utter a word, he dips his head and presses his lips onto mine.

I close my eyes involuntarily as our lips meld into one, giving each other comfort where no words are needed. And not long after, our kiss becomes more heated, more passionate, and more needy. I reach for his hand, and I take him inside the building and into the apartment, feeding off from his lips on the way.

We reach my bedroom where I quickly lock the door behind us. We both undress, our hands just as hungry for contact as we caress and grab whatever skin we can touch.

"Magnus …," I whisper as he runs his moist tongue on the curve of my neck.

"You'll always be mine, Isabelle. And I am yours … only yours," he murmurs hungrily.

We are both lying in my bed, naked, our bodies intertwined, trying to get as much skin contact as possible. His deft fingers find their way down, making me moist for him with every stroke on my clitoris. He groans as I massage his hard cock with both of my hands, biting on his lower lip like a woman possessed. I raise my leg up, bending my knee to give him better access to my pulsing need. I moan when I feel his two, then three fingers inside of me, stroking my inner core with such precision that I feel an inevitable orgasm building up.

"Come for me, Isabelle. I want to feel you come," he urges, looking into my eyes. And I heed, coming so hard that I bite on Magnus's shoulder, eliciting a throaty groan from him.

"Aahh!" I arch my back, still trembling when he moves downwards so his head is between my legs. Then I feel his tongue on my clitoris, prolonging the waves rushing out of my body. I gasp at the sensation of his warm tongue as it enters my slick core.

"Fuck, Isabelle, you taste so good," he huskily groans, as I watch him savor my throbbing pussy. The visual is too erotic that I climax once again.

Afterwards, he leaves light kisses on my inner thighs before kneeling between my legs.

"Go on all fours with your ass in front of me."

His commanding voice is rough, and the way his glazed eyes devour my whole body, makes my core throb in anticipation. I do as he says, raising my ass upwards, swaying it in front of him. I lick my lips with excitement at what comes next. He leans down, covering me with his body, and then he holds me by the neck, coaxing me to lift my head upwards to meet his. The act arches my body in an almost cat-like position, and as he bends down to give me a deep kiss, I feel his hard cock plunge deep inside me, deeper than I thought possible, filling me up completely. Hot damn, it feels incredible!

"Tell me if it's too much." He looks into my eyes, with my head still lifted upwards, his hands on my neck gently holding me firmly, but not painfully, in place. With powerful strokes he thrusts in and out of me.

I shake my head. "Ahh, no, it feels so good, baby," I mewl.

The deep eye connection we have is mind-blowing, like I'm completely letting him take over ... and it doesn't scare me one little bit. In fact, it gets me even closer to another orgasm.

Who knew it's even possible to come these many times?

I can see from his expression that he's closer to coming, as well. He squeezes his eyes shut, and gently lets my neck go, his hands gliding down my arched spine before holding on to my hips. I drop my head down, closing my eyes so I can savor every inch, every thrust. Then his speed increases, and I raise my hips further up, so my breasts are now brushing against the linen. The sensation of my nipples rubbing against my duvet feels so good that I muffle my moans on the bed.

"You … feel … amazing … my … beautiful … fucking … temptress," Magnus growls with every thrust.

I grab on to my duvet as his lunges slam me at the hilt, hitting that special spot. This is it, I can't hold on any longer.

"Let me feel it, baby." And as he reaches down for my swollen clit, my body explodes, shattering my whole being in the most delicious way.

"Yes, … Magnus!" My cries are thankfully muffled by the duvet, and before long, I am panting and out of breath.

"Hold on, fuck!" And with one hard thrust, he follows, filling me to the core.

We pause for a moment as we try to even our breathing out. Then we shift positions so that I'm lying on my back while he places his head between my breasts. A contented sigh escapes his throat, making me smile in return.

"So does this mean we're good, baby?" Magnus traces circles around the fleshy part of my breast, leaving goose bumps on my still sensitive skin.

"Yes, we're good, Magnus. And I'm sorry if I jumped into conclusions earlier. I do trust you, I do. It's just harder for me to get there." My voice trails off, unable to continue, hoping Magnus will understand without me explaining why.

Magnus raises his head and looks at me, and I'm sure he can see the trepidation in my eyes. But then the corners of his mouth begin to twitch up. "Well, at least I know your body's quite trusting of me already." Then he squeezes my breast, making we gasp.

I playfully slap him on the arm, thankful that my just-fucked blush is masking my embarrassed one.

"Hah, you wish!" I giggle.

"I don't wish, baby. I know." He leaves small kisses from my chest to my lips, lingering for a few seconds before he rolls over and gets off the bed. He grabs some tissues and does his ritual for me. Then I follow him with my eyes as he steps inside my bathroom. I lick my lips at the way the sinews on his back moves. And his ass ... that rock-hard ass. It's just not fair that one man can be this good-looking, sexy, and intelligent, and be a beast in the sack as well!

And he wants to fight for me ... for *us*.

He returns with a self-indulgent grin on his face, knowing that I've been watching his every move. Without thinking, my eyes travel down his cock ... semihard, but still formidable. I turn away, not wanting to get caught gawking at him like this. He lifts the duvet and joins me in bed, spooning me with his naked masculine body. The warmth emanating from him is comforting, and it doesn't take long before my body starts to give in to exhaustion.

"Goodnight, my Isabelle." Those are the last words I hear before my heavy-lidded eyes close.

I wake up to the sound of my alarm clock going off. I frown as I reach out to press the *Snooze* button. I turn around, wanting to give Magnus a morning embrace, but I'm stunned to realize he's gone. I check outside my bedroom. No sign of him. I check out the window for his car. It's not there either.

My frown grows, and I go back inside my room to check for any notes. None. I finally check my phone and lo and behold, there's a message from Magnus. '*I'm sorry I had to leave early. I have a very early breakfast meeting today, and I didn't want to wake you. I know how tired you must be, and I plan on working you even harder later.* ;) *M*'

I roll my eyes after reading his message but cannot wipe the big smile on my face. Seriously? He's winking at me? I send him my own brazen reply. '*Where do you plan on 'working me' harder, exactly? In your office, boardroom table, or my office desk? *wink**'

Not even five minutes after my message is sent, I receive another one from him: '*All of the above! Btw, I am in the middle of a meeting, trying to cover up the hard-on you just gave me.* ☹'

I gasp at his reply, covering my mouth to curb my giggling. I can't believe I can get him hard with just a text message! I love this playful side of him! It makes me look forward to getting to work to see if he's really going to live up to his word.

For someone who has almost zero hours of sleep, I'm feeling very buoyant today. I guess knowing that all is well between us, has given be the extra boost.

I get up from the bed and make my way to the kitchen with a spring on my every step.

Ethan is awake, and he walks to the kitchen with uneasy steps, still hazy from last night's slumber. It makes me hope he didn't overhear anything last night.

"Good morning, handsome! Did you have a nice sleep last night?" I ask as I prepare his favorite cereal for breakfast.

He sits down at his usual seat at the dining table, and he gives me a sweet but still sleepy smile.

"Yeah, I wanted to tell you about this awesome dream I had but now I can't remember it."

I breathe out a sigh of relief. This means his sleep was deep enough that he didn't hear anything.

Michelle walks in the kitchen with a look that clearly says, 'We have to talk.'

I give her my 'Don't start with me' look in return.

"I know you don't want to, right now, but we need to talk," she tells me out of Ethan's earshot.

"We *talk* all the time, Michelle. Don't worry, I got this, okay?" I snap back at her, hoping she'll back off.

But I instantly regret it. I know she's just after my best interest.

"Look, Michelle, seriously, Magnus and I are fine. We worked it out. You know I just have some trust issues that I need to work on."

"I just hate to see you go back in that bad place, Billie." Michelle's voice is full of concern, and I stare at her in stunned silence.

I remember vividly that time in my life five years ago, and it involved a lot of pills and I being taken to the hospital with a very worried best friend and a none-the-wiser two-year-old son holding a vigil by my bedside. I don't remember much of it, but apparently, I saw something in the news about Cooper's father running for the Senate, with my family behind him. And *he* was there, right behind his father, next to my parents, with a fucking dignified look on his face. Like he never did what he did to me. Like he wasn't the sick bastard that he was. Knowing that my parents seemed to have moved on perfectly fine without me, and supporting the family whose son broke me, made me want to erase the image ... permanently.

But maybe I didn't really want to die because I took most of my prescription sleeping pills during the day when I knew Michelle was going to be back home from her errands.

After that distressing event, Michelle found Dr. Mitchell and booked me to see her, and the rest as they say, is history. God knows I still have my awful moments, but with Dr. Mitchell's guidance, and my loved ones beside me, I refuse to fall back into the darkness.

"I promised both you and Ethan that I will never go back there, and I intend to keep that promise. Dr. Mitchell will help me. And now I have Magnus. For what it's worth, Michelle, he *does* make me very happy."

Michelle just gives me a nod. And that's the end of that talk.

CHAPTER 15

I'm just coming back from a meeting, but I stop short at the sight of a tall, sexy beast of a man in a tailored gray suit, half-sitting on the edge of my desk with his arms crossed and a panty-moistening smirk on his face. His stunning blue eyes are solely focused on me, and me alone. Like I'm the only one in his line of sight, like I'm the only one who counts.

I think I just moistened a little bit more. But as much as I want to jump him, I keep my distance and maintain some form of professionalism.

Magnus stands to his full height and approaches me instead. "How do you feel about coming up to my office for a late lunch? I got us some Italian, if that's alright?" He lifts a brown bag, and the aroma catches me and makes my stomach rumble.

Oh shit, is it past lunch time already?

"Hold on, so *you* bought us take-out?" I ask with amused scepticism, trying to ignore the mix of disapproving and curious stares from colleagues passing by.

"Okay, you got me. But I rang the restaurant, and they delivered, even though they normally don't. And I *did* pick it up from the front desk."

"Of course." The humor in my eyes mirrors his own amused gleam. Shrugging, I add, "Well, I'm due for lunch, so ..."

I turn and head towards the elevators, but my breath catches when I feel his warm hand on the small of my back. It makes me self-conscious, and I instinctively look around me to check if anyone sees his intimate gesture. Then my whole body tingles when I feel his breath on my neck.

"Let them see, Isabelle. Don't be afraid because I'm not." Magnus's hand glides from my back, and I follow his movements as he finds my hand and entangles his fingers with mine.

I sneak a hesitant look towards him, and he gives me a reassuring smile. This feels right. He feels right. He *is* right.

Squeezing his hand with my own, I raise my head so I can give him a confident smile. "So are you taking me to your office for lunch or what?"

In his office, he unpacks all the food on the small table by the window—salad, wild mushroom pasta with truffle oil, buttered rolls, and a yummy-looking tiramisu for dessert.

I make myself comfortable on one of the chairs across from Magnus and grab a buttery bread roll.

"You know people are already talking about us, right?" I tell him pointedly in between bites. I twirl a forkful of the pasta and shove it in my mouth, nodding and moaning out aloud at its creamy goodness.

He chuckles lightly. "I love that you always have an appetite. It's very sexy."

I blush at his compliment but keep to the subject. "Seriously, Magnus. All of my hard work might be discredited because now, they'll say I got this job because I'm sleeping with the boss."

"Charles knows about us. And he knows I won't interfere when it comes to you, on a professional basis, of course. He's a good man, but he's also very upfront with staff under his department. He will let you know if you're doing a shitty job, regardless of who you are, or whom you're connected to. That's why I trust him because he's upfront with me, and his concerns about us. But I made it clear with him, that as per your wish, I will not interfere. Has he said anything to you about your quality of work so far?"

"No, he hasn't."

"Then you have absolutely nothing to worry about. If anyone does start bothering you, let me know, and I shall deal with that person myself."

"I can fight my own battles, Magnus." I meet his gaze head on.

He smirks and his eyes soften. "I know. I bear the brunt of that many times."

I feign shock towards him before eating another forkful of the delicious pasta, licking my lips to clean off the sauce left on my mouth.

"I wanted to talk to you about something which I'm sure is pretty important, but the sight of you eating with such gusto is fucking turning me on, and now I forgot what I wanted to say."

The tone of his voice seems different now, and I see no humor in those darkening blue eyes which are now focused on my mouth.

How can something so mundane like eating, turn him on? But any doubt I have is shut down when he stands up, and I see the bulge on his crotch burgeoning. Then he grabs a remote to make his window shades go down, giving us complete privacy.

"I want to try something," he tells me in his low silky voice. He kneels in between my legs, and my breathing starts to quicken as he pushes my skirt further up to my hips.

"Magnus, what …"

"Trust me," he whispers not to me, but to my crotch. As if his only focus is the apex in between my legs. Then his fingers hook down on the sides of my panties.

"Lift your hips up." He looks up to me, his expression hungry, but not for food. I feel myself getting wetter by the second.

I do as he says, and he gently takes my panties off, exposing me out in the open. I try to close my legs, but he holds me firmly.

"By all means, continue eating your lunch. I wouldn't want you to go hungry." His eyes gleam wickedly as his lips turn up into that smirk of his.

"On second thought, here, let me feed you." Magnus grabs the plate of pasta and carefully twirls it on the fork before positioning it carefully in front of my mouth.

I open my mouth, and I allow him to feed me the forkful. As I start to chew, he puts the plate back on the table and kneels back in front of me. Then Magnus's head dips down and I feel his wet tongue run across the length of my crevice. I instinctively move my hips backwards, and I let out a muffled gasp. I'm still chewing when he repositions me before he starts flickering his tongue on my clitoris.

"Mmmm," he croons against my crevice.

"I want you to feel both indulgences, Isabelle. I want your taste buds and your pussy tingling with pleasure at the same time."

Holy cow, this is amazing! I chew my food, relishing the taste of truffle oil and the creaminess of the mushroom sauce on the pasta, just as much as I'm relishing Magnus's tongue on my moistened core. He's so right. It's a mind-blowing experience, with both my mouth and pussy feeling varied forms of pleasure.

"Oh. My. God!" I breathe out when I feel his fingers thrusting inside of me, feeling the buildup to ecstasy happening all too quickly.

"Yes, baby. Feel it," his voice is thick and rough. "Does it feel good?"

I nod and blurt out, "Yes!"

"Then show me. Come for me, Isabelle. Come for me now." Like a dam bursting, I climax. And if I didn't cover my mouth, they might have heard my screams outside his office because … damn!

"Come here." Still throbbing inside, I grab his arms to haul him up. I need his mouth on me. I tangle my fingers in his hair and push his head down to me. I lick his already open mouth, still able to taste myself, mixed with a little truffle oil. It's the sexiest, most decadent thing I've ever tasted. And the hands that were just holding me in place earlier, are now circled tenderly around the curve of my neck. He gives me a deep and passionate kiss, the kind that I feel from the ends of my hair to the tips of my toes.

I try to make a grab for his trousers, to release his hard cock from its cage. But he chuckles sexily, murmuring, "I'm good, baby. That was all for you." Then he deepens our kiss even more.

But not long after, he gently pulls back, our foreheads still touching. "I just remembered what I wanted to ask you before I got distracted."

"What is it?" I ask breathlessly.

"Move in with me."

"Wh—what? That's … that's not exactly a question." Is he joking? He's joking, right?

"Move in with me, Isabelle," he repeats, but there's no hint of humor in those blue eyes of his. God, he's serious. I break away from his stare, feeling vulnerable and shocked and unsure of what to say. That's when my eyes find the clock on his wall.

"I … I have to go," I mutter, pulling away, gently easing myself off the seat so I can stand up. I wince involuntarily at the slight soreness between my legs, but I'm too distracted by what Magnus just said right now to even register the pain. I search everywhere for my panties so I can get dressed.

"Looking for these?" Magnus holds up what I'm looking for, dangling it at the tip of his finger. I try to get it from him, but to my surprise, he puts it straight in his pocket.

"Magnus!" I scowl at him. But he walks away and grabs some tissues, then he twirls his finger indicating me to turn around so he can do his post-sex ritual of gently wiping me clean.

"Why do you always clean me up after we have sex?" I finally ask, wanting to satisfy my curiosity and needing him to forget his question.

"Because this is part of me, taking care of you." He shrugs and kisses the back of my head after he's done, returning my panties in my hand.

"I think it's very sweet. Thank you. Do you do this to all the girls you've dated?" *Shoot. Good one, Billie!*

He looks at me like I've said something odd. Then he shakes his head. "No. Only with you."

But he's on to me, and he knows what I'm doing. "Think about what I just said."

"Let's ... let's deal with meeting your family at the charity event on Saturday first. I mean, don't you think we're moving too fast?"

Magnus closes our distance once again and holds me close. "I know I shouldn't have thrown it out like that. I was caught in the moment, and it felt like the right thing to say at that time. I mean it though. You and Ethan ... with me."

I open my mouth, wanting to reason out with him that it's too soon ... too quick. But no words are coming out.

"But maybe you're right. Let's take this one step at a time," he quips.

"Really? Okay. One step at a time sounds good," I reply. And Magnus bends down to kiss me tenderly.

"But after the gala, you're staying over at my place." He walks over by a door that is disguised to look like it's part of the wall. I follow him out of curiosity, and I'm surprised to see a generous-sized bathroom with a closet inside.

He tidies himself up in front of the mirror, and I can't help but stare. It blows my mind how effortless it is for him to look gorgeous and pristine.

"You'd like me to stay over?" I ask, realizing I'm still holding my panties. I step inside the secret bathroom to put them on and look presentable. He stands right behind me. I exhale contentedly as he wraps his arms just under my breasts, bending down to lay his chin lightly on my shoulder.

"Yes. Will that be a problem? We can stay at your place too. It's just that I'd like to fuck you senseless right after the gala, and if we stay over my place, you can be as noisy as you want." He winks at my reflection in the mirror. The playful look on his face is so adorable.

He knows I'll say yes.

I turn around to face him and look him squarely in the face.

"Well, since you put it that way, Mr. Grant, I have no choice but to say yes."

Magnus lands a kiss on my lips, a smile lining his face.

"Now I'm *really* looking forward to Saturday. And I have a person who can help you with the gown, so you don't have to worry about that."

"A gown?" I ask before pulling away to fetch my heels. "Oh, you don't have to help me out. I'm sure I can find something within my price range."

"It isn't a suggestion, Isabelle. This will be our first official outing as a couple, and I want everyone to see you the way I see you— like Aphrodite."

I roll my eyes at him. "Magnus, I'm hardly a goddess. But if it makes you happy, then you can help me with the gown, okay?"

I note the look of relief on his face. He carries me up and sits me next to the basin, then he fetches my shoes and puts them on my feet.

"Thank you for humoring me about the gown thing. Anyway, afterwards we can go back to my place and take pleasure in peeling each ridiculous article of clothing off of each other."

His hands continue up my thighs and ends under my buttocks, squeezing my cheeks and making me gasp. I playfully push him away before his caresses progress into something more, and I won't be able to get back to my work.

"Fine," I answer, hopping off my perch. "I'll go to your mother's event wearing a gown of your choosing. But if I may be perfectly honest, I'm more nervous about meeting your mother and the rest of your family."

Magnus hands me my purse. But as I grab it, he pulls me close against his body.

"Don't be nervous. They'll see what I see in you, and it's incredible. *You're* incredible." He bends down to give me a kiss. Then he buttons his suit jacket. I can't help but swoon at how damned good-looking he is … like he just stepped out of a fashion shoot, minutes after our little lunchtime romp. In the meantime, I look down at my clothes, and even after several attempts at fixing myself up, compared to Magnus, I still look like a rumpled heap.

I'm not thoroughly convinced that Mrs. Grant will be impressed by the mess of a person Magnus will introduce her to, and it thoroughly scares me.

What happens when she finds out about my past? Will she think that I might taint Magnus's image? The most likely answer to the last question saddens me.

"Are you alright?" he asks, his expression showing concern. "You seem to have drifted off there."

I shrug slightly. "Sorry, I'm just having a weird moment, that's all." I turn and start heading towards the door with Magnus walking close by.

"I'll talk to you later?" I turn to him before opening the door.

"Of course. I'll take you home as usual."

"Okay. See you then," I answer, giving him a small but awkward wave. I'm still unable to shake off my worry about the gala event, but I head straight out of Magnus's office before I risk giving myself away.

I head straight to the elevators, and I'm thankful that as usual, Denise isn't at her desk. I reach my floor and head straight to my workspace, relieved that I still have time to compose myself. My phone vibrates. Is it a message from Magnus already? '*No good-bye kiss? Naughty girl. You'll pay for that … M*'

I smirk after reading his message. This message is typical Magnus—frustratingly arrogant but swoon-worthy at the same time.

I respond with a quick message. '*Sorry, baby. Do you take cash or credit?*'

With a silent giggle, I put my phone back in my purse, just in time to see Charles come out of his office and towards my desk. He informs me that he has to make an urgent business trip to Dallas, so I get on to organizing his travel arrangements. I don't have to go with him, thank goodness. I can't imagine how I'll feel about flying back so close to my hometown.

The rest of the day flies by and before I know it, my workday is over. Alex is waiting by the Cayenne as I exit the building. He gives me a smile before opening the car door.

"Mr. Grant will be right out, Ms. Morrison."

"Oh, okay. Thanks Alex," I reply, slightly disappointed that Magnus isn't here to meet me.

My disappointment is short-lived, much to my delight. Magnus leaves his building, talking on the phone with a frown on his face. He looks like he's giving the poor person on the other line a good earful. He nods at Alex gruffly when he opens the door for him, still wearing a scowl. But when Magnus sees me inside, his face softens immediately. He says his good-bye to the person at the end of the line and hangs up.

"Well, hello there, Mr. Grant. Nice of you to join me," I tease with a coy smile giving him a kiss on his cheek, hoping to lighten up his mood.

Unexpectedly, Magnus lifts me from my seat and places me on his lap. He grabs a handful of my hair and pulls me down to his waiting lips, kissing me with so much passion that it leaves me breathless when he pulls away.

"Mmm, much better. If this is the sort of thing that's waiting for me at the end of the day, I'd be a very happy man." He beams at me before settling me back on the seat.

I can't help but give him a big smile back. Magnus sure knows how to make a woman feel special.

"Bad afternoon?" I place my hand on his thigh, feeling his tense muscles ease from my touch.

"Just having a few complications with a new acquisition. But it's nothing that can't be fixed. And how was your day?"

He sounds tired, even if he tries to appear nonchalant about it.

"Charles has to fly to Dallas tomorrow and won't be back until Monday, so I made the travel arrangements for him, and made sure everything is ready before he leaves tomorrow."

"Well, you know that complication I was referring to just now? Charles has to fly to Dallas on my behalf. Mother's event is this Saturday. I want my family to meet you. And trust me, they will love you." He intertwines his hand over mine, keeping them on his thigh.

I give him my best smile, albeit knowing it's more for his benefit. His family will love me ... but what about you, Magnus? Do *you* love *me*?

"You know, Charles initially wanted you to go with him in Dallas," he mentions, his eyes regarding me intently.

Magnus's remark has me in a panic. "I can't go back there, Magnus," I whisper, my voice shaky. He should know that the last thing I want is to return to the place where my nightmare began.

"I know, I know," he reassures me. "I just told Charles not to ask you because you're going with me to the charity event."

He places his arm around me, and all traces of panic begin to dissipate. "Don't worry. If Charles needs to go back to Dallas, I'll be there with you too. I promised to keep you safe, and I intend on keeping my word."

He squeezes my hand to reassure me that everything will be okay. Sadly, I know it'll take a long time before I believe this to be true. But somehow, with Magnus beside me, I know I can get there eventually.

"Are you coming up?" I ask Magnus as the SUV stops in front of my apartment. Alex gets off to allow us some privacy.

"I'm afraid I can't tonight. I still have some issues to discuss with Charles before he flies out tomorrow. Say hi to Ethan for me?"

"Of course. Thanks for dropping me off." I give him a smile, hoping to mask my disappointment.

"I'll be out on meetings the whole day tomorrow so Alex will pick you up at eight in the morning. You'll have enough time to drop off Ethan as well."

"Oh, it's okay, I can just …"

"Seriously, Isabelle. Can you just accept it by saying yes and thank you?" he asks with frustrated authority.

I roll my eyes. "God, you are so incorrigible sometimes!" I huff, as I unbuckle my seat belt.

He grins. "That's why we go so well together, my dear." Then he cups the side of my face so I turn to him, and my mouth parts at the sight of him staring lustfully at my lips. He caresses my lips with his, before his tongue enters my waiting mouth.

I hear a deep growl from Magnus's throat telling me he wants more. But he pulls away and he clenches his hands onto the leather seats, stopping himself from going any further.

"You make it so easy for me to lose control, Isabelle. I definitely need to put a stop to that somehow," he whispers in a husky tone.

"Why would you do that? Think about what we could be doing tonight, if you didn't have to leave now," I whisper back.

He regards me with serious look on his face, like he's considering it, but he closes his eyes and shakes his head, sighing deeply.

"You really are a temptress. But I'll see you tomorrow, Isabelle."

I shrug. "Okay, suit yourself." I reach up to give him a kiss but only on his cheek.

He utters an expletive under his breath, making me giggle softly.

I give Magnus a small wave as I move up the steps to my building and feel an immediate sadness as soon they drive off.

If we lived together, we won't have to miss each other so much.

Why does my subconscious always tell me things I really need but don't want to hear?

Ethan is busy watching the children's channel on TV, but as soon as he sees me enter the apartment, he's on his feet and in my arms.

"Hi, Michelle!" I shout out while squeezing my son playfully.

"Hey yourself!" she shouts back.

Smiling, I turn back to Ethan, who starts tugging at my arms.

"Mom, guess what? Almost everyone I invited to my party's going!" he tells me excitedly.

"That's great, Ethan! In no time at all, you'll be seven!"

Michelle walks in looking fabulous in her bodycon dress and sky-high heels.

"Whoa, looks like someone's got a hot date!" I exclaim in appreciation.

"Right? Nathan will be picking me up soon. Ethan's had his dinner, and yours is in the oven."

"Does Nathan know how extremely lucky he is to have you?"

"Oh, he knows, baby girl. He knows," Michelle answers with a wink.

Nathan arrives and after some small talk, they head out to this new restaurant at Brooklyn Heights. Seeing them together and so happy, makes me miss Magnus even more.

"Where's Magnus, Mom?" Ethan asks, seemingly able to read my mind.

"Magnus is busy with work, honey, but he did ask me to say hi to you."

"Oh, okay. I wanted to play with him. He's really nice."

My heart warms up at Ethan's innocent words. "He *is* a nice man, honey. So is it okay with you if I see Magnus more often then? You know Mommy likes him a lot too."

He shrugs, beaming at me. "Yup. Is he your boyfriend? Like Nathan is Michelle's boyfriend?"

I stare at this little man in front of me, who never ceases to leave me gobsmacked with his questions and candid remarks. I have to be honest to him. He's too smart, and he'll know when I'm lying.

"Yes, Magnus *is* my boyfriend. How do you feel about Mommy having a boyfriend?"

"Well, you never had one before … but I like Magnus. So I guess it's cool."

I give him a big kiss on the head, too happy to speak. Finally feeling hungry, I make my way to the kitchen to get my dinner from the oven. Then I sit next to Ethan, and we watch a movie together while I'm eating my dinner.

Before the movie finishes, Ethan's head is already on my lap, ready to go to sleep. Good thing he's changed into his pj's and brushed his teeth. I carry him back to his room, realizing with every step that he's getting heavier every day. I tuck him in bed, and he sleepily gives me a sweet kiss on the cheek.

After doing the laundry and doing some cleaning up, I start to feel quite exhausted. So I head straight to my bedroom. I'm tired and ready to sleep. After a shower, I change into a well-used tank top and pajama bottoms. I stop at the edge of my bed, just staring at it for a couple of minutes, imagining Magnus lying next to me. I have a queen-sized bed but with him on it, he practically dwarfs the whole space with his size and length.

What I'll do to have Magnus spoon me right now. With his body, naked and warm, and his cock, hard against my back. Just thinking about it is getting me wet.

I attach my phone into its charger, checking for any missed calls or messages. Magnus hasn't tried to call me nor has he left any messages on my phone. Disappointed, I check the time. Ten o'clock. Surely he'd be done with work by now. Feeling like a schoolgirl, I take a deep breath, and I call him, hoping for no rude surprises like the last time.

He answers after only the first ring.

"Isabelle," he sounds pleased with my call, but his voice hints some weariness as well.

"Hi, Magnus. I hope I didn't disturb you."

"You didn't. I'm in the study about to finish up with some paperwork then I'll call it a night. Are you in bed now?"

"Mmhmm," I answer, suddenly feeling shy.

"Wish you're waiting in my bed, naked and wet for me." His voice is practically guttural and muffled with desire.

I feel a hot flush creep up my neck, and my core gets wetter at his suggestion.

"Hmm, that sounds tempting. But I'd rather be in your study, sitting on your desk, naked and wet for you." I'm starting to sound breathless, my heart beating faster after every word.

His breath hitches. Is his imagination getting the better of him, as well?

"What are you doing, distracting me like this? I have a fucking major hard-on right now, and my woman is in another borough." He sounds quite frustrated, trying to maintain control.

"Why? Will I be a distraction if I'm wearing nothing?" I ask innocently. I feel my nipples perk and my chest heave. I squeeze one of my breasts without thinking, wishing it were Magnus's hands instead of mine.

"You can distract me anytime, naked or otherwise. You know I'll just fuck you with my tongue, then my fingers, then my hard cock, right?"

"Will you now? Hmmm … if you continue to talk like that, I might come right here and now," I tease.

"Isabelle, are you being selfish about your orgasms? I should be the one to give them to you, so I should be the one to enjoy them as well."

"Goodnight, Magnus."

"Goodnight? You're not going to leave me hanging, are you?" he asks, stunned.

"Whatever do you mean?" I ask, feigning innocence.

He sighs loudly, "Are you making me suffer for not staying over at your place?"

"I don't know what you're talking about," I answer with a muffled giggle.

"I'm beginning to regret my own decision as well," he answers in his sexy tone.

My body tingles all over, concentrating at the apex between my legs.

"I'll take your word for it, Mr. Grant," I reply. "Goodnight."

"Do not masturbate, Isabelle. I'll know if you did. Save your orgasm for me tomorrow."

Wow, Mr. Bossy sure knows how to make me feel frustrated and turned on at the same time!

"Isabelle?"

"Yes, baby. I'll save my orgasm for you."

Sounding relieved, he answers, "Sweet dreams, my beautiful temptress."

We hang up at the same time. And I'm left feeling a dull ache in my chest … and a throbbing core waiting for release.

I decide to read a book I've yet to finish, needing the diversion of a romance to placate my sexual frustration, and hopefully allow me to sleep sooner rather than later.

CHAPTER 16

Knock knock knock! I wake up in a haze, scrambling to check the time. God, it's only four in the morning.

"Mommy? May I come in?" I hear Ethan's voice on the other side of my bedroom door.

I get up and open the door to find Ethan looking frightened and in tears, tightly carrying his favorite teddy bear in his arms.

"I had a nightmare, Mommy," he says with a quivering voice, as I quickly usher him inside.

"Oh, honey, what did you dream about?" I lift the duvet so he can get inside the bed. I soon follow, wrapping my arms around him.

"I dreamed of a big man, and he's scary, and he wants to get me. But I ran away," he retells with fright. In no time, he's in tears again.

"Oh, it's just a dream, sweetie. Do you remember what the man looks like? Have you seen him before, like maybe in school or on the way home?" I ask calmly but deep inside, my mind is filling up with alarming scenarios.

"I can't see his face, but I'm scared of him. He tried to get me, Mommy."

"Shh ... shh, it's not real, baby. No one will try to get you. Mommy will protect you, no matter what. And Michelle will protect you too. Don't worry. Okay, honey?" I comfort him softly while gently stroking his hair. This always helps him relax and I'm hoping it'll still work this time.

He nods against my chest. I reach for some tissues on my bedside table, and I wipe his tears and help blow his nose.

"Sleep now, my brave little man, and think of fun things. Shhh ...," I whisper, feeling his body go limp as lethargy finally sets in. After a few sniffles and shudders, he's back to sleep.

I gaze at my son, so terrified that his nightmare felt so true that it led him to tears. As much as I can try to comfort him and convince him that his nightmare isn't real, I know for a fact that scary men do exist. I was a victim of one. And to this day he still haunts *my* dreams.

I have to make sure Ethan is safe and that nothing or no one will harm him, at least not when I'm around. Without thinking, I give my son a tight squeeze, making him shift his position in protest. So I let him lie on the pillow beside mine, continuing to watch him sleep, until my own body gives in, and I close my eyes once more.

A few hours later, I wake Ethan up to get ready for school. I ask him about his dream over breakfast, but he vaguely remembers anything. My instincts take over, and I remind myself to ask Michelle if she knows of any odd men lurking around Ethan's school. However, she didn't come home after her date last night. So I leave her a text message to confirm if she's picking up Ethan this afternoon. Thankfully, she texts me back to confirm that she will.

We leave for Ethan's school, grateful for Magnus's insistence that Alex should take us. After Ethan's episode last night, I feel safer knowing we have someone who will look out for our welfare. We get to the school, and I walk my son inside with the intention of speaking to his teacher, Ms. Branson. Ethan seems to be in good spirits now, which is a good sign. It can just be a one-off thing, but I can't be blamed for wanting my own child safe. Ms. Branson assures me that she hasn't noticed anyone suspicious within the school grounds, nor has she noticed any odd behavior where Ethan is concerned. But she'll let me know if anything remotely suspicious occurs.

I notice her disappointment though, that I've come without Magnus. I leave Ethan's school not only feeling overprotective of my son, but also of the man so many women seem to covet. Thankfully, my thoughts of violence towards these women have dissipated by the time I reach the Grant Corp building.

With Charles away on a business trip, I spend the whole day buried in my work. It's great because with Magnus off-site the whole day, being busy keeps me from missing him too much. But by midafternoon, Denise surprises me with a visit at my desk. She hands me a single long-stemmed rose with a card enclosed. Inside is an invitation from Magnus to have dinner at his place tonight. It also states that Alex will pick me up after work, and he will take me straight to the penthouse where Magnus will be waiting. Feeling excited to see him again, I text back to confirm our date.

Towards the day's end, I call Michelle and speak with Ethan about tonight. Thankfully, they give me the go-ahead on my dinner date with Magnus. Then I make my way down to meet Alex in front of the building. But as I reach the main lobby, I break into a big smile at the sight of Magnus standing by the front desk. He's talking to one of the managers I recognize from the sales department, but as soon as he sees me, he excuses himself and starts walking towards me with deliberate swagger and a wicked gleam in his eyes.

"Ah, Miss Morrison, you're here," he says in a voice loud enough for people around us to hear, "Thank you for being Mr. Dune's proxy for an important business dinner tonight. Shall we?" Magnus offers his arm out for me, and motions me to follow him.

Still stunned and speechless by his act, I hold on to his arm and follow his lead with a smile frozen on my face, until we're inside the car and the coast is clear. As soon as Alex drives off, I breathe out a sigh of relief.

"You okay?" he asks, laying his arm around my shoulder.

"Yes, I am now," I answer back.

"I'm sorry I had to do that," he adds sheepishly.

I turn to him with a big smile. "That was brilliant, actually. Thank you for picking me up without being too obvious, oh, and for the beautiful rose you gave me earlier." I kiss him on the cheek, which earns me a kiss on the lips.

We reach his building in record time, much credit to Alex and his great driving skills. But then his phone rings as we enter his penthouse. He frowns at the name on his phone.

"Excuse me, I'll just take this in the study. Rosa's gone for the night, but please help yourself to anything you want." He kisses my forehead distractedly before heading to his study. All I hear is his gruff answer as he turns the corner, and then he's gone.

I stand at the foyer for a minute before slowly heading towards the kitchen. I pass by the formal dining area where the table is now set. In the kitchen, I notice a pot on a stove where a lovely aroma is coming from. I lift the lid and sure enough, there's beef stew inside. On the bench next to the stove is a freshly-baked loaf of bread. The food instantly makes my mouth water.

Then an idea hits me, and I begin to work. The table is already set, so I'll just make sure dinner will be at the table when Magnus is finished with his call. I open a bottle of shiraz and grab a couple of wine glasses, helping myself to a glass like what Magnus suggested. Then I rummage through the cabinets for the serving bowls, but just as I'm about to transfer the stew, I hear Magnus's footsteps heading towards the kitchen. So I pour him a glass of wine and turn to hand it to him with a smile on my face. But my smile disappears as soon as I see the deeply troubled look on his face. Before I can utter a word, he takes the wine glass off my hand and fists his hand in my hair. With a painful groan, his mouth smashes on mine so roughly that our teeth knock against each other at first. With his suit jacket gone, my hands cling to his shirt, holding on for dear life.

"I need you, Isabelle," he tells me with yearning.

"I'm right here," I whisper against his mouth.

Magnus lifts me effortlessly, and my arms wrap around his neck. Before I know it, he's carried me upstairs and we're lying on his bed, our clothes tossed to the floor. He is impatient, as I am, but I feel that Magnus needs to have his release more than I do. So I let him and offer my skin, my mouth, my whole self, as a vessel for what he needs. Now is not the time to ask questions.

Without a word, he lifts my hips and enters me completely, making me thankful that I'm always wet for him. His thrusts are aggressive and urgent, but I take them all and move in rhythm with him, opening my legs wider so I can take him deeper.

"I want you to come first, Magnus," I moan out as he suckles my jutting nipple.

"No, … I want you to come. I need you to come first," his hoarse plea, and the way his thumb is doing it's magic on my clit, sends me over the edge so quickly that it even surprises me. I yell out his name as my fingernails claw at his muscular back.

"Fuck … Isabelle!" Magnus follows, and I feel every single spasm of his cock as he fills me with his come. He slumps on top of me, out of breath, just as I am. He's still inside of me, and I love the feel of his whole being enfolded around me, inside and out.

"I'm sorry if I hurt you," he mumbles against my neck while he licks and nibbles at it.

"I'm a big girl. I can take it, Magnus. And I doubt that you could ever really hurt me," I whisper while leaving light kisses along his jaw.

Something I said must have affected him because he stops what he's doing and avoids my eyes as he pulls out of me and lies down beside me, looking up the ceiling in deep thought.

Has what we have done just now, not help him at all? I turn to my side, lifting myself so I can have a better look at his beautiful but hardened face.

"Did I say something wrong, baby?" I ask while grazing my thumb against his clenching jawline, thankful that my touch seems to soothe him and his expression softens. But his eyes are anxious when he turns to face me.

"How can you be sure I'd never hurt you? God, Isabelle, if I ever say or do something—"

Before he can finish his sentence, I hush him with my finger. "Let's not talk about me because I'm not going anywhere. I want to know what's worrying you. Maybe I can help?"

Magnus just looks at me, like he's searching my face for an answer to my own question. But then he smiles and lifts himself up so we're face-to-face. He pushes strands of my hair away from my face and cups my cheek.

"You *have* helped me by being here with me. You don't need to be burdened by my work problems. I can handle it."

"I know, but …," I gasp when his hand quickly moves down to squeeze my exposed ass cheek.

"And what a glorious butt you've got." He offers me a suggestive grin before pressing his mouth on mine with his tongue sliding along my lower lip … still swollen from the assertiveness of his previous kisses.

"Mmm … hungry?" he asks, and I nod, biting my lower lip. The worry I have for him is replaced by sudden grumbling of my stomach. "Well, our stew awaits!"

Downstairs, I'm wearing nothing but a silk robe Magnus happens to have in his closet. It's a brand-new robe which I suspect he bought for me, judging by its girly shade of pastel pink. He's wearing only a pair of boxers and has no shirt on. I say a silent prayer of thanks to the heater for working so well that even if it's chilly outside, Magnus doesn't need to wear anything else inside. We opt to eat at the kitchen breakfast bar, making our dinner more relaxed. After eating a healthy share of the stew and bread, and sharing some laughs and stories in between, I place all our dishes in the sink.

I sense that familiar pull, the way my body reacts whenever I feel him close. Magnus is right behind me. Feeling bold, I undo my robe's tie and turn around, allowing the robe to open on its own accord.

With my arms akimbo and widening my stance to show more skin, I ask, "What? Enjoying the show?" It's an ode to a previous remark he made in what feels like ages ago.

Magnus smiles mischievously as his eyes take in every inch of my exposed skin, making me feel adored and aroused at the same time. And from the tenting of his flimsy boxers, I'm giving him the same effect. He steps closer, and his hand reaches down to cup my pussy, which is already wet for him. I sigh when I feel his feather-like fingertips on my inner folds. I'm still a little sore, but I pay no mind to it because I'm already so hot and so ready for him.

Still gliding his fingers on my moistness, he dips his head to graze the tip of his tongue on my trembling bottom lip.

"You get so wet for me so quickly, Isabelle. But you're sore, and a little swollen. As much as it gets me harder that you're sore because of me, maybe I should take care of you some other way."

"But it's okay, Magnus, I want you inside of me." I rub my hand on his hardened cock, feeling his heat over his boxers.

"Hmmm, maybe we should wait." His eyes are closed while I'm stroking his cock. Then his hips start to move in rhythm with my hand, the pleasure I'm giving him is written all over his face. And I want to see more of that on his face. I want to be the only person giving him this kind of pleasure.

"Or maybe, I can suck your cock and help you change your mind." I nudge him, so his back is against the kitchen island, his eyes open wide with surprise. But judging from his smile, he likes where this is heading ... and holy shit, so do I.

I pull his boxers down, and his cock springs to life, throbbing, and waiting for me.

"So big," I murmur, as I hover my head over it, my hand holding him firmly.

I lick the very tip of his hood, where a droplet of his essence sits. "Mmm, so tasty."

He groans my name, squinting his eyes with pleasure. "Talk some more, baby."

I take my cue. "Oh, so you like that, do you? Me talking about your cock?"

"I just like your dirty-talking mouth on me," he hisses.

With my eyes fixed on his face, I kneel down and wrap my lips around his cock, sliding him as deep as I can. He moans and throws his head back. Then he grabs me by the hair, trying to control how fast and deep I'm going.

He moans in protest when I pull away and smack my lips against his hood. Then I lick and kiss my way up to his sculpted stomach, his nipples, his neck, and his collarbone. Then I reach his mouth on my tiptoes. His hand is still gripping my hair, deepening our kiss. I give him what he wants, sucking his tongue the same way I've sucked his cock a minute ago.

Then Magnus takes the lead, shifting our positions so I'm against the island, engulfed by his large frame. He gets rid of my robe and sits me on the island so we're easily face-to-face. And then we kiss, just kiss, for goodness knows how long. His shaft is rigid and warm against my inner thigh as we rub and slide against each other's bodies.

Then the way he kisses me becomes less urgent, and sweeter … eloquent, even without speaking any words.

Then he pulls away but his arms are caging me. My brows furrow in protest but placate when I notice a different kind of intensity in his eyes. He's seeing *me*. It makes me feel like a spotlight is on me, and I can't help but feel self-conscious and vulnerable.

"You are so beautiful, Isabelle. I can't believe someone so beautiful is mine." His fingers travel from my cheek, to my neck, and to my collarbone, then stopping on my waist.

"Tell me you're mine. Body and soul …," he whispers before his mouth finds mine once again.

He settles me in the middle of the island so I can lie down before he effortlessly lifts himself up and over my body. Then he's pushing my legs aside and slips his cock inside my hot opening. I gasp at the initial sting of pain, exhaling slowly so I can fully let him in. But the pain is quickly replaced by the pleasure of fullness that only him being inside me can bring. He thrusts gently, taking his time, and kissing me lovingly … a polar opposite to the roughness from earlier.

I leave his mouth momentarily, licking the length of his jaw before nibbling at his ear. We're both so close to climax, with my breathing getting heavier as his thrusts go deeper and faster.

"I'm yours just as much as you're mine, Magnus ... body and soul ..." *And heart.* But I leave the last one out. He's the one that has my heart, not the other way around. And I'm not about to embarrass myself once again. I break our contact, nibbling on his shoulder and squeezing my eyes shut, erasing the saddening thought. We move in sync, with his mouth kissing me in the right places, and his expert fingers rubbing me where it matters. I cry out his name as I reach my climax, mewing with my every shudder. Not long after, I feel his body stiffen in the buildup to his own climax. And then he comes, whispering my name so sweetly over and over again against my ear.

After we both settle down from our orgasm high, he waits a minute or two before pulling out, kissing my nipples and making me giggle softly. Then he gets off the island to wet some paper towels, cleaning me in the caring way he does.

By this time, I begin to feel lethargic. My eyes are already half-closed when Magnus carries me up to his bedroom. And by the time he spoons against me, I have already succumbed into a sweet dreamless slumber.

CHAPTER 17

I open my eyes to the now familiar room. The sun has barely hit the skyline. I check the time ... six in the morning.

Shit, I slept too long! But then again, I probably had one of the best sleeps in years.

Magnus's arm is resting over my breasts. His leg is slung over mine. Even in his sleep, he's still overprotective. I can't help but smile at how he spoons me. However, the call of nature is getting louder by the second, and I just have to answer it.

The moment my feet hit the hardwood floors, I wince at the sting. Sitting down hurts which means I must really be swollen down there. Then the pain in between my thighs makes itself known as soon as I start walking to the bathroom. Sitting down on the toilet to pee, hurt my thighs like a motherfucker.

But as soon as I'm back in the bedroom, I watch Magnus sleep so peacefully in bed. Knowing how his mouth, his hands, his whole body is capable of instilling such a reaction with mine, the pain I'm feeling becomes circumstantial. I know in my heart that I won't be able to find anyone else who can make me feel the way he does.

So as long as he wants me to be his, then I will give him all of what's his. Do I expect the same in return? Well, a girl can always hope, right?

I grab my clothes off the chair, putting them on as carefully as possible, cursing to myself once or twice while I'm putting my underwear on. Even my breasts feel heavy.

All ready to go, I sit myself carefully next to Magnus. I don't want to wake him, but I can't leave without leaving him a kiss. I plant a light one on his slightly opened lips, but it's enough to stir him into waking up.

He squints his eyes, adjusting his focus towards me. His arms automatically wrap themselves around my waist. He frowns as soon as he sees me fully-clothed.

"Something's wrong with this picture. You're supposed to be naked in bed with me." His voice is low and rough, still dazed from sleep. But damn it's so sexy that my insides react instantaneously.

I smile awkwardly, trying to ignore my body's reaction. I reach up and caress his face with my hand. "I have to go. You know I always take Ethan to school. I don't want him to get disappointed."

He sits up, the frown still on his face.

"So were you just going to leave without waking me up, then you're heading all the way to Brooklyn at this hour, and you expect me to be pleased?"

I shake my head. "I didn't expect you to be pleased, I'm just hoping you'd understand."

He loses the frown, but his mouth is still set in a hard line. "I'll drive you."

"Magnus, I don't want to make fuss. You should just go back to sl—"

"Isabelle, I'm taking you home, end of discussion." The finality in his voice makes me clamp my mouth shut. And is it wrong for me to find his bossy behavior sexy?

He gets out of bed to head straight to his closet. He returns with what looks like a black pinstriped tailored ladies business suit, which he lays in bed. It's expensive-looking, possibly Italian and definitely out of my price range.

He deliberately stands in front of me, so his cock is only inches from my face.

"You have new clothes in here. We can shower together and head to Brooklyn. Is that okay with you?"

"You bought me a ... oh ... why do I even bother asking? Sorry ... I mean, thank you." His brow is raised. He knows he's distracting me into submission.

Master manipulator. Ugh, why does he have to be so blatantly sexy doing so?

"So, why aren't you naked yet?"

I open my mouth to say something in return, but if Magnus wants me naked, I will be naked for him.

With a satisfied smirk, he goes back to his closet to pick his own clothes. When he comes back to the room, I've already taken the last article of my clothing off. He stops on his track and observes me from head to toe and back up again.

"What? It's nothing you've never seen before." I laugh a little self-consciously.

"I'm never going to get over how beautiful you are." He stands inches from me, running his forefinger on my lips.

"Your lips are a little swollen." His fingers travel straight down to my crotch, sliding two fingers along my folds. "And these lips are swollen too. Moist, which is getting me excited, but swollen nonetheless. Are you feeling very sore?"

I bite my lower lip. His fingers down there are disrupting my thoughts.

"I've experienced childbirth, Magnus. This is like a walk in the park!'' I reply, shrugging. I want to remove the worry on his face. I wrap my arms around his waist, burying my face on his chest so I can hide my grimace. My arms feel like lead, but I don't care. I just hate to see him worry so much.

Magnus sighs and hugs me back, planting a kiss on the top of my head.

"I have to wait until you're ready before we do this again. I'm so sorry for being so rough last night." His voice is soothing, and do I hear a hint of regret?

"Don't. I told you I'm okay." I look up to him with a teasing smile on my face. "You know, I *am* stronger than you think."

Magnus smiles back, his eyes tenderly looking back at me. He pushes a strand of hair off my face and tips my chin up to kiss me ever so lightly.

"I know. You're so strong it scares me sometimes," he whispers against my lips.

I break into giggles. "Ha! Me? Scaring Mr. Magnus Grant? That'll be the day!"

He smiles back once again but this time, his smile doesn't reach his eyes. Before I can ask if he's okay, he changes the subject.

"Come, we'll go and have a nice warm shower. It should help relieve you of some of the soreness, then have a couple of painkillers before we leave."

I can't help myself. Overwhelmed by my feelings for him, I show him the best way I know how. I go on my tiptoes and hold onto his hair, pushing his head down for a kiss. And I give all of myself in that kiss. He reciprocates, our tongues dancing a crazy tango. It's hot, too hot that I feel it down my core. Our lips are still pressed together when he carries me to the shower, skilfully putting me on my feet and turning on the water without breaking the connection. Our hands are everywhere, with the water, soothing off our bodies but not our desires. Then Magnus starts shampooing my hair and soaping my body, taking care especially on the sore spots.

"Can I soap you too?" I ask him while he's cleansing my back.

"I'd like nothing more, but there's always next time. If you lay your hands on me, I doubt if we can leave this shower, let alone this apartment, for a while."

"Hmm, that doesn't sound so bad," I answer back, giggling.

He smacks my ass sharply, making me squeal.

"Naughty girl. Now rinse off so we can leave soon."

We're on our way back to Brooklyn, with Magnus behind the wheel of his Tesla S. I'm looking out the window, absentmindedly fiddling with my fingers. At the lights, he quickly checks something on his phone before squeezing my leg to get my attention, and looks at me with a wicked grin on his face.

"You're smiling funny. What's up?" I ask him with squinted eyes.

"What do you mean?" he innocently asks me, but his eyes are betraying him. He's definitely up to something.

"You're kind of looking like you're about to prank me or something."

Magnus smirks at me. "I'm innocent until proven guilty. Or is it the other way around?"

I press my mouth into a thin line before lunging at him to pinch him on the side, which is pretty hard to do to someone with practically zero percent fat.

"What?" He laughs, still able to maintain his course. I notice his handsome face transform into an almost childlike innocence. It's breathtaking, to say the least.

"You're up to something. Lucky you're hot enough I can let it pass … for now." I give him a mock scowl before letting a smile pass my lips.

"Oh, so you think I'm hot, huh?" He raises his brows at me.

I scoff. "You know you are! And every single woman in New York City who have eyes, will agree with me on that."

He suddenly tangles his hand with mine and brings my knuckles to his lips to press a loving kiss. "I only care about what *you* think, Isabelle."

Oh. Tiny prickles shoot all over me, and I find myself at a loss for words. Thankfully, we make it back to my place, affording me the opportunity not to respond.

It's still early enough when Magnus and I make it inside my apartment. I hear some commotion in the kitchen and sure enough, Michelle pops out to greet us in.

"Hey, girl! Ethan's still asleep … Hi Magnus." She gives Magnus a warm wave.

"Oh, good. I don't want him looking for me when he wakes."

"I can't believe you came all this way just for that. But at least you're here. A package or something came for you. I put it in your bedroom." Michelle looks at me, then briefly at Magnus.

"Okay, I'll check on my baby first." I don't think much of the parcel as I make my way to Ethan's room, only peeking through the door's opening, as I don't want to wake him up just yet.

I gasp as soon as I open my bedroom door. Hanging on my closet is a large dress bag, while on the bed, is a light brown box of shoes bearing Christian Louboutin's insignia. I check the contents of the box. It's a beautifully-crafted multispiked pair of heels. I've had Louboutins before, but I left them all in Texas. This, however, this one screams sexy. Then I gravitate towards the dress bag, which upon closer inspection, has a major designer's name printed on it.

What the hell?

There's only one person I can think of, who's capable of sending these to me … and I can sense him standing by my bedroom door. His arms are crossed, and he's watching me intently.

I turn to him, feeling puzzled. When did he get a chance to do all of these?

"Open the bag." He waves his chin towards the dress bag.

I'm almost afraid to do so, but I push down the zip of the dress bag, anyway. That's when I see glimpses of embellishments and lace but it's not until I take the dress bag off that I squeal, with my hands on my mouth.

Wow … just wow!

The gown is all black, with long sleeves. It's transparent on top with a deep v in front. Decency is kept safe with some delicate lace and embroidery covering the chest area. These are all held together by very fine tulle from the front, draping low at the back, almost down to the waist, making the back bare. A thin leather belt separates the top from the long georgette skirt with a thigh-high slit at the front and center.

Now, *this* is magnificent. I try to check for the price, but it's nowhere to be seen. But it doesn't matter. I have enough knowledge of high-end fashion from back in the day, so I know the value of a gown like this.

And it's too much, way too much.

"I know what you're thinking. I can see it on your face." Magnus closes the distance between us. "This is my present for you, to wear for the charity event."

"Can you hear the irony of what you just said? You seriously have to return it. I don't feel comfortable accepting something so extravagant."

"You'll do no such thing," he answers abruptly. I hear him breath deeply and his expression softens. He cups the curve of my neck and caresses my cheek reassuringly. It gives me comfort, and I close my eyes to appreciate the feeling.

"You don't have to feel guilty when I'm trying to spoil you. I *want* to do this because it makes me happy. I know it sounds selfish, but—"

"I get it," I cut in, holding onto his wrist resting on my shoulder. I give him a smile conveying my understanding.

"And I'm sorry for sounding ungrateful. Thank you … really. They're all so beautiful. I just hope I could do this gown justice. It's magnificent." I run my fingertips over the delicate handcrafted embellishments.

"Only fitting of the woman who's going to wear it."

"Magnus …" I shake my head at him. It makes me wonder if I'll ever be comfortable hearing his compliments.

"You'll find the sizing should be perfect, but by all means, you can try it on right now." Magnus's tone suggests indecency, as he sits at the edge of my bed with his hands propped behind him, and his legs wide open.

Before I can respond, Ethan rushes inside my room with a wide grin on his face.

"Mommy! Magnus!"

"Hey, buddy, how are you?" The welcome Ethan gives Magnus is not so different from the welcome he usually gives me. What *is* surprising is that Ethan goes straight to Magnus first instead of me. Somehow, it doesn't make me jealous. It actually warms my heart to see Magnus receive that welcome so wholeheartedly.

"I'm so happy you're here. Are you taking me to school?"

"Sure am, buddy!" Magnus ruffles Ethan's hair playfully, causing Ethan to giggle aloud. Then Ethan wraps his little arms around me and pulls me down to give me a tender kiss on my lips and on the tip of my nose. It makes my heart flutter like only my son ever could.

Michelle pops her head in as well.

"Ah, the prince is awake. Care for some breakfast, sweetie?"

"Good idea. I'm feeling famished as well. Magnus, are you hungry?" I intercede.

"Yes, I'm definitely hungry." I might think nothing of it, have I not seen the intense look in his eyes as they gaze up and linger on my slightly opened mouth. I feel the electricity between us as he closes the gap and rests his arm around my waist. He is definitely hungry but not for food.

Michelle rolls her eyes and gives us a knowing smile, before heading back to the kitchen.

"You ready to eat, buddy?" he asks Ethan, who nods with a big grin on his face.

After taking Ethan to his classroom and enduring a few more gawks from the teachers and mothers at Magnus's direction, we lace our hands together to walk back to the car. It just feels so natural to do so.

"This is nice," he comments.

"You like taking Ethan to school?" I ask teasingly.

He gives me a sidewards glance as his mouth curls up to that sexy smirk, and he draws my hand to his lips and gives my knuckles a lingering kiss.

"Yes, I do … but *this* is what I'm talking about," he answers, holding up our linked hands and kissing mine once again.

Our hands stay locked together while sitting in comfortable silence on the drive to work. On the occasion that he has to use two hands to steer or change gears, he places my hand on his thigh, which I stroke once in a while, giving him a coy smile whenever I see the effect it's giving him.

After he parks in his usual spot, he turns me to him and gives me a deeper kiss, one that we simply cannot do in front of Ethan or anyone else for that matter.

"Mmmm, I want to have that every single minute," he whispers, his eyelids lowered and his voice low and suggestive.

"If you're a good boy, then you will," I whisper back, and he lets out a small laugh before getting out of the car.

We step inside the empty elevator, our hands still linked. The electricity between us is palpable that only a fool can ignore it.

I don't hesitate as a rush of adrenaline overcomes me, and I stand on my toes and wrap my arms around his neck. I grasp his hair, pushing his head and I can see his astonished expression towards mine as I kiss him hungrily … greedily, thanking myself that I only wore lip gloss and not lipstick. He reciprocates with a growl as he swoops me up with one arm on my back and the other under my buttocks, leaning me on the wall for support. Our tongues touch and tease, tasting each other's warmth and moist tenderness. I moan at the deliciousness of his lips, lightly teasing it with the tip of my tongue.

"Isabelle ….," his groan is so thick with emotion.

Ding! Magnus quickly lowers me on the floor, and we straighten ourselves up just in time before the elevator door opens. He grabs my hand discreetly and moves me with him to the back wall as a group of people make their way inside. A handful of suits recognize Magnus's presence, and they all greet him accordingly. I move backwards a little to make room for more people, until I'm pressing against Magnus's chest and his undeniable arousal. I sneak a look up at him, and he meets my eyes as if warning me not to try anything scandalous.

For some reason, I am undeterred by his warning. In fact it begins to excite me. Looking ahead nonchalantly, I swing my hand to my back, closing my fingers on the thick, hard outline, wanting to break free from his custom-made suit trousers. His body tenses, and he squeezes my other hand, warning me yet again. I glance up at him, and I see his mouth pressed into a thin line, and his jawline tensing. His eyelids are constantly blinking as I slowly stroke his length over his trousers. Yes, he is definitely enjoying this … and he can't do anything about it.

Ding! I stop moving my hand as a few people step out of the cab. Thankfully no one else enters in. I continue stroking him as discreetly as I can while all eyes are in front, stopping my movement at every floor the cab stops. He subtly leans against my ear.

"Unless you want to finish what you started, you better get off your floor now," he whispers, his low voice sending delicious tingles down to my core.

Ding! That's the sound of the elevator stopping at my floor which also signals the end of my discreet hand job. He exhales loudly, sounding off his frustration, or relief. I'm not quite sure. I turn my head to him, biting my lip and smiling. He has his sexy smirk on while shaking his head, with disappointed dark pools of blue watching my every move as I step off.

As soon as the elevator door closes behind me, I quickly snatch my phone from my purse, and I head towards the ladies room. I lock myself inside one of the cubicles, and I take a picture of myself using my phone, suggestively sucking my forefinger inside my mouth with a wicked look in my eyes. I quickly write a short message with the picture. *'If you promise to wait, I promise to make it worth your while ... in here. Yours and only yours, Isabelle ... PS: I meant my mouth.'*

I giggle to myself before hitting *Send.* I leave the ladies room and head to my desk, knowing my cheeks are a little pink. I barely reach my cubicle when my phone vibrates. *'Good things COME to those who wait. And COME I will. All yours in anticipation, Magnus.*
PS: I meant to COME in your mouth, as well."

A squeal escapes out of my mouth which I abruptly cover with my hand when a couple of curious heads pop up.

"You okay, Billie?" asks one of the girls, her face showing mild concern mixed with curiosity. I think her name is Trina something or the other.

"Yeah, I'm alright, I'm alright" I answer while waving her off lightly.

With our spicy messages still in my head, I start my work with a dopey smile on my face.

Charles left me a number of e-mails to look into which relate to some interdepartmental issues which has given me enough work for the whole morning. He'll be flying back Monday and will be back in the office the next day, so I decide to make sure all his instructions and to-do's are done before his return.

At quarter to twelve, Magnus calls me to ask if I have plans for lunch because he's taking me out. Since I have nothing planned, I agree to our lunch date, telling him to surprise me.

At lunchtime, I head downstairs to meet Magnus, but when I reach the lobby, Jess and Marla are chatting right by the entrance, making it impossible for me to leave without them seeing me. I had to blow them off earlier when they asked me if I wanted to go to lunch, and if they see me, they'll know exactly why.

So I throw caution in the wind and head straight towards them. But I stop walking as soon as I see Magnus coming out of another elevator. He sees me almost immediately, but his eyes shift towards the same direction I was heading to. He sees Jess and Marla, who are now watching our every move.

Magnus must've picked up on my panic, so he walks past me instead, giving me a discreet wink to let me know he's going to keep his word. That's when he heads straight to his waiting car outside and as he does so, he sends me a text message. *'See you around the corner, to your right ... M'*

Breathing a sigh of relief, I head over to the girls.

"Hey ladies. Off to lunch?"

Marla raises her brow, "So are you guys being discreet? We haven't said anything because I don't want this shit to blow out of proportion. I just don't want any angry women working in here to pounce on you."

Jess adds, "Yeah, I had to insist that we keep it quiet ... for your sake, at least. If this goes pear-shaped, this will look worse for you and we really don't want that to happen."

Touched by their concern, I give them both a big hug, "Thank you both so much. I really do appreciate it. You have no idea what this means to me."

"I do ... you still owe us drinks!" Marla jokes.

"Done, let's all go out next Friday," I suggest excitedly.

Jess tries to help by adding, "Hey, at least Boyd can stop pestering you since you're dating *the* boss, huh?"

Well, it didn't help at all.

"Um, I have to go, sorry. Drinks ... next Friday ... your choice, my shout." I reiterate with some finger pointing in the air. And with a tentative wave, I turn around and walk out of the building and around the corner, happy to see Alex waiting by the Bentley. He opens the car door and gives me a smile, to which I reciprocate.

Magnus holds out his hand as I step inside the car. The warmth of his hand relaxes me, and I close my eyes for a moment, laying my head on his arm.

"What happened to your car?"

"Alex usually drives me around during the day. It's easier than having to drive myself from meeting to meeting."

I reach up and give him a quick kiss on the cheek. "Thank you for that."

He turns to me with a solemn look on his face. "I get where you're coming from, but sometimes I wish our circumstances were different. You're supposed to be my girlfriend, and I can't even be seen in public with you."

My chest feels heavy all of a sudden, "I'm sorry, Magnus, I thought I was ready, but … well, my reasons are justified. Are you having regrets? Because if you are, I will understand if you—"

He cuts me off, "No, don't do this. I told you I'm fighting for the both of us until you're ready. And that's what I'm doing. I'm not going anywhere, do you understand? I'm. Not. Going. Anywhere."

He pulls me closer in his arms and kisses my temple, comforting me instantly.

It doesn't take long before we pull up in front of Bryant Park Grill. It is situated behind the New York Public Library with Bryant Park as its backdrop. The iron beams on its façade are contrasted with a lush green vine cover and colorful manicured overhanging flora. It's a beautiful restaurant and practically an institution. It's a good choice by Magnus, of course. A well-presented maître d' leads us to a corner table in a discreet section of the restaurant.

While seated, two gentlemen wearing expensive-looking three-piece suits come over to our table to shake Magnus's hand and to make small talk, congratulating him on his recent acquisition of SonneSys. I am reading the menu but discreetly admiring how he's gracious and accommodating with his peers. And he knows when to cut off their conversation without coming off as rude. It makes me admire him even more.

"Sorry about that. I guess this isn't the restaurant to go to if we wanted privacy," he apologizes as he reaches for my hand.

"I don't mind. I actually like watching you in your element." I move forward so only Magnus can hear what I have to say. "It's such a turn on," I whisper with a wink.

He lifts his brow in mild surprise and moves forward as well so our faces are only inches apart. "Baby, I'm always at my element when I'm with you … and you know I'm not just talking about business." He reaches up to caress my hand.

We pull back as our waiter stands by the table. "Good afternoon, Mr. Grant and Ms. Morrison. My name is Marco, and I'll be your server today. Would you like to start with some drinks?"

I decide on just going straight to the entrées, which Magnus agrees with. I order the grilled stacked mahimahi while Magnus orders their signature sea grill. Magnus also orders a bottle of sauvignon blanc, my favorite type of white wine, to supplement our meal.

"I can't wait to see you in your gown tomorrow," he says right after Marco leaves.

"I can't thank you enough for it. What made you choose that particular gown, anyway?"

"The designer's is a friend of the family. He dresses my mother and my sister at a number of gala dinners and parties. So I thought to call him before I take you shopping. He asked me to describe you for him." He sees the curious look in my eyes, and he pulls one of my arms that are crossed in front of me towards him. Then he starts to caress the length of my forearm, leaving a trail of electricity where his fingers have been.

"I told him that she is on the cusp of petite, with long, luscious deep auburn hair, milky smooth skin, ample breasts, and a sexy derriere. I also told him that she is the most beautiful creature I've ever seen and that her gown should do her justice. Oh, and that you are a perfect size six. So, being the genius that he is, he sent me a photo of a gown from his most recent runway show, and I knew that I needn't look anywhere else."

My cheeks go a deeper shade of red. "Wait, you didn't really describe my um … body parts like that with designer, did you?"

He shrugs. "He wanted an exact description of you," he says, like there's no other way to do it.

"But compared to someone like Martine or Sofia …," I protest but before I can finish, he holds up his forefinger and raises his brows, prompting me to stop.

"Isabelle, don't succumb to comparing yourself with anyone."

I drop my gaze. "I just wish I could see what you see."

He holds my chin with his forefinger, tipping my head back to meet his eyes once again.

"From now on, you will stop doubting yourself," he says in a commanding yet gentle way. "If I have to tell you every single day that you're an amazing woman, I would. Just so there's no more doubt left in your head."

He gives a polite smile to our server as he places our food on our table, while I sit here speechless. Then Magnus looks back at me with a smile on his face. "So, how's your day so far?"

We start talking about work, first about mine then about his. His day sounds more exciting compared to my more mundane one. But nevertheless, he shows great interest in my stories, laughing when I tell him about a funny incident that happened at work.

The mahimahi is delicious and melts in my mouth. Magnus's sea grill looks delicious, as well. We delight in tasting each other's dishes, like any ordinary couple sharing their food. It leaves me giddy, knowing how normal this feels.

We finish our meals with flourish. And as he's wiping his mouth with a table napkin, I can't help but watch him lovingly with a smile on my face.

"Do I have something on me?" he asks with eyebrows raised.

"No, it's just, you know, this lunch date, us tasting each other's food, our conversations throughout the meal, and how comfortable this feels ... It's nice." I say, shrugging.

He gives me a warm smile. "We have all the time in the world to do more nice things together."

His words make my heart skip a beat. Does this mean he sees me in his future?

We decide to skip dessert, opting to walk our way back to his building. Midtown is buzzing with office workers in suits, students, and tourists everywhere. New York City can be overwhelming and intimidating to newcomers—with its tall skyscrapers, locals who take no shit from anyone, and life running in fast-forward, that if you don't know any better, you'd be left behind. It's true what they say— you either fall in love with New York, or despise it. I for one love the adrenalin rush of it all which is so completely opposite from Texas. And that's just how I like it.

Magnus holds my hand before crossing the street, moving to the other side to block me from any cars going in our direction. Again, his simple gestures leave me feeling cherished. We reach his building, and to my relief and consequent disappointment, he lets go of my hand. We step inside his building and into the elevator. He discreetly reaches for my hand and squeezes it before letting me go once again so I can get off the cab. Not long after, Magnus sends me a text message saying he'll see me later and that he intends on collecting on my promise. Just thinking about what's to come sends a rush of thrill throughout my body.

The rest of the day is pretty easy, albeit a tad odd. I confirm Charles's flight back, I also prepare for a meeting he'll be having with Magnus and the acquisitions team upon his return from Dallas. Apparently, there are quite a few issues that need addressing, but Charles doesn't want me to do anything until he gets back. Being Charles's PA makes me privy to almost everything that happens in the company, but this particular acquisition has piqued my curiosity because of how problematic it is and how I'm told very little to nothing about it. There's nothing useful in Charles's files either so I'm assuming he brought all the files relating to the Dallas acquisition with him together with his laptop. Because Charles is so hands-on, and this appears to be a sensitive procurement, maybe he prefers to take care of this directly with the head of Grant Corp's acquisitions, who also went with him in Dallas.

I decide to divert my attention and stop the conspiracy theories in my head. I know I'm just curious because the company they're trying to buy is so close to my hometown. Can this be me, being homesick? I shiver at the thought. There's nothing for me back home anymore. At least, that's what I try to convince myself.

My head is pounding by the time I'm out the building on the way to Magnus's Bentley. Alex opens the door, and I see that Magnus has beaten me again and is already waiting inside for me, with a big smile on his handsome face.

And just like that, his smile manages to make the worries go away. God, how does he do that? How does he manage to always make me feel like everything's okay?

"Not driving tonight?" I ask Magnus after Alex closes the door behind me.

"No, Alex took the other car home. I need my attention focused on one thing only," he answers, his voice smooth as silk and making me quiver all over.

"Really? What is that?" I ask.

"Oh, so we're playing games tonight, aren't we?" The wicked gleam in his eyes is unmistakable.

Oh ... *oh!* My mind is so preoccupied since this afternoon that I completely forget about my 'promise' this morning.

And the way he's looking at me, so hungry and in heat—he wants me, and I know I want him just as badly. Being with him makes me feel good ... so good it's almost addictive.

Yes, I'll play Mr. Grant. With my heart racing, I look back at him coyly. "Have you been good today, Mr. Grant?" I ask him softly.

Magnus doesn't answer. Instead, he unbuckles his seat belt, and shifts over to my side and pulls down a seat that was once flushed in the wall in front of me. *Wow, this car has a lot of surprises ... just like him.* My heart starts to beat faster as he sits in front of me, holding my thighs in place with his hands. He bends forward and kisses me hungrily.

"I've been looking forward to this," he murmurs on my lips, and I throw my arms around his neck in return.

His mouth travels down the crook of my neck, nibbling my skin and tasting it. His hands start to slide up the length of my thighs, hitching my skirt up to my hips, opening my legs. I moan at the feel of his lips on my skin and his capable hands massaging my inner thighs and making me tremble under his very touch.

"Magnus," I gasp when he starts tugging my panties off and then deposits it inside his trouser pocket. Then he takes his coat off and throws it on the other seat.

Before I know it, he's kneeling in between my legs.

My chest is heaving with anticipation, because I know that I am ready for him. He leaves small kisses inside my left thigh, and the electricity is shooting through me and intensifying with every contact. I groan as soon as I feel his tongue on my crevice, and I tremble when he starts flickering my clitoris. My hands are on his thick, silky hair, gripping it as if trying to gain some control of what he's doing to me.

I don't want to come yet, but he feels too good, *he* is too good. And I need the release. This pent up tension inside of me is cracking like a dam unable to hold the force that is Magnus's tongue.

"Let go, Isabelle. Don't fight it," his urging takes me to the brink, and I breathe out his name as my orgasm unfolds, my eyes wide open and looking up the ceiling.

Wow ...

His eyes are hooded when he looks up at me, still in between my legs, but his smile is satisfied, like a vampire full after his feed.

"So, Magnus, time for *your* reward." I hold onto his face with my hands, and I kiss him with ardor, my senses on overdrive at the mingling of my scent with his.

"But, baby, I *have* taken my reward." And in one lingering kiss, he pulls away and sits back on his seat, leaving me perplexed and slightly annoyed.

"Wait, but I want to please *you*," I voice out, my brows furrowed.

"You did, by coming while I'm pleasing you," he replies calmly.

"That doesn't make sense," I answer, getting even more confused and annoyed. Why can't he see that I want to give just as much as he does?

Magnus realizes my frustration and turns to me. He takes my hand in his and kisses my knuckles. "The look on your face whenever you reach your orgasm is so beautiful, Isabelle. You look so ... free. And after what you've been through ..."

"Magnus ... don't ...," I whisper, my voice trembling.

"My reward is to see you come. Because I know that at that moment, I helped make you happy ... I helped you feel free."

The honesty in his light blue eyes was enough for my tears to form. He wants me to be happy, by all means possible. Is this man for real?

"But I'm a very selfish person too, baby. I want you to come because of me, and only me. I want to own all of your orgasms."

Oh. "Hmm, well, that *is* pretty selfish. But how can I say no to that when I absolutely feel the same way?" My voice crackles, even with humor in it. I'm still too moved by his revelation that my chest feels like it want to burst.

The look of relief on his face is unmistakable. He reaches the back of my neck and gently pulls me towards him. As our lips meet into a tender kiss, tears start streaming down my cheeks.

He pulls away with concern on his face. "What's wrong? Why are you crying?"

I shake my head as he wipes the tears from my cheeks with his thumbs. "God, I'm such a cry baby, sorry! I'm just happy. I never thought anyone could care for me in so many levels. I definitely wasn't expecting someone like you," I whisper.

"I wasn't expecting someone like you either, but you're the best surprise I ever had," his lips curve into a slow smile, and he takes my hand and laces my fingers with his.

Just then, the car comes to a halt. I look out and notice that we're parked in front of my apartment building. Back to reality with a thud, I hesitate before untangling my hand with his.

"Stay the night with me?" I ask, touching his arm.

He looks at me with a spark in his eyes. "Are you sure? Will Ethan be okay with that?"

"He likes you a lot. I'm sure it'll be okay." I answer reassuringly.

"Will you be staying with me tomorrow night?" he asks back.

"I'll check with Michelle and Ethan, but I'm sure it'll be fine." I notice the wrinkling in between his brows. "Don't you wish right now that you hooked up with a single chick with no baggage? Life would've been a lot easier for you." I add jokingly.

He chuckles. "It wouldn't matter if the chick has baggage or not, as long as you're that chick."

I bury my face in my hands, a little unwilling for him to see how much I've fallen for him even more.

But Magnus pulls my hands down and regards me seriously. "I'll come down to say hi to Ethan, but unfortunately, I'll be heading back home after. As much as I want us to finish what we've started tonight, you'd still be a little swollen and most likely sore. So I think it's prudent for us to just wait until tomorrow," he sighs aloud and rakes his hand through his hair. He's as frustrated as I am. But I can't argue with him if he's right.

Magnus opens the door on his side and walks around to my side. Alex, who is already waiting by my side of the car, nods at Magnus and walks back to the driver's seat. Magnus opens the door for me, and helps me out. As I'm straightening my skirt, I realize I'm missing an essential part of my clothing.

"Magnus, my underwear! You still have it!' I tell him softly with gritted teeth.

"You can have it back tomorrow," he answers with a naughty smile on his face, with his hand protectively inside his trouser pocket. "I might just put this to good use while I'm alone in bed tonight," he whispers to my ear before discreetly nipping the tip of my lobe.

I gasp before covering my mouth to soften my giggles. My mind is suddenly filled with thoughts of him doing damage to my panties, and surprisingly enough, it's getting me hot ... and very jealous of my own underwear.

"Wouldn't you like to know what I'd do with it?" he growls at my ear as if reading my mind. He wraps his arm around my waist, holding me close as we walk up the flight of stairs to my apartment.

"Um, surprise me?" I answer back with a brow arched for added effect. He lets out a laugh before kissing my temple.

The minute we get in the apartment and Ethan sees Magnus, he quickly jumps off the couch and greets him. With no hesitation, Magnus picks him up and flies him around like he's an airplane, and Ethan's not exactly small or light. But the sheer joy on Ethan's face melts my heart and my tears start to brim. I manage to get myself together just before Magnus puts Ethan back on his feet.

"That was so much fun, Magnus!" Ethan tells him excitedly.

"We'll do that again next time, okay, buddy?" he says while lightly ruffling my son's hair.

Ethan nods happily. At this moment, he realizes I exist and that I'm standing right next to Magnus.

"Hi, Mom!" He gives me a big hug and reaches up for a kiss, which I happily give him.

"Oh, so you finally notice I'm right here, huh?" I tease him while hugging him tight.

When Ethan manages to wriggle out of my arms and runs off, that's when I notice Tasha sitting on the couch with him, which means Nathan's here as well.

"Hey, guys!" I call out as we walk to the kitchen where Nathan is letting Michelle have a taste of whatever he's cooking. It makes me smile at how normal and domesticated they look together.

"Oh, hey, Billie." Michelle waves to me. I give them both a kiss on the cheek.

"Here, try this. I know it's missing something, but I can't figure out what it is." Nathan playfully rests his arm on my shoulder, and the fact that his touch isn't affecting me negatively is a happy surprise. He scoops a small spoonful of what looks like pasta sauce and directs it to my mouth.

"Hmmm." I smack my lips. "Needs more basil, I think," I reply.

"See, I told you!" Nathan laughingly makes his point out to Michelle, who playfully puts a hand to his face.

A cough interrupts our revelry. We turn around to see Magnus with a scowl on his face, his eyes set on Nathan's arm, which is still on my shoulder.

"Magnus! How are you, man?" Nathan awkwardly removes his arm off me, wiping his hands on a kitchen rag next to the stove, before walking over to Magnus to shake his hand.

Magnus nods and takes Nathan's hand, but his eyes are on me.

"Sorry to interrupt," he tells me, giving a sidelong glance at Nathan with his steely blue eyes. "But I have to go, Isabelle."

I steer Magnus out of the kitchen, away from the bemused expression on Michelle's face and straight to my bedroom.

"Please stay for dinner," I ask him softly.

"Are you sure you want me to stay? Nathan seems only too happy to have you around," he coolly tells me with his mouth set in a hard line.

"Oh, for God's sake, Magnus! You know he's with Michelle, right?" I answer exasperatingly, walking towards the window and crossing my arms defensively.

"I don't appreciate other men touching you. I thought you don't like being touched by other men either?" His cold blue eyes are as hard as the expression on his face.

"It's not that bad with Nathan. I'm comfortable around him and only because he and Michelle are really serious about each other. Please Magnus, there's no malice in his actions."

"Any man's touch will be malicious in my eyes when it comes to you, Isabelle. I can't stand other men touching you. It fucking kills me, and then it makes me want to kill him!"

I walk back to him tentatively, wrapping my arms around his waist and pressing my cheek against his hard chest. I close my eyes, listening to his heartbeat as it starts to slow down, his chest eventually relaxing. Finally, he sighs and wraps his arms around me.

"God, Isabelle. I never felt like this about anyone," he whispers against my hair.

"Neither have I, Magnus. Sometimes it scares me," I answer against his chest.

"Why does it scare you?" he asks softly, tipping my chin up so I can look up at him. His expression has softened.

"Because I don't want to upset you enough that you'll hurt me. And I don't want to lose you," I answer softly.

Magnus tips my head up, and a mixture of concern and anger is written all over his face. "Wait, did he ever hurt you when you were together?" he asks softly, but his jaw keeps clenching tightly.

I avoid looking at him, embarrassed by what I'm about to say, "Sometimes. Usually when I push him too hard. So I know it's my fault when he hurts me. He always told me he doesn't really want to hurt me, so when he does, it's because I've forced him to."

"That motherfucker," he hisses harshly. "No wonder you put yourself down so much."

Magnus places his hands on my shoulders and looks me straight in the eyes. The anger from his eyes is gone, replaced by pure concern. "I want you to understand this, and if I have to, I will repeat it over and over again until it's instilled in you," he pauses. "Isabelle, there will never *be* an excuse to hit a woman. Never. He is a coward and a poor excuse of a man. Actually, no, he's a poor excuse of a human being to break down someone else's spirit like that because of their own insecurities."

I close my eyes in an attempt to stem my tears from falling.

"Open your eyes, baby," he urges gently. "As long as I'm around Isabelle, no one will hurt you, physically or otherwise. You are an amazing person, and whatever demeaning bullshit he threw at you are all false and untrue. He did it because he was too much of a weakling to let you think for yourself. And he knew it. He knew you were way too good for him."

"Stop ... Magnus ..." I place a shaky hand on his chest.

"I will never lay a hand on you like that, Isabelle." He kisses my trembling lips softly, reassuringly. "And you will never lose me. Never." He kisses my temple gently and holds me close.

"I believe you, Magnus. I really do," I answer back.

We hold each other for a few more moments, until my gaze somehow travels and lingers on the gown hanging on the other side of my room.

Magnus follows my gaze. "I can't wait to see you in that gown tomorrow."

"I hope I make the designer proud," I think out aloud.

"Isabelle, you can be wearing a paper bag and you'll still be the most beautiful woman in the event."

Knock! Knock! "Mommy? Magnus? Are you in there?"

"Yes, Ethan. We'll be out soon." We pull apart hastily before opening the door to let Ethan in.

"Are you staying for dinner, Magnus? 'Cos Tasha and I are setting the table." Ethan looks at Magnus expectantly.

Magnus looks to me with an unsure expression on his face.

"Mom, can Magnus stay?" Ethan asks me instead.

"It's entirely up to him, honey. But it would be wonderful if he could stay for dinner, right?" I look up at Magnus with an encouraging smile.

"How can I say no to you, or your mom? Count me in, buddy." They give each other a fist bump which makes me chuckle softly, earning me a smile from Magnus.

Dinner is thankfully pleasant, but it's more to the credit of the kids for making the atmosphere lighter. Magnus manages to act civil towards Nathan, who still has no idea that he was *this close* to getting seriously hurt. How? Because I read a feature article about Magnus on GQ, and it said he studied mixed martial arts. Yeah, he was close to going UFC on Nathan. That would not have been a pretty sight.

After dinner, Magnus expresses his apologies and excuses himself so he can head out. He promises to see Ethan soon, and thanks Michelle and Nathan amicably for a delicious dinner.

"Thanks for not hurting Nathan," I jokingly tell him near the stairs outside my apartment.

"Thanks for stopping me," he answers with a wry grin.

"So, is your invitation to stay tomorrow still open?" I ask, chewing my lip while waiting for his answer.

He tugs my lip free and runs his thumb gently across it.

"That invitation is indefinitely open only to you," he answers in his low voice, his eyes fixed on my mouth.

"Oh ... well, I've decided to accept it," I answer teasingly.

His eyes light up, and his smile makes me swoon. He draws me to him with an arm around my waist, and he plants an affectionate kiss on my lips.

"You don't need to bring change of clothes. Just leave it up to me," he whispers in my ear, nipping at my lobe gently and making me sigh. God, he knows how to turn me on just like that. After one more kiss, he heads downstairs and out of the building.

"Okay, what is up with Magnus earlier?" Michelle asks once we're alone. My poor son is too exhausted and is sleeping already. Michelle and I are sitting on the couch with some hot chocolate and marshmallows ... because it's that kind of Friday.

"What do you mean?" I ask, feigning innocence.

"Girl, he looked like he wanted to strangle Nathan while we were in the kitchen. Wait ... hold up ... is it because Nathan put his arm on you?" she asks incredulously.

I shrug but remain silent, concentrating on sipping my beverage instead.

"Oh, shit, it is. Was he jealous of that? I was right there with you guys, and I didn't think anything of it. Was Magnus jealous?" She grabs my arm and shakes it, as if she's trying to wrangle an answer out of me.

"Yes, well, he doesn't like other men touching me." I shrug.

"*You* don't like other men touching you. You two are *the* perfect match, oh my God!" She laughs.

"I tell you what though, there's nothing sexier than a hot man getting all protective on your ass. Nathan's pretty easygoing most times, but I've seen his jealous streak. And it is hawt, girl! In your case though ... just remember there *is* a fine line between being overprotective and being obsessed." Michelle gets serious and cocks an eyebrow at me.

"You're not telling me anything I don't know already," I answer back. "He really likes me, Michelle. Maybe that's why he feels the need to protect me, especially since ... well, he knows."

Michelle nods and sips her hot chocolate. Then she looks back at me with excitement in her eyes.

"So, have you decided on what you're going to do with your hair and makeup for tomorrow night?"

My face lights up with the same excitement as I describe what I have in mind. Michelle is a genius when it comes to makeup and hair, so I can't wait to see if I can pull off the style I want.

While she's practicing different hairstyles with me, I suddenly realize that I haven't told Michelle I'm sleeping over there.

"Hey … I just wanted to ask you … about tomorrow night … I've decided to stay at Magnus's after the charity thing. I was wondering about Ethan …"

"Don't worry about it, baby girl. You know that I know you better than yourself sometimes," she laughingly tells me.

"I kind of thought you might want to celebrate your 'first event as a couple' at Magnus's anyway. Don't worry, Nathan and Tasha are staying over for another slumber party tomorrow night. It should be fun … for both of us!" She giggles, and I can't help but giggle with her. I have an amazing friend.

I raise my head to look up to her. "I love you, you know that, right?"

"Oh yeah, I know it!" she laughingly answers.

We talk about other things, catching up on this week's stories, and what style I'm planning on for tomorrow night. When we finally decide on what hairstyle works best, we both agree to head for our bedroom for some much needed sleep.

CHAPTER 18

I feel numb. I can't open my mouth anymore, can't cry out. I'm so tired, with a constant dull pain down my groin. I can't find the strength to struggle as he defiles me, over and over again. He must be so high because no human in his or her right mind will do this to another human being. Or maybe it's because he's just an animal.

He says he loves me, even breaking down in tears, apologizing a few times. And he heeds me and lets me drink water once in a while. But what he really does to me isn't brought by love. Or maybe it is, I don't know anymore. All I know is that I want this to end. I'm so tired ... and dirty. I feel so dirty.

My face is wet with tears because they seem to flow endlessly. I'm still tied to the bed in God knows where. I don't even know how long I've been here ... has it been days?

Then I hear him come in the room again. Cooper ... I know it's him. He's not admitting to it, but I know it's him. I know his smell, the way he kisses— hard, impatient, clumsy, and selfish.

"Please ... Cooper ... no more ..." I beg of him.

He laughs out aloud, like what I said was the funniest thing he heard.

"Don't worry your pretty little head, Autumn. I'm very, very satisfied. You're going home soon."

He sits next to me, and I feel my skin crawl just sensing him this close.

"Listen, I'm going to cut you loose, then I'm going to take you to the bathroom where you'll take a shower. You will follow what I tell you to do, and you will not, under any circumstances, remove the patches I've taped over your eyes. If you do," he says, his mouth now inches from my ear as my breathing starts to quicken. Then a cold, pointed object is pressed on my cheek, as he continues, "I will kill you. Do you understand me?"

I nod without hesitation, my whole body trembling with fear. He cuts off my restraints, and I hiss at the sting of release, my wrists throbbing too much. The restraints on my ankles are next, and it takes me a while before I realize they're free. They must be so numb from the tightness of the rope. But he also removes something else from my wrists and ankle.

"Awesome, not a mark on you. Who knew wrapping foam around them would work?" he says, sounding sickeningly proud of himself.

He drags me up on my feet, and I wince at the pain shooting up my legs. My stomach still hurts so badly from where he punched me.

"Wait ... wait." My legs start buckling from the numbness after a few attempts, and I struggle to get up.

"Shit, c'mon. I haven't got all day!" he snarls impatiently.

He carries me over his shoulder like I'm a sack of rice, and my stomach bears the brunt. But I keep the pain to myself. What if he hurts me again if I complain?

Finally, he puts me down on some cold tiles, and I stretch my arms out to find a wall or something to hold on to so I don't lose my balance and slip.

Then I hear a creaking sound, and I shriek as cold water starts splattering all over me.

"Oops, haha! Here, let me mix in some hot water for you!" My tears threaten to spill out. Why is he treating me like an animal? How can he say he loves me and treat me like this?

"Now scrub yourself from head to toe!" He hands me a bar of soap. With shaky hands, I use the soap to wash my hair and my body, scrubbing harder around the places that he touched, that he hurt ... that he invaded. I'm scrubbing so hard that I'm feeling new pain from the friction, but I don't care. If I can remove the layer of skin that he touched, I will.

"Stop! I don't want any more marks on you. I made sure your arms and ankles have nothing on them. Don't you fucking mess it all up now." He grabs the soap off me, and I gasp as he pulls my hair and jerks my head towards him.

"Hurt yourself again, and you'll see what happens," he barks at me.

"Yes, okay, I'm sorry." I throw my shaky hands up in fright.

"Good, now rinse up, you're done."

***

My whole body is shaking, and my face is wet from the tears. The pillow I've buried my head in muffles my sobs. I slowly open my now heavy eyes. I'm back in my bedroom. But it doesn't make me feel any better. I feel so unsafe, so alone.

I wish Magnus were here with me. I never had these dreams when I sleep with him. I need him with me. With shaking hands, I note down the details just like Dr. Mitchell asked me to do.

Knock! Knock!

"Billie? Are you up?" It's Michelle. I get up and open the door for her.

"I heard you crying. You had another nightmare, didn't you? God, I want to kill that fucking son of a bitch!" Michelle exclaims as we sit on my bed.

I shake my head weakly, bringing my knees up to my chin. "He's not worth it. And good luck trying to get close enough to him. He's a son of a senator now, and would be flanked by security."

"Damn it, Billie, I'm just sorry this keeps happening to you. It hurts me so much to see you go through this constantly and not be able to do anything about it."

"You being here is helping me. And Magnus is there for me too. He doesn't have to, but he cares for me enough to hang around, you know ..."

Michelle wraps her arms around me. "I can see how much he loves you."

I pull away slightly, my eyes widening. "Who says anything about him loving me? There you go again. He doesn't, Michelle. He just cares for me, that's all. "

"Mm-hmm. Honey, you've got it bad. But I tell you what, I would gladly eat my favorite pair of heels if he doesn't admit that he loves you."

I don't say a word. I just lay my head on Michelle's shoulder, and we sit in silence for a few minutes.

"Would it help if I slept here with you? It's only four in the morning, and you need your beauty rest for tonight." She helps me back under the duvet, and she follows straight after.

"Thanks for staying," I tell her softly.

"Well, I'm neither tall, handsome, or rich, but I hope I can make do," she says with her brow cocked and a smirk on her face.

I reply by giving her a big hug and a kiss on the cheek. "You will do just fine, Michelle ... you'll do just fine!"

I wake up at around seven, still a little groggy from a few hours ago. Michelle is still sleeping beside me. I grab my phone and carefully get off the bed to check on Ethan, who's thankfully still asleep.

Excellent, this gives me a chance to prepare breakfast for two of my favorite people.

My mind wanders towards Magnus, and it makes me wonder if he's awake. I take my phone, and I send him a morning text. *'Good morning, Magnus. I hope you're well rested. I miss you, and I can't wait to see you tonight."*

I put my phone on vibrate so I don't wake the household in case Magnus texts me back. And not long after, I feel the phone vibrate in my pajama pocket.

He isn't texting me back. He's calling me.

"Hey, I wasn't sure if you're awake so I just sent you a text. How are you?"

"Better now that I'm hearing your voice," he replies, his voice a little rough.

"Did you not sleep well?"

"I seem to sleep better when I'm with you."

"So do I," I answer wistfully. "I'm so happy you called back though," I say, trying to sound lighthearted. "Luckily, my phone was on vibrating mode. I kind of enjoyed it though. Actually, I should've let it ring for a little bit more," I add.

"Oh, really? Now you're making me jealous of your phone? I better get over there and put it in it's place." He growls playfully.

I giggle before putting on my sexiest voice. "You can remind me later tonight … all night."

He pauses for a second. "Don't talk to me like that, Isabelle, especially when I'm so far away. You know what happens when you talk to me like that!"

"Down, boy," I answer in a low voice, loving the effect I have on him.

"Better eat a lot of protein and carbs today because you're going to need all of your energy for what I have in store for you tonight."

"You make it sound like I'll be doing the triathlon," I answer jokingly.

He chuckles softly, making him sound so sexy that my core tightens. "My darling, once we're done, it'll feel like you've done all the events of the Olympics."

"Hmmm, can't wait!"

"I'll pick you up at eight. See you then, beautiful." And we both hang up.

Oh. My. God. I think to myself excitedly, my heart beating so fast in anticipation.

Feeling energized after speaking with Magnus, I start on breakfast. Just as I finish up with the omelette and toast, Ethan comes shuffling in the kitchen, rubbing his eyes.

"Good morning, Ethan. Did you have a nice sleep?" I wrap him in my arms and kiss him on the top of his head.

"Yes." He nods.

"Wanna help me set the table?"

"Okay."

He walks off and slowly sets the table while I finish chopping off some fresh fruits to eat with some muesli and vanilla yogurt.

By the time breakfast is ready, I check on Michelle, who is starting to stir in bed. "Michelle? Breakfast is ready, okay?"

"Okay," she answers, her eyes still closed.

At the table, I sit opposite Ethan.

"So what would you like to do today, honey?" I ask Ethan.

"I thought you have a party to go to? Magnus asked me if you could go," he answers while chewing on his toast.

Magnus asked my son's permission? That man is full of surprises! "Did he? That won't be until tonight, honey. So you and I can hang still have our 'Saturdate' today."

"Oh, oh, I know! My friend Cody says he goes to Karate class, and I wanna do it too. Can we check out the classes?" he asks me with expectant eyes.

"Sure, buddy. I'll look up the closest ones online, then we can go check them out. How does that sound?" These classes can be expensive, and I don't get paid until next week, but it doesn't matter. It's a good idea for Ethan to take martial arts classes, anyway, so he can learn how to defend himself. I wish I took one myself when I was younger.

Michelle finally joins us for breakfast. When we're all done, I ask to borrow her laptop, and she waves at his desk where her workspace is.

I have to remind myself to get a laptop too, so I won't have to hassle Michelle so much.

I google Karate classes within our area and pick up three prospective ones, checking the class schedules on each. Luckily, they all have Saturday classes for Ethan's age group. It's just a matter of finding one he's comfortable with, and then we can go from there.

While I have the laptop, I decide to sneak a search on Magnus Grant as well. I must be missing him too much that I have to do a search for him online. His images come up, and most of them are just him, on his own, with an occasional pretty young thing beside him at galas or movie premieres. I check the dates on these photos and thankfully enough, they were from months before.

Then my stomach turns when I see a photo of him with Sofia Meier, his hand on her back. I know Magnus reassured me that their relationship is completely platonic, but knowing that they've shared a night together still makes me feel sick with jealousy. But like a masochist, I scroll down where a few more photographs come up that upset me even more. But one photograph in particular leaps out. It appears the photo was taken for the social pages of the New York Times, and it's Magnus sitting beside Sofia, with her hand on his knee and his arm at the back of a red leather couch. The background looks familiar. She is smiling and full of class while Magnus has small smile on his face making him effortlessly good-looking. But his smile doesn't reach his eyes. They are almost disarming with how cold they are, like he sees something displeasing to him but covering it up with a smile. I've seen that look before, more than once. I check the details of the photo: 'CEO of Grant Corp, Magnus Grant with Sofia Meier: two of Cirque Club's favorite VIPs.'

This is when I realize that the date proves that it's the same night I was there with Jess, Boyd, and Marla! Was this picture taken before or after he saw me in the club? When I saw him, he was happily chatting with Sofia. What changed his mood? Did seeing me in the club dancing with Boyd upset him? My heart flutters at the thought. He had his eyes on me, all along!

With a new sense of self-satisfaction, I close the window and Michelle's laptop.

Ethan is watching his Saturday morning cartoons, so I use this chance to help Michelle out with the dishes in the kitchen, and to have a little chat.

"Thanks again for staying with me," I tell her softly as I dry off the clean plates.

"You know that I'll always be here for you. You're my sister from another mother." She gives me a bear hug. She's right. Since my family abandoned me seven years ago, Michelle has become my family, and I love her for that.

"So what are you guys doing today?" Michelle asks.

"Ethan wanted to sign up for Karate classes, so we're gonna check out a few dojos. Then I'm taking him to Brooklyn Mac. And if we still have time, maybe we can chill at the park on the way back. What about you?"

"Well, I just have to do some finishing touches on this coffee ad, then I'm seeing the girls."

The girls are Tahni, Clara and Remy. I've known them since I've known Michelle. All four of them were established friends and they welcomed me with open arms as friend number five. I go out with them once in a while, but not often, since it's not always easy getting a babysitter. It also didn't help that most of my previous jobs had odd working hours.

"The girls! Tell them I said hi, and tell them I miss them."

"Tell 'em yourself. They'll be here tonight as your fairy godbitches," Michelle announces with a big smile and a wink.

"No way, really?" I exclaim excitedly. "But wait, so you told them I'm dating Magnus?"

Michelle shakes her head. "All they know is that you got invited by someone from work to a super formal event, and they all volunteered to give you a makeover. We're doing a party out of it right here with margaritas and everything!" She giggles. "I cannot wait to see the expressions on their faces when they realize who's taking you."

I shake my head at Michelle's mischievous plan. But it'd be wonderful to catch up with our friends. And it doesn't hurt that Remy is a professional stylist, so there's a very good chance I'd look presentable enough for Magnus and his family tonight.

I give Michelle a kiss on the cheek and thank her for her surprise. Then I tell Ethan to dress up so we can leave soon.

After visiting three local dojos, Ethan and I agree on the one closest to our apartment. I find the sensei as somewhat of a gentle soul, but watching him teach his class, he has a very commanding presence that his students seem to respect and look up to. And it's also a bonus that their fees are affordable

After our mac 'n' cheese lunch, we pass by the park since we have a couple of hours to spare, and I let Ethan play with the other kids at the playground. I sit at the bench nearby so I can keep an eye on him. As I watch him play with a big smile on his face, it just makes my heart want to explode with joy. Sometimes I thank the heavens that even with the horrific experience I had, I am blessed with a child who's so good and understanding. Ethan's my constant reminder that silver linings do happen … even in the worst of situations.

All of a sudden, my phone buzzes. My heart flutters upon seeing it's a message from Magnus. *'Counting the hours. Yours, M.'*

Short and sweet. I bite my lip as I reply back. *'Counting the minutes. Yours too, I.'*

I can't wipe the stupid smile on my face. I check the time. Four o'clock. Time to head home. I signal for Ethan, who does one more round on the slide before running to me. We walk home holding hands, with me feeling so lucky that I have a son who loves me regardless of my faults as a mother, and a man who's cares for me regardless of my past.

We can hear the happy chatter as Ethan and I reach our apartment. The girls give us enthusiastic hugs as if we've never seen each other in years. It's nice having the noisy bunch here.

Tahni is a very talented chef of Jamaican and Spanish descent, who owns a tapas restaurant at East Williamsburg. She brought her five-year-old son Henry, which is great because he and Ethan have been pals since Henry was born. Unsurprisingly, they head straight to Ethan's room to play. Clara is tall, tanned, and classically beautiful, with blonde hair and hazel eyes. She works part-time as a model to pay for her law degree. She's also in a long-term relationship with Remy, also tall, with pale skin, and jet black hair, which is shaved on one side and long on the other. She's a successful stylist for the music industry and especially on high demand for music videos. We're a rambunctious bunch, and it's always a party when we're all together.

But other than Michelle, they're the only friends who know about my past. I was apprehensive at first on opening up to them about the real reason I moved to New York. But they never judged me, and welcomed me like a sister.

We catch up with what's happening in the past weeks over tapas and margaritas, courtesy to Tahni. Unfortunately, we are having way too much fun catching up that we lose track of the time.

"Oh, my God, Billie, you have to get ready!" Remy exclaims, and I jump up when I see it's almost six o'clock.

"Okay, I'll just hop in the shower," I hurriedly say as I rush to my bedroom.

"Make sure you shave! You wanna be nice and smooth for your stud!" Clara shouts out, giggling.

"We've got kids here, Clara, God!" I could hear Michelle reprimanding the girls, making me snicker as I close my door.

Inside my bedroom, I quickly take out my overnight bag and throw in items that I might need for my overnight stay at Magnus's place. So I toss in my toiletries, hairdryer, a dress, flats, my sexiest underwear, and my red satin nightie, which I bought months ago on a whim but never got a chance to use.

After showering and as Denise says to make sure I'm nice and smooth, I open my bathroom door to find the girls gawking at my gown.

"Holy shit, that's a really high-end gown!" Remy exclaims with her mouth still gaping. She looks at me with wide eyes and a sceptical look on her face.

"Michelle told us he bought you this and the Loboutins? First of all, how rich is this stud that he can get you this gown fresh off the runway, with limited edition heels? And no offense but are you sure he's not gay? I only ask this because his taste is fucking exquisite!"

"You'll know who he is soon enough, Remy, so get your nosy ass off of Billie's case," Michelle interrupts with sass, giving me a wink for good measure.

"Oh, and he's definitely not gay … trust me," I continue pointedly with a grin. "Now, let's get this over with, shall we?"

Denise claps her hands excitedly. "Let the makeover begin!"

After close to an hour, the girls step back to inspect their finished 'project.' They don't want me to check the mirror until they're done, but from the proud looks in their eyes, I feel it's time to check the end result.

I gasp at the sight of myself in the mirror. My hair looks so different, like an actress from the forties with one side smoothed and flattened with hidden hairpins, while on the other side, my long auburn hair flows over my shoulder just covering my lace-covered left breast as it falls in big lush waves. My makeup is kept minimal with just eyeliner with a slight wingtip, nude eyeshadow, some rouge on my cheeks, and deep red lips.

And my gown, wow! My gown fits perfectly and hugs the right curves. Even with the long sleeves, the gown shouts sexy, with the deep v-neckline and intricate lace and beading covering my chest in the right way. The back is cut so low that I'm practically bare from my neck down to my waist. The slim leather belt cinches my waist, and the thigh high slit in the middle of the billowy georgette skirt, with the help of the spiky black heels, shows off just the right amount of skin without being scandalous. I turn around slowly, checking every angle and giving myself a little smile.

'Aphrodite.' Magnus's reference echoes back to my ears. Is this how he truly sees me? The thought brings a big smile to my face and tears start to well up in my eyes.

"Hey, hey, honey, don't cry. You'll ruin your makeup. What's wrong?" Michelle holds me by my shoulder, her face concerned.

I shake my head. "I'm okay, just overwhelmed. It all looks beautiful. Thank you so much, girls. You did an amazing job!"

Remy gives me a quick hug. "Baby girl, we didn't do much. This is all you. You actually scrub up nice."

"I am the luckiest girl on Earth to have you all as friends. I hope you know that," I tell them sincerely, my tears threatening to fall but I quickly blink them off.

"Stop it, you're gonna make me cry!" Tahni pipes in, fanning her face with her hands exaggeratingly.

Ethan and Henry, hearing the commotion, run down from Ethan's room. I laugh when I see Ethan look gobsmacked.

"Whoa, Mom! You look so beautiful. Like a princess!" He gives me a tight squeeze on my waist.

"Thank you, honey. That means a lot." And I lightly kiss the top of his head.

"Here, you can borrow this purse." Michelle hands me her Alexander McQueen knuckleduster evening clutch. The contrast of edgy and elegant compliments what I'm wearing. But it's too expensive for me to borrow, plus this is Michelle's favorite clutch.

"Michelle! This is too much!" I try to hand it back to her.

"Shut up, you're using it, no questions asked!" She waves her finger at me. I can't argue with her when she's like this.

"Ok, ok ... Thank you," I reply, smiling back at her.

Just as I'm putting my phone and other necessities in the borrowed purse, the phone rings.

"Is it him?" Clara asks enthusiastically, so I hold up my forefinger to my lips for some quiet before answering the call.

"Hello?"

"Hello, Isabelle. I'm downstairs. Buzz me in."

My heart starts to thud so hard that I think it might leap out. All three girls rush to the front window before I can reach the intercom button to buzz him in.

"Ho-ly shit!" cries Tahni. "That's Magnus Grant! *He's* the guy from work that asked you out?"

"Damn straight! He's not just any guy at work. Our girl has done well!" Michelle exclaims mischievously.

I glare at all of them when I hear the knock on the door, hoping they quiet down.

"Let me open the door. Stand over there, so he can see you first thing," Michelle whispers, beating me to the door.

Here goes nothing. I take a deep breath and stand where Michelle asked me to.

She opens the door, and there he is. As soon as Magnus lays his eyes on me, his mouth gapes open.

And in that moment when our eyes meet, everything else seems like a blur.

"Hi." I walk towards him, gaining confidence with every step.

He looks beyond handsome in his black tailored tuxedo suit. His shiny black hair is slicked back, and groomed so stylishly. Blood rushes to my cheeks at the intensity of his blue eyes as they drink in every inch of me.

"You ... look ... breathtaking. Absolutely breathtaking," he whispers as he closes the gap, brushing his warm lips on mine. I've been aching for his kiss in what feels like forever but it's only really been since last night.

"Oh, my God," Clara gasps, and Remy quickly shushes her, effectively breaking the moment.

"I'm sorry, where are my manners?" I respond breathlessly, blinking my eyes way too fast. "Magnus, I'd like you to meet the girls—Tahni, Remy, and Clara."

Magnus graciously shakes each of their hands. "It's a pleasure meeting all of you …. Michelle." He nods at Michelle with a small smile on his face before holding me close, his hand settling on my bare lower back.

"We know who you are," Remy adds. "You are a rock star, man. I've actually styled for a couple of editorials for Flair."

Magnus nods approvingly. Flair is a popular magazine for urbanites, featuring mostly fashion, as well as socially relevant issues. Grant Corp also owns the publication.

"I'll make sure to check your work. And if you helped style Isabelle, then I'm already a fan," Magnus answers graciously.

His answer makes Remy blush, which is a rare occurrence.

"So how long has this been going on?" Clara blurts out, with a stunned expression still on her face.

Magnus cocks a brow at my direction with a suggestive smile, waiting for my answer. I squint my eyes at him playfully before answering Denise. "Not that long, but it's … it's been amazing." All the while, our eyes never leave each other.

"Well, if you don't mind, I'm going to have to take this stunning woman away for a little while."

The girls start talking at the same time, asking him questions. So I take the opportunity to excuse myself to go to Ethan's room.

"Honey, we're going now."

"Hey, buddy," Magnus manages to break away from the girls and greets Ethan from behind.

Ethan walks to us and gives us both a hug. "Have a great time! I love you!" Then he scuttles back to the game he's playing with Henry. Ah, boys and their toys.

As we head out the door, Magnus carries my overnight bag while I grab my purse, before giving all of my girls a hug.

"Don't worry about Ethan, okay? Nathan and Tasha will be here shortly. You enjoy yourself now," whispers Michelle.

Magnus and I are hand-in-hand as we walk to his vehicle, this time a limousine. The driver waiting is unfamiliar to me. He opens the door for us, before depositing the bag inside the now open trunk.

"I gave Alex the night off. Which means we have the penthouse to ourselves later. We're using father's car tonight." Oh, suddenly I'm feeling tightness in my core at the very thought of having him all to myself in a few hours.

Inside the limo, we've barely made it out to the road when Magnus presses a button for the privacy screen. He turns towards me as I wait with baited breath. He raises one arm to rest behind me while his eyes follow the trail his forefinger touches—from my cheeks, brushing on my lower lip, down to my neck, towards the deep v of the bodice, straight down my stomach, and stopping just above my groin. My breathing becomes labored as his finger moves down to the tip of my thigh high slit, deftly pulling them apart to reveal my skin. He draws circles around the exposed thigh, making my skin increasingly sensitive to his touch. I close my eyes to control the trembling of my core.

"Open your eyes and look at me, Isabelle," he gently commands as he raises my chin with the same forefinger.

I do as he says, instantly drawn to the intensity of his eyes.

"Feeling nervous about tonight?" he asks.

"I am. I'm meeting your family. That's pretty nerve-wracking," I answer with a shaky laugh.

He regards me thoughtfully.

"Do you still feel sore?" he asks gently.

"No," I answer, shaking my head.

"Good, because I'm going to make you come now."

"Oh!" I gasp as his fingers make their way inside my dress through the slit. He starts to trace patterns on my crotch, still protected by my panties, making me hot to my core and practically panting.

Before long, he slides my panties off me and smirks as he lifts it up. "Thongs ... I never appreciated these things until now," he teases before tucking it inside his trouser pocket.

"Will I be getting that back, Mr. Grant?" My brow is cocked and my lips upturned in a coy smile.

"We'll see," he answers back, before his hand travels up my inner thigh, grazing the sensitive skin and making my insides throb. I gasp as his forefinger slides up and down my moist crevice, finally circling my clitoris. I close my eyes involuntarily from the pleasure it's giving me.

"Open your eyes, Isabelle," he firmly commands me again, and I comply.

"I can feel how much you want this too." He licks his lips slowly as he uses my wetness to slowly slide his finger inside my core.

"Oh." I bite my lower lip, my eyes fluttering momentarily. He feels so good, like he's meant to have this connection with me. I can see how pleasurable this is for him as well. He bends his head and lightly flickers his tongue on my lower lip, convincing my mouth to open.

He directs my other hand to his crotch, and I feel his hardened length twitch underneath his tailored trousers. His eyes follow my eager hand before gazing back into my own.

"You do this to me, every time," his voice is husky and low ... and maddeningly sexy. His adept fingers quickly circles around my clitoris, pressing, and increasing the speed, making my legs widen with surrender. My orgasm is building up and I don't know how long I can hold on. I mew, and I move my hips to mirror his hand movements.

"Look at me, Isabelle. I want to see your incredible green eyes when you come. I want to feel your insides throb against my fingers."

"I'm so close," I whimper as my fingernails dig into his coat sleeve.

"I know, baby. Let go."

"Magnus!" I cry out his name, as I shatter to a billion pieces. I feel my core shuddering, and my hips buckling.

"That's it, baby." His eyes are hooded, and his mouth is slightly open. I know how turned on he is by the way the tip of his tongue licks his front teeth. God, he's so sexy, it's driving me mad!

Unable to resist, I move forward, meeting my tongue with his, my lips nipping at his lower lip. He tips my head up, deepening our kiss and making me moan against his mouth. I run my fingers through his hair, pushing him down, needing more of him. He slowly pulls his fingers out from inside of me and detaches his mouth from mine. But then he starts sucking on the same forefinger and middle finger. It turns me on so much that I stare at his fingers in hunger.

"Here, baby. Taste yourself." I open my mouth with no hesitation. The reaction on his face as I suck both of his fingers with enthusiasm is priceless, giving me some bravado to grab his wrist with both hands and slide his fingers in and out of my mouth. His breathing becomes raggedy, his eyes fixed solely on my mouth.

I start unbuckling Magnus's trousers, and he lets me take control as I set his throbbing manhood free, pushing his trousers down to his ankles.

"I want you inside me, Magnus," I breathe out, as I leave kisses on the palm of his hand before kissing him hard in the mouth.

"Sit on my lap." His voice is thick with unbridled desire as he stands me up and lifts my delicate skirt aside by the high slit. I let out a long, satisfied sigh once I let his hardness slide inside me, filling me up completely. My skirt billows down over the sides of our legs, concealing our actions under silky georgette. I move forward to kiss him, meeting his every thrust with my own, moaning in sheer ecstasy, knowing his cock feels so damn right inside of me.

Now I understand why he wants this connection. Why he wants me to keep my eyes open for him. His blue eyes speak volumes, locked against mine. It's nothing I've ever felt before. It makes my heart want to explode.

"Isabelle," is all he utters as he comes, the throbbing of his cock tips me over the edge and I join him. I let my eyes shut tightly, my head thrown back at the overwhelming release.

"Magnus … that was so … intense," I whisper against his ear, still breathing heavily. His arms are wound tightly around me, and we hold each other like this until our hearts pump a steady beat.

"Still feeling nervous?" he asks, his eyes soft, but observant.

"No, I actually feel ready," I answer brightly.

A slow smile reaches his face, and that's when I realize what he's done.

"You made me come for a reason, didn't you? You wanted me to lose the nerves."

He doesn't answer me, but continues to regard me with affection in those stunning blue eyes. That in itself, speaks volumes.

"We're almost here, baby," Magnus whispers against my ear as he gently lifts me off his lap and sits me next to him.

He starts pulling his pants up and tucking his dress shirt in. He grabs a couple of tissues so he can clean me up, as per his ritual of care. Then he thankfully hands me my thong, which I quickly put back on.

"I personally prefer the just-fucked scent on you, but considering the circumstances …" he remarks with a wicked gleam in his eyes.

I roll my eyes at him and shake my head in mock disappointment. "Like I said before, you are incorrigible, Mr. Grant," I exclaim before chuckling softly.

Thankful that I brought my compact mirror and lipstick, I correct my smudged lips and notice pink hues on my cheeks and lips. I try to smoothen out one side of my hair, making sure there are no strays. *I probably look ravished.* I just hope it won't be so noticeable once I meet Magnus's family.

"So how do I look … do I look okay?" I ask Magnus. We arrive at the venue and about to pull up at the entrance.

Magnus looks at me adoringly, making my heart skip a beat. "Okay is not exactly the word I'd describe you, Isabelle. Exquisite, I think, is more appropriate." He raises my hand and kisses my knuckles. The electricity from that small kiss still manages to send shockwaves through my veins.

I love this man so much. I can't help it, I really do love him so much … even if he probably doesn't feel the same as I do.

"Are you ready? Or would you prefer the side entrance? It's your choice, baby," he says softly, still keeping my hand in his while we wait for our turn in the line of cars.

I shake my head. "No, I can handle this. I've got you, right?" I ask tentatively.

"You sure do, my temptress." Magnus shows me his confident smile, and that's all the convincing I need.

"Let's do this then."

An attendant finally opens the limo door. Outside, there is a red carpet and waiting photographers on the other side of the red velvet ropes.

I exhale deeply. *This is it.*

"Time to show you off to the world, Ms. Isabelle Morrison."

He gets off the car first, holding his hand out for me to take. The flashing lights from the cameras overwhelm me. This kind of reception is only fit for celebrities. With his sexy good looks and achievements in the business world, it's no surprise that Magnus is a regular in media outlets. He's used to the limelight. But I am most definitely not.

While walking the red carpet, one of the organizers asks us to stand in front of the event backdrop so we can be photographed. I try to step back, preferring to watch him in his element. After all, this is his mother's event and I'm trying to stay anonymous. But Magnus keeps his arms around my waist and refuses to let me go.

"I want you beside me, Isabelle. I want everyone to know that you are with me. And if you're still worried, don't be. I'm here to keep you safe, okay?" the way he whispers those words in my ear, eases my apprehension. I *am* a long way from Texas. If they ever release our photograph, it will only be for the local papers …. at least that's what I'm counting on.

"Mr. Grant, over here!" one of the photographers yells out.

"Miss, who are you?" Another asks. "Mr. Grant, who are you with, tonight?"

Magnus nods to me reassuringly, and I nod back at him so he can go ahead and answer.

"All you need to know is, this amazing woman right here is someone very, very special to me. Thank you."

"She's gorgeous, Mr. Grant!" I hear someone shout out randomly, making me blush.

"Thank you. I'm a very lucky man." I catch Magnus looking at me with adoring eyes, and I know for sure my cheeks are now red.

"You didn't disclose my name." I look up to him with both delight and curiosity in my eyes.

"Ah, but I did answer their question. They asked who I am with, and I answered accordingly. I didn't hear anyone asking specifically for your name," he explains mischievously.

We both chuckle softly. *This night is turning out to be unforgettable already.*

He leads me further down the red carpet towards the entrance of the Damrosch Park tent, with my nervous heart pumping a thousand beats a minute.

'Oh, wow!" my mouth drops at the extravagance before me. The venue has been transformed into something out of *Midsummer's Night Dream*, with Swarovski chandeliers, lush flora of various shades of earthy red, orange, and yellow. It looks like an autumn wonderland. I swallow hard.

"Hmmm, autumn." I feel like icy water was thrown on me, hearing Magnus speak of my former name.

"S ... sorry?" I stutter.

"Autumn. The theme for tonight's event is change, so it's like the autumn season," he pauses, then nods slowly, "and I've just realized the double entendre," Magnus looks at me with an apologetic smile.

"I'm just blown away by all of this," I explain, waving my hand around weakly to emphasize my point.

Magnus chuckles. "Well, my mother likes to make her fundraisers an event to remember. It helps raise a lot of money for her charities, so I suppose it's a necessary evil. Come, let's go find her so I could introduce you to her." He takes my hand and holds it securely, as he leads me through the sea of guests, who, at $10,000 per plate, should be at the upper echelon of society.

"Magnus! Wonderful, you're here!" We turn towards the direction of the warm voice, where a tall and elegant woman excuses herself from the couple she's talking to, and opens her arms wide as we approach. She has jet black hair tied in a neat chignon, with a streak of white hair running on one side. I've seen her before, in one of the photographs that came up when I googled Magnus the other day. And judging from her striking features, there is no denying it, this woman is Magnus's mother.

"Good evening, Mother," Magnus's voice is warm and relaxed. You can actually feel his affection towards her. It's beautiful and painful at the same time, as it reminds me of how it was between my own mother and me.

She gives Magnus a full embrace, with kisses on both cheeks before realizing that I'm standing a step behind her son.

"Mother, I'd like you to meet my girlfriend, Isabelle." Magnus guides me in front of him, which would have been all right, if I don't feel so nervous.

"So you are *the* Isabelle Morrison." She holds out her hand, and I accept it firmly. My eyes widen as she uses this to pull me close for a hug, patting my back gently and instantly easing my anxiety.

"Magnus has spoken about you on numerous occasions." Her kind eyes sweep me up and down gracefully. "And I dare say, I can understand why. She's gorgeous, dear." She looks on to Magnus and back to me again.

I feel a blush creep up my cheeks. "Thank you, Mrs. Grant. That's very kind of you," I reply nervously.

"You're welcome. And please, call me Miranda." Her smiling eyes are a light shade of blue. Magnus has definitely taken his looks from her.

"Now if you'll excuse me, I have my hostess hat on, so I should mingle. You two should do the same. Have fun!" She gives Magnus's arm a light squeeze and me a small wave before moving on to a power couple in the entertainment industry.

"Your mother is beautiful. I see where you got your looks from," I tell him openly, my nervousness easing down as we make our way to our table.

"So you're telling me that I'm good-looking?" he teases with his brow raised.

I roll my eyes at him. "Oh, please, let's not pretend for a second that you don't know you are!"

I gasp as he grips me tightly around my waist.

"Its just aesthetics, Isabelle," he whispers in my ear. "I'd like to think I have more substance than what I physically look like."

I turn to face him. "If it weren't for this, and this," I gently touch the side of his temple and the left side of his chest successively, "I wouldn't be with you right now. And as for your looks? " I shrug and give him a wink. "Well, I can't complain."

Magnus laughs out aloud, and my smile widens because I love the sound of his laughter especially when I'm responsible for giving it. Then he looks down to me with a hint of a smile and heat in his eyes. He rests his hand on the crook of my neck, tilting my head back so he can give me a tender kiss, making every part of my body feel like butter.

"Oh, puh-lease, get a room, you two!" A bubbly voice from behind us makes me jump, but Magnus doesn't pull away. Instead, he looks past me with a slight annoyance in his eyes but only for a second as the grim line of his mouth switches to a lopsided grin.

"Isabelle, I'd like you to meet my sister, Regan, whose timing, as always, is yet to be desired."

I turn around and I see yet another tall, attractive woman. She is most likely my age if not slightly younger than me, with hair as dark as Magnus's cut in a pixie style which suits her statuesque frame. And when she smiles, her whole face lights up and her blue eyes sparkle.

"Hello, there." She gives me quick, enthusiastic hug, and my polite smile widens. "It's good to finally meet you, Isabelle."

Does Magnus talk about me to his whole family? "And it's great to meet you too, Regan. But please ... call me Billie."

"Billie ... I love it! And you know what? This is the first time I've seen Magnus get all handsy with another woman in public, especially in Mom's fundraisers. He's super uptight on good days."

"Regan, this really isn't any of your business," Magnus snaps at her with a crease on his forehead.

I scowl back at Magnus for snapping at his sister.

"We'll try to keep on our best behavior from now on." I nod at Regan with a smile.

"I like her a lot, Magnus. Billie knows how to reign you in." Regan beams at him before turning back to me. "We should catch up over drinks one of these days. You have to give me your number."

"Um, sure. That'd be great." She hands me her smartphone, ready for me to enter my details.

"Regan, don't impose," Magnus sternly warns her.

"It's not an imposition at all, Magnus." I enter in my details and hand the phone back to his sister.

"Where's Father?" Magnus asks Regan while looking around the venue.

"Mingling. Well, I have to go find James. I'll see you at the table!" She gives Magnus and me a quick kiss on the cheek before flittering off in her beautiful red gown.

An announcement for everyone to make their way to their seats comes on. Not surprisingly, we're seated at the head table, together with the rest of Magnus's family. I'm seated next to Magnus and Regan, who introduces me to her boyfriend, James. They met six months ago at a mixer at Columbia University where they're both studying medicine. All this time, Magnus's hand is interlinked with mine underneath the table. Then he raises his head and stares at the man of strong stature and dark good looks walking towards us. He has graying temples on his otherwise dark brown hair. The man approaching us reminds me of actors back in the fifties—dashing and debonair. Beside him is who I assume is Gerald, Magnus's younger brother and the middle child of the family. He is shorter than Magnus, but still commands attention with his stance and attractive features. Magnus stands up and lets go of my hand, and I follow his lead. Both men are now right across the table from us. The elder offers his hand out to Magnus.

"Son, how wonderful to see you." Magnus shakes his hand firmly.

"I try not to miss Mother's fundraising events." Magnus's voice is polite but detached.

I'm suddenly feeling awkward at their exchange. I glance over at Regan, who's busy talking animatedly with James.

"So who may I ask, is this vision in front of me?" His hand is open, waiting for mine.

I oblige and place my hand in his. "I'm Isabelle Morrison. Billie, for short. It's a pleasure to meet you, Mr. Grant."

He places a light kiss on my knuckle, eliciting a loud exhale from Magnus. "The pleasure is all mine. Just call me Carlton, by the way. Where have you been keeping her, Magnus?" Carlton winks at me playfully.

I notice Magnus's face harden and his jaw clench, watching his father's movements closely. Possibly sensing the hostility, Carlton nods to both of us before taking his seat next to Miranda at the head of the table.

Gerald steps closer to us with a slight smile on his face. He offers his hand out, which I also accept, and he shakes it firmly.

"Well, it's nice to meet you, Isabelle. I'm Gerald." He leans closer, obliging me to do the same. "I would be careful about Magnus if I were you," he whispers, and I give him blank stare.

Magnus notices my reaction and literally blocks me from his brother. "I hope you're done with the introductions?" Magnus icily regards Gerald.

"Bro, I'm just trying to reduce the body count." Gerald raises his hands, snickering.

"Don't start with me, Gerald." Magnus's voice has a hint of quiet menace so nobody else but the three of us can hear. I instantly hold onto his arm, hoping to calm him down.

"Don't worry, I won't. Oh ... and by the way," Gerald pauses, "you'll never guess who I was talking to just a few minutes ago."

I look over to Magnus, but he looks just as puzzled as I am.

"On second thought, I'll keep it as a surprise. It's just more fun that way, don't you agree?'

And with that, Gerald gives him a mock salute before walking towards his seat with a self-satisfied swagger.

Sensing that all is not right, I brush my hand against his arm.

"Do you feel like talking about what just happened between you and your father, *and* you and Gerald?"

He turns to me, his jaw clenching. He seems unwilling to divulge anything.

"I'll tell you about me and my father eventually. I don't want to ruin tonight by talking about business."

"Okay," I nod in understanding.

"As for Gerald, he continues to give me a hard time about Martine ... among other things." he whispers gruffly.

"Why would Gerald give you hard time about Martine? You've been broken up for five years now, right?"

He doesn't answer. Maybe I'm pushing him too far?

"Don't worry, it's okay, maybe—"

Magnus interrupts what I'm saying, "Gerald has been in love with Martine from back then, and even more so now. He pursued her, but she wanted me, and he never got over it. And when we had that accident, he blamed me for it. He doesn't even know about the miscarriage. Martine and I decided to keep that between us."

"Magnus, that's his problem if he can't let go, not yours." I gently cup his face, trying to smooth the troubled lines that creep up.

"What about you? Do you ... do you still love her?"

He looks me straight in the eyes, blinking slowly, as if considering his answer.

"I did love her. But that was years ago, and whatever love I had for her, disappeared the minute I left her."

I should be happy with his answer, but what if those feelings return now that she's back for good? No, I can't allow it. I'm not giving Magnus up without a fight.

I reach up to give him a kiss on the lips before wrapping my arms around his shoulders. I want him to know that I'm just here if he needs me.

He sighs, settling a hand on the small of my back and on my arm with the other. We hold each other for what seems like hours, when it was only minutes. The announcement about the program starting brings us back to the now, so I straighten up on my seat while Magnus takes two flutes of champagne from the drink server and hands me one.

The emcee of the show introduces Miranda Grant to the stage, and we watch as she glides to the podium in her lavender gown with a grace and stature only accomplished by a former prima ballerina.

Miranda starts with a speech, thanking everyone for attending the fundraiser, especially since it's a $10,000 a plate event. She hopes to raise enough money to sponsor more scholarships for the less fortunate but talented students who would like to pursue a career in the arts. Then she goes through tonight's program—an auction of artworks from already sponsored students, a fashion show from up and coming fashion designers where all gowns to be featured will be up for sale, another auction of experiences, from a full day at the spa, to two VIP tickets to the Knicks game at Madison Square Garden. And last on the list is a performance from a Grammy award winning singer/songwriter.

Each auction coincides with each dinner course, and by the last course, and throughout the proceedings, Magnus has been attentive and affectionate, never leaving my side no matter how many times his attention has been sidetracked by people he knows, or by unabashed women blatantly hitting on him right in front of me. Thankfully, he ignores the latter. But by the tail end of the auctions, Magnus becomes too engrossed in a conversation with a hotshot lawyer, that I have to excuse myself to go to the ladies room.

After my trip from the ladies room, which took quite awhile because of the long line, I notice Magnus isn't in his designated seat and is nowhere to be found. I look around the venue hall full of revellers, thinking maybe he's come looking for me. Some guests are now dancing, and the singer is performing a song I want Magnus and myself to dance to. I decide to check if Magnus is in the men's room, and the closest one is along a hallway leading towards the side exit. On the way, I'm taking in the opulent décor and appreciating the amount of work made on this one event, when I feel two taps on my shoulder. *Magnus!* With a ready smile on my face, I turn around.

Only, it isn't Magnus staring at me from head to toe with malevolence in his eyes. It's the man I've been trying to escape from. But now he's right in front of me. *He's found me.*

"Well, well, well." He steps closer. "I heard Autumn is beautiful in New York, but I wasn't expecting this. Miss me, princess? Because I sure as hell did!"

No! No! No! This isn't happening! "Stay away from me, Cooper!" Even in shock at the sight of my living, breathing nightmare, now standing inches from me, my brain still works as it pushes my feet to move away from him as fast as I can.

"Oh, come on. But I wanted to catch up on lost time!" That voice I've been trying to erase from my memory seems to be getting closer. So I run. I run like a mad woman in my high heels, towards the crowded dance floor, hoping I'd get swallowed by the crowd. In my haste, I bump into some of the dancers, but I ignore their shocked expressions. I find the hallway I was looking for, where the men's room and exit door are. I look back and I can't see Cooper. Maybe I lost him. So I turn towards the hallway, peeking out to make sure I'm safe. I run further down the hall to be sure, but the shock and the running have left me short of breath. I lean my back against the wall. That's when I notice a door that's sightly ajar. Thank goodness I brought the clutch with me! Maybe I can hide in that room and call Magnus. But that also means I have to finally come clean about Cooper Thornton, because he found me. And if the Grant's have any links with the Thornton's, then Magnus needs to know. I look beyond the hallway to make sure I'm not being followed, then I move towards the room with the open door.

But it appears the room isn't empty. I hear voices raised, in what sounds like an argument. But both voices sound familiar to me.

Wait, is that? I quietly close in on the two voices, opening the door ever so slightly so I can hear them better. That's when my stomach clenches because those are Magnus's and Martine's voices arguing inside. The door is open by a crack, but I can see them both—they're in what appears to be a dressing room, with Martine sitting on a couch and Magnus standing a few feet away with his arms crossed. A part of me wants to turn back and not listen because I'm being nosy, and this isn't my business. But a bigger part of me, the proprietary part of me, is adamant at staying because Magnus *is* my business, and if he needs me to back him up, I fucking will!

"Magnus, please, just stop this charade already! Can't you see that we're meant to be together?" Martine whines.

"I've moved on, Martine and I suggest you do the same."

"You're just making me jealous. Fine! I'm jealous! There, are you happy?"

"The sooner I leave this room, the happier I'll be."

My heart does a somersault at the way Magnus refuses Martine's advances. I lift my hand to open the door so I can save Magnus from that trifling bitch, when she starts speaking again.

"Magnus, I know the fucking truth about her. I know you only pursued that Texan redhead because her father owns the company you're trying to acquire. I know you're just using her as a drawcard because she's a runaway and her parents want her back. So what are you waiting for? Just do the trade already so you can stop this charade and we can move on with our lives!"

What? Suddenly, I feel the walls are closing in, my chest is tightening, and I can't breathe!

Still shaking, I sneak a peak inside as Magnus takes his phone from his pocket to call someone.

"Are you calling Isabelle's father? Good, you're doing the right thing," Martine says, sounding satisfied.

No! Not you too, Magnus! You're different from all of them, right? That's why I've fallen so hard. So please say something! Deny the whole thing. Please! Let me hear you say she's lying. Just ... say ... something ...

Magnus isn't even denying it, nor is he fighting with Martine about it. All I can hear is silence from his side. Complete and absolute silence.

That's all the confirmation I need.

CHAPTER 19

Have you ever had a moment in your life when you wish that everything stopped at a certain point? Because that certain point of your life was your happiest and you're afraid another moment will turn that happy experience into shit?

I wish my life ended right before we came to this charity event. Because now, I realize that every … single … point … in my life since I met Magnus was a lie.

No wonder he never opened up about his work issues. Why would he, when they relate to me. Maybe I'm part of the problem. Pretending to like me was too much for him. *Oh my God, what did I do to deserve this?* I'm still having trouble breathing. I hold myself against the wall as tears start to gush out of my eyes. I try to muffle my sobs with my hand, pulling myself up to steady myself because I can't be here. I have to get out of here! I stagger down the hallway, my vision impaired by my cloudy eyes. And just when I thought things can't possibly get any worse, a lone, yet frighteningly familiar figure is walking towards me.

"There you are, princess! Aww, are you okay, baby?" the sadistic monster calls out for me in a voice oozing with sarcasm.

"Stay the fuck away from me, Cooper!" I manage to cry out before I quickly turn the other way and run towards the exit door. But then I trip on my heel and I stumble. Just then, I hear a ruckus behind me, but I refuse to look back while I remove my stupid heels. And then I run, as fast as my wobbly legs can go without looking back, until I'm finally out the door.

But he's too fast, and his arms fasten around my waist from behind, and he carries me kicking and screaming.

"Let me go, Cooper, you monster!"

"No, Isabelle. Please stop. It's me, Magnus. Is Cooper the guy I knocked out? Well, that asshole won't bother you again." He's still walking away with me in his arms, and I'm still struggling because I know what happens when Magnus touches me, and I can't let him do that to me. Not anymore.

"You don't understand, do you? You fucking put me down, you lying motherfucker, or so help me God, I *will* scream rape!" That gets him to stop walking. He puts me down carefully, and as soon as my feet hit the ground, I turn so my hand connects with his cheek. Hard. The loud crack on contact gives me momentary satisfaction, as does the red mark I left on his cheek. I welcome the throbbing pain in my hand because that slap is worth it. Magnus touches the reddened handprint on his cheek before raising his head at me.

"So you heard," he speaks quietly.

"So it's all a lie, huh? From that time in the restaurant I was working at, until tonight, it was all a lie? You're just using me as a pawn to your twisted acquisition strategy? Did you and Martine have a good laugh at how much of an idiot I am?"

"Isabelle, it's not like that." He reaches for me, but I quickly step back.

I scream at him, "Don't you fucking touch me! I can't stand your hands on me!" The shock and hurt in his face is just as painful to see because I just compared him with every single man whose touch made me feel sick. But I need to lie. He deserves to feel the same pain he's giving me.

"Please, if you'd just let me explain ..."

"I don't need you explanation. For all I know they're probably lies, anyway. Why don't you go and take your explanations to hell, *Mr. Magnus Grant*?"

I turn to walk away, but he grabs my hand, and I hate that he still affects me the way he does. He still makes my whole body want him, and I hate it because it's all based on a lie.

"Please, Isabelle." Suddenly, his hands are cupping my face and his lips are on me. "Don't tell me that what we're feeling when we kiss isn't real. This is real, Isabelle. Please hear me out." He starts kissing me again and my traitorous body responds to him. Why does this have to feel so right? But thank goodness my brain still works and that bitch inside of me who I switched off is telling me to get ... the fuck ... away.

So with all my remaining strength, I push him away, and he fumbles backwards. With him not touching me I can think clearly.

I'm not giving him another chance at breaking my now irreparable heart.

"I'm done hearing you out. I opened myself to you, Magnus. I bared my whole fucking self to you. You, on the other hand, had plenty of opportunities to explain everything to me, but now it's too damn late. You want to know why? Because you didn't trust me enough to make that choice, and I would've chosen you! What you did is heartless. No wonder you couldn't love me." My voice breaks as fresh tears pour out from my eyes.

I'm such a fool to think I deserve love.

Magnus tries to step forward but hesitates, roughly raking his hair back. "Isabelle, I fell in love with you the moment you dropped those files in Charles's office. But I couldn't tell you without coming clean. And I was scared that if I did, you won't believe me, and you won't love me back. When you said you loved me right before you fell asleep but took it back the next day, I knew I couldn't come clean yet. That's why I asked you to be sure before you say it. Because *I want to deserve your love*, Isabelle. Please give me chance to deserve your love. I never meant to hurt you. If you let me explain, you'll understand why I had to keep all of these from you. Please, Isabelle. Don't do this." He slowly kneels by my feet, his eyes pleading. This powerful man, with thousands of people under his wing, is kneeling in front of me, begging me to give him a chance.

My heart, shattered as it is, still manages to skip another beat. Magnus never said he loved me, but I felt it in his actions, in his beautiful words. But now I realize they are based on falsehoods. I fell in love on false pretenses. I won't allow myself to fall for him or anyone like him again.

"Stand up because I want to look you straight in the eyes with what I'm about to say."

He hesitates, before doing as I ask. I take one deep breath before I start talking.

"You don't love me, Magnus. It's not love you're feeling. It's greed. I believed in everything you said to me because I thought you were different from all the other men. I thought you were genuine, and you made me feel safe. But you're just the same, if not worse. Now I'm scared for me and my son's life because guess what? That guy you apparently knocked out, is my ex, Cooper Thornton. He's the very monster who abused me like I'm a piece of dirt. That son-of-a-bitch found me through you, Magnus.

Because you let me open up to you and you used it to gain advantage for your business. You made me fall for you, you made *my son* look up to you, and for what? For Grant Corp's profit? Well, guess what, Magnus? Fuck you and fuck your profit!" I start backing away from him, and he's too stunned, too speechless to follow.

I turn to walk away but stop midway and I turn back to Magnus. Seeing him still frozen in his spot, with his shoulders slumped and his handsome face wet with his own tears, just makes me want to reach out and comfort him. I've never seen him this vulnerable. But how can I still feel so much love for this man who betrayed me? I have to start thinking about myself and about my son and stop caring for the man who shattered my heart and pounced on each broken piece.

"You ruined me, Magnus! Cooper might have broken me, but you *ruined* me. You knew how damaged I am, and you exploited it for your own gain. What did I ever do to you to deserve this? Is it because I fell in love with you? Is that it?" I pause for a moment as I take a breather, making sure my voice won't break with what I'm about to say next.

"Just so we're clear, it's over between us, Magnus Grant. I don't *ever* want to see you again. And just like what Martine said, you can end this charade and go back to her. She's all yours. You fucking deserve each other."

With that, I turn and walk away for the last time. One foot in front of the other. In the corner of my eye, I see Magnus pacing unsteadily back and forth, his hand above his eyes. He turns towards me, and he calls out my name, promising things that I know will never be fulfilled. The agony in his voice tugs at my very being. But I keep moving until I manage to hail a cab that will take me as far away from this place, and from him, as possible. That's when I let my tears fall once again. And as I distance myself away from the man responsible for making me whole again, only to shatter me with his betrayal, I begin to wonder if it's even possible for me to pick up the pieces and rebuild myself once again.

******

Thank you for reading my debut novel, *Autumn Falls*. If you enjoyed reading this book, you'll definitely love the final book in this two-part Autumn Series: *Autumn Reigns*, coming in September 2014.

AUTUMN FALLS PLAYLIST

Music has always been a big inspiration in my life, and now, into developing my stories. With *Autumn Falls*, the following songs were constant in my writing process because they define the emotions I wanted to convey within certain scenes or chapters. I hope you enjoy listening to these songs as much as I did.

'Autumn' ~ Paolo Nutini
'Your Song' ~ Ellie Goulding
'Beautiful Girl' ~ William Fitzsimmons
'First Train Home' ~ Imogen Heap
'Can't Take My Eyes Off of You' ~ Cary Brothers
'Sparks' ~ Kristina Train
'Because of You' ~ Kelly Clarkson
'Hold You in My Arms' ~ Ray Lamontagne
'Glory Box' ~ Portishead
'Earthquakey People' ~ Steve Aoki
'Lights' ~ Ellie Goulding
'Feels So Close' ~ Calvin Harris
'She Is Love' - Parachute
'Open Your Eyes' ~ Snow Patrol
'Cross That Line' ~ Joshua Radin
'Near to You' ~ A Fine Frenzy
'Breathe Me' ~ Sia
'Where I Stood' ~ Missy Higgins
'Say Something' ~ A Great Big World
'Gravity' ~ Sara Barellies
'Manhattan' ~ Sara Barellies

The *Autumn Falls* playlist is available on Spotify.

ACKNOWLEDGMENTS

My journey into writing took awhile to come into fruition. All my life, I've been trying to search for my niche. I sang professionally at a tender age and was offered to sign a recording contract when I was given an opportunity to migrate. I chose to leave a promising career behind, throwing caution to the wind, and started my new life elsewhere, putting my creative endeavors at the back seat. But my creativity itched and I had to seek other venues. So I went from web designing, to interactive multimedia, to fashion designing, and even into cake art. And although these endeavors gave me a certain amount of happiness, the feeling of fulfilment seemed far-fetched, evasive even.

But a story in my head kept lingering, distracting me, until the yearning to write it, got the better of me and I decided to go for it. As soon as I started writing my first sentence, it was like a dam of words and ideas flowing out of me without letup. Before I knew it, I've written almost nine hundred pages! Once my story was laid down on a manuscript and formatted, fresh ideas for new stories began popping up inspired by songs, photographs, travels, and various interactions with other people. It was like a bulb in my head has been switched on and now it's impossible to switch it off. Yes, I have finally found my bliss.

Looking back, I remember when I was a little girl, how my mother and I would make up all sorts of stories, just by watching people we did not even know. My mother, an educator, is an academic author/editor as well, and a very successful one at that. So Mom, thank you for introducing me to books and storytelling at a very young age. But as you know, I'm very stubborn and independent, always trying to discover things my own way. So finding myself where you were at about the same age is like coming in full circle. Thank you so much for your support, for your patience, for your constructive comments and analyses, for editing my humble novel … and for not looking at me differently after reading the whole thing! To my dad, thank you for supporting my each and every undertaking. I totally understand if you pass on reading my book though, since I know I'll always be your baby girl, and baby girls know nothing about 'adult situations,' right?

To my son, you are my very own Ethan. I wrote him with you as my inspiration and model. I hope I did you justice. To my daughter, everything that's sassy about Michelle, I picked up from you. Thank you for understanding why Mom couldn't play with both of you sometimes because I had to be in my writing cave. I love you both so very much!

To my friends and family, thank you for your support and feedback throughout my writing journey. I know you'll continue to support me because that's just how awesome you all are. I love you all tremendously.

To my beta readers, Kitch Ponce and Tonette Davis, your comments and suggestions were invaluable. I hope you're game enough to read the next instalment!

To my fellow authors, both indie and traditional, who had inspired me in more ways than one, thank you so much! You all kick butt, and I hope to meet you all personally in due time.

To my very own Magnus Grant, my husband … when I wrote my leading man, I wanted to emulate your personality into him. Thank you for supporting my every pursuit, knowing there's a chance I might give it up if it doesn't make me happy. Thank you for reading my rough drafts and loving the content, even though they were that—pretty damn rough. Don't worry, I'm seeing this one to the end, babe, I promise.

And lastly, I'd like to give a big giant 'Thank you and kisses' to you, the readers, who spared some of your time and money to read this book. I hope you enjoyed reading about Magnus, Isabelle/Autumn, and the other characters whom you could have identified with, as much as I enjoyed writing it, and I hope you'll continue to support *Autumn Reigns* … and hopefully my other books as well. (Keeping my fingers crossed!)

ABOUT THE AUTHOR

I am a purveyor of romance, of tragedy, of laughter, of sassy women and swoon-worthy men. My goal from this day forward is to make my reader's heart skip a beat or two. Actual skipping is optional, but most welcome.

I am married to a wonderful man, and a mother to two gregarious children. I love to cook, read, bake, and run when I have any spare time, the latter of which, in between my full-time job, house chores, and writing, is well, almost nonexistent. Yes, my life is busy, but I wouldn't have it any other way. And once they invent a pill that can make people function relatively well without sleep, then my life will be absolutely perfect!

If you would like to know more about me and my upcoming novels, please check out the links below. Your feedback and comments are more than welcome. It would be lovely to hear from all of you!

Website: esmariawrites.wordpress.com
Facebook: https://www.facebook.com/ESMariaAuthor
Email: author@esmaria.com